The Brothers Silver

The Brothers Silver
A Novel

Marc Jampole

Owl Canyon Press
Boulder, CO

© 2021 by Marc Jampole
First Edition, 2021
All Rights Reserved
Library of Congress Cataloging-in-Publication Data
Jampole, Marc
The Brothers Silver — 1st ed.
p. cm.
ISBN: 978-1-952085-07-9
Library of Congress Control Number: 2020952242

Owl Canyon Press
Boulder, Colorado

Disclaimer

CHAPTERS

ON THE COLD HILL'S SIDE

I count the dust rings floating down the beams of rusty sun, pouring into lofty windows, running over wooden billows in the surface of the floor, down a wooden hallway to a wooden door.

Lee attacks the black and charcoal hounds-teeth of my sport coat's arm and shoulder.

"Black punch buggies no punch backs!"

"Where's the punch buggy?"

"I saw one tomorrow."

"Here are ten I'll see next week."

On the dark creaking wood we wrestle, fake hits and gentle sacks, joking blows, tugging clip-on ties, tickling underarms and slugging backs. We dash across the floor, we thrust and poke.

"Time out to get my shoe, Jules."

"Hear that echo, Leon?"

"It's a Grand Canyon of oak."

The lawyer takes us, shirttails tucked back in unevenly, to a room of darker wood that echoes every step, past dark wood pews, empty save for our parents. They sit in different rows. He takes us by dark wood rails, up worn-out wood steps to dark wood chairs. A stout judge presiding from his dark wood lair above us gravely composes questions for me: "How is it going? How is school? How is Boy Scouts? How is life with Mom? Do you give her a helping hand? Are you ever suddenly sad? Ever exposed to something you don't understand? How was it last time you saw Dad?"

I speak with all the confidence I have, quickly, brightly, words rehearsed, bulldozing through. I want to get them right, these assorted game-show questions from this courtly Bennett Cerf.

Same questions now to Lee, and his answers come more slowly, after frowns and squints and sighs that make his drowsy brows connect to form a long and bushy print above his eyes.

My knees begin to twitch, and then my thighs, like every time I have to sit too long. Leon softly bops my knee to make me stop it.

Momma's forehead kneels against the steering wheel. Her fingers push against her temples as if she's trying to stanch a leak. Automobiles make squeaking stops behind our Plymouth, frozen in the center lane. The drivers peer at us, shake their fists, and rant.

Momma weakly chants, "My brain, my brain! My brain, my brain!"

Cars are screeching, veering, whining, staring, swinging, soaring past our Plymouth. The drivers bore the air with sideways-circle crazy finger signs.

Momma's hands explore her pocketbook for pills I know she already took. She pries at the plastic vial. Her leg is shaking. She grabs a pill and slips it through an aching smile.

She starts the car. It lurches forward, teeters slowly home, yard by yard, mile by mile, while cars and buses pass and beep, pass and beep, pass and beep. Turning at our street, she jolts to a stop, then creeps slowly to a spot before our house, stops the car again, slumps against the wheel, and falls asleep.

I open her door, shake her. Shake her again. "Try to stand. It's time to go inside," I command.

"Another minute, Jules." She slurs her words and pushes back my hand.

Inside, sleeves above my elbows, tie unclipped, I search the fridge and cabinets for something we can eat. Eggs to scramble, grated cheese, some onion dip, a box of Cream of Wheat. I talk of Mantle's injuries to Lee, Howard at the plate replacing Yogi, how Whitey with a mighty curveball put a collar on Sherm Lollar, why I think the Reds will tank, why Matthews is as good as Ernie Banks, Cepeda, McCovey, other Giants. I speak to fill my brother's silence.

Momma staggers into the house, litters the kitchen table with the contents of her purse looking for another pill, and skitters down the stairs to the basement. She curses bitterly, a shrieking fanfare about Dad deserting us. The TV clicks on, and now its steady blare.

Dad leans against a kitchen chair, gripping plastic bags from Treasure Island. An unlit Camel lines a corner of his lower lip, as he asks Momma, "Signed the papers yet, Ethel?"

"It's none of your business." She glowers.

"Are you out of your mind, of course it's my business."

"I won't take pressure, no duress."

"No duress, just sign the papers, Ethel, please. We're racking up the lawyers' fees." His eyes address Lee and me.

"You can't presume to tell me what to do anymore."

"I don't presume to tell you what to do."

"You do presume, you do presume," she says, and bangs the wall. Leon leaves the room.

"Sign the paper! You're behaving like a filly kicking up a storm in the stall."

"I don't want to hear your horseracing analogies. You can't tell me what to do!"

"Okay, okay, you win, you win. My apologies! I'll never tell you what to do."

"And spare me your shit-eating grin." Both my Dad and I break out in kingpin smiles.

He lets the plastic bags tumble to the floor and starts to open the back-door. "I'm going, Jules. Please keep the tags in case something doesn't fit and we need to take them back."

Momma runs at Daddy, spitting words like flak. "You can't abandon your kids, you egomaniac."

"I'm not abandoning them. Jules, I have to split."

"You dirty, no-good, low-life bastard!" My mother speaks her searing words directly to his face, an inch away.

"Do you know what he's done, your dear father? He didn't let you take painting lessons, didn't let your brother take ballet. Said he feared it would turn you queer. He didn't see your last school play. Let me rot in Bellevue six months after Lee was born, let me rot while you screwed that shitty snot-nosed jailbait at the Ocean City boardwalk on a cot. That whore who wasn't even pretty. The next-door neighbor in the living room, Uncle Max-ie's fiancée you finger-fucked on the bathroom floor on Thanksgiving, the baby-sitter's mother, the titless wonder at work...." Dad's only reaction is to keep smirking.

She places two fingers in the cleft of his chin and thunders, "I'll make your children hate you as much as you hate your father."

All trace of cool bemusement drains from his visage, replaced by an angry fireball. He heaves her hard against the wall. Her fists are pounding at his face, pounding, pounding, pounding, pounding, and he heaves her hard against the wall, her fists are pounding at his face, pounding, pounding, pounding, pounding, and he heaves her hard against the wall, pounding, pounding, pounding, pounding, her fists are pounding at his face, like a mumblety-peg knife against dirt, and he pushes her hard against the wall and she falls to the ground in a heaving ball of arms and legs.

He carries her to her bedroom and slams the door. He comes out minutes later, bounds across the floor, and leaves.

I wait a few minutes, and then open the door and see her unconscious on the bed, her back cleaved against the edge, her legs expanded wide beneath her dress, her lacy panties down and dangling slanted round her feet at the bed base. A smile of absent, distant stupor crowns her face.

"It won't be bad. It won't be bad." My father's answer to a question no one had. He speaks by phone from somewhere in New Jersey. Coursing in the background I hear a tony nasal voice calling a horse race, and I imagine his hands counting cash, a Camel prancing at his mouth, blessing air with ash. "I'm living in a pretty tiny room south of Jersey City till I find a bigger place, one that has room for you and Lee. But in the meantime we can go to ballgames and the putting green, that Chinese spot you like, the trampoline. I know it's hard, but it could be a helluva lot harder. At least you've got food stocked in the larder and a couple of bucks in your pocket, not like when I was your age and my mother spent the welfare check the first day on thick, nicely-trimmed steaks and roast beef swimming in gravy, then fuck you, rots-a-ruck, it was her brackish boiled chicken, and then slim pickings and fend for yourself for the rest of the month. It's best to snap to it. No groans or buts. Focus on your schoolwork and the Scouts. Focus on the things you like to do. Life's not a walkover, so don't get caught napping. There are other horses racing and the winners will always be those best at adapting."

Numbered paragraphs, knotty declarations. A crimson X is halfway down the final page near a line for Momma to sign: *Decree of Separation.* The reason she has rotted downstairs for days. I can hear the bleating of the TV. The burger stew I made on Saturday is gone. All I can find for dinner is Cream of Wheat. On the dirty dishes mold is growing, the dirty laundry basket's overflowing.

"You didn't do your art homework because you want to hurt me," Momma shouts at Leon.

"I didn't do it because the teacher is a jerk."

"And now, something even worse! You've started stealing money from my purse. How could I be such a failure?" She is certain she is at the heart of every action.

"Fuck you," Leon curses. "I didn't lie! I didn't take your cash! I didn't do it! You're living on Mars or somewhere else in outer space!" Leon roughly spews ugly, poisoned, blackheart words as Dad does when he's mad. "Instead of making accusations, change your clothes, go to work, and clean this place."

He races up the basement stairs, slams the back door, and doesn't shiver back home till after four. When he enters, she immediately hugs him with one of her long mothering body embraces that make you feel as if space has collapsed and the walls are pushing against you, smothering you. Leon stands zombie stiff and sad, shoulders grazing ears, bushy eyebrows matted fearfully. She smiles and mutters tearfully, "I've been bad, I've been bad."

The next day she cleans the house, irons clothes, takes a bath, paints her toes, does her face, makes a roast and spaghetti sauce, bakes ginger bread, stabilizes a fence post, arranges flowers in a vase, chats with Aunt Hope and Aunt Hedy, cleans the doormats. She mopes in bed the day after that, and the day after that and the day after that.

Swish of turning pages. Plank and Salinger, Henry Steele Commager, de Tocqueville, mechanics, *A Shropshire Lad*. I sit inside a fort I made of college books, all Dad's when he worked full-time and also went to school. Leafing through the volumes I sometimes stray upon pages full of childish crayon swirls and spools, my unfenced invention at three unfurled in red and gray.

Vladimir Horowitz brightly playing a quaking crescendo, Liszt's *Second Hungarian Rhapsody*, while Lee and I grappled up and down the stairs, fake-fighting Bugs against the bears and lions, punch-pulling, flipping up and down, and shaking the house so much with our roughhouse choreography that the needle skipped. Then we ripped the covers off our sleeping Dad and Momma, shook their bed until they tripped downstairs. Momma made scrambled eggs and crunchy bacon strips, while Dad would lecture us through brunch.

He'd sip his coffee, smack his lips and quip that thermodynamics explains the universe, explicates all things: how a doorbell rings or how a bluebird sings. A speech he would repeat week after week. "Thermodynamics teaches us the how, reveals the why. The zeroth law says, if two things reach the same heat as a third, they are the same temperature, if the system is sealed."

"That's the transitive axiom in math," my brother squeaks with zeal. How does he know number theory that I'm only just starting to comprehend?

"Yes, good," Dad affirms. "Now the first law imparts that neither matter nor energy is created or erased, but in the end just rearranged from one form to another, a flow chart of heat changing to movement, movement to electricity, electricity to work, an energy chain. You can never rake in any excess or record a gain. That means no matter what, the best you do is break even. The second law stresses that all things tend toward maximum entropy, which is a measure of disorder. That means you won't even break even, because every action makes a bigger mess. The second law is the house we're all always betting against. Take the baking-hot sun, transmitting miscellaneous heat towards earth. Plants use it to grow. We eat the plants, burn the energy and turn the rest of it to shit and piss."

We start to giggle, which makes him more excited. "So in the end, everything always turns to shit."

"Dad said sh... sh... shit," I fake a stutter, nervy and delighted.

"Now we can say entropy when we mean shit," Leon observes.

"Want to play a game of Bull Entropy?" I ask in a high-pitched, girlish squeal, then swerve to my deepest register and mutter, "No, I have to take an entropy."

"Boys, boys!" Momma pokes me to silence.

Daddy, soaring with visible joy at his science, continues, as if unaware that his audience of scions is making jokes. "The third law states the entropy of a system approaches a constant value as the temperature approaches absolute zero, the coldest possible temperature."

"I've always had trouble going in the cold," I boldly roar, but everyone ignores it.

He pokes his cigarette in the air to underline his words. "I have little use for metaphysics or psychology, which is like "breaking your balls through your mind." But thermodynamics—his only real love, his cause for "How a watch unwinds... How a highway is designed... Why an ice cube thaws... The flight of birds... The smell of turds... The color of skies... The action of eyes... How coffee brews... How a lathe bit bores... Why a plane can soar... The erosion of the shore... The gloom of night... The vroom of motors... The head of spume on a raging flume... Why nature abhors a vacuum."

After breakfast Lee would spend a lazy morning helping Dad fix a rheostat, wire a lamp or replace some window glaze, while Ma and I would cook a stew. Cube the veal, slice away the fat, then braise. Sauté garlic, peel carrots, dice potatoes, salt to taste, add half a can of tomato paste. The yellow onions would make her cry, "Happy tears because I know how good it's going to taste for my three dears."

On the dirty dishes mold is growing, the dirty laundry basket is overflowing.

She finally signs the separation papers. She has me take them to the drugstore notary, who signs the papers even though he's not supposed to do it, with a side trip to the A&P for ice cream, chocolate sauce and Dream Whip, for sundaes we call tuesdaes from Leon's question he would never skip: "Why call them 'sundaes'? We're eating them on Tuesday."

A day later, she returns to work.

We play hamburger-treat with cousins Dave and Petey, Pete's idea. The mattresses on Petey's twin bed are slices of bread, Dave's a ground beef patty. We place Dave sideways between the slices so that his head and feet stick out, pile on pillows and jump up and down on top to spread the imaginary mayonnaise and flatten the meat.

Pete gives me bear hugs all the time. He coughs his laughter and smiles like he's in tears. He complains that his mom, Aunt Flo, lets his older brothers, Steve and Joe, beat him up and call him queer. "It'll toughen up the little mutt." he says she says. Momma tells me that when she first met Flo, she was leaning forward on a concrete stoop biting a cigarette butt. Flo blew a stream of smoke at her and said "Fuck you, Edwin's latest Betty Boop. Ooo-poo-be-doo, fuck you!" Momma said for dinner Flo would drop a plate of cutlets in the middle of the table, say "Go!" and let her four boys battle over who got what.

Petey reminds me of the cousins' club I created—the Naval Hogmen. We vow to eat as much as we can without getting sick at every family event. "Admiral, Jules," Petey falls to bent knee, "Command us to eat!"

"Let us feed on the tiny peas, strips of beef, and potato balls like crows of the field tuck into seed," I reply. "Let us find room in our bellies to consume the lemon squares and petit fours. Let us suck them in like air."

Freckled breasts are falling from the scooped-out neckband of the blouse of the chunky woman resting her head against my Daddy's shoulder, as he regales my Uncle Gene on the cheapest way to fix the lock on his car trunk, his hands impaling air. This couldn't be the *titless wonder* Momma is always wishing choked to death on burning sand?

Flo and Gene have a hairy, hang-dog mutt, part cocker, part setter, and Daddy lets us keep a puppy from her latest litter. My birthday gift that I will split with Lee, unfairness that angers me. Leon never has to share *his* presents. We name him Rocky for the flying squirrel. Momma says we're old enough to train him, but we can't seem to do it right. When he makes his mess, we rub his nose in it, beat his snout and throw him on newsprint or into the yard. But it doesn't matter how hard we try—how long we put him out or walk him in the street. Rocky fights us. He doesn't seem to want to learn and I end up cleaning up the flop days later when I find it in the corners of Dad's old shop or underneath the washroom sink. School begins again, which means Rocky is home alone to go in secret spots, and soon the basement stinks.

Momma dials a number in the kitchen. Like waggling bees, her legs flit a mile a minute. Her fingers squeeze an unlit Newport. "Edwin Silver, please....

You only sent forty and the court order says ninety.... What do you mean? I deserve every dime!.... I'll phone your office any time.... I'm going to call my lawyer, get a writ.... You've never changed, you're just a little ghetto shit. I should have foreseen this!.... I want your number at home.... I won't let Flo be a go-between and wait for you to call.... That's debatable!... That's just great! What if something happens to the boys?.... What about your children?.... You are not a good father.... You're a dreadful father, and your children hate you.... Don't do this to me, Edwin Silver ... Ed ... Ed ... Ed... Ed ...."

Lips grating, eyes dilating, both legs shaking, fingers raking forearms on the floor by Leon's bike. Momma berates the phone receiver dangling at the wall, tells the quivering, curling wire how he was just a gutter kike who happened to be smart, smarter than her older brother Henry, which is why she loves him—correction—loved him, but apart from the photographic memory, he was just a ghetto upstart with nowhere to go, no way to grow, before she made him what he is, made him take the test for Cooper Union, taught him what to say in interviews, made sure he went to classes and graduated, taught him what was tacky, what was chic, how to write a letter, how to answer phones, how to enunciate with a short, flat, Mid-western tone.

His betrayals with the titless wonder ... the trampy redhead ... the well-heeled vamp ... the slut and the nutcase ... the hag and the dishrag ... the blonde ... and the blonder ... the rube from Rutland ... the one with sagging boobs....

How he gladly signed the forms for surging current through her body....

Let the doctors tie her tubes....

I'm fixing foreign stamps in pages of my album, while Leon watches cowboys camping on the range, then switches channels, hopscotching through *Candid Camera* and stopping at Lucy and Ethel dressed as tramps at a highway on-ramp.

"That's a stupid show. Change it back," I demand.

"Quit your bitchin.' You weren't even watching."

"I'm watching now."

"You always get your way."

"Just because you say it, doesn't make it true," I tease, then turn the cruelty in my voice up a notch. "Okay, I'll let you watch your Lucy Ball, so I don't have to hear you bawl."

"I'm not bawling."

"Bawl baby Leon, bawl baby Leon!"

He grabs my album, knocking over a table lamp, and starts to pull out pages. I yawl at him to stop, which just enrages him more. He rips the stamps and paper into chum.

Momma stumbles in, hair hanging in a tangled mess, in the knee-length button-in-the-front pastel blue housedress she's worn for days. "Why the bedlam?" she says in a tired, lame voice. Can't you boys stop your brawling and play nice? Don't make me dread coming up here."

"He's ripping up my stamp collection!"

"He called me names!"

"If you loved me you wouldn't fight!" Her answer seems both drained of energy and enflamed with derision. "You wouldn't blame each other for every little effing thing. I know you do it out of spite. You do it just to hurt me and that hurts the worst, like frostbite or an incision that bursts, something so unbearably painful," she declaims with tiny head flourishes as if on stage or staring at a mirror, then takes flight down the basement steps to the blaring television.

Manhattan—dreamland of theaters, stores, museums, inviting deco buildings craning towards the clouds like mammoth stalagmites. Contentment watching seals and bears in Central Park. Awe confronting massive Cubist paintings in museums. Joy trapped inside a crunch of spritely walkers flapping and twisting 'round midtown after dark, bunching at corners, then unraveling into small groups at dapper storefronts, at once alone and yet together with these loud, enticing fellow travelers. Manhattan—dreamland of Aunt Hope and Uncle Jack's apartment, their cluttered paradise a blissful respite. Momma seems calmer in the presence of her older sister. Bus to subway, E train to Times Square, A train to Washington Heights, elevator to a newsstand on a hill, hook right and across the little park and up a steep slope, then climb four flights to Aunt Hope's books, Uncle Jack's playbills, his stamps, his coins, his model trains, his racks of hotel soap and bottle caps, plastic replicas of Cadillacs and Pontiacs, windmills, telescopes, crawler cranes, Eiffel Towers, Grand Canyons, Taj Meals, weather vanes, submarines, and seaplanes. To Jack's indecent tales of mixing drinks for sexual powers, newlyweds making love for hours, Martians doing it by shaking hands, one-night stands, women sporting giant feet and tiny mouths, chorus girls in pedal pushers hitching South, salesmen caught in snowstorms at farmhouse doors, death-bed confessions of husbands and whores.

Hope is the opposite of Momma, always in control and not afraid of anything. Short and stubby, she picks up litter in the subway, confronts the offender, flings it at his hands and blusters, "This train's a public place, not your private dumpster!" Once a month she sends chatty letters on pieces of unlined paper to all her brothers, sisters, nieces, nephews, cousins, uncles, aunts, and friends.

Lee and I teach their daughters *Bullshit*, but Momma makes us call it *I Doubt It*. She tells us to put a sock in our tough language and not play rough, especially not to knock about or throw their Barbie dolls. We play fake fist-icuffs in the herbal garden at the Cloisters, while Uncle Jack hoists the girls onto the stone retaining wall. We watch the river, and Jack talks of running through the oak and pine before they built the Henry Hudson, swimming by a sandbank, fishing at the bend, cranking liners over treetops off a boy-hood friend "who had a cup of coffee with the Yanks." Afterwards, we walk back to their place for deli: pastrami, salami, corn beef on rye, pickles, chips, soda, strudel, key lime pie. "It's not as good as Mom's or yours," Hope tells Momma. Jack shows us his collections: stamps, coins, old photo postcards, model sailboats. Out of many mounted pennies, nickels, dimes and quarters, he selects ten or twelve vintage coins that have real collector value, in the hundreds of dollars. He gets them counting through all the change at the restaurant where he works as head cashier. He's looking for the Holy Grail of collecting, a 1909 VDBS penny, but in twelve years he hasn't found any.

"Remember the time that Emil tried to make strudel? He must have been eight and I was sixteen," Momma says, and she and Hope begin to laugh.

"I would never have helped that dopey poodle clean up the mess like you did," Hope asserts. "There was flour everywhere, and every plate was dirty."

"It was my fault," Momma serenely confesses. "I had shown him how to do it a dozen times, and the time before I had let him roll out the dough."

"But you didn't have to take the blows when Pop-pop counted three eggs missing and went wild."

"As I said, it was my fault," Momma smiles. "Besides, it was all the same to me. They were always blaming me for everything that went wrong. I was the bad child, Henry the exalted one." Momma pantomimes expressions of pride and regret when she mentions herself and her older brother. She doesn't look assaulted when she speaks these words. In fact, she seems to feel better than in weeks. "I love talking about the times Momma was alive and we were all still together," she beams.

My fingers nearly yank the rook beside my king to bring it to the seventh rank where it can take my brother's isolated pawn. But the board keeps breaking into disconnected squares, pieces spawning other pieces, swimming in a muddy soup that makes it hard for me to concentrate. I decide to play it safe, retreat my queen, and regroup. Leon slides his bishop into checking me, then checks again with his other bishop. I evade, but Leon brings his castle out, forcing me to trade. My king is now too far away to fight his dreaded pawn advance, backed by dancing bishops and a well-positioned knight. I make many forced moves, each more biting than the one before, until I shed my will to fight and, once again, I lose a game of chess to Lee.

"I guess I should have pushed the rook," I say, and my younger brother quickly demonstrates seven different moves I might have tried and how he would have fried me after each of them.

The man presenting us our trophies for first and second place says we do not look like brothers. It's true. I resemble our mother, a soft, round face of teeth that can only show a smile, sleepy eyes beneath my curly reddish hair, tall and pudgy. Leon is short and wiry, limber, like Dad, ploughboy arm and shoulder muscles bulging like an "after" picture in a body-building ad, oily black hair falling over eyes, angled face of burnished bones, bushy eyebrows. "Like Adonis," Momma says, embracing him.

Leon drops his trophy from his bedroom sill. It lands in pieces underneath a basement window grill.

Aunt Bernie breaks the news that Dad and Momma have to light a candle on the cake together at Cousin Jake's bar mitzvah reception, or none at all, since she considers Ethel, "like my own blood." Dad says no, which starts a flood of tears from Momma. For days before the feast, I hear her wending through the house past midnight, sometimes pacing slowly, sometimes faster, frantic like a harassed and frightened grouse or hartebeest released from a large cage into a smaller one, lamenting what she calls "the symbolic final feast of my holy union with my genius lord and master, my beautiful beast, my beautiful beast."

My father brings a woman to the party whom I haven't seen before. Momma gets drunk and bellows, "Edwin Silver's latest and greatest whore" to her face. On the way home from Leonard's, she races through a yellow light, hits a traffic cone headlong with the fender, spins the car around and halts, the car facing in the wrong direction. She threshes around the house for hours in the dark on all fours wearing nothing but a scanty red mesh bra and matching panties, squawking pieces of a half-crazed story in which my father is a snake that gallivants around her naked thigh in bed, a hawk's head that swallows her whole, an elephant's hoof that squashes her, a bull's teeth that rips her flesh to shreds.

I josh my brother again. "Hey, Leon, it's your turn to wash."

"But I did it last time."

"Yeah, two plates and a pot! I did a week's lot twice in a row. That means it's still your turn."

"I don't want to wash these slimy dishes. I want to dry." I can see his eyes are burning.

"But we're taking turns," is my cruel reply. "Washing's harder when the pots are crusted."

"It's not up to you to make the rules," Leon says, his face turning rust.

"I make dinner every day," I push a little more churlishly.

"I can make my own. I'm no fool. Frozen peas and fish sticks."

"As if you could work the stove or find the freezer! Will you eat them raw? Or will you use a flavor straw? Since you can't even wash a dish."

"Stop teasing me," Lee emits a feverish banshee call and unfurls a soaking dishrag at me, but it hits the wall.

Momma appears in fuzzy slippers, socks, and a half-zippered housecoat. A long, burly scarf is wrapped around her throat and drags along the floor.

"What's wrong now? Would you two stop your uproar?"

"Tell us who should wash and dry," I say.

"Oh, no, you don't! You won't play me for a fool that way by putting me in the middle of your fight."

"What are you talking about? That's ridiculous," I answer for both of us, a guilty ache driving through me that I incited my brother.

"I know you do it out of spite, so one of you will hate me for siding with the other. It's part of your grand scheme with your father to drive me mad!"

"We don't hate you, Momma," I carefully state. "If you tell us what to do, we'll do it," Leon glides a few steps towards me and shakes his head in agreement, glassy-eyed, his face a mask mixing sad with mad.

"Then why do you fight about tasks? If you loved me, you'd collaborate on your chores."

"We love you, but would it be so bad if you decided who did what? That's all we're asking."

"Don't pull that crap on me! No wonder I'm too depressed to work, with ungrateful sons who never listen anymore."

She slams the basement door, and soon I hear the TV louder than before.

Rocky stays a runt and refuses to be trained, so we can never keep the basement clean. Leon, giggling like a muskrat, calls him "Homunculus of turd." I call him "Our midget shit machine."

Epoxy's bitter smell feels like old times: pouring polyethylene liquid into molds and watching viscid purple fold and flatten. Back in Daddy's lab again, for the first time in many months. We bake the casts on green ceramic slabs until they harden into sateen leaves and rubber soldiers, Dad explaining every step of the complicated process. Afterwards, we eat steamed mussels and raw oysters in a long and narrow barn-like restaurant bending east towards the Far Rockaway shore, owned and operated by the waiters jaunting and clattering through the rows of tabletops that never seem to begin or end, but go on as far as I can see down the long banquet hall. Dad explains the chemistry of everything we did, spinning chains of molecules on paper napkins.

This time his woman has green-specked eyelids, teased black hair, a tiny jaw and narrow chin, a sleeveless dress, scoop-top showing freckled skin below a string of tiny pearls, a fold of flesh where her lightly pitching breasts begin to break and separate, tan and freckled, looking soft as sponge cake.

I dream I awaken from a dream-dead sleep of drinking shoals of mist, wander to the bathroom, unsnap my pajama bottoms, lean a hand on the sink stand and tinkle in the bowl, and wake up pissing in my bed like Denny Knoll. Momma catches me twisting the balled-up sheets and spread into the washer and acts like she knows what happened. "It's normal," she insists, sipping orange juice from the small glass in her hand.

"No, it's not," I calmly say. "It's an aberration, and it will never be repeated. Next time I'll know that I'm asleep even if I'm dreaming, and I'll leap from bed and run to the john." Explaining myself drenches me in a perspiration of exasperation, like a skittish faun.

"But it's normal, normal," she drones on.

"Don't worry. Next time I'll know I'm dreaming about dreaming about dreaming to pee and I'll sprint to the toilet."

"There's nothing wrong with what happened."

I clench my fist and squint my eyes. "Of course there is," I repeat, with a hint of disgust, "but I'm certain it won't happen again."

Ma starts to squall, "It's normal, it's normal," and hurls her glass against the wall.

I hear a roar from the kitchen. Momma's fallen on the floor, phone receiver dangling, banging against the wall where the molding meets the door. She grasps a kitchen towel in her fist and rasps mechanically, as if in a deep slumber, "Edwin Silver doesn't work here anymore and has left no forwarding number. Edwin Silver doesn't work here anymore and has left no forwarding number. Edwin Silver has abandoned his wife and sons. Edwin Silver left them for the titless wonder Marilyn, his boss's wife, but he wasn't rich enough to make her leave her privileged life. Edwin Silver was a shakedown artist when he forced me to have my tubes tied because that stupid doctor said I'd have another nervous breakdown, and a liar when he promised we'd adopt a baby girl. Edwin Silver wanted other men and women in our bed.

Edwin Silver wants me dead. Edwin Silver wouldn't let me fly to my mother's funeral, passed at forty-two from cancer. I never had a chance to say goodbye. She loved me less than she loved the rest, blamed me for nothings, always said I disobeyed, shamed me when I said a plumber touched me, when cousin Melvin touched me, when I said I saw Pop-pop screw the maid. Edwin Silver doesn't work here anymore and has left no forwarding number. Edwin Silver doesn't work here any anymore and has left no forwarding number...."

Dishes crusted with dried spaghetti sauce, oatmeal, and mustard gloss fill the sink. On the kitchen table are envelopes with bills and another bulky document that compels my mother's frightened ramblings: *Decree of Final Divorce*, there for a week like a force of nature that makes Momma sleep all day, watch TV all night.

The phone rings. It's her boss. "Where's your mother? Is she all right?"

"She's been sick in bed with the flu. She thinks it may be a flare-up of indigestion. Something she ate." I start to recite imaginary symptoms.

"Why didn't she let me know?" His interruption ensnares me in my lies, and my skin blossoms heat.

"I guess I was supposed to call you. Please don't tell her I forgot." He trusts my story and spares me further questions.

"Tell her to get better. I need her to do the inventory."

"She's sure she'll be better in a day."

I turn the spigot, soap up the sponge, begin to spray hot water into pots and scrub. I rinse away the brownish filmy grunge. Leon takes a towel and starts to dry and put away.

My teeth bite into a stringy strip of pot roast, dripping with brown sauce. The salty, slightly burnt taste swells my insides with well-being. The kitchen seems familiar and strange at the same time, as if under a tinselly, chintzy spell—cleaner than it has been in weeks, free of worry, full of the luscious smell of blintzes and Mario Lanza singing "The Student Prince." "How was your day, Leon?" Momma asks. He shrugs, stares at his plate, and says, "Okay."

"Jules?"

I'm chewing carrots, and before I can answer she launches into the details of her evening's plans. She's going to make chicken soup, pan-fried kugel and salmon croquets for dinners for the rest of the week, iron her blouses, bake cookies for our Boy Scout troop, and finish cleaning house, so she'll be free tomorrow to attend the synagogue sisterhood meeting and study the details of the portion for the Talmud class she's taking. "That will give me time

Saturday afternoon to take you boys to roam the Queensbridge Projects and sell more light bulbs for the Boy Scouts, after I get home."

"We're already first and second in sales, thanks to last Saturday," I remind her.

Leon takes the city math test for his grade and gets a perfect score. Momma tapes his letter from the school board to the freezer door.

They make me leader of a Scout patrol and give me seven tenderfeet, including Lee, plus Denny Knoll, my friend who wets his sleeping bag at camp and utters one of two words in response to everything, "Boss" or "Neat." Instead of naming us an animal, tribe, or kin, I propose the Zestabs as our pseudonym, after Mighty Mouse's favorite vitamin.

I nudge my bike up Suicide Hill. At the summit runs a barbed wire fence. On this side, descent to trees and garden apartments—the other side, a dark and dizzy plunge to landfill and the Grand Central Parkway. When lots of kids are there, we trudge to the back of the line and skiff down, one guy at a time. We all know about the time two boys tracked too close together. One bike clipped the other, and one of them took a spill and lost control. The rocks ripped the boy's brains apart as he rolled inertly down the hill, stopping stiff and bleeding at a doorsill.

On my bike now, rattling handlebars, spinning spokes, feet spread wide. The wind resistance chills my face. I glide sweat-soaked down the hill, past bushes and choke weeds, cold and tense with the fear and thrill of jolting speed.

My bike is shaking over stones and bumps, going ever faster as I advance. Wind is droning at my back. Tires are thumping over clumps of grass. Metal parts are straining, groaning like a grunting antelope, as I tack to steeper slope, eyes wide and trained on the bottom.

Acceleration fills my heart like freedom—not freedom of speech, not freedom to vote, not freedom of religion, to live where you would, not to read a book nor buy a boat, not to take an action, nor to do some good, but freedom to be free, freedom to be here, the freedom of tearing through space and time with verve, the freedom to rumble swiftly down the hill, by myself, dash towards the courtyard of apartments at the bottom, and at the final moment, swerve to avoid a crash.

Manhattan fountains. These water chutes and sprays reveal chaotic flow through space. A million water bubbles bounce my way. I sit on the concrete edge and trace water's jumps and twists in lapping pools, the coolness over hands and wrists, walkers passing through a sunny mist. Uncle Jack escorts me on this tour of midtown fountains in the city he adores. My mother's family always jokes that Jack gets nervous every time he leaves Manhattan, even if it's just to go to Queens or Staten Island. Jack is so different from my father, whose rule is to avoid the sun and never exercise, even though he was a football star in high school.

Jack has his winter walk, mostly indoors, from overpass to tunnel to subway transfer point of boutiques hawking flowers, papers, candy bars. Scent of fry and coffee wafts from donut joints. Fly up the stairs and through the far end of Rockefeller Center, ride an endless escalator underground. We cross half of midtown hardly ever outside.

His favorite walk is a dirty joke-filled Times Square stroll, but he doesn't take me on this tour until I turn twelve. We ramble past open bins of 45's, rock-and-roll and soul, gambol by movie theaters that only play Sci-Fi, their loggias specked with seedy guys looking like they just got out of jail, cameras and tchotchkes in carts on closeout sale, refugees from tour groups crowding streets and stores, shoals of cajoling back-seamed, spike-heeled whores.

I prefer his jaunt down Fifth towards Greenwich Village. We cross Madison Square Park, haunted by junkies, and the Flatiron Building, turn to Union Square, past outdoor shelves of used and discontinued books. Now back to Fifth, restaurants in nooks, elegant townhouses and apartments dead-ending at the benches and fountains of Washington Square overlooking soccer games and street performers, clenching couples, grandmas caressing toddlers, seesaws, deadbeats on soap boxes proclaiming revolution or condemning the theory of evolution, knockabouts deep in chess games, rummage tables, roasted chestnuts, salt-lick pretzels, all-beef hot dogs with sauerkraut, pigeons pillaging crumbs. We walk until his island's edge, where raindrops pock the surface of the river at the Brooklyn Bridge.

Momma's on the phone all evening, calling the ladies in the Sisterhood, reminding them to shop the seconds sale. She asks that they put their cash contributions in the mail, all the while her fingers sewing buttons on our pants or needle-pointing doilies—Hanukkah presents for aunts and uncles—after which she makes a stew for Tuesday.

We're waiting for my dad, who's late for his monthly visit. "How little he loves you," she fumes.

"Not a word about my father," I reply, and Leon leaves the room.

"I just don't want you and Leon hurt when he doesn't deliver on whatever he's promised you or treats you like dirt."

Now we're in the car with Dad, and he asks, "What kind of bullshit is she asserting this week?"

"Not a word about my mother," I curtly say.

"It's time you learned that women cheat and play unfair. They always want to trap you. They hurt and scar. The only thing they're good for is to plow."

"Just shut up with your crap," I lower at him. Leon gazes out the window of the car.

Isaac Schreiber, English class, utters long, unusual words, like *pusillanimous, supercilious, preternatural,* and *hypochondriac,* that send me to the dictionary every day. He totes enormous volumes in a sack, all of which I check out from the library and read: *The Stranger, The Dead, The Grapes of Wrath, The Red and the Black,* which makes me teary, scared of my inconsequential fate, wishing I were dead. Monsieur de la Mole would never think of me to memorize confidential secrets of state and thus escape a weary life of hardship in the back country. Instead, he would ask my brother with his photographic eyes, embossed with every word of every page he ever read.

Denny Knoll and Jerry Loft are singing my songs: "Dominique-nee-ka-neek, you are a fink, a fink, a fink. In fact, I think you stink-a-stink-a-stink.... Hey, hey, Paula, I wanna suck your tit.... Hats off to Larry, he broke a fart.... 'Cause I'm uh-huh stuck in you.... It was an itsy bitsy teeny weenie yellow cannellini peenie.... I feel shitty, oh so shitty, I feel shitty and farty and tight.... Look at me, I'm as restless as a horse that has to pee. On my own, would I have to use my hand to stroke my bone?... Nothing could be finer than to be in her vagina in the morning, nothing could be sweeter than for her to suck my tweeter...."

Momma is typing out meeting notes for the Sisterhood while watching *Hello Pea Pickers.* Watching her watch Tennessee Ernie Ford sing with bittersweet yearning, "Sunny Side of Heaven" makes me aware of how great things are when she's all there—when she's feeling all right, not burning with nervousness, not taking many pills, just enough to fall asleep at night and kill the nightmares. She plunges twists of boiling fudge through frigid water at the perfect tipping point, without a thermometer. She whips egg whites and oil with effortless wrist spins. Creates endless games with blocks, balloons and pieces of paper on rainy afternoons. Peels pears and oranges for children and adults she loves, likes to take a lengthy bubble bath, falls to knees in mocking wrath and points her index finger above her head and shakes it to emphasize a discrepancy in height. She listens as others tell their woes far into the night, always sympathetically, never offering advice. She plays Stravinsky and *Carmen* with Leontyne Price, knows the biographies of all the classical composers, nineteenth-century novelists, and Impressionist painters. She taught us funny words to the "Toreador Song": "Toreador-oh, don't spit on the floor-oh! Use the cuspidor! Whaddya think it's for?" She loves to talk about the books she reads, loves to feed the ducks and feel big wet raindrops fall on her hair and head in open fields. She repeats what others think of her and thinks of what they think she thinks they think. She says nasty things when she drinks too much, then seeks forgiveness so sincerely that people like her more for her apology. She stews on snubs that no one else can see.

Shadowing everything we do together and everything I do myself is a feeling that all is fragile, that every happy moment could explode, that every now could be the last of everything: last movie, last museum, last ball game, last bowling frame, last subway ride, last rippling tide, last baseball slide, last blossoming countryside, last moon tide, last ice cream, last sunbeam, the end of every friendship, of every camping trip. All of it could flip to dream, or slip away. Nothing lasts beyond this moment, past this day.

Cramped in the cloakroom of the synagogue, Dad hands us brand-new winter coats. They fit way too big and the outsides are daubed with snow and slightly damp. Dad says we'll grow into them. A cigarette is bobbing at his mouth, smoke floating towards the ceiling. He says he's glad to see us since, it's been so long. "Thirty-nine days," my brother notes.

I want to hide myself behind the folding stool concealed behind a row of hanging coats, hide in the sweet and wet bouquet of soggy wool, hide from memories of my father. Like the time he wouldn't bother helping me practice pitching since he didn't think I'd make the team. How he'd bitch at me for not refolding newspapers to make them look new, steamed that I was up before him reading them first, and all the way through. He always offers Lee the chicken breast, which really shouldn't matter since I like dark meat best. He didn't bother teaching me how to make a free-throw when I couldn't do it naturally the first time. He told my uncles I was yellow because I wouldn't fight Russell Rusheim. Then there was the time he yelled at me at dinner for dropping Jell-O on the floor. A piece of his fell by his chair, and I saw his feet furtively push wobbling green towards my seat, trying to ambush me, but I beat him to it and barked, "You dropped some, too." Or when he cracked Momma's head against the tub ... when he called her stupid when she flubbed the checkbook balance ... when he rapped her mouth ... when he slapped her silly ... when he had to be a scientist and cruelly tell me every detail when she slit her wrists and Leon found her gurgling in a pool of blood ... when he gave his stupid talks about desire and focus ... when he left us.

A guy named Donald comes for dinner. He and Momma giggle office politics—about the sinners and the saints, the winners and the "aints," the friends and the adversaries, the goldbricks and the disgraceful, who should get a bonus, who has the onus of dishonesty, the soulless rat race, then about raising kids without a mate, problems with his wife, how her coldness grates him, her alienating comments meant to put him in his place. For a change my Momma's knees do not vibrate. Her eyes, large and graceful, follow the expressions on Donald's face.

He removes the TV case to fix the picture, which plays nothing but fuzz. Leon holds a flashlight in place, while Donald tugs the tubes from molded metal. "That's the one," my brother says, as Donald battles with a tiny chromium-gilded globe.

"Why that one?" Donald asks, while probing for the other tubes.

"My Dad replaced it when it happened before."

"We'll take them all. Go get your mother!" I hear a tightness in Donald's voice, as if he's swallowed an enormous ice cube.

At the store we test the tubes, and Lee is right. "We'd have to buy another one of those if it was brightness," Lee says to Donald. "This one if it was the sound," pointing to a round and metal-coated bulb with grounding cotter pins. Momma scratches Leon's head, beams her pride and says his mind's a blotter. She buys us chocolate sauce and pecan ice cream.

They sit together on the couch, so close their knees are about to touch. They slouch and laugh and sip red wine. Donald sasses her, and she enjoys it. She drips the ruddy liquid into Flintstone glasses, dripping, dripping, dripping. They're sipping, sipping, slow and shaky, cozy, boozy, Donald tipping to the side, gripping Momma's thigh.

I leap from bed, panicked that I've overslept. I run downstairs to wake Momma for work. Her bedroom door is open wide, two Flintstone glasses at the headboard, crusty purple residue circling the sides. My careful feet glide closer, squeamishly. I see her naked arms and legs and murky pubic darkness underneath the sheet, lightly moving, swishing under the light fabric, mattress groaning, ingratiating, as if in a blissful dream. A blinding brightness penetrates the window grate and streams through the whiteness of the sheet. "Here, my sweet," she hisses, still in sleep.

Noiselessly I back away and shut the door, wait a second, knock hard, and yell to Momma that it's getting late.

"I'm not going." She sounds groggy and disoriented, as if my ears were waterlogged

"You have to go," I raise my voice so I can be heard through the door.

"Too tired," she mewls through the wood. "I won't survive a grueling day of work."

I regard the closed door—the door I closed—in a confused fog. Finally, I say, "You can't shirk it off. You have to go."

"I don't have to do a thing."

"You have to go to work."

"Don't castigate me, Jules. It's not your place to talk to me that way and I won't take it."

I wake my brother, make us breakfast, walk to school. We meet at synagogue for a Boy Scout meeting and then go home.

A bitter stench attacks us in the kitchen. Tubing packed behind the stove runs through the inner alcove to Momma's bedroom, disappearing underneath the crack below the door. It's shuttered tight and we can't rive it open, blockaded on the other side by jammed-in shelf brackets. We push, shove, drive. We push, shove, drive. We push, shove, drive. With a loud scraping whoosh the door finally swings wide to reveal our mother, motionless, silent but still alive, on the floor, a slightly bent and hissing tube scotch-taped to her nape.

"I know where the gas valve is," Leon says.

"Shut it," I command and start to batter at the tape decked about the window jam, use my hand to ram the window up, pop it open, shattering glass. I rip away the tubing crammed against her face and it stops wheezing.

I seize Momma by the shoulders and move her through the hallway slowly, a little at a time, by pushing her up and letting her flop and fall forward into a funerary frieze. Push, flop, and fall. Push, flop, and fall. A few feet. A few more. Finally we're at the kitchen where Leon stands, shivering. "See if the Friars are home, then give me a hand," I command.

I spin her weight across the kitchen floor. Push, flop, and fall. I'm exhausted. I take a moment to breathe deeply and catch a fading whiff of gas.

Scott's enormous pot-bellied dad is at the kitchen door, Leon behind him. He greets me with a drag from his half-inch stogie, tosses it behind him on the stoop, enters, tucks Momma's drooping body neatly over his shoulder with his lifeguard arms, carries her to the yard and flips her like a rag doll onto her feet. He stands her up and holds her straight against the fence, tells Scott's mom to "Bring a pot of coffee and something sweet to eat. And get me another cold beer. But don't call an ambulance."

Mr. Friar walks Momma along the lawn, slowly, her much shorter body sandwiched between his brawny side and shoulder. Momma's head begins to roll. He rides his elbow under her arm as support. Her mouth begins to groan, and then to chortle, half groggy, half sassy, "Ha, ha, Hal, it's you who guards the gates of hell.... Ha, ha, let me go ... I ha, ha, left ... theft the gas on ... can't you smell it ... swell it?" She staggers freely along the grass.

"We took care of the gas."

Her arms are flapping upward.

"And what about the bastard who made me turn it on? Did you chase that louse from the house?"

"We took care of him, too, Ethel. He's gone."

She sees me on the other side of the lawn and staggers free from Mr. Friar. "Jules! Are you okay?"

She's sliding on the grass. She stumbles forward, falls beneath our tree. She crawls on hands and knees, creeping closer, head upraised to me, make-up smeared, hair in disarray. "Are you okay, Jules?" She's braced against the fence. Her fingers crawl up the links. She's walking upright, woozy, wobbling, towards me, falling. Her arms are sinking around my waist and I climb into non-thinking.

It's been a week since she's disappeared into the basement, climbing the steps sometimes to get a bite to eat and pace a bit, start a fight or throw a fit, or make an ugly face to the hallway mirror. A week of tearful drones about why she's alive when her mother's dead for years. A week of bemoaning her flaws, bonehead wife, pinhead parent, airhead driver. She's a drain on everyone, plain compared to curvy sister Hedy who won a beauty contest, just a dope compared to brainy, well-read sister Hope with her Master's in Englishurbation. Always pushed against the grain. Always feeling pain too quickly. Unable to appease her parents, unfit to please her husband. Easily stressed and presses too much. She can't set boundaries for those spiteful monsters, her curse to raise alone, her delightful little geniuses who deserve a home-cooked dinner every night, deserve a house that's clean, a basement that doesn't stink, deserve mended clothes, deserve a stable life. She drinks too much. She can't fend for herself. She goes on and on, then descends to the blinking TV light.

Harlan Schwartz pulls his winky out in class and starts prancing round the room and pumping it. Leon jumps behind him, thrusts in sync, low-kneed like a wiry Groucho Marx. Lee obscenely gestures with his tongue and barks out Pi's first digits, over and over, "Three…point…one…four… one…five…nine…three…point…one…four…one…five…nine…three… point…one…four…one…five…nine…three…point…one…four…one… five…nine…." He's suspended from school a week.

Momma's on the phone, but she doesn't speak. She just stands and listens to the other side and shakes her head. With an unexpected violence, she throws the phone receiver at the wall and pounds a chair with her open hand. When I leave for school, she's crawling by the kitchen table, wearing a robe and a pair of socks. Radio blare is drowning out her bawling. Three cigarettes smolder in a metal ashtray on the floor.

When I get home from school, she's still on her hands and knees in the kitchen, now forcefully scrubbing molding in a corner of the doorway with a coarse soap pad. She gazes up at me and whispers hoarsely, eyes ablaze with remorse, "I was fired today."

Lee barfs his breakfast all over the back seat of the car, and Momma blames herself for driving like a maniac. She hugs him, calls him her Adonis. His eyebrows link to form a thick black scar, his shoulders hunch together stiffly, an arch in his back as he tries to shrink away from her.

Someone swipes the side of our parked car in the parking lot of the five and dime while we're inside shopping. Momma blames herself, gripes she parked too close to the double yellow stripe.

Leon stops wearing underpants and nips his dick in his zipper teeth, which masticates a tiny bit of sheath. He needs three stitches for the nasty cut and gets a gauzy penile cast. Momma says she caused it by letting the dirty laundry pile up.

Slippery feel of soap on ceramic tile, slippery feel of shoe soles on a wet slab of linoleum, sudden stiffened gait, start and stop of body, awkward panicky grab at a spinning, falling disk. Inchoate dizziness. Slow-motion shattering of a wet plate. I stand agape and shivering like a wet Lab for a minute, looking at the various irregular shapes radiating across the floor, all sharp and ready to stab.

"Did you do that on purpose?" Momma pronounces these words in an angry, pounce-on-prey voice, biting each syllable off slowly and deliberately.

"What?" This false accusation confuses me. I try to guard my shame even as it makes me speak defensively. I bend over and start apprehensively to pick up the larger shards with my fingers.

"What did you say? Don't use that language with me."

"All I said was 'What?'"

"I'm not hard of hearing. I heard you use the F-word."

"No, I didn't!"

"It wasn't a bird who chirped it. You're becoming just like your father. Uncultivated and disrespectful. You owe me an apology"

"I don't agree. I don't know what you heard, Momma, but I didn't use the F-word and I didn't drop the plate on purpose."

"You can't use that language with me." Her voice becomes more and more grating. I wish she would believe me.

"But I didn't say anything." We bicker back and forth, until she kicks the wall and retreats to her bedroom. I look at the broken mess. It's my fault, but it's not my fault. Nothing is accidental, but sometimes there are accidents. No malice precedes the action but precedents exist. I didn't plan to do it, but it happened. I did it, and it exhausts my sense of shame. The words I speak get lost in bleak complexity. I didn't curse. But it's the perverse opposite of a tree falling in the woods and no one hears the snap and crash. Did it make a noise? If someone hears you say something, does that mean you said it even if you didn't? You can explain every mishap, every adverse thing with a cause. Every burning has a flame, but does it have to have a blame? There are laws, but there are also exceptions. What about the truly random—a flash of light in the eyes, rain from the skies, a momentary perceptual deception, a sudden explosion, a gradual corrosion, a sudden wind, a sudden pain? I am drowning in blame and misgiving, guilt attaching to every action like hydrogen to a carbon chain.

Momma churns the key in the car ignition, and the starter chews itself and stalls. She has it hauled to a garage, but it costs too much to fix. We replace it with an ancient Dodge.

Rocky jumps from Leon's bed towards a chest of drawers and catches a hind leg on the herringbone spread. He runs around the room in circles yipping, dragging his haunches like a sack of stones behind him, pissing everywhere, ripping the sheets to shreds with frenzied chewing, collapsing underneath the bed with a frightful moan.

The vet's exam reveals he's broken several bones. "Five hundred to set and he'll always limp. Why not have him put to sleep?" the vet suggests.

Leon stands without expression. I say that I don't want to keep him. "I'm tired of cleaning up his messes."

Momma resolves to save the squealing shit, because she "Cannot kill a thing that thinks and has a name and answers to it." I count the dollars in my mind, all five hundred, one at a time, and then I do it dime by dime. How many weeks could we make it last? How many gallons of gas? How many boxes of shredded wheat? How many loaves of bread? How many pounds of meat? How many peaches and pears? How many subway fares? Every time I see his stupid dog grin, I think that Momma doesn't have a job. His crooked bumpkin dog smile, his splat and stuttering way of running now, like *Gunsmoke*'s Chester hobbling after Sheriff Matt. I think that Momma doesn't have a job. My stomach spins and scats with queasy worry, like when you've eaten too much candy. Momma doesn't have a job.

I say, "I'll trade my green and purple lots for the orange one you've got." Two monopolies for one I offer Scott. Majestically I wave my hands across the board. "Five hotels and all you have to do is hoard a little cash, which won't take long. Come on, take the plunge!"

Leon squeals like a squeezed dripping sponge, "Don't do something rash.

You're nearly broke, and Jules has cash to buy hotels. People land on green a fraction of the time they land on orange!"

Leon knows the odds, but I keep poking, prodding. "Have you seen the high rents on green?"

"Don't do it! He'll build his hotels right away!" My brother sounds alarmed, frenetic, yipping like a cornered wolverine.

"But you'll have two monopolies. You'll have it made. What do you say?"

"Agreed, I'll make the trade," Scott resolutely tells us, and we swap our cardboard deeds. It's my turn and I start to grin, because I know I'm going to win. Leon knows it, too, and shows it in his eyes, a smoldering chagrin. I give the bank my dough, drop hotels on the orange properties, roll the dice and land on *Go.*

Leon rolls a seven from Electric to New York.

"One thousand even. Fork over the shekels," I chortle.

Thwack—something decks me. Leon's hands tug my neck, choke me. His knees have pinned my forearms to the rug.

"Let me go! Let me go!"

But he presses down his knees against my arms and I can't move. Tugging, kicking, screeching, gagging, gurgling, reaching frantically, then tingle in my legs and arms, ringing in my ears ... a seething sting ... a distant bark ... a distant brattling ... something rattling ... an embattled starkness screeching ... groggy ... blurry ... reaching darkness....

Awake but dazed, on the basement chaise, looking up at Leon's teardrops spattering my face.

From fridge to stove to hall to fridge to stove to hall, Momma strides across the room, settles at the table, stands again, walks around the little alcove, then stalks another triadic passage from fridge to stove to hall.

"I didn't think I'd even get a call, but when I did I had to cope with driving sixteen miles to Westbury. When he asked if I had college, I said I hoped it wouldn't disqualify me."

From fridge to stove to hall, she talks and smokes and paces. "He asked about the latest place I worked and some other things that I forget. I told the truth without regret and said I took ill for several months. When he dialed my former boss right then and there and asked him why, my hands got wet, my throat went dry."

From fridge to stove to hall, then she charges to the counter top, starts to form a meatball, drops the spoon and starts to pace again from fridge to stove to hall. She stops and looks upwards into space, hands raised, looking half crazed.

"My heart was racing. My head was throbbing. I wanted to crawl away," she sobs. "But then he hangs up the phone, smiles, and says he wants me starting Monday and I have a job!

Tranquil half-slumber, subway's rock and sway warms and numbs me. My heart begins to rumble, racing Leon up the subway steps and through the booming vastness of the deco lobby of the Hotel St. George, zooming past the shops and armchairs to the locker room. Reek of chlorine serves as invitation to joy expanding, the lashing blithe sensation jumping in the giant waterfall that's crashing from the pawls under ceiling sluices at the shallow end, pouring water on my head and arms, pouring, pouring, pouring, pouring, pouring. An eternally thunderous profusion of water soars and falls into splashing contusions. A pleasantly dreamy exhaustion in the steam of Turkish bathing, old men wrapped in towels or wearing jockstraps, mashing cigars in teeth, hashing their ancient irksome jokes about their wives and bridgework. Back to Queens, tranquil half-slumber, subway rocking.

Denny throws a wobbly pass to Lee, who slides through Jones Beach sand, jumps and stretches high for the football and catches it, but glides across a chair and lands astride a smoking barbecue and sears a grid-shaped pattern in his arm and hand.

A court complaint against my Dad stands open on the kitchen table, conspicuous like a wart or stain you're unable to explain. Nonpayment of child support. If Momma signs, a sheriff could throw him behind bars anytime, anywhere in New York State. "It's not the man I hate, it's the situation. He's the father of my children. I don't want to see him go to jail, so it's hard for me to sign and put it in the mail."

For months, we haven't seen him. He lives in Northern New Jersey and calls us once a week and doesn't speak to Momma, even if she asks for him. Momma hasn't gone to work in days. She doesn't cook, she doesn't wash the dishes, doesn't dust, doesn't shop, doesn't do the laundry. Finally she ascends from the basement. Her hair spews out in all directions and she talks in disembodied low inflections, like a zombie, sagging skin exploding blood-shot eyes. "He must be taught a lesson. Today I'll sign the sheriff's order and hope he comes around and finally pays. That way, everyone's a winner."

When she signs, she makes a flourish in the air, then flays the paper with the pen, making a dull, hard scratching sound. She sends me out to get the legal papers notarized from our friendly pharmacist, and to buy some food at the A&P. She takes a bath and straightens up the house and then makes brown meat and kasha for dinner.

In the middle of eating, she stands up and proclaims, "I'm ready to make a big announcement. I'm not missing work anymore, but I need your help around the place. Make your beds, do the dishes, walk the dog, no long faces. When I say do your homework, don't get sore or make a lame excuse. And please, don't bog me down with your constant blaming over little crap. I want a truce. We'll do it together. Now come here" She lifts her arms out and expects us to rush to her so she can enwrap us in them, one on each side. I see Lee start and then freeze. Her hands give beckoning waves, fingers fluting back and forth towards palms. I move to her side and Lee follows suit. The arms wrap around my shoulders. It feels safe and steady, but also like a teasing trap.

The Boy Scout jamboree, four hundred fifty patrols and all with one goal: to win one of twenty-five blue ribbons. A sense of desperate urgency imbues me, as if I'm stuck in the middle of a packed auditorium and have to pee, except it isn't an antsy bladder, but the totality of my mind and body on the edge of nervous activity, my senses like a threatened yak at the moment of attack. We must win a blue. I design our camp to be an outdoor living room and give the plans to Leon, who lashes wooden benches, equipment racks, and a hanging pantry, while Denny sets up tents with trenches. The rest of the Zestab crew searches for wood. I make a stew in metal coffee cans tossed directly on the fire for twenty minutes, and there's barely enough for us, since all the judges want to try it. After we clean up the campsite, I put together Zestab teams for the next day's competitions, making sure that every kid does what he does best. I stare at the pegs battered into the ground on all sides through the night, listening to raccoons tread the forest floor and crickets rub their legs, remixing and rematching my teams in my head.

In the eight-man relay after Michael Denver trips and drops the stick, Leon picks it up and races desperately from sixth to third. We come in second in the talent show, singing my funny words to a Steve Lawrence ditty in our underwear, a bare-chested Denny beating on the bongos, *Go Away Tenderfeet, go away Tenderfeet, You're not supposed to make a tent from sheets.* We're the fifth patrol to find ten different locations in the woods using just a compass. Leon and I must fight off seven other two-man teams and lift a watermelon creamed with lard onto wooden beams at the deep end of the swim zone. I remember what my father always says—get your butt between the ball and the other guy. When we gain control of the bobbing white oval, instead of trying to carry it like the other teams do, we trap it between us and slowly maneuver it to the pier by slapping it back and forth, all the while fighting off the others. At the pier, I put myself between the greasy globe and the other teams and block furiously, slashing, splashing, throwing elbows, while my brother swims underneath it, pushes up and lifts it onto the wooden planks. We win a blue ribbon and from our troop a special prize: Swiss army knives complete with case and whetstone. "Today the Zestabs are the Yanks," I tell the guys.

Momma washes walls and baseboards. She digs toothbrush and tweezers into corners on her hands and knees. She scrubs the floors, defrosts the freezer, and rubs away the smell of Rocky's messes. She designs, addresses, and sends the invitations, sews her dresses, makes new curtains for the kitchen, and cooks the food for eighty. All the family specialties— liver fricassee, goulash, paprikash noodles, Viennese strudel, roast potatoes, porcupine balls with onions, red cabbage sautéed in wine, white cabbage served raw as slaw, all for my Bar Mitzvah party, which we have at home to save money. She rents extra flatware, napkins and plates, gets a special centerpiece from out of state, buys the booze and pumps balloons.

All her favorite tunes repeat on the stereo hours on end—*Scheherazade, West Side Story, Peer Gynt Suite, Carmen, My Fair Lady,* Sigmund Romberg. She gaily sings along while mopping to the beat, "My desert is waiting, dear, come there with me. ... Love came to me, gay and tender, love came to me, sweet surrender. ... Give me some men who are stout-hearted men...."

Momma paces through the lobby of the Greyhound station, chasing looks around the doors and at the schedule. I ground my eyes inside my book, but trace the faintest shadow of her fretting strides across the pages, bounding back and forth before the letters. We wait for Aunt Hedy and her family, expected from the Jersey Shore: my cousins Guy and Teddy, and Uncle Mark, a few months older than me, who went to stay with Hal and Hedy after Grandma passed away when he was three, and Pop-pop, who owns a failing linen store in a sordid section of the boardwalk near the jail in Atlantic City, an unloved cache of decorator napkins, percale pillow cases, table cloths, bandoliers, gloves and doilies Momma said he bought before the market crashed more than thirty years ago.

"He embarrasses his family on purpose and it's shameful," Momma wails while we wait. "Leaving false teeth on his plate. Wearing plaid with stripes. He dips his fingers into platters, wipes them on the table cloth, and sips from other people's cups. When he makes a mess, he never cleans it, but covers it up. He forgets to flush. He fixes everything with spit and twine. His whiny singing in the synagogue, always a beat behind. Lies about his business, age and education. His false claims that we're descended from the Dukes of Budapest. Everything he says is fabrication, and every moment with him is a test!"

"Don't get upset in advance," I have heard Hope say to her with her usual aplomb. "Wait until he drops his bomb, whatever the taunt or stupidity, and even then, don't react and don't attack. That's precisely what he wants, so stay calm."

"Yes, that's smart, you're right, that's good advice." Momma's legs start to scurry in place like rattled titmice. Momma holds her knee to try to tame the tremor. "But it's not easy. He's always tearing into me."

"It's as easy as pie. Just don't let him entice you into playing his games. Practice the fine art of not caring. That's why he's never preyed on me. I haven't cared what he thought or said since I started seventh grade."

But Hope isn't here at the bus depot to tame Momma's nervous fury and she paints herself a canvas of worry.

Eight of us packed inside the Plymouth motoring on Union Turnpike, my smaller cousins sitting on laps. Momma is trying to enter the left-hand lane to make a turn. She looks to her left, sees a black Caddy beside her and burns the brakes to fall behind it, jolting everyone forward and waking the snoring Pop-pop. But the other car drops back, too, so she accelerates to pass and doesn't see a fat pothole. As the right tire whacks into it, the side of the car suddenly dips and we start to hear a loud, lacerating clack. Pit-a-pat, pit-a-pat … flat tire. Pit-a-pat … pit-a-pat…. Momma rolls the car over to the side of the road. We wait along the shoulder, while Uncle Hal jacks up the frame and mounts the spare. Momma paces round the car and gnaws a fingernail

Pop-pop says, "Try to calm down, honey, all's well," in a frail, cajoling whine.

"Dad, I'm fine," Momma inhales a sea deep sigh.

"Calm down, honey," Pop-pop says again and starts following Momma as she paces, noisily thumping the concrete with the bottom of his shoes. "All's well. Hal will change the tire and we'll be on our way without being towed. It's just a momentary miscue, a minor bump in the road. We can refuse to get upset or let it get to us. We can choose to remain calm and in control. Don't make more of it than what it is. Our goal in life should always be to seek peace, not strife." He speaks sweetly, but in a persistently hectoring croon, like argumentative sheep in a Bugs Bunny cartoon. His bleating begins to chafe on all of us. I see it on the faces of Hedy and Momma, who look ready to kill him.

"Dad, I'm calm." She halts to light a cigarette, her hands unsteady, then begins to pace again. Pop-pop starts to follow behind but Hedy, peeved, pulls him back by the coat sleeve. "Stop needling her."

"I'm not. I'm trying to help. Calm down honey, calm down."

"How can I keep calm with your constant hectoring?"

"Calm down, honey, don't blame yourself. It's not your fault. It's your cheapskate husband who won't buy you a decent car," he niggles in a high-pitched wheedling assault.

"I don't have a husband," Momma's voice swells with sadness.

"You still do in the eyes of Adoshem. He's just not a good one."

"Go to Hell," Momma shouts into his face, and all the kids giggle.

Pop-pop pulls his false teeth from his mouth and sets them on his place-mat at Friday dinner. Momma growls at him, "Put them back in or leave the table." Pop-pop picks up the foul mess and lets it drop, retrieves it from the floor, and expresses an oily remorse, "I forgot."

Momma discovers Pop with his hand on a plate of apple strudel on a basement stand. "Can't you wait until tomorrow?"

"I'm moving it to make some room." He rotates both arms and lifts the glass tray, opens his hands wide and lets it fall. The platter bends and shatters as it hits the tile. On the floor around him splay flakes of glass and clods of crumbs. Hedy smacks him across his bum, as if he's still a child. Momma paces and talks to herself a while.

Pop-pop pushes through a group of people gathered in the aisle to kiss the Torah scrolls in synagogue, stumbles over Marty Hellman's big-boobed older sister, rolls his forehead on her lap, remains an instant, and brays, "I'm sorry!" in that achy whine with which he talks and prays and sings, a beat behind—just like Momma complains—and in a different key.

I see him among the dozens milling outside the men's bathroom in syna-gogue, yelling to the porter about clogged pipes, stamping his feet and wav-ing his hand in the air like he's wiping away a bad aroma. Jerry Luft comes out, hands still damp from washing them, swipes his hand across my shoul-der and stamps his feet, "Yipes, it smells like something died about six years ago in there, and I think your Zayde killed it."

Pop-pop sees us pillow-fighting at the party, orders me to stop, so I boldly flaunt an unwritten rule that Bar Mitzvah boys can do whatever they want. Pop-pop balls his hands into a tight fist, thumb inside his palm, like my father taught me not to do, sways on the balls of his tiny feet and whines, "Tough talk from a tough guy. Wanna fight about it?" then drops his hands and takes flight.

A circle of aunts and uncles tell their stories about me: the time when I was three, my hands smeared with chocolate, running towards Aunt Hope's new pink chair and Jack scooped me up just before I got there, zoomed me round the room with his extended arms and to the kitchen sink. The time I asked my Momma if we could visit Hope, who must be in the hospital death-ly sick, because her birthday card to me wasn't in the mail. The time I mem-orized a book of dirty limericks. When Momma asked Aunt Hedy where the library was as soon as our bus sailed into Galloway, and Hedy asked her why: "Because sooner or later every day we'll have to go there for Jules." "That's ridiculous, just tell him *No*! Tell him we have rigid rules," relenting twenty minutes later after I bombarded her, she says, with question after question on her garden dirt, until her forehead started hurting. She drove me there herself "to make him shut up," she groans. My use of *valence, quadrille, exquisite, recompense*, and other words Aunt Mamie sighed would make her dart straight to the dictionary after visits to their Brownsville brownstone. When I was eight, and Momma said I identified every painting we saw in the Museum of Modern Art.

The start of Aunt Bernie's story about my slipping on Petey's muddy shoe, losing my balance, and flipping down a flight of stairs in cartwheels is interrupted by a high-pitched grinding squeal of steel, followed by a violent thud.

Pop-pop, reeking of booze, sits behind the wheel of our Dodge, the bumper of which is embedded in the back of the Lodges' Cadillac.

"I was backing out the car so these nice people could go," right hand patting heart, he whines to all eighty people at the party, now outside in the driveway or on the lawn. Momma bellows a bone-crunching catharsis fit for a Greek play. A chorus of aunts start to calm her down, Hope embracing her, Hedy, Bernie, Beryl, Mamie, Bunny, and Lilly surrounding her like a clowder of villagers forming a protective circle around one of their own who has had a peek at something awful. Aunt Flo propels her nose an inch from Pop-pop's jaw, screaming loudly, "You shitty little pipsqueak, you dinky fuck-faced clown!"

There's a sudden shriek of an invaded bobolink and Cousin Helen races from the house. She's found a food-drenched set of false teeth soaking in the bathroom sink.

My father explains by phone that he didn't come to my Bar Mitzvah because he didn't want to get arrested, even though Momma promised not to call the cops. He says of all the books he's ever read, he's sending me the tops, the very best, now that I'm old enough to understand it. If I read it carefully, I'll always be riding under wraps and land on my feet. Weeks later his package waits for me in his car when I get out of school: a paperback of *Atlas Shrugged* and fifty one dollar bills wrapped in a paper band.

But it's not his car anymore and he's not in the driver's seat, but his friend Joey, hands on the wheel. I find the gift sitting on a mass of girly magazines, racing forms, three-ring binders and other crap, curled pages covered in shoe prints and coffee rings. Joey leans out the window and sings out to me to hop in the car and we'll stop at Sterling Optical to get new glasses.

It takes an hour for the glasses to be ready, and we pass the time in the front seat of the car in the Lake Success shopping center's parking lot. Joey buys a deep-fried breaded hot dog and some fudge ice cream for me, while he slurps pureed bananas and peas from small greasy glass jars. Joey drains the sludge with milk straight from a carton. My father likes to ridicule Joey's ulcers and his disheartening bad luck with get-rich-quick schemes. "Every guy has a friend who's a schmuck, and Joey's mine," Dad always says. Joey sits without talking, burping his meal and groaning. The sky teems, then begins to drop a steady rain. I fit the gift under my coat and watch the puddles pool. The parking lot could be an ocean, the car a poorly sealed boat, and I could be afloat on it, completely abandoned, drifting aimlessly between islands in an uninhabited archipelago.

Leon gets suspended from Hebrew School for fighting and from public school for lighting up a cigarette.

Momma roils the car key in the starter. The engine sputters weakly but it doesn't turn. The chassis starts to reek of burning oil.

"That bastard couldn't help it, could he? He had to ruin my car like he ruined my mother, like he made her life an unbearable toil."

Momma plunges an imaginary knife into her side as an emphasis to every syllable, both hands riding a shadow blade, "Like...he...makes...ev...er...y...thing...wrong...like...he's...ruined... ev...er...y...thing...he's...e...ver...touched...." She murmurs a hollow, catatonic sing-song: "Dragged us up and down the Atlantic coast with his trashy linen stock and his Eastern European shtick, after losing most of our savings in the 1929 crash, which doesn't stop him acting rash whenever he scrounges extra cash. He made my mother sick by knocking her up year after year, and then he started screwing some piece of trash who worked where he bought his beer. I found them going at it on the floor underneath a table in his linen store, while Momma was delivering Emil. Even when the louse was out of work, he never did a thing around the house. He would appear in the kitchen empty-handed and command that Mom could now clear the dishes off the table. I caught him crouching sadly on the weed-infested slope behind the bathroom looking through a window, peeking at my sister Hope. He didn't listen when I told him Cousin Melvin touched my spot. He got mad and punished me and said—'It's for your own good, honey.' In jail for my high school graduation, arrested in a hotel lobby for solicitation, he's to blame for everything that's bad...."

She buys an ancient Chevy with my Bar Mitzvah money.

Another speech from Momma, bleary-eyed, perspiring, lurching aimlessly round the kitchen in a sprawling peach housecoat. "Leon, Jules, my boss just called. He bawled me out and warned me that if I miss work again, he'll fire me. I need your help to get up in the morning, Jules. And both of you, don't get mired in endless brawls about dusting or the dishes or your other tasks. Please make your beds every day without my asking."

We both say okay.

"Let's celebrate by making sundaes!"

"But it's Monday," Leon says.

"Okay, we'll make 'mondaes,'" Momma concedes.

"But it's already Tuesday in Calicut," Lee proceeds. They banter back and forth while Momma doles out the ice cream, chocolate sauce, and nuts over pound cake.

Next morning, and I'm at her door to wake her.

"Go away!"

"It's time for work."

"I can't today."

"But you'll be fired!" I insist, and she goes berserk, screaming and shaking a fist like Pop-pop's, thumb awkwardly hidden. She throws a pillow at me. Her eyes are leaking banshee tears. "I can't, I can't, I can't today. I need a break. I can always find another job, but I cannot leave my room today," she shrieks.

She stays in bed all week.

Lee takes a flashlight to bed. He holds it with one hand overhead for light and dives into a thick, weighty science tome far into the night. He brings home a note from school: *Leon falls asleep in class almost every day.* They want to speak to Momma, but she doesn't call.

Momma starts for work, but the Chevy stalls and she turns back home.

The principal deprives Lee of extracurricular activities for throwing a ball in the hall.

I'm Wally in my dream, hanging out with the Beav in the backyard, building up a pile of snowballs, except we're not in Mayfield, but underneath the elevated track on Livonia Avenue and the train is barreling by above, unsheathed rails vibrating between supporting beams, sparking at rust-stained ferrules. The bundled-up dream Beaver looks like Lee and he's laughing loudly, bellowing guffaws that drown out the train, his mouth opened wide and exhaling black steam.

Momma tells me that my father went to Belmont with Aunt Flo to bet the ponies. Aunt Bernie knew they were there and called the cops. They caught him in the parking lot and escorted him to jail for nonsupport. He spent the night locked up, "elbow to elbow with a throng of low-lives and free-loaders, where he belongs." At daybreak, he went to court and paid the alimony he owed. "He just wrote a check. I knew all along that he could pay it without hardship or delay."

Momma goes on a shopping spree, shirts and socks for me, pants and shoes for Lee, underwear and sweaters for all, dresses for herself, a magazine rack, a stack of books, a rake for the yard, brakes for the car, asparagus with Roquefort and skirt steaks for dinner, cheesecake for dessert.

I turn my bike into the driveway and see Leon holding Momma by an arm, walking her along the grass. Momma talks some gibberish about the cold. The inside smells of gas.

Prayer by rote in hours of fasting service, sweating under sports coat on a Yom Kippur day more like summer than fall. Brainless from hunger, Denny and I are tired of braying and beating our chests with our fists, reciting lists of sins, or milling in the lobby's heated din of moms and pot-bellied bards.

We walk to my house. The basement's cooler than our sun-soaked yard.

"It smells like Philip Simper!" Denny says.

"I wish that fucking dog were dead."

"I'm sure that Russ would take his BB gun and shoot him in the head for twenty bucks."

"It'll only take a sec to clean it." I get a pail and trowel and look for piles. It's been a while since I've done a search, so pieces have dried. When I twist the blade to wrench them up, their undersides release an acrid reek that makes me lurch, dizzy from the sulfurous stench.

"I'll do that, Jules." Momma appears, skin blanched from lack of sun, hair teased and pushed to one side. She's in a housecoat open at the knees.

"That's okay, I'm almost done." I fake a smile.

"But it's Yom Kippur. You're fasting."

"It's okay, Momma, let me finish, please!" I continue my exploration for smelly piles.

"You'll ruin your clothes, don't make an issue of it!" she bleats.

I don't want to make an issue of it. I don't want to have a scene. I don't want to start an argument. I just want to clean it up. Walking bent over, I stumble on a dip in the concrete.

"Jules, I'm capable of doing this," her shriek a mix of hurt and mean. She seizes my trowel and some of the foul matter drops to the floor.

"It's not about you or your capabilities," I implore.

She slaps my cheek. The sting rips venomous claws through bands of tender flaming flesh on fire, sharply threshing the hidden wires that align my emotional frame.

I start to hit her. I don't want to do it, but I can't stop my aimless, fistless palms from bearing down on her, smacking and slapping, hacking and rapping, many blows landing on her head and hands. Denny shouts, "Jules, it's your mom!" His voice sounds far away, like the sound of distant whitecaps flitting at the shoreline. Denny's right, but the more I hit, the more I want to hit. The more I hit, the more I want to hit. Momma shrinks defensively but underneath her outstretched hands I see her smiling grandly, as if she planned it. When I see her lips, grinning as if in victory, I stop my hitting, run upstairs and outside. I sprint back to the synagogue at full speed. Runner pangs are splitting my sides. I'm gasping for air.

I see Steven Kander on the sanctuary stair. I race to him and bash him in the jaw, bang, bang, and say, "Wipe the bugger off your face! Oh, that's no bugger, that's your nose." He raises a fist. My left arm tautly blocks. My right, left, right, left, right, left blows knock him on his ass, like my father taught me years ago when a bully socked me after class. Jerry's father takes hold of Steve and Mr. Hiken pulls me back, leans into me, and whispers, "I understand that Kander trash fighting *yontev*, no better than a goy, but you're a good boy, Jules, a mensch not a schmuck. You know better than to lash out like dat. So tuck your shirt in, *geh* bench, *geh* pray."

Sitting on the wooden bench along the aisle in the sanctuary, I fixate on the blood between my knuckles and smile.

Rocky scampers out the kitchen door before I have a chance to shut him in. "Go inside, I have to go to school!" I beg, but he doesn't listen. Instead, he spins around in circles, twitches his tail, shows his tongue and drools, then slows a bit and licks his butt and spits. I flail my arms to catch him, and he peg-leg hop-steps to the side and wails, kicking up his bad leg like a pogo stick. "I'm going to miss my friends, you stupid mutt!" I scurry up and down the driveway to trick the shit machine. He jogs along and barks his blissful, mocking bark. I run behind the back-yard gate. He approaches it, but brakes in time and doesn't take the bait. I run and stand, run and stand, run and stand, then stop and go straight at him. But he sails right through my hands, jabbing his twisted leg fleetly into the air, as if flaunting my defeat.

"Fuck it, fuck you!" I say and cross the street.

Rocky tails me at a distance, yapping and prancing, cautiously close enough to follow, but zigzagging, and still far enough away not to get trapped. I turn up Union Turnpike. I shoo him home every few lawns. Tail wagging, he yawns at me, shifts directions, and drifts away but stays in view.

When I reach 265th Street, I cross the road to where my friends are wait-ing. Too scared of screeching cars to breech the curb, Rocky leaps and glares at sidewalk's end.

"We were going to leave without you! Hey, that's your dog streaking around across the street."

"He sneaked outside the house and won't go back inside. I keep telling him to go away, but that ratty shit hog won't obey! He thinks we're playing hide-and-seek."

"Shit hog. You said that about your own dog!?" Denny laughs.

"Fuck that freak, let's go. He'll jog back home when he's good and ready."

After school, and Rocky is still not home. Momma says to look for him around the neighborhood, but we hang out at a nearby playground instead. We don't leave the door open overnight for him. Momma doesn't call the pound. A week later, I clean the basement floor. I hope he's dead.

I drift in and out of sleep, radio humming. In my head, vignettes and moods seem to sift and spin, twists and frets from songs exuding a thin membrane of dream: *Don't think twice, it's all right ... I get around ... See that funny little clown ... with no particular place to go ... He's so fine ... in that warm California sun ... Do you want to know a secret? ... A change is gonna come ... she'll have fun, fun, fun ... from morning, noon and night ... Walk right in ... Someone, somewhere tell her it's not fair ... Catch the wind ... she's not there....*

Our letter holder on my mother's nightstand is stuffed with bills: electric, sewer, Macy's, Penney's, phone. In my hand, each invoice feels as heavy as a corner curbstone. Bright red block letters splatter every envelope spelling, "Payment on Demand."

Momma complains of insomnia, but she refuses to take her Librium. She says she is saving them, so she can have some extra in case she gets a job and needs to stay calm. She frets that she's afraid to fall asleep, afraid that she will never wake again, afraid of creeping through nightshade in a dream that never ends. At night she walks the house and watches TV ghouls and talk shows. She's asleep when I get home from school.

The three of us watch TV together, sitting on the basement sofa bed. We see stunned expressions of grief on the faces of dozens of talking heads. A procession of mourners. Flags and flags. Jack Ruby appears out of no-where, points a gun at Lee Harvey Oswald, and bags him. Shoots him dead. Seeing Ruby double over and struggle with the cops makes me think of my father, who hated JFK and insisted that his father was a Nazi lover and the Pope was in his ear. I don't repeat his words, not even to my mother, having learned from the blistery reprimand by my fifth grade teacher Mrs. Klein when I bandied my father's twisted view on Hiroshima: that it would mean nothing in the vast scheme of natural history.

Desire to play Oberon in the school play claws at me. This hunger doesn't rest, to say out loud in front of everyone, "*At a fair vestal thronèd by the west ….*" To a mirror twin, I exclaim my lines for hours. Audition day I stand outside the gym gnawing, pining, and whining to myself my shapeless, aimless shame. I watch the other kids, but can't go in.

My spastic hand dials wrong numbers, again and again, unable to complete a call to Kate, guileful friend of Penny, Marty Hellman's older sister. I want to ask her to meet me in the park sometime. Last week she stole my glasses when we were playing billiards at Marty's, put them down her blouse and didn't fight when my fingers splayed apart inside her bra to feel her ladybird breasts before retrieving my sight.

I pull out three tens and seven ones. There're only seven twenties left in Momma's wallet. At the supermarket, I load up on low-cost food, day-old white bread buns, packaged cookies, eggs and chopped meat, canned instead of frozen vegetables, a bag of carrots, Cream of Wheat.

Another task, the laundry: hang the wet clothes in the basement, drop the dry ones in a basket, which I carry to the living room, where I dump my freight. I have homework and I want to watch *The Fugitive*. Folding can wait.

Three Bs, two Cs? I know this stuff. How could I make so many stupid mistakes? Not carry the one. Transpose the date. Write *nitrogen* when I mean *nitrate*. Write *brake* instead of *break*.

A monitor escorts me to a messy office to chat with the school psychologist, Dr. Cassander, immense, in a formless tent dress, with golden bracelets twisted round her fatty wrists. "What's wrong with your brother? He sits in class listless and never says a word. But when his teacher mentioned reading *Brave New World*, Leon hurled his books and pens across the room and shouted how he hated the Huxleys, hated the Jameses, the Alcotts, and the Alous. He kept berating the teacher and she didn't know what to do. He ripped his notebook to shreds like a hungry goat; then, without being asked, he took his chair into the hallway, sat and read a book the rest of the day. Neither of your parents has replied to my note."

Wait a minute! What about me?! Didn't you notice I'm finding it hard to stay afloat? Aren't my grades a wreck? You'd never think to check on me because I'm not the genius, not the Perfect Lee.

But then I think about the many torments that have been my brother's fate. It was Lee my father's pit bull bit along the arm and on his gut when he went to shut the gate one scary, storm-lit night. It was under Lee that the ground gave way and he landed on his butt nine feet down an open sewer line while trick-or-treating and I had to pull him out. Lee who caught his prick in his zipper, Lee who tripped on a barbecue grill, Lee who got crabs, Lee nabbed repeatedly for stealing candy bars, Lee awakened in the middle of his tonsillectomy. Lee who discovered Momma, wrists cut through, and twisting in a swill of blood. Lee who saw our father bang her brains against the tub. Lee whom she drubbed with a bent coat hanger before her stay at Bellevue when I was two. At least that's what my father maintains.

It's not the same. Am I lucky, or luckier, despite what I've been through? How can I compare the two? I can only guess what others feel inside, what Leon feels, from the expression on their face and what they say and do. I have no way to titrate their pain. There's only say and do. Say and do.

But I don't reveal how I feel. I talk instead about the way my mother is. I don't conceal the facts about the things she does and doesn't do. I talk about my father, too, his absence, his silence, his distance. Dr. Cassander breaks a flimsy smile and says she isn't sure what anyone can do. She grabs my hands and places them inside her cold, flabby ones, graced with golden bands, and whispers in a voice suddenly full of warmth, "Don't blame yourself, Jules. You can't save anyone who wouldn't save themselves without you. It's the hardest lesson to learn in life, take it from me."

On the front steps Leon stands, tossing a football hand to hand. "Let's play behind the Hillside Manor parking lot," he demands.

Between the garages makes a perfect spot for punting back and forth. Our spirals tack a chilly wind that freezes the face. Back and forth, we fake, hike, kick, and catch. The sunlight backs into roofs and detaches into red and orange spikes, turning blue, then stark black.

I kick through murky spotlights by the dumpster, then pedal back to track the flipping, flopping of a shadow football rising, falling, bouncing at my feet as a spinning top or an excited molecule resonating heat. I pounce at it, follow in a turkey trot, jouncing side and front across the lot. Side and front, side and front, side and front. Pick it up, point my foot and punt to a flash of eye-whites at the other end, this vague sign of my brother bending up and down, a blurry darkened stain that bounds after the ball. I stagger, chase, pick up, punt, stagger, chase, pick up, punt, ignoring hunger pains, listen for the thud of Leon's kick, then chase the shadowy tumble of the ball somersaulting towards asphalt.

Finally too tired to chase the ball, I say, "I'm getting hungry," and I lay a perfect spiral towards him. Leon's answer: our first catch in many tries, a bull run at me, slamming into thighs and middle with his shoulders, ramming forward squarely into me, grasping, clasping tightly as heaving lungs will grasp at air.

Scattered in a tattered Macy's box—our photographs in black-and-white, spanning epochs, that Momma never gets around to arranging in an album: Her with girlfriends exchanging orange blossoms. Dad in army gear leaning against a rail at Chelsea Pier. A history of their marriage that we put together with paste and paper for his thirtieth birthday, everything looking normal. Momma cradling babies. Momma ladling soup for Dad. Dad in his company baseball team uniform. Night clubs, racetracks. A costume party when they dress like Baghdad sheik and concubine. Neon signs of Broadway plays. Sipping wine. The cabin in the Catskills. Dad flipping a steak, Momma cutting a bun. Their children—Lee and me—on a street in East New York, strutting on horses, dressed as cowboys, Jules the Ranger with a badge, Lee the Desperado with a gun. Both of us in leather coats and caps with flaps over ears on a teeming Brooklyn corner near a pylon holding up the monstrous El, my right arm tightly round his shoulders, both smiling, me with a lips-closed beam, Leon openmouthed in jolly yelling laughter, as in my dream about the Beav and Wally. The dogs we had: Honey the pit bull, Pretty Boy the terrier. Leon sits on a tree branch. Lee dissects a frog. Lee unclogs a drain. Jules in loincloth steps a Hopi rain dance. Jules strides on stage, dressed as a single reindeer pulling the sleigh in the kindergarten Christmas play.

Many photos of the four of us together: seders, ballgames, beaches, Prospect Park. The boardwalk in the stark of winter, miles of driftwood, sand and snowflakes. At Daddy's college graduation party around the cake. Photos I know very well, photos I've arranged in my mind many times, photos that now seem new and strange, photos that now all look the same to me. All seem to share a grand design: within the camera frame, an ironclad triad formed from the sightlines of the three of them looking at each other, grinning madly, and the sightline of a fourth one playing with the camera, smiling brightly, as if trying to put the audience at ease, as if to say, "I'm one of you, take me, please." I'm the one apart, and I feel apart, feel as if I live in reality by day and slide into a gloomy, gory, putrefied death-dream after school when I go home and reenter the real world when I ride my bike to the store or start for school again. It really is three worlds like Dante created: Inferno is the basement, Purgatory the rest of the house, and Paradise the real world waiting outside.

The triad of my family's eyes is filled with suffocating quicksand. I want to reach out my hand and extricate my brother. But he's sinking deeper, and I'm not brave. I don't have the skill or strength to help, and I want to get myself to solid land more than I want to save him. My eyes are begging for a rope or rig to dig me out and help me stand. Yet I also crave to jump inside the quicksand, to be with them.

I dump the photos in the box, leave the house coatless, scarfless, bleary eyes filled with bleak tears, streams of snowfall stinging through my sweater, steamy breath burning cheeks, until I get to Suicide Hill, where I sit against a tree and watch parades of lights slink past me through snowy, star-smeared night. Watching and not watching, thinking and not thinking. Thinking I was in a normal family where everything was good, living in a normal home in a normal neighborhood. I imagine the normal ever-repeating features of my normal family life—agreeable, amenable, ample, lucky—parents and children eating a strifeless dinner at the same time every night, children doing homework on neat desks, mother doing dishes, father tucking in the children, husband kissing wife.

As I sit by the fence that separates the highway from Suicide Hill, shadowy amoeba-like lights begin to flop across my heavy eyelids like sea anemones painted in the walls of an ancient cave, slowly, numbly, moving left to right, become a car, then skid to stop. Someone in the car waves to me.

I climb the fence and hop to the ground. I roll my body down the hill, arms tightly held at my side, shoulders squared, eyes plastered wide open. My heart beats like a subway rumble. Gliding past the boulders, my body tumbles faster, faster, faster. At last the grass incline begins to flatten. I close my eyes and play the old game of chicken with the highway, unafraid of scraps of glass and half-buried boulders I pass in my fast descent, digging hands into the ground to stop myself only when I feel the gravel surface of the highway shoulder.

I open my eyes in a ballroom full of round tables and a dance floor. Each table sports eight serving sets in lime and a flower arrangement. A six-piece band pounds out songs from before my time, like Momma's 78s.

People I recognize crowd the room. At one table, Aunt Hope is writing letters with a plume and inkpot. Uncle Jack's unfolded palms hold a tiny plastic Thinker, Taj Mahal and Grant's tomb. Their daughters kneel on the floor and dress Barbie dolls in lace. Other cousins dress as Naval Hogmen: Petey, Herbie, Howie, Steve and Stew, Ira, Gary, Michael, Keith and Lou, all jogging around in rubber boots and full-body wetsuits, waving lamb ribs and yellow petit fours on spears, playing a game of triple hamburger at the edge of the hexagon dance floor. Smiling Petey ambles off the swaying pile of mattresses, hollers fearlessly to his fuming mom across the room, "I already made my bed tomorrow," and then resumes his slamming. Uncle Mark sits with a corps of younger cousins, Robin, Rhonda, Danny, Sonny, Lynne, playing cards and board games—checkers, Scrabble, chess and donkey pin— wearing candy canes around their necks. Next to them, aunts and uncles play Hearts and drink gin. While Beryl, Peter, Izzie, Bunny, Joe, and Nancy booze, Aunt Pam and Uncle Douglas rumba dance, Douglas counting steps and glancing at his shoes. Aunt Hedy belly dances. Pop-pop lances hora kicks in place, both his hands clenching dripping plastic teeth, outside the ladies' bathroom beneath a winding staircase. Uncle Emil leaps Cossack style to a four-four beat, thrusts out one leg, then the other, one two one two one two one two, trusting his doubtful balance to rubber feet, one two one two, tail-bone scraping the ballroom floor, his tie and belly squalling gusts, his knees gaping, while Aunt Virginia's face turns as ruddy as her flaming hair to see her burly husband's clownish pace, smiling what my Momma calls "her good girl smile," standing graceful and modest in a bathing suit that flattens her enormous breasts, beneath a palm tree, bare feet in sand. Uncle Henry, al-most-famous scientist, in synagogue Yom Kippur at 7:00 am, dryly remarks that the early ones compete for god's attention. His wife, the Cajun Bridget, sitting on a bench, breast-feeds their first-born at Kitten's wedding. Kitten in her wedding dress, bouquet in one hand, the other one caresses Uncle Len-ny's wedding band. Uncle Morris's flopping, flabby body in a swimming pool tentacle-hand-chops at Lee and me, drooling, roaring, "I'll get you, Captain Ahab." His wife, Aunt Bea, on our veranda, blabs about the fast expanding galaxies and astral swarms. Skinny Uncle Alfie in a tee-shirt, pack of Luckys bulging at his arm, leans against a door portal, then stretches over a table with his Super Eight, making groups of relatives immortal by turning to-wards him, smiling, waving. Aunt Bernie raves loudly as the image flickers on the wall of naked female infant cousins bathing. Aunt Flo, hair in curlers, on a brownstone stoop, smokes her Camels in rapid takes between her angry pouts, puff and pout, in and out, puff and pout, puff and pout. Her bearish husband, Big Gene, on his truck route, lifts boxes from a shipping dock. Uncle Little Gene and Aunt Lilly, on folding chairs, observe the airplanes overhead that rock their house and yard on course to Idlewild. Uncle Hal is bending over his elaborate model trains, tracks extended over two-thirds of an airplane aisle. Bubby offers me a plate of tasteless boiled chicken, "Just like your father likes it." Momma's best friend Mary Byrd, before she got sick, waits with me at the central post office for first-day stamps. My father's friend Joey is leafing through nudie magazines and eating from a jar of baby food. Jerry Luft displays cartoons of lewd vamps and spacemen tramping over hot volcanoes with purple heads, bola arms, and twisted toes. Jerry's father Rudy asks a cross-country skier under maple trees exuding sap if he can stand on the long and polished planks so that for once in his life he can say he's been on skis. Marty Hellman carefully folds his handkerchief and puts it on the stoop before a game of two-hand touch. Freckled Randy Pearlstein, broken leg on crutches, the night the Boy Scout troop camps at Valley Forge—it's midnight, and Mr. Luft admonishes our tent for noise and warns that the chaplain will evict us if we don't keep quiet, and wise-guy Randy yells as boisterously as he can that if the chaplain tries complaining once again we're going to cut him down to size and circumcise him. Steven Deutscher at the corner of the schoolyard brandishes his crossing guard captain shield a month before he catches hepatitis at the beach and dies within a week. His mother's tears appeal to me not to say a word, as she serves me soda at the Purim Carnival a year later. Fatty Stephen Spigmann in his swimming suit gives a goofy backwards Scout salute after he breaks the camp swimming record for the mile first time in the water. Toughie jag-off Marty Magnus, soaking wet, holds his dripping sleeping bag and pack after we attack his tent, rip it from its stakes, and drag it to the woods the instant it starts raining. Marvin Tanz and Michael Denver settled on a cot, their rookie fingers struggle painfully to tie a simple square knot. Harlan Schwartz is grabbing at his zipper. His older brother Barton holding a flashlight on his homework late at night inside our cabin, grips his pencil tensely. Denny Knoll, his brown hair center-parted, shows off expensive two-toned shoes he got with money earned collecting bottles. Eric Golden takes a snooze seated at his Bar Mitzvah bema. Danny Mott intones Del Shannon a cappella into his closed right fist in front of Dr. Slavin's sixth-grade class, his knees bouncing up and down, his slicked black hair reflecting classroom lights, groaning, "I'm a walkin' in the rain, tears are fallin' and I feel a pain." At the desk facing mine, Nancy Siskin writes the answers to the spelling test upside down for me. Isaac Schreiber reads *The Shahnameh* in Farsi. Robby Reiner has his elbow up a girl's skirt. Russell Rusheim hurls a younger kid through the glass door of the synagogue, glass flying everywhere, but no one gets hurt. Philip Simper, his corduroys down, his ass shivering, waits for Russell to spank him with a shoe after Russell paid him two bucks one rainy afternoon when we were in Philip's basement with nothing to do. That boy in first grade on the playground who pulls off his belt and flicks it at the other kids the last day of school. The thugs who once surrounded me, made me drop my books, and punched me in the stomach, only now they're bunched around a switchblade in the dirt playing mumblety-peg. The horizontal fat kid I dragged across the finish line to win a three-legged race and a silver dollar.

Jacky Nussbaum giving me a quarter after accidentally hitting me with a baseball bat. Bobby Porter dives for a ball at short, catches it in the webbing of his glove, pulls it out, stands erect, and throws it overhand to first. His twin sister Sandy directing my feet on her bedroom rug the day she tries to teach me how to twist, while I'm waiting for Bobby to finish his arithmetic. Debbie Diamond beckons me to join her for a kissing session in a plush arm chair to "Our Day Will Come" by Ruby and the Romantics. Mary Byrd's daughter Shelley in an alluring bathing suit showing curly strands of reddish pubic hair. Denny's mother standing at their front door in a translucent dressing gown revealing umber nipples, teal blue panties. Mrs. Klein, large-breasted fifth grade teacher who only wears skin-tight black, who ranted at me after I told the girls jokes on menstruation that I heard from Uncle Jack, now sitting topless in a dunce cap on a stool, two wonderfully wide and lightly quaking spools of flesh. Penny Hellman's friend Kate completely naked, lying on the Hellman pool table. My second-grade teacher, Mrs. Stephenson, big-bellied pregnant in her kitchen baking brownies, asks me to read aloud from Aesop's fables. Mr. Hughes, his blue and yellow polka-dot bowtie, leans against his desk contriving phrases that exemplify the differences between a simile and a metaphor. Bald Dr. Slavin sits on his tall stool by a blackboard crammed with chalk parabolas and slopes, beating out Beethoven's Fifth in the air with his yardstick. Bald Dr. Kleiner offers me his stethoscope. Robert Young is handing Bud the car keys. Dr. Stone and Donna contemplate what to say to Jeff about his cheating on a test. Andy and Opie, feet in lake, under pine, hook their bait, then slowly reel out fishing lines and jabber, while they wait for shad and walleye. Ricky pours the milk while Harriet dishes out the apple pie. Jon Provost smiles and scratches Lassie round the neck in a field, surrounded by his mother, father, granddad, a police officer, and the next-door neighbor Lassie pulled from a car wreck. Danny Thomas scoops Rusty Hammer from the floor and swings him in the air, as Rusty combs his curly hair. Beav and Wally on a stoop, punching baseball gloves, discussing how to help a friend who's in a mess, Beav defending him, "He's got that dumb expression on his face, but he's really not as goofy as he looks." Dick Van Dyke hooks his yoyo body over chair and stumbles acrobatically across the floor, bounces up and lands at mock attention facing Laura and little Ritchie. Herbert Gillis, Dobie's Dad, embraces Maynard's shoulder, sighs, and regrets that his luck with girlfriends wasn't any better when he attended Central High. Our Miss Brooks is teasing Walter Denton for ornate language in his essay on "The Lorelei." Phil Silvers flings his undaunted arm around a grinning ding-dong-dumb Doberman, squeezes the private's shoulder, and singsongs with wired but oily cajoling that Doberman "is like the son I never had," or was it the son he never wanted? Spying George Burns, talking to a TV, flicking his cigar ashes, tells the image of his college boy he's fired because he wrecked the car, "And you're fired, too, Harry." George takes another puff and zings, "And you're fired, too, Gracie," Gracie startled, shivers, toys with scarf. Bugs pulls a rabbit season sign from shallow water and hammers in a duck season sign, which makes beady-eyed Elmer Fudd swing his gun away from Bugs and towards a sleeping Daffy Duck in water reeds. Goya's callow dwarf. Madame Charpentier with sweet Paul and Georgette. Those sweaty children creeping on the floor in Steen's saloon. The broken-hearted kids following the flight of William Beard's lost balloon. Breughel's drunken farmers underneath a tree beside a half-harvested field of wheat. Picasso's little Maya. His family of saltimbanques lost in sand dunes, looking wistfully at the water. De Hooch's family of musicians plays a tune. A Monet family pressing down a gravel path between two fields of giant wild flowers that tower over them. A fat Franz Hals child. A family dressed in Sunday best picnicking on the Isle of the Grande Jatte. And still more behind them swelling towards me tenderly.

They welcome me and enthusiastically grab my hand. They kiss me on the cheek, congratulate me for being so unique. They put an arm around my shoulder, smile with pride. They ask if they can sit beside me. They praise all of my accomplishments, pat me on the back, and tell me how great I'm doing. They call me, "Dear old chum," and give me the thumbs up. They hand me ribbons, trophies, plaques. They present me plates of yummy food and serve me first. They include me in everything, accept me, protect me, support me, escort me. They believe in my abilities. They quench my thirst, put me first, put me at my ease, esteem me, beam at me, embrace me and grace me, a unanimous vote—all in favor, none opposed. They love me, love me, love me, love me.

I burst with the freedom of rolling down Suicide Hill, feet off pedals and eyes closed. I want to share my joy with everyone I see and everyone else in the world alive today, everyone who's been and everyone who'll ever be, pushing from behind, polite but insistent, swelling forward to get a better view of me. I unlock my mouth to speak, "My family, my friends, my world, my life, it's my turn to say that I...."

At these words, everyone starts to streak away from me quickly, all of them, horrified at my voice. As they recede, they swiftly lose their shape, shrinking, blanching, fading into shadowed landscape. Some wave, but most have turned their backs to walk into an avalanche of black. I reach out to them. To everyone. To anyone. But they're too far away to touch. I try to speak, but the words hide in my mouth. There they go, everyone, everyone,

everyone already a sinking horizon of waving hands, already a distant world missing parts and sliding into nothing, already a receding tide swirling salt, already lost forever, and I awake *on the cold hill's side.*

I drudge home, burning like dry ice in open air. It's past midnight. Lee and Momma are playing cards and eating sundaes topped with fudge and sliced bananas. Leon wins a hand and starts to grin. No one asks me where I've been.

We lug our camping gear inside. The kitchen is as cold as the street. The sink is full of the dirty dishes we left two days ago.

I yell, "Momma...."

No answer.

"Momma?"...

I trot downstairs.

She languishes motionless on the sofa bed, wearing a pair of Dad's green pajamas, four empty vials of Librium by her pushed-up head. The TV blinks "The Price is Right" on a rolling screen.

"Momma, Momma!"

I nudge her slinking arm. It drops to the floor, and she doesn't budge, so I get behind her, pull her upwards by the shoulders. She bends and doubles over. "Momma, Momma!" my voice ascends another notch. I nudge her once again, but she remains still.

Leon's knitted eyebrows watch me as I try to wake our mother. "Momma, Momma!" shouting loud enough to make my throat ache. "Momma, Momma!"

I leave her flopped upon herself and we go upstairs. I take the phone to call Aunt Hope, but the dial tone doesn't come. I try to dial without it but nothing happens. Not a sound, not a hum, not even static buzz. "Okay, Lee, let's get this stuff cleaned up."

We change our muddy clothes from two days camping in the rain into dungarees that Daddy bought large, so they still don't fit, and sweaters Momma knitted. We throw our dirty garments in the hamper, throw our camp utensils in the sink, and fold our sleeping bags. "Do you want something warm to drink?" I ask.

Leon smiles and shakes his head yes. I look for something to make, but there is no hot chocolate, no tea, no Ovaltine, not even instant coffee. I open the fridge to find it's almost completely empty, except for condiments and caked-on condensation. No milk, no eggs, no bread, no fruit, no meat. I fill the kettle and set it on the stove and spoon some sugar into coffee cups with pictures of the Cliffs of Dover on them. I turn the faucet warm to wash the dishes but a winter storm flows over my hands. The water on the stove is hot and I pour it on the sugar in the cups and place them on the table, stir and have a drink. I take our jumbo pot from underneath the sink, let the frigid water slosh into it until it reaches the top and set it on the stove on highest heat—warm water for washing.

I seat myself at the kitchen table with my brother, who stares into space, rigid and frowning. We sip our sweet warm water, which tastes good. We look at each other and utter not a sound. I know I should do something, try something, say something, but I think about nothing. Sometimes Leon's bushy eyebrows push together, relax, push together, relax, push together.

We sit for an eternity, silently sipping, absolutely still. The room grows chilly, then cold, as the sun outside recedes. The water starts to creak, then boil on the stove, bubbling boldly as if in a samba groove.

It turns to night outside, but I don't move.

APRIL 1969

Things are rapidly turning to shit. I had hoped Leon would straighten out after our long conversation at the Chinese restaurant. He seemed finally to understand that he was harming himself using drugs and fucking up in school. Instead of accusing me of trying to control him, he seemed—finally—to realize that quite the contrary, I give him more free rein than most parents give 17-year-olds. The dinner went so well, I let him have the last piece of roast pork. I was certain that he would stop taking drugs, certain that the incessant quarrelling when we were both home would cease, certain that he would start doing his chores, certain that his self-destructive behavior would stop.

It did. For three days.

Then he fell right back into his old ways. He stopped making his bed. He left his clothes strewn around the hallway and the bathroom. He didn't screw the toothpaste cap on the tube. He left the bathtub faucet dripping. Didn't take out the trash or wash his breakfast dishes. Cigarette ashes sat in neat piles on the carpet. All stupid little things he did intentionally, and, when I chided him about it, he took offense. His manner became brusque and haughty. He stayed out late, sometimes all night long. His first report card at the community college was a cold deck. One D, one F, three incompletes. Great performance from a kid who got a perfect score on the College Boards! He didn't try out for the wrestling or track teams. A kid with his natural athleticism—the way he runs—powerful, beautiful.

I'll lay three to one that he's taking drugs again.

Maybe a week ago, I'm watching the Bulls game, frustrated at my idiot foreman for screwing up, and anticipating more frustration when Lee gets home, because I haven't seen him in two days. That's his pattern when he stays away. When he comes home, usually before I do, he always leaves his nasty tracks. Leaving the light on after he's left a room or burning incense— the shitty little shitty stuff he does that he knows bugs me and will set me off. He's as predictable as a low roller with an ace high.

But there are no signs of the kid. No dripping faucets. No crusty dishes in the sink. Not even an ashtray filled with crushed Camel butts. I figure he's at an extended hippy party, smoking pot and balling hippy chicks. At least he's getting laid. That is, if he isn't too doped up to get a hard-on.

I'm trying to watch the game, when the phone rings. It's Sam Nash's mother, sniffing and sobbing. She asks whether I've seen her son, a long-haired punk a few years older than Lee who always wears dirty tee-shirts and greasy blue jeans. I tell her point blank that Sam isn't allowed in the house after the time I caught the two of them smoking pot. She says he's been living at home the past few weeks since he was kicked out of his apartment for making too much noise. Two nights ago, Sam and his father came to blows—not the first time—after the older Nash discovered a plastic bag filled with marijuana in Sam's dresser drawer.

Dad slapped son across the cheek. Son responded with a punch to Dad's jaw. Dad is a big guy, a machinist at Allis-Chalmers, and he clobbers son with a quick combination that sends him to the floor. Not out like a light, more humiliated than hurt from what I can gather. But what's that got to do with *me*, lady? It's *your* kid. If you want to unload on someone, call your priest. He's paid to listen.

I'm about to cut her off and hang up, when she finally gets to the point. Yesterday, she found a note by the phone from Sam that said he and Lee were moving to San Francisco and he'd send their address in six months. She has no idea how they got the money for the tickets. I would make book Lee and Nash have been selling drugs. How else would they raise the dough?

Mrs. Nash is bawling into my ear, and I want to get her off the phone so I can think straight. I ask her if Sam is eighteen, knowing that he's close to twenty. Yes, she says, and I shoot back, "Then there's nothing you can do because he's legally an adult. But *my* kid is only seventeen, and I intend to call the Frisco cops and have them find him and ship him back home." Then I give her the bum's rush I reserve for office equipment salesmen and say, "When I hear from Lee, I'll phone you with any information I get about your son. Thanks for calling me, Mrs. Nash. Take care, Mrs. Nash. Good bye, Mrs. Nash." Fuck you, Mrs. Nash.

I wanted to hit someone, but there was no one to hit. I couldn't hit Leon. He was two thousand miles away. Besides hitting the kid would only make things worse. Maybe when I was younger, I might have gone to a bar and picked a fight with a faggot, like when I failed the physical for West Point because of my poor eyesight and I realized that I was going to be stuck living in that henhouse with my mother and my six older sisters unless I enlisted in the dog shit version of the army.

What pissed me off most was that Leon didn't even have the common courtesy to leave a note. He didn't have the decency to tell me he's running away from home. I don't mean a thing to him. Is the kid that fucked up?

At least he never raised his hand to me, like Jules did the summer before he went away to college. We were talking politics, and I said that I read that most of the Viet Cong were really Chinese soldiers. He called me a liar. Maybe I was stretching the truth a little, but you don't call your father a liar. It shows no respect. It used to be, the boys just believed whatever I said. Why all this questioning? It made me so angry that I raised my hand, more to menace than anything else.

Jules catches my wrist in his hand and holds it mid-air and raises a fist of his own, which I grab with my free hand. We just stand there, like two wrestlers, each trying to bring the other down. I didn't know the kid had gotten so strong. Then I walk away. You win some and you lose some, right?

My hands ached to move. To act! To control the situation. But it was out of my hands. My beautiful, brilliant boy is in San Francisco, drug capital of the world, high on who knows what and guided by that slimy punk Nash! And there's nothing I can do about it. Not a fucking thing.

Maybe the police can do something. I call the San Francisco Police Department. They keep me on hold for ten minutes, even after I explain I'm calling long distance from Chicago. A detective named Liberty finally comes on the line. I tell him that my underage son has run away to San Francisco. I want to give the Frisco police his description and wire a photo, so they can find him and send him home, on my nickel, of course.

Liberty laughs at me, a piercing sarcastic cackle. As if he were talking down to someone stupid, he asks if I know how many people live in the city of San Francisco. How the fuck am I supposed to know? "Look, Mac," I say, "I'm paying for this call and I don't want to piss away my money on guessing games."

"Don't take offense, mister. I just want to show what we're up against. There are seven hundred thousand people living in San Francisco, and we estimate that about one hundred thousand of them are underage runaways. We have the largest transient population in the country. Larger than New York City's," he says with civic pride. "We have rooms full of missing person files from parents with runaways who think their little darlings are in the Bay Area."

"Don't they all flow into the same part of town, the hippy neighborhood—what is that, the Haight district?"

"Sir, it's 1969. The entire city is a hippy district. I'll take your information and make a file. If we arrest your kid and we're able to match the files and he's still under 18, we'll give you a call, collect! Many of these runaways get busted for prostitution or shoplifting. There are a lot of amateurs out there right now."

I figure that, like most big cities, San Francisco is pay to play. Five years ago, I gave a thousand bucks in small bills to someone in the Johnson re-election campaign and suddenly my divorce case was on the docket in New Jersey a week later and the judge reduced the ninety bucks alimony the New York judge was making me pay to forty a week. So I say to Liberty, "Okay, I get the idea. How much is it going to cost me?"

His laugh is even louder now. "I'll pretend I didn't hear that. You parents with money are all the same. Look, even if we took bribes, we couldn't help. There are just too many of them out there."

I hang up the phone. I feel a strange emptiness not having him here, a constant nervousness when I think about him in San Francisco, hanging with the wrong crowd, maybe shoplifting. Maybe worse. Thinking about it makes me feel skittish, like a filly in heat.

I have an ace up my sleeve, though one I don't want to use. One that I never want to use. But sometimes the stakes are so high, you have to go all in. Maybe my father knows someone who can help. The old man is supposed to be a bigshot in the California Masons. I heard from one of my sisters that he was Grand Wizard or Worship Master or some such crap.

I could call him. I have his number.

But what do you say to someone you've seen once in thirty years? One time since he left my mother and the ten of us kids and ran away in 1940 to California with one of his girlfriends? One time, in the late fifties, when he was visiting New York. We didn't talk much. What do I have to say to a man I never knew? He wasn't around much even when he lived with us. He'd spend weeks away from the family. He was a real cunt hound. It's like I tell Leon and Jules, I'm a whoremaster, but not a cunt hound. The difference? A whoremaster won't sell his children for a piece of ass.

The old man taught me chess when I was six and once gave me one of his old racing forms. A few days before he skipped town for California when I was ten, he caught me smoking on the fire escape landing and we smoked one together, blowing rings across the small space that separated our apartment from the building across the alley. He gave me advice about betting the horses. I computed some odds for him in my head. He beamed with pride, patted me on the shoulder, and offered me one of his Pall Malls.

After he left, my mother badmouthed him. Your father's no human being. May he only find bitterness in California! May he rot with whatever whore he's shacked up with!

Only when I returned from active duty did I learn the truth from my older brother Mel. My father had given every one of my six older sisters the clap, and he did it the old-fashioned way. Turns out I was born with congenital syphilis he gave my mother, or maybe she gave him. The old man didn't run away from the family. That fucking degenerate was running from the law, after the nurse at the elementary school diagnosed my twelve-year-old sister Marlene.

Lucky fucker, he got to Los Angeles exactly when the boom began. Back then there weren't many master electricians around Southern California with twenty years' experience working in a real place like New York. It was like holding two aces in the hole with two showing. The old pervert broke the bank—made a lot of money wiring the mansions and haciendas of Beverly Hills and Westwood. Says he plays cards with the Lennon Sisters, Artie Shaw, and Melvyn Douglass. Now in his old age he plays the big shot when he makes his annual pilgrimage to New York. I'm glad I'm living in Chicago now, so I don't have to see him. My sisters tell me he invites their kids to live in LA. Says he'll get them jobs or into USC. The Masons are everywhere! Maybe the old man has some connections with the Frisco PD. It's worth a phone call. At this point, anything is better than doing nothing.

The old man is very happy to hear from me. It gives him a chance to bloviate about his latest operation. He fell apart about six years ago—heart attack, diabetes, and emphysema, all in the span of a year. His voice still sounds strong, as if he's booming out directions from the top of a roof to a service van in the street. I tell him about Leon's disappearance and he gives me some very useful information. Last year when Jules and Leon visited Los Angeles to see their mother, he saw Lee twice. The first time they all went out to dinner and the old man liked both Jules and Leon. He said they were well-mannered, handsome, intelligent, athletic looking. Real Silvers. As if he would know! The second time, after Jules had returned to Chicago for his summer job. He and his wife had Ethel and Lee over for dinner. Leon didn't speak to his mother the entire evening. When she asked him a question, he failed to even acknowledge her existence. Doing dishes with Ethel, his wife Anne learned that they had an argument about something three days earlier. Since then Lee was giving Ethel the silent treatment. Ethel thought he would act differently in front of other people, but that didn't work.

Maybe that explains why Leon acted depressed when he got back last July. But I don't say anything to the old man. It's none of his fucking business.

"It's no secret that Ethel is slightly wacko," the old man says.

You don't know the half of it, I think. But I'm not going to spill my guts to that old pervert. Besides, I want to keep my eye focused on the ball. I detail the bad treatment the Frisco police gave me and ask if he knows anyone.

He says that he knows the ex-Mayor, who is still the most powerful Democrat in the state and has a lot of union connections. How much is it going to cost me? I ask.

"Put your wallet away, Ed. Sometimes the only way to get things done is through friendship. Friendship is the lifeblood of business. I've scratched his back plenty times. You know what they say, one hand washes the other and they both stay clean. Do unto others and they'll do unto you. No one minds being screwed a little as long as they can afford the Vaseline." He goes on with these little turds of wisdom for a while, then moves to a new subject, how he got my sister's kid Petey into USC and how ungrateful the kid turned out to be. He didn't go to classes and managed to knock up two girls in the same week, which cost the old man a few hundred bucks for abortions.

The old man is beginning to sound tired, strained. The weakness in his voice grates on my ears. I don't want to listen to him piss and moan. This phone call is costing me a small fortune and I really don't care a wipe about Petey or my father. I want him to get off the phone and call his bigshot.

As it turns out, my father isn't such an old fart after all. Not ten minutes after we hang up, I'm watching the game and the phone rings. It's the ex-Mayor of San Francisco. Not his flunky, not his secretary, but the fucking Mayor himself, and it isn't a collect call. He says he sympathizes with me and makes a solemn statement about the challenges raising children today. After this brief political speech, he tells me that he'll contact someone in the police department immediately and request that they do more than the standard file and forget. I'll believe it when I see it.

I put down the phone and return to the game, but before my ass hits the sofa, the phone rings again. This time it's the public affairs director of the Frisco police, and again, it's his nickel. Person to person! He apologizes for the impolite treatment I received and asks for the name of the officer. I tell him I'm not interested in hurting anyone's career. I just want to find my kid. He assures me that "the SFPD will offer as much assistance as is required to locate your son in a timely fashion." Yeah, and suck my cock, while you're at it.

He dials the head of the juvenile division on another line and I hear him explain that my underage son ran away to San Francisco and I'm trying to locate him. After he transfers me, the head of the juvenile division also expresses his sympathies and begins to bullshit on the deplorable influences that can lead children astray nowadays. These guys are all politicians, but since it isn't costing me, I let him go on. Finally we get down to it. He takes descriptions of both Leon and Nash, gives me his private teletype line to transmit photos and says he'll make sure that Lee's case gets the highest priority, whatever the hell that means. More apologies, assurances, expressions of support, and caveats about the overwhelming challenge of finding a runaway in a city of runaways.

A few days later the phone was ringing off the hook when I got home. It was Leon, calling collect. I accept the charges.

"Hey, dad. I'm calling from San Francisco. Isn't it a trip?" He sounds a little smug.

"Are you okay?"

"I'm fine. Just a little hungry."

"You're not in any trouble, are you?"

"No, man. No trouble at all. Just a little hungry."

"Where are you staying?"

"In a cheap hotel that rents rooms by the week. It's pretty crummy, but it's a place to crash."

"With Nash."

"Yeah," he answers, a little irritated. "With Nash and some people we met." A real hippy hoedown, I imagine, with drugs and hot and cold pussy running from the tap. "Hey, listen, old man. I ran out of money. I'm pretty hungry. Could you send me some cash?" There isn't a trace of contrition in his voice, no apology for running off without leaving a note, no admission that he's acted foolishly. He speaks in an off-handed manner, as if asking for his allowance a day early.

But at least he isn't being high-handed. He knows I hold all the cards, that I have control. He can't pull any of his usual shit on me. Of course, I'm concerned that he may be going without food. That could be crap, though. Maybe the real reason he wants the money is to buy hashish or LSD or whatever it is he's on. I want to feel him out. "What did you do with the money you had?"

"Spent it. Wasn't that much to begin with."

"And what have you been eating?"

"Mostly brown rice. It has a lot of vitamins and it's cheap." The hippy ideal! Sit on the floor of a squalid, roach-infested room of a fleabag hotel with a bunch of sleazy, long-haired punks, take drugs and eat brown rice. Peace, love and all that good shit. At least until the money runs out.

"What did you think you were going to do in San Francisco?"

"I don't know, old man. It sort of just happened. Nash said he wished we could go to California and I said, let's do it. We copped a ride on the college ride board and made it out here in three days."

"Didn't you think about how you were going to support yourself?"

"We thought we'd get jobs, but there aren't any."

"Have you been taking drugs?"

"I keep telling you, old man, I don't take drugs. I was storing that sheet of acid you found for a girl I was balling."

"What about when I caught you and Nash smoking pot?"

"Come on, old man, am I on trial?"

"You're not on trial, but I'm concerned with your well-being."

"Besides, drugs cost money."

"Everything costs money."

"You're going to wire me some cash then?"

"What I'll do is send you a one-way ticket back to Chicago."

"You just want to control me, as usual."

"Now hold on. I didn't make you hitch to Frisco with no money in your pocket."

"Hey, I'm out here. I might as well stay a while and see some of it!"

"You like Frisco?"

"Yeah, it's a far-out city."

I'm not annoyed by this dancing around, because I can lead us to where I want to go. Besides, as long as he doesn't raise his voice or insult me, it's a good conversation.

"Wire me enough bread for a week—maybe fifty or seventy-five bucks."

"Can't you borrow the money from one of your new friends?"

"Everyone's broke."

Like a bunch of fish tapped out chasing longshots. Time to move in for the kill, subtly, coolly. "I'll wire you some money, but only under the condition that you tell me the name and address of where you're staying."

Leon starts ranting at me. "Fuck that, man. No way I'm telling you where I'm staying. So you can call the pigs and have them pick me up? That's really fucked up. You don't care if I starve to death, but you want to throw me in the slammer and then ship me back to your prison. You want everything your way. Eat your way, sleep your way, shit your way. You don't care about me. You just care about your control trips. It's all bullshit!"

Blah, blah, blah. I hate this shit. I hated it when his mother used to go on in this way, and I hate it when he does it now.

Maybe he is hungry. But he may have plenty to eat and want the cash to buy drugs. But if I don't give him the money, he might get caught ripping off a store, or worse yet, suck some guy's dick for a ten-spot. But if I give in, he'll call when he's broke again and ask for more and I'll be helping him remain in Frisco. But I don't want to get a phone call from the cops saying they found him dead of gun wounds in the middle of street. I can't get the image out of my mind of Lee down on his knees in a piss-soaked alley with some slimy, uncircumcised, middle-aged cock in his mouth. Damned if I do and damned if I don't. Damned no-win situations. Just like Ethel.

Leon has stopped shouting and the phone goes silent. He's still on the line. I hear him breathing, not heavy as if he's spent himself of rage, but slow and steady, under control. He must really need the dough, since he hasn't hung up yet. I let the silence between us continue. I'm leaving him out there on a limb, but I'm not going to saw it off. After a while, I say, "I'm not trying to control you, but I am concerned about your safety."

More silence.

"I will wire you twenty bucks. I don't absolutely have to know where you are staying."

"Twenty bucks?" He sounds disappointed, as I knew he would be.

"Twenty bucks should be enough to see you through a few days. If you need more, just call collect."

"Sure, fine, twenty bucks is cool. I'll pick it up at the Western Union office by the bus depot. Thanks old man, gotta split."

And he hangs up without even asking how I'm doing, the selfish little prick. He doesn't give a shit about anyone but himself. Makes me want to puke. But it also makes my longing to see him unbearable.

Something is wrong with the whole fucking generation. Rampant drug use, strange clothes, long hair, no bras, free love, communes, anti-war demonstrations—what the fuck do these kids know about war? Most of the kids I know are fucking up. My sister Molly's daughter is a heroin addict and her boy quit college after one semester. Francine's boy Pete evidently fucked up at USC, and her oldest son Steve is in the slammer for armed robbery. One of Bunny's kids quit high school. Mel's oldest has been bumming around Long Island for five years. They all smoke pot.

Jules seems to be doing alright—all A's at Wisconsin—but when he's home he's always on his high horse about the war and civil rights. He goes to demonstrations and rock concerts all the time. That's not good. Everyone does drugs at those things. I don't like the kids he hangs out with. One of Jules's friends from high school was caught with a high-powered rifle on top of Humphrey's hotel at the Democratic Convention last summer. His roommate Bob Turob quit last semester and ran away to San Francisco. His pal Adam Kadman is also quitting school. He's joining the Naval Reserves to stay out of Viet Nam. That's a real schmuck. One thing I learned in the army is you don't volunteer.

When I was growing up, you couldn't afford to fuck up. No second chances in the Depression. We didn't think about spiritual fulfillment or fixing the world's problems. We thought about survival. My shoes had holes. I stuffed cardboard in them, so I wouldn't get my feet wet walking to school. Of course, someone stoned might not even notice his socks were soaked. I remember thinking a pencil was something to cherish. Now they give them away. If you find one on the street, you don't even bother picking it up. But in the thirties, if you found a pencil sticking out of a pile of dog shit, you picked it up, wiped it off with a piece of newsprint and thought you hit the Trifecta. We always had food to eat, if you can call my mother's cooking food, although at the end of the month we had to scrape by on peanut butter sandwiches and her awful boiled chicken. Eat it, you always liked it, she still says. That was some other kid of yours, lady! But yeah, we worried. We worried that Con Ed would turn off the power. I worried about it, even as a twelve-year-old. Then the niggers started moving in and the streets weren't safe anymore. Things got easier when the war ended. Molly and Bunny went to Philly to work for the Feds. Fewer mouths to feed. My other sisters all got jobs in Brooklyn. The war ended and all my brothers and sisters married and we all had to make a buck. I was pretty lucky—too young for World War II, and by the time the Korean War came along, we had Jules and I had left the army. I didn't pay anything to go to college, but I already had two kids, so I had to hustle for the almighty dollar just as much as everyone else.

Sure we had fuck-ups back then. Like my younger brother Donny or my brother-in-law Arnie, both potheads before it was hip. Some people, like Ethel, were just too sensitive to live in the real world. They blew their brains out or ended up in institutions. Or, if they had money, they drank themselves to death or ran business after business into the ground. Or sometimes they ended up like my friend George Brown. He would steal hubcaps and throw them on the tracks of the subway late at night. He asked me to come along on these midnight escapades, but fuck that! I wasn't going to end up in jail. This was a good-looking, charming boy who wasn't Jewish, so he could have gone to Harvard. But he pissed it all away, like a bridge-jumper betting on a long shot. Asked him once why he got into so much trouble. He told me that because of his standardized tests his parents expected too much of him, but when he was bad they expected less. I lost track of him when he dropped out of Brooklyn Tech and graduated to armed robbery. Or there was that girl who liked to lay down in a parking lot after dark and take on a bunch of guys. One after another. It was disgusting. Always got there early, so I could be one of the first five. So sure, we had our fuckups, but not that many. Not like today when the entire generation is fucked up.

Sociologists and psychiatrists like to blame it on poverty, overcrowding, inattentive parents, overly strict parents, crazy parents, no parents, the class system, the pressure to succeed, the fear of failure. But they're all blowing it out their asses. A lot of people grow up under these conditions, and not every one of them turns into a dope addict or an alky or a criminal or a sensitive flower that wilts under any pressure or a fucking loon. I think there's something in the genes. Some people can be put through real hell for long periods of time and come out of it well adjusted. Others crack under the slightest stress.

Some people fuck up and some people don't. It's that simple.

It doesn't matter how many shrinks you see, how much money you have, how many people sacrifice to meet your every need, how perfectly your life is set up. If you're a fuckup, you fuck up. And anyone who tries to help a fuck-up risks being destroyed himself, like Ethel almost destroyed me. The best thing to do with fuck-ups is to write them off completely, like a piece of ass you're through with.

Ethel is a fuck-up. My brother Donny is a fuck-up. Jules's friends are fuckups. Bernadine Dohrn—fuck-up! Charlie Whitman, that maniac who climbed the University of Texas Tower with a cache of guns and killed 14 people, picked them off like sitting ducks, bing, bing, bing—a royal fuckup! The kids who threw pig's blood out the window at the cops at the Chicago convention—all fuckups. The kids who shave their heads, don clown suits, and dance up and down Michigan Avenue chanting Hare Krishna—fuckups, one and all. The Chicago Eight—the biggest fuckups of all, fuckups in every flavor and variety, fuck-ups for the Age of Aquarifuckups.

Kids nowadays don't know what life is about. They think that the world is their sugar tit. They've never known deprivation. They think the abundance around them is created magically, without effort. They don't believe the laws of physics apply to them.

I have news for them. You can't create something from nothing. That's the first law of thermodynamics. You create money from work. You trade the money for food and shelter. If you don't want to bust your ass laying carpet or installing toilets like the rest of my family, you go to college. You can't go to the Dean and say, Dean Schmohawk, look at me, I'm a genius. I'm a good person. I deserve my diploma right away. You can't go to your boss and say, Mr. Schmuckbucks, I don't want to work for that customer because they're manufacturing fart-blowers for the army. Can't miss work for four days and say, sorry, I was so stoned I couldn't move. Or like Ethel, you can't say, I'm too depressed to go into work today. Please don't fire me, though, because I'm a good person. It's the last time, I promise. I've changed. I'm better. I've learned so much about myself. I know why I was depressed and how to stop it. It won't happen again. Until the next time, you lazy, soul-sucking bitch!

Leon's acting just like his mother. Both take the path of least resistance.

Go with the flow, as the hippies say. But the flow is always towards maximum entropy, which means stasis, which means shit. It's the second law. As long as things are going perfectly for Leon and Ethel, they're fine. But as soon as it takes work or discipline, they just quit. They just go with the flow. They dissipate their resources without thought of the future. Lee is always asking me for extra money. What do you need it for? "I want to see a movie." When did you find out about the movie? "About a week ago." Why didn't you put a couple of bucks aside for it?" Here comes the shrug and the off hand, "I guess I forgot." He guesses he forgot! What if I forgot I had a kid and I pissed all my money away at the track?

His hey-whatever-happens-happens attitude screwed up his first year of college. In the beginning Lee is very enthusiastic about attending. He aces his first exams, which basically review high school material. But he parties around, chases pussy, smokes marijuana, stays up all night. He forgets he has a paper to write. He falls behind in his readings and begins to cut classes. It's easier to sleep in. Besides, he thinks he's so smart that he's going to continue to ace the tests. Soon he stops going to school altogether, so now he needs an excuse. He says he doesn't like the classes. They're too boring. He blames the restrictive school, the fascist professors and the greedy capitalist society that puts too much emphasis on achievement and money. He proclaims in that dramatic voice he likes to use when he's feeling good and self-satisfied that he doesn't want to be a cog in the military-industrial complex, which is all college trains you for. He blames everyone. But it's his own fault, and he knows it.

It's even money Leon's a fuck-up. I'm afraid his problems go deeper than growing pains. I'm afraid his problems may be genetic.

I'm afraid that all the years living with Ethel took their toll.

I'm afraid he'll never be able to live without drugs, alcohol, or some other crutch that gives momentary relief to imaginary suffering. Afraid that Leon has already taken so many drugs that they've destroyed his ability to reason.

Afraid that his lack of discipline will prevent him from having any type of a life above the gutter.

If I could only talk to him. We could discuss things rationally, break his problems down to their parts, and solve each part. Act like rational human beings!

I used to talk with both my boys. We discussed physics, engineering, history, war, politics, philosophy, economics, chess, sports, and women. They used to love to listen to me. We sat around bullshitting for hours. I thought to myself, my boys are lucky they have a father who talks to them honestly, who tells them the truth instead of filling their heads with crap. I was pretty lucky, too, to have two boys I could talk to as adults. When they lived with me for six months after Ethel went into the nuthouse before they moved to Miami, we had great times together. Like the day we went to see the Mets play a double-header against the Giants. It was overcast and we didn't even know whether they would play even one game. We thought we might change our plans and go to the New York World's Fair, literally across the street from Shea. In the first game, Juan Marichal took care of business like a real thoroughbred. But the second game lasted twenty-two innings, the longest game by time in Major League history. We left after the Giants put two men on base in the fourteenth inning with no outs and Orlando Cepeda hit into a triple play. A triple play! The kids were going fucking nuts. But it was already very late, so we decided to leave. First a subway to the Port Authority, then a bus back to Passaic. We picked up the car at the park-and-ride lot and drove back to the apartment and turned on the game. It was the top of the twenty-second inning and there were men on base. Jim Davenport hit a slicing double and the Giants were ahead. The Mets went down in order in the bottom of the inning, and it was over. Jesús Alou, the Giants' right fielder who had played every inning of both games, retrieved a long fly ball at the wall and threw a perfect strike home. No bounce. That made Lee and Jules stand up and take notice!

Great times, and less than five years ago. What the fuck changed?

They were always real thoroughbreds. Jules was always a mudlark who likes a heavy track, but I thought Leon was a Triple Crown winner, a stud. Turns out he may be an early foot, quick out of the gate but soon yielding the lead to other horses.

Jules does foolish things. He was awarded a large scholarship. Instead of working this summer to pack some bucks away, he plans to fly to Los Angeles and visit his mother, then hitchhike back home. What a schmuck! I bet he hops a plane the first time he freezes his ass off standing on the side of the road for a few hours.

Another dumb move—he's talking about filing as a conscientious objector once he graduates. I keep telling him that Nixon is going to end the war soon, so all he has to do is serve his two years. As a conscientious objector, he'll be a marked man for life. No one will hire him.

He's such an idealist, which may just be another way to fuck up. A few years back, niggers destroyed university property during a demonstration at another Wisconsin campus. The administration kicked them out of school. Three of them wanted to take classes again, but the regents said thanks, but no thanks. Jules got his face on the evening news leading a demonstration at the regents' meeting. He says they should have allowed the admissions office to review each case on its merit and not make an a priori decision about the group. He reasons that to deny someone admittance because they are part of a group is inherently racist. He's missing the point. These niggers broke the law, and they have to pay the consequences. But think about it: he risked his scholarship for a bunch of niggers probably too dumb to attend school without affirmative action. That's my definition of a putz.

Besides, there's no chance his side is going to win, and the winners always write history. No one is going to remember this demonstration. Hell, no one is probably going to remember the civil rights or the anti-war movements at the end of the day, and even if they remember them, they'll think it's an aberration, because the establishment is going to win and write the story. Take the Old Testament. It tells us how wonderful and pious David was, how wonderful Joseph and Jacob were, but they all won rivalries and therefore got to control the telling of the tale. Think about it—Samuel, the religious leader of the country and a very bright guy, selected Saul as King. Saul must have had some competence in matters important to the state—military and organizational prowess, or the ability to stir men's hearts to the defense of the twelve tribes. Undoubtedly a thoroughbred himself, David used the army of his country's enemies to take the throne, an entire horde of ringers, which is a helluva lot worse than shaving points. David then sent his best general on a suicide mission so he could screw the guy's wife. Which of the two seems more legit? Saul or David? History presents David as a young multi-talented genius and Saul as a cranky old man, but that's clearly a whitewash. And we know that Ishmael fathered a nation even more fruitful than Isaac's, and thus was just as deserving of Abraham's favor, at least in the abstract. And we know that Esau was a great hunter, a skill greatly prized in early nomadic cultures. He had skills, yet history, written by Jacob's descendants, presents Esau as brutish compared to the sophisticated, cunning Jacob. There was a lot of sibling rivalry back then that determined the dispensation of flocks, lands, and slaves. Apart from inheritance, how else could a father reward a favorite? Winners and losers. We don't know what really happened in history, because the winners sanitize their actions and denigrate the losers. The only thing we can be absolutely sure of is that Joseph really did fuck Potiphar's wife. I know I would have.

Jules is always breaking my balls about some cause or another. He's not around much anymore. And Leon doesn't confide in me at all. When we had our talk in the Chinese restaurant, I thought I was getting through to him. He's a great chess player, so I explained to him the ways that chess resembles life. You make small goals for yourself that lead to the big goal, like occupying the center to attack the king or getting good grades to win a scholarship.

You can't win at anything if you divide your forces or overextend yourself. You always overprotect your strong points, strengthen your strengths, as Nimzowitsch said, and then build from a stable position of power. There's always a limit to what you can do with your material at hand—you can't attack the king's side with just a queen and you can't buy a new car with two hundred dollars. Every position you strengthen causes a weakness someplace else, which is another application of the first law of thermodynamics. Matter and energy cannot be created or destroyed, only transformed from one form to another. You can't create something from nothing. And you can't forget that timing and position are as important as strength. You have to be at the right spot at the right time, in chess and in life. And, of course, it helps to be white!

He laughed at my joke. He conceded that everything I said was true, and enthusiastically swore he would make a new start in school. I'm beginning to believe that Lee was agreeing with me as the easiest way to get out of a tight spot. Imagine that, Ed Silver bullshitted by a snot-nosed kid.

He disagrees with everything I say. But when I disagree with him, he yowls ad hominem attacks at me. About a month ago, I mentioned that I read about a report that shows that marijuana use causes acne breakouts, something that happens to Lee a lot. It's a damn shame to see such a beautiful, square-jawed face marred by so many pimples and pockmarks. Now I didn't really read such a thing, but how would Lee know? Right away, he says that cigarette companies must have paid for sham scientists to fake results. I changed the subject to current events. I mentioned my objection to George McGovern accusing the establishment of leading us into the stupidest and cruelest war in all history. It's a patently absurd statement for a former history professor who must have studied the Crusades and the Peloponnesian War. Lee called me a fascist and started rattling off some bullshit about self-determination and the Vietnamese people. I wish he'd put a muzzle on.

One afternoon, I get home from work and notice my beautiful rosewood dining room table has a black burn-hole in it. Next to the hole is an ashtray full of cigarette butts. Only someone crushing out a lit cigarette directly into the table could have made the hole. The table means a lot to me, because I got it half-price after accusing the furniture store of bait-and-switch advertising. I used to love to tell the boys the story of how I pulled it off, first pretending to be dumb, then citing a phony law to the stupid salesman.

I had stayed at Melinda's the night before, so I didn't know for certain that Leon had been home. A lot of times he doesn't come home at all and says he's stayed with a girl, which is really fine by me. But all the evidence points to him having spent the night here. His bed is unmade and I know the schwarze made it the day before. His bath towel is on the bathroom floor. The radio was on when I got home. He must have been home, and he must know how the table top got ruined. But I don't want to confront him about it right away. I want to trap him.

When he gets in, I'm sitting in the armchair with the news on. He tries to sneak quietly behind the chair. I let him get to the hallway before I say, as disarmingly chipper as I can, "Leon, how are you?"

"Hey, what's up? I didn't see you."

"Want some dinner?"

"Yeah, cool, in a bit."

"You look pretty bushed. Where did you sleep last night?"

"I had a test this morning, so I studied at the library late at night. To tell you the truth, old man, I met a girl at the library, and she snuck me into her bedroom at her parent's house."

"You sure you didn't sleep at home last night?"

"What is this? Another cross-examination?" Notice how he changes the subject by taking the offensive. But I'm not going to lose my temper.

"I'm not cross-examining you. I'm asking one simple question, because I'm your father and I care about you. I just want to know where you slept last night."

"I told you, old man, I crashed with a chick."

"But Leon," I move in for the kill in a friendly, unbelligerent way. "The cleaning lady made your bed yesterday morning and now it's unmade."

"What's today?" he says, rubbing his hair and squeezing his eyes in mock confusion, so that his thick black brows connect.

"Wednesday."

"Wednesday?"

"Yes, Wednesday."

"I guess I did sleep at home last night. I got the days confused. The test was yesterday, and I was real tired after studying and balling the night before."

"You confused the days."

"I guess so."

"Are you too confused to tell me how a hole got in the dining room table?"

"What hole?" He looks like a puppy that knows it's supposed to shit on the newspaper but goes on the carpet anyhow and puts on a silly grin, pretending he doesn't know why the room stinks.

"Come here." He follows me into the dining room. "This hole, right here! The one that goes right through the finish and deep into the wood. This hole, right next to this ashtray filled with butts and ashes."

"I don't remember seeing a hole."

"It's a pretty big hole to miss."

"I was sitting here a while last night, reading and smoking."

"And you made a hole in my table."

"Look, old man, it was an accident. I dozed off, and when I woke up, the cigarette was lit and sitting on the wood."

"The way you describe it, the hole would be shaped like a crescent moon, but it's a full circle the size of a cigarette, as if someone purposely crushed it into the wood and let it smolder awhile."

"You're accusing me of purposely making the hole?"

"You explain it."

Leon begins to laugh derisively. "Get off my case, old man. You know, you're really fucked up."

"I'm fucked up? I'm fucked up?" I raise my voice a little, like a prosecutor moving in for the kill, not like someone losing it. "You lied to me like a four-year-old. Now *that's* pretty fucked up."

"I didn't lie. I forgot. Besides, it's only a table."

"That's an expensive rosewood table. To get rid of the hole, I'll have to have the entire table refinished. And you tell me *I'm* fucked up?"

Leon raises his voice to a level that must hurt his lungs, "Fuck you, old man. It was an accident. It's only a table, you asshole." He walks out, slamming the door as loudly as he can.

A few days later, we're having dinner together. I don't want to have another fight, so I decide to wait for him to begin the conversation. We'll talk about what he wants to talk about. I wait for him to start, but he remains silent. He seems to be lost in his own world. He looks down at his plate. Our eyes never make contact. All I hear is the clanking of flatware and the sound of my own chewing. Maybe he's stoned and trying to hide it. His plate empty, he gets up from the table—without taking his things to the sink—and begins to saunter away to his bedroom. Then he turns, looks down at his shoes, and says, "Hey, I'm a little short this week. Can you front me an advance on my allowance?"

All he wants to do is bilk the National Bank of Dad. But I don't want to get into another argument, so I let him have his money early.

A few more days pass, and he's home for dinner again. Silence shrouds the dining room. The silent treatment bugs me more than the arguments, because I have no idea what he's thinking. The lack of conversation becomes so unbearable that I have to say something. "You haven't asked me how my day was," I venture.

"If you wanted me to know, you'd tell me."

"Well, how was *your* day?"

"Nothing special. Do you really care, old man, or are you looking for an excuse to start pontificating?"

I ignore this insult, and we lapse into silence. Now comes one of his favorite tricks: the dawdle. He loves to do things as slowly as possible, because he knows it bugs me. He'll take a forty-minute shower or offer to make dinner and then do it so slowly that we don't eat until after nine. His favorite dawdle, though, is at the dinner table. He was always a slow eater, even as a child. He chews his food very slowly, like a three-day-old foal. Between bites, he pushes the peas around his plate and then stares into space. He takes a short sip of his milk, then looks at his plate and moves his hamburger to the other side of his fries. Now he takes another bite and chews for an excruciatingly long time. He knows that I would just as soon get the meal over with, but since I have complained often in the past about Jules abruptly leaving the table in the middle of the meal while others are still eating, he knows I won't leave until he has finished. If I do leave, he knows I know he's going to start raging about my double standard.

I sit there, stuck in another no-win situation. But he's in one, too, since he'll keep dawdling and not get up until I do. He is trapped in his trap. It's as if we're wrestling and have reached an equilibrium in which neither side can win. I'm Jacob wrestling an angel, except the angel is my own flesh and blood.

We sit there silently, me waiting politely and Leon chewing and sipping as slowly as he can. I'm getting frustrated, because I want to go ball Melinda. I have to end this stalemate, but I don't want to give him a chance to get on his self-righteous high horse. No choice but to raise the ante. "Did you hear?" I say. "It turns out the commies were behind the anti-war demonstrations in New York and across the country last week. Paul Harvey reported that the Socialist Workers Party was instrumental in organizing the protests."

"So what, old man?" he says, gets up, a third of his food still on his plate, and walks out the door, leaving me with the dishes, as usual.

"Where are you going?"

"What do you care?" he says, and slams the door.

That was a wash—no winner, no loser. I give Melinda a call, even though she's starting to disgust me. I get to her place a few minutes after she puts her daughter to bed. She's wearing nothing but a housecoat, which she opens wide as soon as she closes the door. She leads me into the bedroom, takes off my clothes, works on me until I'm hard, and then gets on top and says, "Hit me, Ed. Slap me in the face!"

"What do you mean?"

"Hit me! As hard as you want. I like it" There she goes again, telling me about the other guys she's screwing. She's really going downhill fast. She was reluctant to let me go after we officially broke up and I moved across town and told her I was seeing other women. Fucking another guy was the only way she'd move on. I had my friend Joey fly in from New York, and we got her completely smashed one night and did her one at a time, me first since I hate sloppy seconds, but that didn't help. Flash forward six months, and now she's telling me about fucking a lot of guys and she's supplying details. She's trying all kinds of stuff—like she shaved her pussy because one guy said he liked it. She thinks I give a shit who she sleeps with. I stopped caring about you a long time ago, lady! I couldn't care less how many guys you ball. You ain't my old lady anymore.

I slap her lightly across the cheek. "Harder, Ed."

"What the hell? Do you want me to hurt you?"

"That's the idea. What's the matter, are you hung up?' I wonder who taught her that hippy expression.

"I'm not hung up, whatever that means. I don't want to hurt you."

"But it feels good. I do what feels good."

"How does your mother feel about that?"

"She's just happy I'm not involved with a Jew anymore."

"And what about your priest?"

She starts to frown and stops grinding her pelvis. It feels good to lie on her bed in the dark completely motionless, with her on top of me and me inside her, listening to incomprehensible sounds emanating from the television in the living room, meaningless waves. The sound of a multitude of horse hoofs racing down a fast track. The sound of the dust they kick up. The sound of entropy.

"I liked your friend Joey. Bring him around next time he's in town." She's taunting me now. But the joke's on her. She's the one turning thirty, which is already over the hill for women, whereas, at thirty-nine, I'm looking distinguished and prosperous. Men keep getting better looking until we're well into our sixties. Lots of young chicks like an older guy who reminds them of their daddy and has money to spend. But a thirty-year-old broad doesn't look as good as a twenty-five-year-old broad and a twenty-five-year-old broad doesn't look as good as a twenty-year-old broad.

Yet I still have a physical thing for Melinda. When we lived next door to her, I would shoot over to her place to spend the night every evening after having dinner with the boys. Although she was married when I met her— to a truck driver who beat her—and had already had one affair, she never enjoyed sex before me. I made her orgasm the first time, and she was my slave. She was so hooked on me that she'd do anything I asked. Sometimes I would piss on her floor and make her crawl through it and beg for a taste of my cock.

It was convenient having Melinda close by when the boys were still in high school. She washed our clothes, knitted sweaters for them, and made us Sunday dinner. She baked cakes and pies for us. All I had to do was keep giving it to her, which I did with pleasure.

But after a while, I got tired of her bullshit. It wasn't one big thing, just a bunch of small ones. Like always campaigning for me to make an honest woman of her, but never agreeing to convert. She is too close to her mother and father, both of whom like to make derogatory comments about Jews. Like the father wondering why all Jews wear glasses. It's because we read a lot, you *schicker*! She does nothing to discipline her daughter, whom the entire family spoils rotten. I never liked that she goes to church every Sunday—I told her that she was now a Jew by injection! Listening to her complain about her boss all the time screeched like nails against a blackboard. And let's not forget her predilection for keeping everything super clean, which could be a royal pain. She vacuumed every night, while I was trying to watch TV. She changed the bedding after every fuck.

Now she comes for every Tom's hairy dick. But I didn't turn her into a whore. She was a whore when I met her.

Let's face it. All women are whores. They play the prim and proper, pure-as-fresh-snow virginal creatures who expect to be treated with respect and dignity as they uphold society's most cherished notions, but in their dark hearts they're nothing but cunts.

I slap her face with the full force of my right hand. Her head jerks away from her neck and she screams, "God, Ed, you don't know how good that feels." She groans and begins to tighten.

I move faster. I want it to be over, so I can leave. Her cries of "You're still the best" mean nothing to me.

I haven't seen her since.

Now I'm sitting in the dark, trying not to think of any of the irritations that seem to be scraping me like sandpaper. I haven't eaten yet. I'm just sitting here in my underwear, lights off, no radio, no TV, waiting for the call that I figure will come tonight or tomorrow. Leon must be getting down to his last dime and ready to hit me up again. I'm slumped on the sofa waiting for the call and thinking about what I'm going to say.

I have to reel Lee in slowly, like a big fish. Keep giving him a few bucks at a time until he trusts me. Soften him up. Ask him what he likes about California, what things he's seeing. Pretend to care about what *he* cares about. Pretend that I'm sincerely interested in what he's doing in Frisco. Maybe I can get him to tell me where he's staying, and then I'll let the cops know. I read somewhere—was it *Popular Science?*—a Greek engineer patented a way to identify the phone number of the caller. Maybe I can contact this guy and put together a black box I can plug into the line. Leon will call, I'll grab the number, tell the police, and they'll pick him up.

I won't send him more than twenty at a time, that's for sure. I'll keep him on a semi-tight rein, enough to maintain control but not so tight that he bristles and bucks and stops calling or does something stupid.

Once I get him home, I'll have to figure out a way to dry him out. His brain needs to defog, so he can start thinking straight. Maybe get him committed for a few weeks. But I don't want any shrinks getting near him. Ethel went to shrink after shrink, and all she learned were excuses for acting crazy. It's my father. It's my mother. It's the cousin who molested me. Lady, it's a crock of shit. Just suck it up, like I always do. Forget about your frustrations, your unresolved conflicts, your childhood traumas, your sibling rivalries, your phobias, your emotional pain, your secret sins, your secret desires, your inner turmoil, your hidden perversions, and your other turditivities.

Two years ago when he was wrestling for the state championship at 132 pounds, I was so proud of Lee. What a specimen—his back and chest so chiseled they looked like close-up photos of a snake pit—the spitting image of me at the same age, but even more muscular, more sculpted. He wrestled with a fierce and relentless intelligence. His wrestling coach told me that Leon could watch other kids wrestle and immediately identify all their weaknesses. He was like an assistant coach. Lee had destroyed all his competition and all that stood between him and the state championship was a hick from downstate.

The match starts. Leon doesn't wait to circle, but immediately goes for a take down. He scores a near fall and then a defensive escape and then a defensive reversal. He's up six-nothing. He takes his opponent down again, like he's swinging a dishrag. I'm yelling, "Pin him, pin him, pin him!" Another reverse and another takedown. He keeps scoring points, but he can't seem to pin the guy. It's as if he's toying with him, seeing how many points he can pile up. He's totally humiliating this hick. It's now eleven-oh in Lee's favor. If it gets to fifteen-zip, they stop the match and he automatically wins. I'm standing up, waving my rolled-up program, shouting "Pin him, Pin him!" His opponent scores two points, but allows Lee to get another takedown, making it fourteen-two. My son is in total control. He's dominating, like a big buck stallion humiliating the field. Now they're circling again. Thirty seconds left. Lee is playing out the clock. "I'm shaking the guy next to me and shouting feverishly, "That's my son, that's my son." He's the best and everyone knows it.

Lee's knee buckles and he falls to the ground and rolls on his back, taking his opponent with him. It's as if Leon is pulling the farmer on top of himself. The other kid looks exhausted. His face is dripping perspiration and he appears to be reeling from side to side as he straddles Leon. He's about to faint, but somehow his body gets positioned upright and Lee's shoulders fall flat.

Leon is pinned just as the buzzer rings.

What's worse, Leon has a big smile on his face and he's staring right at me the way kids gawk when they're on a carousel and it passes their parents, or they smack a double and they're standing like a cock-of-the-walk on second base. He blew a 14-2 lead in the state championship with one second left, and he's grinning. I wonder if he was smoking pot even then.

I feel as if I'm in a blind switch, caught in a pocket of horses and facing a tough decision. Do I wait for an opening? Or drop back and try to get around the crowd? I have to do what I always do—put on those blinders and do what has to be done. Keep my eye on the finish line and avoid distractions. Don't let anyone sidetrack me with sleights-of-hand or bullshit.

I still have big plans for the future. I want to find some buxom but proper Midwestern girl and remarry. Buy my own home and stop getting sucked dry by landlords. Fuck my bosses, open my own business, and take all the customers with me. Open up a second factory in Alabama and another west of the Rockies to get national exposure. Maybe take Leon into the business. Let him run the California operation. The Silvers will have a dynasty. I know exactly where I'm going and exactly how to get there. But straightening out Leon won't be easy. At this point, he looks like a long-shot, and I'm more of a chalk player than a dog player. I like the favorites.

MUSIC HIDDEN IN THE SHRUBBERY

"That you, hon?"

"Yes'm."

"How'd it go?"

"Well, all right, I reckon. There was a whole mess of things I wanted to say to Lee when I dropped him off. But I couldn't get the words out right."

"You let him know that, if we had our druthers, he wouldn't be moving into a tent in the middle of winter?"

"That train already left the station, so I held my peace."

"Probably for the best. Work on what you can fix, I always say."

"That's what you always say, Ginny. I needed to make sure he understood he was welcome back with us whenever he hankered for a home cooked meal or a real bed. I told him he's as much *mishpoche* as our own two boys. All he has to do is follow a few simple rules. No drugs on the premises, no smoking cigarettes in the house and clean up your own mess."

"He always followed our rules."

"Maybe not always. I never told you 'bout the time I caught him smoking some wacky tobacky at the edge of the property. He was all aw-shucks, eyes in the dirt. I told him I wouldn't say anything to you about it, but that he couldn't do it again. I really gave it to him about pot smokers eventually turning to stronger stuff, not being able to focus on work, being susceptible to strange behavior, getting arrested, going to jail for years. Then I started cussing him out fearsome about us having two young boys who we don't want taking drugs. Read him the riot act from A to Z and all the letters in between, and he just stood there, taking it without saying a word. He raised his thick black eyebrows from time to time. Looked to me like he was trying to hide a smirk, trying to look serious and sorry. I was angry as a wet cat. Hey, what's so funny? You've got the beautiful deep-dimple smile on your face I love, teeth and freckles showing."

"I'm smiling because I caught him once, too. I never smelled it before, so I didn't know what in blazes he was smoking. I said to Lee, 'That's some skunky tobacco you're smoking.' He told me it was marijuana and said he wouldn't do it again."

"No one can lie to you, Ginny."

"Maybe so, maybe no, but I've picked up that odor a time or two around the property since then."

"You should have said something to me, I reckon. We can't have someone taking illegal drugs in front of Maurice and Miles. I don't care who it is. I might have kicked his sorry butt out if I had known, but first I would have kicked his sorry butt."

"Now, Emil, you know you're just talking. You're as harmless as a dove."

"You think that's why he left? So he could freely smoke that shit?"

"Language, Emil!"

"Yes'm."

"I believe him when he says junior college wasn't challenging and that he couldn't learn anything from the teachers."

"Maybe so, maybe no. But I reckon you have to start someplace. But that's another train that's left the station. Anyways, I told Lee that I wasn't fixing to convince him to reconsider. I know when his mind's made up, he's as ornery as I can be. But I needed to make sure he knew the door is always opened. He repeated his plan to me. He spoke slowly, deliberately, in that deep voice of his, pausing every few words, as if waiting for the thought to sink in. 'I'll bake bread full time, man ... at the organic bakery ... until next fall ... to save up tuition ... then start taking classes ... in advanced math ... which the JC didn't offer.' He has a plan, sure as shit...."

"Watch that tongue of yours, Emil Teller!"

"Yes'm. He has a plan, sure."

"And if he puts his mind to it, he's bound to make it work."

"I believe it. I worked as a short order cook and put myself through college and I ain't got half Lee's *seykhel*. Anyways, I watched him set up camp and pitch his teepee in a clearing on some high ground, near a few tree stumps. He gathered some large stones and piled them up to make a small fireplace. We were about a hundred feet from the Oconee. We could hear the shushing of the river flow against the low shore. I asked him why he didn't place his camp near the river and he said he didn't want to be too close to the water because he didn't want to share his sleeping bag with water rats. He worked slowly, deliberately, an unfiltered Camel hanging from his lips. It gave me a hankering for one, but I knew you'd smell it on my breath. A storm was brewing. He had a plan for that, too, a sheet of plastic he spread on the earth as the floor of his teepee around which he dug a deep but narrow trench. Watching him cut the shovel through tree roots reminded me of his welding."

"Why that boy never stuck with that, at least for a few years, I'll never understand."

"Better money than baking bread. He was a wonder at it, too. And his boss never gave him no sh… sugar."

"Remember how Lee moved so quickly through that welding class. My buttons popped with pride. It was a series of assignments—building different things that involved ever more sophisticated welding techniques. Once a student completed one assignment, the instructor graded it and gave him the next one. The program was supposed to take six weeks. Lee did it in five days and got an A+ on every assignment. And his work was beautiful. I love that metal chair he made for your basement office."

"That good ol' boy Billy Joe Cone who I got to give him work—he sure liked him fine. I stopped by his fabrication shop one day to talk to him about renewing his policies and all he could do was kvell about Lee. Lee was his fastest worker. Lee could read the blueprints faster than he could. Lee's welds passed every test without failure. No cracks, no distortions, no gas bubbles, no incomplete fusions. It didn't matter if he was welding a pinpoint or a beam."

"I was happy he was making good money. In a few months' time, he saved up enough to pay us back what we laid out for the course."

"I told him I didn't want his damn money, so he bought all of us something nice—a beautiful silk shirt for me, some records for Maurice and Miles, a new food processor for you. He got himself a used rusted-out Dodge, put in some new brakes and tuned up the engine real nice."

"He was spending it just as fast as he made it. Every time I asked if he was putting something away, he grunted the kind of yes a kid gives when he's lying. There was nothing we could do about it, though. It was his money."

"We could have charged him room and board."

"But that's not our way, Emil."

"It would have been my way. People think that if you don't pay for it, it ain't worth sh… sugar. Besides, we would have given it back to him when he set up his own place."

"Lee didn't seem to care a lick about money at all."

"He didn't seem to care a lick about most things that motivate people to get up in the morning."

"It's true, hon. At times I wasn't sure what made him tick, except maybe the insecurity of growing up the way he did. He never once wanted to talk about it, but sometimes on Friday night when Maurice was reciting the *bracha* over wine, I could see a tear circling Lee's eyes and his lips tug a little. Then the expression would turn blank and flat. He squeezed together his eyebrows, as if he was fighting the urge to cry. I'm sure he was thinking about what he missed growing up. I don't think he was moved by the prayer."

"No, he always was picking a fight about religion."

"You four boys had some heated discussions, that's for sure."

"He would come at you in sneaky ways. Friday dinner was like a high school debate sometimes, with Lee slyly introducing the topic. He didn't say, 'Resolved: Jews are not the chosen people since they act like every other nation. Or Resolved: the theory of evolution demonstrates that there is no god. Or Resolved: Jewish law has a different set of rules for the wealthy than for everyone else.' No, he'd ask an innocent question, like 'Why do we throw our food out before Passover, but rich folk are allowed to sell their wine collections to gentiles and then buy the wine back after the holiday?'"

"I remember that time. Maurice fell right into it. 'I know,' the poor boy said. 'It's because the value of the wine is so great that the rabbis considered it a hardship to destroy it.'"

"'Isn't it more of a hardship for a poor family to have to throw away all their flour, bread, and 'most other food? Food is a big part of a poor family's budget, much bigger than for rich folk. What's so tough about a rich person throwing away some wine?' Lee would quietly ask."

"'With a little planning, the poor family could work their food supply down to nothing before the holiday,' you chimed in."

"As soon as I began talking, he went right in for the kill. 'And so could the rich person. For example, he could give the wine to his synagogue for a great pre-Passover party.'"

"'I reckon some people have a lot of wine in their wine cellar. Thousands of bottles,' I said, to which he immediately responded like a cat pouncing on a cardinal.' 'And you think they deserve the money it takes to have all that wine, while there are poor people, and people who are worse than poor.'

"'If they made the money,' I said, but the words sounded hollow, even to me.

"'Uncle Emil, Uncle Emil, you know most rich people inherited their money or had connections that got them where they are. You know there's very little economic mobility in any society. So you can't give me that nonsense that they deserve what they have. Especially back then when people tended to have the same profession and social status as their fathers did. No, the rabbis made special rules for the rich, who were paying most of their salaries. It's the rabbis who give rich people a break in the Talmud, but the original Torah talks about the Jubilee, a time that comes every 49 years when all debts are forgiven and all slaves go free. In that kind of world, no one can save up enough money to have more than a few dozen bottles of wine. Perfect for a nice community party.'

"'I agree with Lee,' Maurice announced. 'The Talmud does favor rich people.'"

"The boy was right, Emil."

"But it's the world we live in. Every religion favors those who have money. Lee had no end of radical ideas. But not liking money? That's just plumb crazy."

"Money isn't going to solve his problem, hon. Spending time in a haimish family full of love and respect that keeps regular hours and follows regular habits and goes to Shul Friday night. That's all he's ever needed. He's needed to see people get mad at each other without shouting or throwing things and then make up right away without holding a grudge. He's needed to see people doing things for each other and taking responsibility for each other."

"He was getting a mess of all that good stuff with us. If that's what he needs, he should have stayed with us."

"I know, I know. We can only hope that he's had time to heal in his two years' living with us."

"Time to recover from living with that summabitch Ed.'"

"Emil!"

"You have to let me have that one, Ginny. Ed Silver's the worst summabitch I ever met."

"Lee is away from him now. Let's hope he's ready to stand on his own two feet. Course it could be he just got tired of welding."

"Like he got tired of cleaning bedpans in the hospital, and tired of community college and he'll probably get tired of anything that doesn't use that mind of his."

"Working as an orderly really said it all. He was fired because, instead of calling for a doctor, he delivered a baby by himself. The charge nurse entered the room just as he was pulling it out, and goodness gracious, what a row there was about it!"

"What a way to lose a job!"

"All we can do is hope for the best and be there for him."

"As usual, Ginny, you're right. You can't make someone save their money. Still, you know I was pretty puh… riled when he made his big announcement."

"Yes, I could see you steaming when he said he was quitting his job and moving to Athens to go to U-G-A. You said you reckoned he had saved up a pretty pile of money for tuition. When he said he would have about twenty bucks once he paid for dinner, I could see your teapot start boiling."

"If we weren't in public, I might have blown up at him. 'Course that's why he offered to take us all out to Big Bob. So I couldn't make too much of a big to-do. Anyways, he says, 'I met a girl at the rock concert in Atlanta a few weeks back. She said I could bake bread and wash dishes for the bakery her sister owns. I won't have any expenses, since I can eat at the bakery.'

"'You got yourself a place to stay?' I asked.

"'Got that covered, man,' he said, like a fella playing checkers who knows that, as soon as the other fella makes a move, he's got himself a triple jump. So he's just sitting back, drinking his whiskey and smiling. That's the way Lee looked. 'My friend Danny Zucker's grandmother owns a piece of property on the Oconee River.'

"'The one whose folks own the liquor store downtown.'

"'His grandmother doesn't mind none if I pitch a tent or teepee and stay out there. No rent, no food expenses. Tuition will be no problem at all.' The more he told me about his plans, the less I liked them.

"'You're going to live in a teepee! Cool as a moose,' Maurice shouted, so loud the people at the next table turned around. Maurice giggled more like a six-year-old than a teenager, the way he always laughs when he gets excited."

"Maurice loves both of Ethel's boys to death. Miles does, too. They've been a good influence on them."

"Mostly. Don't like their politics much, but I reckon that'll change once they get some skin in the game. Don't like Lee's pot smoking none either, but he swore to me the time I caught him that he would never do it with the boys. I reckon he wouldn't break his word about something like that."

"No, no, I don't think he'd do something like that to us. He knows we'd have to cut all ties with him."

"And you're always calling *me* the tough one."

"You have to be tough about some things."

"Amen to that."

"Some of his ideas are just as dangerous as smoking wacky tobacky. I didn't like it none when he talked up living in a teepee. 'Maybe I can live in a teepee instead of the dorm when I get to Athens,' Maurice said."

"'I don't think so,' Miles piped up. ' You like to take long hot showers too much.'"

"'The boy's right. We all like our comforts,' I said."

"'Well, I don't know,' Lee said softly, in that deep voice of his. 'It's a Thoreau kind of thing. I want to simplify my existence. Live close to nature, away from the entanglements of the city.'"

"We're hardly living in the city on the outskirts of Macon on a couple of wooded acres, which is exactly what I told him. 'If you want to be close to nature, you can always camp on our land instead of living in the basement.'"

"'It's not the same experience,' he said. 'In my heart I would always know I could come inside to take a shower or get a hot meal anytime I wanted. This will be the real thing. I want to try to experience the natural world the way it really is, unmediated by social constructs. To be in nature and of nature. I want to live in fresh air, not the stale air of an air-conditioned, oil-heated house soaking in perfumes, air fresheners, soaps, hairsprays and other artificial odors. I want to see and hear reality without the distracting noises and images of civilization, the constant human chatter from radios and televisions, the constant buzz of engines, thrum of motors, background music, and the constant exhortations to buy or believe something. I want to be able to listen to the voice of nature. I want to learn to play nature's music. I want to learn how to distinguish that which is inherently good and beautiful from that which we are brainwashed to believe is good and beautiful.'"

"'Won't you get awful lonely out there living by yourself?' Miles asked."

"'There's a big difference between being alone and feeling lonely,' Lee answered. 'You can feel mighty lonely in a crowd of people if you don't know anyone and everyone else is dancing and eating and drinking and having fun and no one is talking to you. And you can be all by yourself, with nothing but your thoughts and the millions of stars stretching above you across the sky, and be filled with a sense that everyone and everything is on your side. *Alone*—that's a matter of physical presence. But *lonely*, that's a feeling.'"

"It wasn't often he said more than a few words, but when he did, he sure did go on."

"That he did, and it made living in the woods sound inspiring and beautiful. But it's going to feel right cold sticking his behind out the teepee when the ground's froze over."

"I'm glad you didn't say that in front of the boys."

"Didn't have a chance to. He kept going on. 'I also like the idea of living off the grid which means living off the land,' he said. 'Build my own furniture from wood I cut down, collect my own firewood every day, do a little fishing, gather the wild berries that grow along the roadside, maybe plant a garden if I can figure out a way to keep the deer and varmints out.'"

"He wouldn't let anyone else get a word in edgewise. He had a speech to give about what he was doing, and he was going to deliver it."

"'It's simpler out in nature,' he told us with the conviction of a dog sniffing around outside a butcher's shop. 'Sure, there's no running water and you have to squat over a log to do your business, but you don't have to worry about ever fixing a leaky pipe or jiggling the toilet handle to get the damn thing to stop whistling Dixie. And you don't have to worry about paying a bunch of bills. What with all the rats and other varmints, you have a mess of pets and you don't even have to walk or feed them. If you want to read at night, you can do it by candlelight or firelight, like people did for thousands of years. Well, I don't rightly know, but maybe we've taken a wrong turn piling up material possessions that own us more than we own them. Like Freud said to those who marveled at the telephone connecting people thousands of miles away: they wouldn't be apart if it weren't for the railroad. Early humans knew things that we've forgotten, because they lived in nature whereas we visit nature every once in a while. It's a knowledge you don't read about in books, but the knowing of it connects you to all things.'"

"'I'm going to do it,' he concluded emphatically. 'I bought my teepee and all the equipment and utensils I need to live out there and I'm set on trying it out.' I wasn't happy about him striking out with the same twenty bucks in his pocket that he had when got here two years ago."

"At least you paid for dinner, so he had seventy-five."

"I also slipped two hundred in twenties into his bedroll."

"I'm glad you did that, hon."

"Driving home, I thought about Ethel. I wished I had said something to Lee about her when we were sitting out there on a log in front of his teepee, waiting for the rain to come, watching the clouds gather together and grow dark. We just sat there in silence for a while. I was thinking of telling him that he should let his Momma know directly where he's living, that it was wrong to leave it to us to be the ones to tell her. I was thinking maybe I could get him talking about what went wrong between them that he should shut her out."

"You've tried to talk about Ethel to Lee before, and he just walks out of the room. You know, whenever she's called or we call her, he's never wanted to speak to her. Sometimes he made an excuse and sometimes he just made himself scarce. Her letters from California arrived about twice a month. Did he ever answer any of them? I really can't say for sure, but the times at the beginning when I tried to give him a gentle reminder, I could see him bristle, his shoulders hunch together defensively. I stopped asking after that one time I was cleaning his room and found a bunch of her letters in a drawer, under a pile of clothes, all still unopened. At least he didn't throw them away."

"I spoke with him a number of times about the responsibility that every Jew has to honor and respect your parents, even when they aren't honorable or respectable. You can't shut them out. It's not right."

"It's not right. It's like cutting off your nose to spite your face. A person who hates their parents can't be happy. Your parents are the first people you see, the first people you love, the people you need for everything for the first few years of life. You can't be happy if you cut them off. It's impossible. It's like cutting off part of yourself."

"I reckon he has a right to be angry at his father, but not at his mother."

"You know your sister could be a handful. You remember how it was when we were all living in Miami."

"I also remember that, growing up, she was my favorite, because she always treated me fine. There were five ahead of me. They all seemed so much older and smarter. They treated me as if I was always in the way. But not Ethel. But I'm gonna hush up now. I've told you about it a thousand times."

"But you sure do like to talk about those old days. And I like hearing about them."

"Yes, I sure as sugar do. Hope was the oldest. I reckon she's ten years older than me. She was like a second-in-command after Momma, at least for a while. She stopped helping Momma in the kitchen and dressing us young ones in the morning as soon as Ethel was old enough to do it. After that, she stayed in the room she shared with Ethel and Hedy, reading until it was time to go to school. She never came home until just before dinner and then disappeared afterwards, usually to the closest public library or to her bed with the nightlight she bought with her Hanukkah gelt one year. After she went to college, when she came home for visits, or to live with us briefly before she married Jack, she never had any time for me. Then came Henry, Momma's favorite by divine right, as the first son and also by talent and intelligence. I knew I couldn't beat him at school, nobody could, so I was never gonna try."

"Everyone in your family thinks too much about who's smarter."

"Henry set a pretty high bar—Leon kind of smarts. One every generation."

"Henry wasn't the top insurance salesman in his company three years running."

"Ain't the same thing. I worked at it. And I had you to help me do the books. Henry never had to work at anything."

"You had to grow up pretty fast. You were fifteen when your Momma passed. You had to get a job right away and work full-time your last two years of high school and straight through college."

"We all had it tough once we lost everything in the Great Depression and started moving up and down the coast for years, like sharecroppers. Didn't matter none to Henry, though. He was always in his own world and he was king of it. He had two paper routes as long as I can remember, one before school and one after school, so he always had plenty of money, even after giving some to the family and putting some away for college. And there was no doubt Henry was going to college. I don't think he ever got lower than an A on any test he ever took. He won the science fair in a few different schools, always by building mechanized arms that performed simple lifting and carrying functions. He would put them together from spare parts. He always did the right thing, and even when he didn't, he did the wrong thing the right way, so he didn't suffer the consequences. Like the summer he set up a casino in our basement in that big old house we had in Tampa. He somehow got hold of a roulette wheel and a mess of poker chips and took all of Momma's solitaire cards from the credenza in our living room. Henry had Morris and some of their friends hand out flyers to all the kids in Hebrew School and serve as dealers. I made sure the tables and ashtrays stayed clean and collected the soda bottles, so we could make extra money turning them in for the deposit. Henry took the five cents admissions we made all the kids play and sold boys chips at a premium. That's how we made money. He sold a dollar's worth of chips for a dollar ten cents and bought them back at ninety cents. I reckon Henry had it all figured out. During the games, he rolled up the profits in change rolls that he had me pick up at the local bank, so it was easy for him to pay everyone their split afterwards. He ran the game for one Sunday and invited all the kids from Hebrew school, who invited their friends until we pretty much had every Jewish boy in the Tampa-St. Pete area between the ages of 13 and 18. When Mo asked why we weren't doing it again, Henry smiled and said, 'One time is adorable. Twice is dangerous.'

"Henry had a great sense of humor, but a lot of times you didn't get his jokes until you thought about it later on. Like at the end of a romantic aria that Ethel put on the phonograph that seemed to go on forever. The soprano's voice went higher and higher. The orchestra played louder and louder. It all reached a crescendo, and then the music stopped, and Henry chimed in, 'Cha, cha, cha,' with a devilish little smile. I couldn't figure out what he meant until he did it again at the end of a Sigmund Romberg song a few weeks later, and I realized he was making fun of the music. Or his puns, which he would tell with such a straight face that you didn't know he was kidding: 'Egg sample' for 'example' or "real eyes" for "realize.'"

"His humor is drier than a desert in a drought."

"Morris, who comes after Ethel, put Henry on a pedestal and did everything Henry did, stepping right into Henry's footprints four years after Henry laid the original trail, making it even harder for me. He got mostly A's in school and won debating contests. He even took over Henry's paper routes, although he dropped the afternoon one after a few weeks because it was eating into his homework time."

"Mo's humor is cruder than Henry's. We always understand Mo's jokes, seeing as most of them have sound effects."

"For bodily functions."

"Mo has done well for himself. He was almost as enterprising as Henry. I reckon I've told you about how we would catch baseballs that went over the short fences in spring training. We would get the players to sign the balls or sometimes just sign their names for them, then sell them to the tourists. That was Mo's idea, and it worked until a potential buyer questioned the authenticity of a Joe DiMaggio autograph and summoned a passing police officer."

"It was a good lesson for the two of you to spend a few hours at the police station before your mamma fetched you."

"Maybe so and maybe no. Then there was Hedy, *sheyna*, a real beauty, married off to another Hungarian at the age of fifteen. Then me. Kitten is even younger than I am, and always a piddling little nudnik. Mark didn't come until years later, just before Momma died. That's when Hedy took in Mark, Kitten, and Pop-pop, and I stayed in Miami. She was just seventeen, but already married for two years. Henry was twenty-five and in graduate school, and Mo was still in the Navy. In one way or another, they were all living in a different world from me."

"At least until ya'll grew up and became as thick as thieves, as thick as only *mishpoche* can be."

"Ethel always treated me different. She always took an interest in me. My earliest memory is her reading me *Gulliver's Travels* on the porch of that big old house we rented in Washington, D.C. She played with me for hours when I was a boy. She baked cookies and cakes as good as Momma, without having to read the ingredients from a book like Hedy did, and she always let me lick the spoon and bowl. When Momma or Hedy made batter, there was hardly anything left to lick, but Ethel, she left me a whole heap of it. She was always knitting sweaters for me, one a year for the beginning of school. She could fill a rainy afternoon with games she would invent using pieces of paper, trash cans, and folding chairs. Or we would sing songs she taught me, opera and show tunes. Even when I was an awkward but still thuggish fifteen-year-old just before I met you, and Ethel was home on leave from the WACs and it was blowing up a storm, she insisted we gussy up and she taught me how to jitterbug to Benny Goodman records. Henry listened to Benny Goodman all the time and tried to get me interested. Ethel was the one who taught me you could dance to it. When the rain and wind gusts stopped, she took me to a local malt shop for chocolate phosphates. There was a dance floor and a juke box the kids kept plugging nickels into. Ethel pulled me out on the dance floor and we danced every move she had taught me. When we got to the front door after the walk home, she kissed me on the cheek, leaving a smudge of red lipstick, and said, 'Now you can say, you've had your first date. Just don't tell anyone it was with your older sister!'

"She was a wonderful swimmer. She could glide back and forth across a pool lap after lap without raising a splash, just smoothly slicing through the water. Did I ever tell you 'bout the time we were living in Brooklyn and Ethel took me to the beach on Long Island?"

"No, hon, that's one story I don't know."

"'The family that owned the kosher bakery down the street from us had an ex-swabby for a son. I reckon he was in his 30's living at home since his discharge. He had been an amateur swimming champion in his teens. I forget his name, but the bakery was called Horvats, so I reckon that was it. One evening during dinner, Ethel asked Momma if she could go with Horvats to a Long Island beach to swim early one morning, before the crowds gathered. Before Momma could say a word, Pop-pop said, 'Absolutely not. He's twice your age and he's a bum that still lives at home.'

"'What does that have to do with anything? It's just swimming.'

"'There's no one at the beach that early. It's not proper for you to be alone on the beach with a grown man.'

"'Nothing is going to happen. We're just going to swim.'

"'It's not proper. You'll be the talk of the neighborhood.' They went on arguing for a piece until Momma settled it by suggesting that Ethel take me along as a chaperone. I was about ten, which means Ethel was sixteen.

"A few days later, Ethel wakes me when it's still as dark as a black bear's fur outside. No time for breakfast—she slathers margarine on a few pieces of challah and tells me to eat it in the car. Horvats is waiting for us in a shiny new Nash 600 that he bought with his discharge bonus. On the drive out to the beach, we see a beautiful sunrise fill the sky, the sun a big ball of red throwing off pink flames.

"Ethel plays with me in the sand, while Horvats does calisthenics in front of us. Every once in a while he says, 'Watch this' and does a flip in the sand or stands on his head. 'Let me try one,' I say, and he shows me how to stand on my head supported by my two hands. I wished Henry and Mo could see me looking like an Olympic gymnast, proud as a dog with a bone in its maw. Then they take me into the water and we splash and dive into the waves. It's freezing cold, so cold my skin turns red and I can see hundreds of little bumps up and down my arms. But I don't care, I'm having as much fun as a pig in mud. Ethel suddenly says, 'Hush, do you hear that?' 'What? What is it? I can't hear a thing,' I say, and she breaks into song 'Clank, clank, clank goes the trolley, ding, ding, ding goes the bell....' We all start singing it and laughing, like a bunch of drunk hunters. After a while, Ethel says that they came to the beach to swim. I can't make any headway against the current, so they just swim around me for a while, then say they want to take a longer swim. Ethel asks me to stay on our towel and play and makes me promise not to go into the water. Of course, I did, but not any farther than to get my feet wet, because I had felt the waves trying to pull me under before and was a little scared. 'Course, I don't show it none."

"You haven't changed a bit in that way."

"If you want someone to look cool and in control even though he's so scared he's about to cr... to carpet the floor, I'm your boy. I watch them swim out beyond the waves and then head in one direction. When I see they can't see me, I run out into the water, but just a little ways in. I sit in the mud near the shoreline and splash at the dying end of the waves floating over my legs. The sun balances on a greyish yellow pool of light shimmering at the horizon. It seems to be moving towards me, slowly as it climbs the sky. Pretty soon I get cold and run to the towel. I wrap myself in it and look out at the water and then down the beach in the direction Ethel and Horvats swam. Large white birds with long legs glide down and land in the sand, hop along the beach a bit, peck into it, and fly away again, always over the water. Every hundred feet or so I see one of those tall wooden structures that lifeguards sit on, but it's too early in the morning for lifeguards. In the distance stands a pier with a couple of houses at land's end. Other people are starting to arrive. An elderly couple walks barefoot in the mud. They stop every few feet and pick up a shell. Some they throw into the waves, others they put into a satchel the woman carries over her shoulder.

"A few people jump in the water and swim beyond the waves, like Ethel and Horvats. I wonder where they are. It's been a long time. I begin to worry. Maybe they drowned? Maybe I should send someone out to look for them? But I don't want to get into trouble, or get Ethel in trouble. I decide to count fifty waves before I do anything. But those fifty waves come and go in no time flat, so I count another fifty. Pretty soon I've got two-hundred-fifty under my belt. I can feel tears start to form behind my eyeballs and I fight the urge to let them flow.

"I look down the beach again and see three, maybe four groups of people walking towards me. No one looks like them, except for one couple so far away that all I can see are their body shapes—he's tall like Horvats, and she's short like Ethel, but they're holding hands. I squint my eyes to make them out better. They stop and seem to come together for a minute and become one creature, then break apart and start walking again. They're still pretty far away and it doesn't look like them.

"I look in the other direction, thinking maybe I got turned around, but all I see that way is a bunch of birds pecking at the sand. I turn back the other way and that couple I saw in the distance is running now, running towards me. It is Ethel and Horvats. They look dry, but Horvats grabs a towel and starts to pat Ethel dry, as if she just stepped out of the ocean. Ethel does the same to Horvats

"'I'm hungry,' he says. 'Let's get some breakfast before we start back.' 'But we keep kosher,' I say. 'We won't have any bacon,' he says, 'just pancakes.' Pancakes sound great to me. I look at Ethel and beg with my eyes."

"You still do, like a little *mazik*! You bring your eyes down and they seem to water and you put a very small frown on your lips and stick out your chin just a little. You poor, lost little boy!"

"That's the look, all right! I give it to her with both barrels, and she says, 'Yes, that's fine, we still have time. But we can't say a word about going to a restaurant to Pop-pop or Momma. Not one hint!' They were some mighty good-tasting pancakes. You know how being at the water makes you hungry, plus they had some tangy, sweet-and-salty flavor to them that I had never tasted before. Horvats said it was their secret ingredient, and that's why he always came to this place for breakfast when he was on Long Island. I wolfed down my pancakes so quickly that Horvats bought me a second stack, which went down just as easy as the first one did. It wasn't until I went off to college that I found out why they tasted so different and so good. They were fried in bacon grease, not margarine or butter. I reckon that Ethel knew, which is why she had some dry toast and a soft-boiled egg that came in a ceramic egg cup that she softly tapped and tapped, all the while singing, 'You always hurt the one you love.' 'You know all the top songs, don't you,' Horvats marveled.

"On the way home, Ethel led us in a rendition of 'Would you like to swing on a star, carry moonbeams home in a jar....'"

"And be better off than you are.... My mother used to sing that one to me."

"What a grand morning that was. But after Horvats dropped us off, Ethel's mood turned dark, like it sometimes did. I excitedly told Momma about the excursion—the waves, the birds, building sand castles—everything but the part about pancakes. Ethel didn't say a word. When Momma asked if she had a good time, Ethel said, 'It was a wonderful to swim in the ocean and see the beach, but now it's over and I'm feeling a little sad about it.' It was later that day that seven of us were piled into Pop-Pop's old Plymouth Six chugging down Franklin Street, when one of the back doors flew open and Ethel rolled out and along the pavement. Pop-pop slammed on his brakes. So did a few other cars to keep from hitting her. She came out of it with a bump on her head and a few bruises. Pop-pop blamed her for accidentally hitting her elbow against the door lever."

"Whenever you tell that story, I'm surprised that the door wasn't held together by a piece of wire or string that broke."

"I reckon I don't rightly remember, but I know Pop-pop was always trying to fix everything with spit and string and no proper tools. Ethel, she just laughed it off by making herself the butt of a few jokes. She was as funny as all get-out, except when she felt sad or was fixing to throw a fit. Then she couldn't figure her way out of bed in the morning. She did about like me in school. Being a girl with average grades, she didn't get to go to college, but took a bookkeeping job. I was about Bar Mitzvah age when her first boss put her in the family way. The old man fell apart like a one-legged man in an ass-kicking contest. Henry came home from college and took care of everything. I wanted to beat the guy up, that piece of poor white trash, but that wasn't ever gonna be Henry's way. Henry quietly arranged for an abortion and Ethel went into the Army, where she met that low-life piece of dog meat Ed Silver. Before she met him, she was a little *meschugge* from time to time, but she never went into the looney bin."

"Hon, you were a psychology major, too. You know the kind of problem that Ethel has manifests itself in the teens and early twenties. She was twenty-three with two young children the first time she went into an institution."

"Ed was and is and always will be a mean, loud-mouthed, low-down dirty dogova sommabitch."

"You know how much I love your sister, but she can be a handful."

"She's just one of those people who needs a little help from time to time. She's a bit more delicate than most. I thought we could help her and the boys, which is why I urged her to move down to Miami. I remember that first day. She must have driven through the night because they arrived at seven in the morning. They all looked dog-tired, but not so much that Jules couldn't make a big to-do about breakfast."

"I offered him French toast and his eyes lit up. But I didn't make it the way he was used to having it. I made it how my Momma does—just egg and challah. I didn't know you could stir milk into the eggs and add cinnamon. Jules just pushed it away and said, 'What a disgusting mess.'"

"He did the same thing at lunch. I thought the boys would like to try Burger King, since they didn't have any up north back then. He took one bite out of his Whopper, spat it out and said the special sauce was disgusting. He was pretty much an angry young man when we were all together in Miami."

"We pulled him away from his friends."

"He made new ones right quick. He did all right for himself in Miami. Better than I did in high school."

"He was on the student council and the football team…"

"…but he never got to play."

"For a young man, just to be part of the team means something."

"Team or no team didn't matter none to Jules. He came to town angry, and he stayed angry. He was angry the day we put them on the plane two years later to live with Ed. He thought he was just going for a visit over the holidays and was coming right back and live with us for his last semester in high school, while Leon stayed in Chicago and Ethel went into the hospital for another long stay."

"We didn't have the heart to tell Jules he was going to live with his father."

"We didn't tell him, but he must have sensed something, because he was in fine fettle, complaining that his Brussel sprouts tasted rancid, the dressing on the salad was disgusting goop, and the music at the restaurant was for squares. That boy could always find something to bit... to bellyache about."

"You know Brussel sprouts isn't a vegetable young boys tend to like."

"Maybe so and maybe no, but he was and still is an argumentative peckerwood. I remember the time I came over just to check up on them and caught Jules and Ethel in the middle of an argument. Jules was screaming something fierce. From what I could piece out, I reckon he'd been playing one of his forty-fives with the door to his bedroom closed and she walked in without knocking, took the record from the phonograph and busted it in half. Maybe that was a little crazy, but it don't matter none what she did. As soon as he started yelling at his Momma, he put himself right smack dab in the wrong. That was always the rule in our house growing up, and it's the rule in our house now. So first I shout him down to get him to quiet up. Then I tell him that it don't matter none what she did or said or what he did or said, that once he raised his voice to his Momma he was in the wrong and I had to punish him. I told him to drop his pants and lay down on his bed, because I was going to give him a belt-whupping. The boy knew I was right. Even though he was already as tall as me, he dropped them drawers and spread himself across his bed, which was unmade, as usual. I pulled out my belt and whopped him a few times, just so he'd get a taste of it."

"You know I never like it when you take a belt to the boys."

"Sometimes it's the best way to make an impression. I don't mean to hurt them none, just to shame them a little."

"What was it about those boys and making beds? They never wanted to do it."

"Leon would just lie and say he forgot. But Jules would smile his smart-ass Yankee smile and say that it was senseless to make the bed, since you'll just have to do it again the next day. When I pointed out that eating was the same way, that you just had to do it again the next day, he laughed and said that you don't have to make your bed every day to live, but you have to eat every day to live. That's where I thought I had him. I said, 'In my house, you need to make your bed every day to live.' 'It's not your house, though,' he said, and of course he was right. That was the problem. It was Ethel's house, and she wasn't about to lay down any rules, so the boys made their own."

"They weren't really bad kids, though, when you consider everything. Jules did most of the cooking and laundry and cleaning up the dishes. Whenever I was over there, his side of the boys' bedroom was always neat and clean. The rest of the house was a pigsty."

"Near the end, it was depressing to go over there. Ethel looked like hell. She never got out of bed. The carpets needed vacuuming, the furniture needed dusting. Sometimes the kitchen smelled of stale food."

"You did your best."

"You did, too. But it couldn't go on. Then she got another job, but that lasted even less time than her first job, and this time her depression was even worse. Then Jules wrecked the car."

"The boy takes after his uncle. How many cars have *you* wrecked, Emil?"

"My share."

"And mine."

"Okay, okay, but at the time, they needed the car crash like a *lokh* in *kopf*. The family was falling apart. Ethel stopped answering the phone. Lee was playing hooky a lot. He had quit the wrestling and indoor track teams and seemed to be as depressed as Ethel sometimes. He didn't feed his pet rats and they died. He just left them in a cage on the back porch for weeks until I happened back there and saw the stinking mess and cleaned it up myself. Lee didn't holler none, at least not when I was there. But he wasn't doing much of anything but reading. We had no choice. We had to put Ethel in the mental institution. And when Ed said he wanted the boys, we had no choice but to let him have them. He's their father. Besides, we had no room for them."

"We did our best."

"Yes'm, we did, but I still feel bad about it. Especially about Lee…."

"We couldn't stand there and do nothing after he flunked out of college. But the first time we asked him to come live with us, he turned us down."

"The boy changed his mind real quick when that sommabitch cut him off."

"Lee was drifting around Chicago like a lost dog, playing guitar and washing dishes. We told him he could stay with us in Georgia, get a job, and give college a try again when he felt ready. He was even quieter than in Miami and he had become gentle. He walked around the house noiselessly, and would come up from behind you and scare the living daylights out of you. But when he did speak, he said some amazing things."

"That boy has more book knowledge than anyone I've ever met. And he knew how to fix everything around the house."

"Whenever someone was trying to figure out the name of a song or the year something happened, he would let people guess for a while and then tell us the answer in a near whisper. He was trying to give others a chance. He was a kind and gentle soul."

"Except sometimes when he would get angry as a bear with a sore head. Like when Miles told us he was yelling at that driver who almost hit him crossing the street outside the five-and-dime. He sure did like to play chicken with buckets of bolts. Crossing in the middle of the road to make some driver slow down. Like a toreador waving a red cape at a bull, only it was his body he was using to enflame those good ol' boys in pick-up trucks and muscle cars. And when they took the bait and stopped to make something of it, he'd get in their face like a crazy person, yelling right into their nose. It didn't matter how big the guy was, he was bound to be scared off by a crazy fella screaming at him."

"I always knew he had been into it with someone, because he would come home brooding. He'd take the anger home and it would live in him for hours. Like the time he was downstairs in the basement playing his guitar. He was playing the same few notes again and again, in different ways. Different speeds, then different lengths to the notes, then different chords. All of a sudden I heard the sound of glass shattering. Before I had a chance to get down there, he was walking up the steps with a bloody towel wrapped around his left hand. He had smashed it through the window overlooking the easy chair. When I asked him how it happened, he said he tripped and fell into the widow. Bless his heart, I know that was a tall tale. Thanks goodness he only needed a few stitches."

"Billy Joe Cone said he yelled some pretty ugly words to him when he quit his welding job. Burned that bridge right to the ground, pilework and all."

"You never told me that before, Emil."

"Trying to keep your hopes up. You do love that boy."

"He should have stayed with us."

"It suited him just fine. He's walking away from a mess of friends. A lot of young fellas with long hair would just pull up into the driveway and stop by to see him all the time, usually just to schmooze for five or ten minutes. He would take them to the pine trees at the fur end of our land and play the latest tune he was working on or share a smoke. They were all good ol' country boys—liked to roll their own. Lee seemed to fit in just fine."

"He seemed to like the slow, friendly ways we have in the South."

"He sure does like that good-old-boy music! Lee would play blues solos on the guitar which gave his bluegrass group a right different sound. His fingers—bulging with extra muscles, tips as hard as nail heads—his fingers flew across the frets so fast, you could hardly see them. Made that old-timey sound into something new but still old-timey."

"A lot of practice went into toughening up those hands."

"Yes'm, it did."

"The songs they played at the Macon Cherry Blossom Festival had the crowd dancing up a storm. It was an old-fashioned hoedown in the parking lot of the Macon Speedway, lots of people buck dancing or flatfooting it. I reckon they worked up that crowd real good. They were just starting to schlep all over Georgia and South Carolina for gigs at bars and country fairs. It was when he was still an orderly at Macon Hospital. He had plenty of flexibility in his schedule.

"Yes, we could see him slowly making the transition to doing music all the time. I told him that they needed to get a business manager, and he said that it wasn't a bad idea at all. Then he came home one day and said he was fixing to quit the group because the drummer and base player had moved to New Orleans and he didn't want to start practicing from scratch with new folk. But I saw the two of them in the Waffle House a few weeks afterwards."

"Do you know what really happened? He never told me a thing."

"No idea. It's a damn shame, too, 'cause they were purty good."

"Night and day he would go outside to practice, so he wouldn't disturb anyone. He'd sit behind the shrubbery on the sunny side of the yard, light up a cigarette, and just play music for hours. Even when it got hotter than all get-out, he'd be out there *schvitzing* and picking notes. Songs he knew well and songs he was just learning. He'd practice a line for a while, then he'd do another, stopping every few minutes to take another drag from his cigarette. Then he'd put it all together and slowly work out the kinks, as if he were learning to drive, first jerky on the turns, then nice and easy. I didn't know most of the songs. They were old Mississippi Delta blues tunes from the twenties and thirties he discovered in old music books he found at the Chicago Public Library. It wasn't my favorite type of music, but when it wasn't too hot I liked to open the kitchen window and listen to him play. Coming from the buttonbush and the viburnum on the wings of a lazy afternoon wind, it was like the music was playing hide-and-seek with you."

"Or maybe just hiding that he was smoking some wacky tobacky!"

"Maybe. But I like to think the best of people, especially people we love."

"You do, and I reckon I do, too."

"Maybe if he had a girlfriend, he would have stayed."

"Maybe if he had just one. He had lots of girls, but he never had one girl who was special, except for that *shiksa* Lynnette, and she was nothin' but poor white trash."

"Emil, you're not poor white trash if your engagement is announced in the society page with a photograph."

"You are if you go catting around with another man, like she did."

"That other man was your nephew, Emil Teller."

"Don't make it any more right now, does it?"

"No, it doesn't. But Lee really seemed to be in love. He was seeing her all the time. She'd drive up in her car and they'd head off for a walk in the woods and wouldn't get back for hours. They were so cute the time she had dinner here, darting quick looks at each other, then looking down at their plates red-faced. A real case of puppy love. Lee, usually so quiet at dinner, chatted up a storm about the origins of the music he was playing. She seemed very easy-going and the Baptist version of what my Momma called haimisch, especially for a Baltimore girl."

"It's still the South."

"With perfect manners, asking to help set and clear the table and volunteering to have her and Lee do the dishes. Like any girl trying to make a good impression on her future in-laws. You could have knocked me over with a feather, when she told us over dessert that she was in town to get married to the youngest son of the Tire King."

"It took me by storm, too, 'cause they were sitting right close and giving each other the dopy smiles that young folk do when they're in love. Then they headed out and he didn't get back for a few hours. Probably parked someplace doing what we used to do under the boardwalk on Miami Beach when you snuck out late at night."

"Remember, we were engaged at the time."

"So was Lynette, just to another man. So everything they did was wrong. Completely *meschugge*!"

"You weren't there, so you don't rightly know what they did. Maybe they were just talking. They both like music a lot and they both seem to have read every book in the library. Maybe they were just talking."

"Young men and women who spend that much time together alone ain't just talking about books. That's the way it was when we were courting, and the sun still rises in the east. When a dog comes sniffin' around, it got more than barkin' in mind. And there was a lot of sniffin'. The dinner the Tire King held for the happy couple the evening before the wedding, she said she had stomach flu. As soon as her fiancé got back from dropping her off, Lee left the party. I was watching with hawk eyes, and I reckon others were, too. It's a small town, and the community of business owners and professionals is even smaller."

"Are you saying that there was gossip going around?"

"No'm, none that I heard. I'm saying that I bet my boots she was having one last fling with our nephew the night before the wedding. He got home just as I was fetching the morning paper from the end of the driveway. He was walking on a cloud, smiling broadly, making no bones about it, and said he had to pack his things and wait for a phone call. I asked him what it was all about and he aw-shucked me, broke out into another smile as wide as the Mississippi, and said he was taking a trip. I reckon he tried to convince her to run off with him and I reckon he thought he had succeeded. And maybe he had. Maybe she said yes, she'd run away with him. Maybe she meant it when she said it. But then maybe she got to thinking about life with a college drop-out with two dollars to his name. And then maybe she thought about how nice and comfy life would be as the daughter-in-law of the Tire King. How nice it would be to join the Junior League. The nice new car she'd get every two years. The nice vacations to Florida and New Orleans. The nice private schools her kids would go to. Lee waited all day for that girl, fiddling with his guitar a little, pacing and smoking a cigarette, looking towards the door like a love-sick polecat, poking out a few more bars of some lonesome-sounding tune. But she didn't come. She never was going to. There were ten million reasons why not."

"Poor Leon. To have your heart broken for money. What kind of girl would choose money over love?"

"Lots of them. Besides, you don't know that she loved Lee. She looked like a good-time girl to me."

"Hush now. You're making the girl out to be nothing more than common trailer trash."

"That's what she is, as far as I'm concerned, in her tight, blue-jean cut-offs and tie-dyed rainbow tank tops showing everything."

"It's what the girls are wearing now. Besides, I saw you looking at her a few times like a cat eyeing a bowl of milk."

"The kind of looking I do, I'm not even window-shopping. I'm as harm-less as a wasp without a stinger. Just an old married shoe."

"She looked like the girl next door in her wedding dress. It's hard to square the sweet glow on her cheeks walking down the aisle with her loving another man. She looked so happy."

"There was a different look in her eye when she was dancing that hip-py dance barefoot with Lee. He was sitting at our table frowning, looking out-of-place in his schmutzy jeans and sneakers. At least he had the good sense to wear a solid-colored shirt with buttons and a tie, even if it did look like something Pop-pop would wear. He was sipping on a beer, his shoulder hunched up to his ears, just staring at her waltzing to a ballad with her husband. The tempo changed and the band started doing a hyped up, rock-and-roll version of Buddy Holly's 'Not Fade Away.' Lynette walked away from her man and directly to our table and offered Lee her hand. She kicked off her heels and they danced up a storm. The expression on her face was bold and sassy, like Bathsheba cavorting in the streets with David. After the dance, she gave him the kind of hug you give your teacher, shoulders touching but torso out so they don't meet. Then she sashayed back to her new husband and gave him a big kiss. Lee didn't even come back to the table, but left the party right away."

"But why didn't you tell me any of this before now?"

"You were there, too. You saw them dancing. Besides, messing around with another fella's woman is a *shanda*, nothing you feel proud about. And maybe he was messing around with a married woman, too, 'cause she came out here maybe a week after the wedding and they drove away for a few hours. You were doing the shopping or something. I didn't say nothing about it to you. I know you love that boy. I didn't want you to think less of him."

"I'm a big girl. You don't have to be so protective. What else haven't you told me?"

"Nothin' I can think of right this minute."

"You should have told me she came by. Nothing he could do would make me stop loving him."

"I know that, but still, it's not in my mind to go telling tales out of school. I reckoned it would all blow over after a while. And it did."

"You think he's leaving for Athens because he's still tore up over her?"

"Maybe so, maybe no. It was only three months ago she got married and left for Gainesville, but I've seen him with other women since, and it's his usual. Girls visiting their Macon relations. Freshman at the girl's college. The hard-looking hippy girls collecting at the bus stop like raindrops in a barrel. That boy needs to settle down and find himself a good woman. I mean *his* good woman, not someone else's."

"He has time."

"When I was his age, I already had two children."

"Not everyone can be as lucky as we were."

"You have something on, me no like. Take off!'

"For heaven's sake!"

"You never heard about that one?"

"Heavens, no!"

"Soon after they first got to Miami, Jules says he and Lee would teach the boys their famous Boy Scout skit. Jules explains that, in New York, they performed it at large campfires where kids from different troops would gather after dark. They begin with Lee sitting with legs and arms crossed, dressed in nothing but a loincloth and a towel draped over his shoulders. He sits motionless in a regal posture, his brown skin rippling with muscles, and stares into space, with a serene expression, looking like a Greek statue. Jules walks back and forth in front of him, as if on a stage giving a seminar to the audience. In an exaggerated New England accent, stately and sounding important, Jules introduces himself as the United States ambassador to Uzbekiteki, a small country in central Asia, and that he is accompanying the King of Uzbekiteki as he tours the country. Jules points to Lee and asks the audience to give the King a gracious welcome.

"Jules then tells the audience that the President of the United States is engaged in complex and sensitive negotiations with the King for Uzbekiteki's mineral rights. The future of the free world may depend on the outcome. The United States government wants to make certain that the King feels welcomed, and so needs a volunteer to participate in a formal welcoming ceremony performed at the Uzbekiteki court for centuries. Both the boys raise their hands. Without hesitation, Jules selects Maurice. Later he explains that it's important to know who your victim is going to be ahead of time. It's got to be someone who can take a little old-fashioned ribbing.

"So Jules says, 'You stand as the representative of all of us here today and of every citizen of these United States of America. It is an auspicious and significant responsibility. Are you prepared to do your sacred civic duty?'

"Maurice enthusiastically says yes. Jules has him kneel on the floor in front of Lee and places the tips of his fingers on Lee's bare knees. 'Now I want you to lower your head and shoulders and raise them again five or six times like you're davening and keep saying, Oh, glorious King of Uzbekiteki, may you prosper until the end of time. And say it as loud as you can without shouting.' Maurice bellows out the words a few times, hands on Lee's knees, head and shoulders bowing rhythmically as he would davening the Amidah. Lee interrupts him, saying in an angry voice like a mean ol' brown bear that's been poked, 'You have something on, me no like. Take off!'"

"For heaven's sakes!"

"Jules immediately takes center stage and says, 'I must issue a humble apology. I forgot to mention that no one is allowed to wear a wrist watch in the presence of Uzbekiteki royalty. Take your watch off and do it again.'

"Maurice removes his watch, and Jules takes it and gives it to Miles to hold. Jules repositions Maurice and exhorts him to start chanting again, 'Oh, glorious King of Siam, may you prosper until the end of time.' Maurice shouts the words, and once again, Lee gruffly says, 'You have something on, me no like. Take off!'

"'In Uzbekiteki, it's customary to supplicate the King barefoot, Jules says. 'I thought it would be okay in the United States not to bother, but I was mistaken. My sincere apologies. Take off your shoes and try again.' Maurice removes his shoes and Jules repositions him.

"Once again Maurice begins to chant. Once again Lee interrupts him with the same words, 'You have something on, me no like. Take off!' This time, Jules remembers that the King doesn't like the color orange, which is the color of Maurice's shirt. Maurice removes his shirt and tries again. Once again, Lee says, "You have something on, me no like. Take off!" Jules suggests Maurice remove his belt, because the shine of the buckle may be irritating the King's sensitive eyes. The next time Lee says, 'You have something on, me no like. Take off!' Jules insists that it's Maurice's socks that have to go.

"In a few minutes, Jules and Lee have Maurice down to his underpants. He's standing in front of us looking like a complete schlemiel, his face as red as his hair, a broad embarrassed smile on his face, shoulders hunched down, knees squeezed together as if he's trying to hide himself. Miles and I are splitting our sides laughing. I reckon I need to stop them before they go too far, but it's at this point that Lee sharply says, 'Ambassador!' Jules bends down and the two have an animated discussion in mime.

"Jules stands erect, looks sheepishly at the audience, clears his throat officiously, and says, 'The King just informed me that the thing that Maurice has on that he doesn't like is his hands on the King's knees while supplicating.' Everyone immediately gets the joke, including Maurice. If it were me standing there in my undies, I might be as mad as a horse chewing hornets, but Maurice was laughing as hard as the rest of us."

"He's always a good sport."

"Takes after his Momma. I warned the boys that not everyone would be as good-natured about the joke as Maurice, especially if strangers were around. 'We found that out.' Jules said. 'We did it a number of times for our troop in New York, and no one cared. But the summer we were living with our father in New Jersey while our Momma was in the hospital, they removed me as patrol leader after we did it in front of a mixed group of Boy Scouts and Girl Scouts. I tried to tell them that underpants were no different from a bathing suit, but they wouldn't listen.'"

"That boy must have been mortified with embarrassment. I sure hope Maurice and Miles never pull that trick on anyone."

"And I hope they do. Boys will be boys."

"I can imagine Lee as an Eastern potentate. He always seemed to be reading books about the East. One day he was reading the *Bhagavad Gita* and

Maurice asked him about it."

"That's one of those books I read in philosophy class but I wouldn't read it for fun, and I can't remember a stitch of what it was, 'cepting it was Hindu."

"Lee carefully explained that Krishna was a big old deity pretending to be a servant, and Arjuna was the best warrior."

"He might have told them that our god would send an angel."

"That's all right. I was just listening and not interfering. The boys got real upset when Lee told them that the book was about a war between cousins, until he explained that they were Indians from the sub-continent and that our family would never do such a thing."

"Da... darn straight. We don't hold grudges in this family."

"He explained that Arjuna was the same way. He didn't want to fight his cousins. But Krishna tells him he needs to be himself, which is the most accurate shot, the fastest runner, the strongest in man-to-man combat, a stone-cold killer. He needs to be himself and be one with his task, regardless of the consequences. Miles was very impressed, but Maurice questioned the very idea of war and killing. 'Whoa there, Maurice,' Lee said, 'I'm with you, man. No war, no nukes. But these guys never really existed. It's a Hindu metaphor for how to live. It's not the way I believe.' 'Of course not, you're a Jew,' Maurice said. 'No, man,' Lee answered, 'I'm more of an I Chin kind of guy.' I think he said Chin or Ching or Chang or something like that. I don't recall it in any of my schooling."

"I reckon it must be Chinese."

"I just don't know what's going to come of that boy. I do worry about him. The idea of going to U-G-A is a good one, but he's had good ideas before. And some bad ones, too. Like when he quit his orderly job to sell Kirby vacuum cleaners door-to-door. He said that his father sold them for about six weeks during the evenings and weekends before he left Ethel—'when we were still all together' were Lee's words. He talked a long time about hearing his father brag about how easy it was going to be to sell the Kirbys and how much money he was going to make. But Ed only sold one and complained bitterly about all the slammed doors, the shameful walks back to the car, and the frustrated rides back from Levittown to Queens. Lee thought he knew the secret of his father's failure—he talked too much and didn't listen. He wasn't going to make that mistake. Lord knows, the boy tried at first—he left early every morning in that beat-up old car, dressed more like he was going to the movies than to sell an expensive product. I suggested he borrow one of your white shirts and tie and wear a nice pair of slacks instead of blue jeans, but he said that he wanted people to feel comfortable. He didn't want them to feel he was better than them."

"I told him that dog wouldn't hunt. If you want to get someone hankering to buy something expensive, then you have to look like you don't need his money none."

"He didn't listen to either of us, and he didn't sell a vacuum cleaner. After one week, he up and quit, long before he should have. He must have felt very discouraged."

"So many things that boy can do well. He probably could have done that well, too, if he just wasn't so ornery. He needed to cut his hair short, get a nice suit, and shine his shoes until they looked like deep puddles of black. He just wasn't willing to compromise."

"Let's not be too hard on the boy."

"No'm, I know. Living in a teepee without a flush toilet or electric lights or the other conveniences we're all used to having. That's not going to be easy for him. We'll see how long he makes it, but I have a feeling he's going to be out there a long time."

"I hope that's what he needs."

"Yes'm. At least our food bill will go down, and we'll be able to put a little bit more money away for a sailboat."

"For Maurice's and Miles's college."

"Yes'm, that, too."

"First for their college."

"You have something on, me no like. Take off!"

"Right now? It's past midnight."

"You have something on, me no like. Take off!"

"How's this?"

"I like it just fine, but I reckon you're right. It's late. How about if I shake you around six. Before the boys start to stir?"

"Anytime, sailor."

THE MIRROR SHATTERS

Jules sleeps restlessly in a room just large enough to hold a Murphy bed and a miniature fridge on top of which sit a hot plate and a toaster oven. He's floating snuggly in a world shrunk to the size of an efficiency apartment, levitating an inch above the creaky, lumpy mattress. Objects float by him—the toaster, text books, a bunch of red grapes, stacks of paper, dossiers on everything in the universe—all past, present, and future phenomena and thought broken down to still photographs and glib phrases arranged in rows of neatly organized piles. He grabs an unframed mirror from a hovering wall shelf, glass warped to funhouse. Inside the liminal surface, his twenty-four-year-old's face stretches sideways and long-ways, elongating his head into an acute triangle in curved space and crushing his eyes to flickering faradic points.

The mirror shatters in his hand. The fragments leap from the floor and morph into tall, thin, bearded young men, all of whom look just like him. They ignore him to bicker among themselves.

Anger: She deserved to die, the bitch.

Guilt: We waited for it to happen and did nothing. And nothing happened. Then the phone rang, and it was Aunt Hope. She told us to go across the street and get Mr. Friar.

Sadness: Hope in a hopeless situation.

Guilt: Don't you understand, we did nothing. We did nothing. I did nothing. All I had to do was go across the street and tell Mr. Friar that she was lying in the basement, unconscious and barely breathing. But I just sat at the kitchen table drinking sugar-flavored hot water until someone told me what to do. I knew what to do before Hope called. But I did nothing.

Shame: I was in a state of shock. Too stunned to move.

Anger: Stunned by what? I'd seen it before. Pills, gas, slashing. How many ways can a person do something and never get it right?

Guilt: No, I wanted her to die. At that moment, I really did.

Anger: Damn right, I wanted her to die, and I wish she had.

Guilt: I wanted her to die and I'll never forgive myself for that. Everything that happened afterwards was my fault.

Fear and Sadness (together): I was afraid of so much for such a long time.

Shame: And I was ashamed of so much.

Anger: Afraid of what? Ashamed of what? I did nothing wrong. I was an innocent victim, a mere child in shock. My mother lay there next to a half a dozen empty pill bottles, motionless, folded over herself like a rag doll, oblivious to the television blaring out a game show. Not again. You bitch! How could you? To your own children? Knowing they'd walk in. Making sure they'd walk in. You must have hated us to do that.

Guilt: Unconscious mother, barking television, plastic vials, glass half-filled with water—I knew it was all my fault.

Shame: Stupid, stupid, stupid, not to see her breathing. Not to see she was still alive.

Anger: I knew she was alive. I wanted her to die.

Sadness: I can hear the groans of the aging boiler gurgling on the other side of my thin plaster walls and try to conjure how Momma must have felt when she swallowed all those pills. The tinny jangle of a few dozen in her hand. The gulps of water filling her dry mouth. The acidic taste down her throat. The bloating in her stomach as she ploughs more and more pills into it, followed by more and more water. The dizziness as they start to act. She stumbles without moving. The sofa bed undulates like ocean waves. The blankets crawl away. The TV screen and walls are moving towards her, then away, then towards her again. Iron weights are pushing at the insides of her eyelids. Crust is forming in front of her eyes. She's up. She's down. She's up. She's down. She's starting to fall into deep stillness....

Panic: ... No, no, no, God no, stop that pounding at my chest, no, no, can't breathe, an elephant is inside my lungs stomping in all directions, can't sit still, I fall to pieces, must move, must hit the wall, take off my skin, please help me rip it off, help me, I can't stand the suffocation of every object casting ominous stares at me, can't sit, can't stand, can't pace, can't keep still, can't stand, can't pace, can't stand, keep go still can't, cold and hot at the same time, perspiration streaming in rivulets down my cold hot thighs, my cold hot torso, my cold hot arms, my underwear soaked, I fall to pieces, and I have to pick up each broken edge from the floating floor, but I have to pee and can't stand still long enough to squeeze and shake it out, I'm cold, cold, it's too hot in here, I'm cold, cold, can't turn off the light, can't stop pacing, searching for my voice, the me of me, of every thought will kill me, but nonthinking looms like painful torments of a hell meant never to end, never to end, cold, I'm perspiring, shivering, and nothing comes out, and I fall to pieces and I....

Shame: I lost control.

Exhaustion: Enough, enough. Enough.

Guilt: Never enough to make up for my sins.

Pride and Anger (together): There's no such thing as sin.

Sadness: No such thing. We agree, for a change.

Anger: We agree more than you think.

Sadness: Now I imagine that she slits her wrists ...

Guilt: ... like she did when I was at Scout camp. I didn't see it, but my father gave me a detailed description, like he always does about everything, of how she looked when Leon discovered her sprawled out on the kitchen floor in a slowly growing pool of her own blood. They had just come back from clothes shopping, and Lee had run ahead into the house and came out again with a confused expression, shouting, "She's on the floor!" My father dispassionately described the ghostly gray color of her skin, the way one arm draped across her body dripping blood, while the other twitched slightly on the linoleum in its own deep red pond, her partial nakedness in a bra and slip, the ovular shape of the pool of blood surrounding her, the placement of the chairs and table around her. All graphically rendered, as if he were writing a lab report.

Anger: My good fortune to have missed it.

Guilt: My bad fortune to have something else to feel guilty about.

Sadness: I try to feel her despair, as she sits in the middle of the floor in the kitchen of the one and only house they owned together. Her fear as she raises the blade to strike. The pain as the razor slices through her veins. The burning as blood spurts forth. The heady feeling, as if riding a whirligig and suddenly slowing down, the wind no longer a medium you cut through like a night train through fog, but a gentle, almost imperceptible massage. Light and ethereal. The sudden tiredness as the blood flows out. The loss of existence....

Panic: ... no stop, stop, stop, no stop, I can't tolerate the suffocating, no stop, waves of fear rolling over my, stop, body, no stop, I can't keep still, attack of little pellets of fear in every direction, must keep moving around the apartment, I fall to pieces, fall to switching on the light, makes it worse, too bright, too dark, too bright, too ... maybe music will help, but it attacks me with savage roars, I fall to squirming pieces on the floor like pithed frogs, there must be invisible soldier pieces nearby, enemies, creeping monsters, hidden specters, blood-thirsting butchers, rapacious flesh-eaters, voracious, fall to pieces, hot, cold, everywhere, with sharp edges ready to flay my skin, hot, cold, I fall to pieces, I can't keep still, murderers coming for me, I can't stay contained in this room, shoes on and out the door, I can't keep still, into the dim hallway reeking of weed, maybe that will calm me down, breathe deeply, once, twice, three times, but it makes the panic more real, more sensual, terrifying, I fall to harrowing pieces, menacing need to rip my skin off my body and jump into nothingness, walk briskly, gingerly, on the empty, hatless, rained-on brutal streets of, I fall to scarfless, Seattle, pieces, can't stop even at a stop light, dash past cars with tires up, rainfall susurrating like steam-splashing boilers turned to cold, cold, so hot I want to rip off my skin, cold, cold, so hot I can't keep still, perspiring all over my body, cold, cold, so hot, shivering as the cold air chills my damp, too hot hair and too cold beard, I fall, so hot that it pierces so I want to rip off my clothes, cold, cold, till dawn arrives, can't stop, must keep moving, at a harbor I fall, knowing the water is so cold it would freeze the anxiety into the nothingness I fear. But I won't fall, can't fall, can't not fall, can't not not fall, can't not not not fall.

Fear: My biggest fear I'd rather never think about.

Anger: The future absence of life. My life. Another reason to be pissed. They brought me into a life that ends. All we get is an eighty-year tease of life, or maybe it's only seventy years or sixty-five. Every number seems too short a time. And then to snuff the happiness out of so much of it with anxiety over coming home from school each day, the worry about next meals, the fear of a blowup or another suicide attempt, the constant walking on eggshells, the barrage of belittling.

Shame: ... the feeling that it was something I did, something I didn't do ...

Anger: ... the desperate attempts at emotional manipulation ...

Shame: ... the shame of shouting and the shame of being bludgeoned with shouts ...

Fear: ... the fear of expressing a desire for something else, even to myself ...

Guilt: ... the guilt of expressing a desire for something else, even to myself ...

Shame: ... the knowledge that whatever I do is wrong ...

Anger: ... the disappointments ...

Sadness: ... the sadness and insecurity of those years and the constant memory of them.

Anger: Another thing they did to us. Another thing they did to me.

Shame: Don't you understand? She didn't do it to us. She did it to herself. She felt inadequate. I know that feeling. Your face burns for hours with the shame of your failings, your smallness, and your insignificance. She thought she could do nothing right. She did it to save me and Leon.

Anger: Why couldn't she do the job right?

Shame: Sometimes people can't do anything right. I know better than most. I went through that in Miami. I couldn't seem to do anything right.

Anger: Miami. The fresh start after our fresh start in New York failed. And that one failed, too. She was great at fresh starts.

Sadness: Fresh starts were like the avocado seeds she would stick tooth-picks into and balance the toothpicks over an old *Yahrzeit* glass filled to the top with water, so that the enormous smooth oval seed would sit halfway in the liquid, pointed end up. A fresh start that sits in the sunlight on the kitchen window ledge, offering hope for the future. Hope that it would soon sprout thin gray hairs below the waterline, then thicker white roots, then a stalk and a single leaf, then more leaves and eventually a full plant that she planned to cover with dirt in a pot and water until it grew tall enough so that its top branches scraped the ceiling. But her avocado would only grow a little before she got distracted or depressed and forgot to water it.

Guilt: At first I might fill the *Yahrzeit* glass when the water level got too low, but then I would stop, too, weighed down by the inertia of everyday life, the sluggish impossibility of change. The enormous seed would shrivel and the side of the glass would take on a filmy white dullness from the salts that the evaporated water left behind. The leaf would turn brown and crumble to the touch. With an aggressive, almost angry flip of the wrist, she would toss the desiccated mess, glass and all, into the trash can.

Anger: All her fresh starts went that way. Her fresh start after she lost jobs. Her fresh start after she got out of the mental institution and we returned to New York for six months. Her fresh start when we picked up and fled to Miami. All shriveled avocado seeds, fit for the compost heap.

Shame: All my fault.

Anger: For not watering the damn thing?

Guilt: No, for falling for her fresh start pleas time and again. If I had said, I want to live with Dad, Leon would have followed along. Instead I insisted we return to live with Momma after she got out of the hospital.

Sadness: We lived in a two-bedroom apartment in our old Queens neigh-borhood because the bank got the house. Momma got another "Gal Friday" job at a small insurance agency. I took the bus and subway to go to high school in Manhattan, and Leon went to the local junior high school. My sev-enth school before I graduated, with two more to come. But I loved Manhat-tan. It was my dreamland: The bins of cheap 45-rpm records all along Sev-enth Avenue near Times Square. The hulking gray rocks thrusting out of the green fields of Central Park. Meeting my cousin Pete in Tompkins Square Park whenever he was playing hooky and staying away from home for a few days. Watching the chess players and street musicians in Washington Square Park. Gawking at all the art deco buildings in midtown. Exploring row after row of Egyptian mummies at the Met. Taking the subway to Washington Heights to have dinner with Aunt Hope and Uncle Jack. Manhattan, my par-adise away from home. But it only lasted a few months. She started missing work and spending her days watching TV in the living room. She lost her job. Uncle Emil visited for a few days in the middle of December. After his visit, Momma announced we were moving to Miami.

Anger: Two more years of hell! That was our home life until we finally moved to Chicago to live with the old man in the middle of my senior year.

Guilt: My fault for making the wrong decision. When she got out of the hospital, we should have stayed with Dad.

Anger: Stop saying that, you fuck-up! It pisses me off.

Sadness: I remember our last day in New York. We packed up the car and headed onto the Grand Central Parkway. I turned on the car radio to hide myself inside the trebly crackle of pop music. The music went mute as we entered the Holland Tunnel towards New Jersey, the passageway from the old life to a new one I didn't want. A birth canal of dingy white tile and small flickering lights, blinding and dull at the same time. As we emerged from the tunnel into the Garden State, the radio signal returned to full blast. The Moody Blues. *Since you gotta go, oh you better go now*, last song as we motor away from unpaid bills, job firings, suicide attempts, days and nights of pacing and watching television, sinks of dirty dishes, hampers of dirty clothes, dusty furniture, car problems. Wipe the slate clean, Momma said. A fresh start. A new beginning. The first day of the rest of your life. *Tell me just what you intend to do now*, rows of globular moving lights exploding past standing ones through winter's early sundown, *Go now! Go now!* Static cymbal bling, piano hammers' harmonic convergence, singer's subtext whimpers stay, please stay. Where we go, *go now, go now*, is Miami, where the land lies too low to build a railway under streets, too soft to support skyscrapers, too warm for changing seasons, *don't you even try*. Will it be any better for her in Miami? Worse for me, without my friends, my school, Manhattan, the soothing subway shunt and rumble ... *before you see me cry* into unknown space ... *I don't want to see you go* already into fade, piano's striding brash finale snuffed out before the solo by the beginning of the next song on the *Hit Parade*. A week later, after a day of watching horizontal shadows bounce on women on the beach, I tossed my sunburned teenaged body in an icebox motel bed, blistered with sunstroke, delirious, in a trance, hearing *Mrs. Brown, You've Got A Lovely Daughter* eighteen times in a row, some DJ's idea of taking a risk.

Anger: Then the vicious cycle started again. A few months of stability during which Momma had a job and went to work every day, followed by a few months during which she stayed in her room, since we didn't have a basement anymore, and didn't go to work or shop or do the laundry, and came out to sputter ugly words and go back in her room again and slam the door. Then a short burst of intense activity in which she appeared to be doing everything all at once all the time, followed by another bout of the blues, all in a downward spiral, each period of depression worse and longer than the one before. And we were back where we started, only now in a rented house near Uncle Emil and Aunt Ginny instead of in the old Queens neighborhood. So much for a fresh start.

Shame: And I found it hard to fit in with Miami kids, who all drove cars, wore stylish clothes, and had more money than we did.

Guilt: And the knowledge that I had made the wrong decision. That things weren't going to change. That she wasn't going to change. That the father who disliked me was a better choice than the mother who loved me.

Sadness: Dad played favorites, and I was not the anointed one. Momma loved me, though, and treated me special. I was her helper. I helped her cook and bake for the holidays or when we were going over to relatives. I helped her fold laundry and clean the refrigerator. We read Shakespeare together. I believed her whenever she said she was feeling better. Every single time.

Anger: Every single fucking time. What a fucking moron!

Guilt: That's why it's my fault. Every single time. When she came out of the hospital and we had to choose between the two of them, I picked the one I thought loved me.

Anger: The old man is an asshole. She's nuts. It was like picking between Scylla and Charybdis. But I believed her bullshit, and that makes me pissed off at three people. I'm pissed off at her for lying about how she really was feeling. I'm pissed off at Dad for being such a cold-hearted asshole about it, and then doing nothing. And I'm pissed off at myself for believing any of it.

Guilt: Two more years of it. I bet that's what made Lee the way he is. It was just too much time in the pressure cooker. His getting kicked out of high school, forced to graduate early or be suspended, his quitting college, his taking too many drugs, his drifting. It's all my fault.

Sadness: Leon was always shaky. Even as a kid.

Anger: What do you mean "shaky"? Don't try to blame *him*.

Guilt: No, it was my fault.

Shame: The old man says he's a born fuck-up. He says some people are just born to fuck up, and that Momma is like that and Leon is like that.

Anger: I guess he thinks that absolves him of all responsibility.

Guilt: No one is absolved of anything.

Anger: I'm being sarcastic!

Sadness: Leon must have been a great disappointment to him.

Anger: Because he never thought about *me*!

Sadness: Yet wasn't living with the old man better than the Miami years? The bills were paid. Food was always in the house. There were long, loud arguments, but they were about politics or economics or lifestyle, not who did or didn't love whom, which seemed to be the sole subject of so many of the fights with Momma. The house was clean, thanks to his girlfriend Melinda who lived next door to us. I still had to cook, except when we ate at Melinda's. I still did the laundry. But it seemed easier than with Momma. Thinking about doing routine chores no longer seemed like confronting a mountain of makatea barefoot without carabiners and rope. Doing the chores no longer made me feel like a car battery in the Arctic, drained of all power. In Chicago, tasks were routine, drab, lacking emotional resonance. That was a relief.

Shame: I didn't feel awkward all the time in Chicago.

Pride: At least not after I had a few girlfriends.

Shame: Not all the time, but some of the time.

Guilt: Little remarks people made didn't fill me with guilt anymore.

Anger: I didn't hate everything anymore.

Sadness: After six months, I went away to college. I felt like I could breathe for the first time ever.

Guilt: Saying it makes me feel as if I've betrayed her.

Shame: When we lived with her, I tried my best to pretend that life was normal, but sometimes the pressure inside me was so great. Trying to be the normal kid at school, but knowing I was flawed, that my family was flawed. Knowing that whatever I said was a little off emotionally. Sometimes too enthusiastic, sometimes too sarcastic. Sometimes too aggressive, sometimes too passive and weak. Clever things in my head became stupid once I voiced them. The fit between my world and the real world was so slipshod that I embarrassed myself almost daily. Asking out girls who thought I was a goof, and only now, in my twenties, recognizing that there were other girls who liked me a lot. Or when I ran for student council president and told the audience of juniors and seniors that the solution to the parking problem was car-pooling. I looked out at the audience of boos and nearly fainted from the exhaustion that shame always brings. You're too tired to defend yourself. You stand there in a shower of reprobation as hard and cold as the thickest hailstorm. My shame disconnected me from the real world. It was a veil, a fog through which I saw everything and saw nothing. I remember standing up in the assembly to complain how stupid recent changes in the lunch program were. As I stood up, I felt a hero, but later on I felt a fool. Or after we moved to live with my father in Chicago, after she went into an institution for the third time in ten years, in the middle of my senior year. The third day in school, I ran for student council representative of my homeroom. As I gave my speech, I perspired nervously, ashamed of every move I made. I felt sweat drip from my armpits and land along the sides of my body, which filled me with even more shame. I smelled like an aging fart. The eyes of my classmates—the disapproving looks. Who is this overweight jackass who thinks he can win an election the third day he's in school? What a stupid, insincere speech. But I couldn't help myself. I kept talking.

Anger: I was angry at having my life ripped up yet another time, but I was determined to have a fresh start. A real one. Not the phony ones she always talked about.

Fear: I was so afraid of failing, but I was more afraid of being afraid. I was determined to run for office, so I had asked a kid I had just met—Irv Opalin—to nominate me. He was a big kid, as tall as I was but much wider, and all of it muscle. As I soon discovered, he routinely performed feats of strength during lunch and after school: Breaking a board in two that no one else could. Lifting a VW bug a foot off the ground. But unlike a lot of football players I knew in Miami, he was a pleasant type. Irv liked nothing better than to hang around talking to other guys about girls. I had met him the day before the election. Our homeroom teacher asked the two of us to deliver a few maps to other homerooms. I thought it would take five minutes to walk from the third floor to the second and back, but Irv took a circuitous route that included the school gym—empty, so we shot some hoops and I watched him make fifteen in a row from the free-throw line. On to the boys' locker room, the nurse's station, and bathrooms on both floors. We stopped to speak with a few kids and the school nurse. Irv had turned our map delivery into a forty-five-minute break from a boring extended homeroom.

Shame: Irv agreed to nominate me, but his speech didn't help. "This new kid Jules from Miami wants to run for Student Council rep and he asked me to nominate him," to which the class responded with loud laughter that made the inside of my ears ring with a sharp pain.

Sadness: My only opponent was the boy who had been student council rep for seven straight semesters. Over that time, he managed to piss off lots of kids. They voted for me.

Shame: I won, which filled me with even more shame. I knew I didn't deserve it. Without knowing it, I played an opportunistic carpetbagger taking advantage of disgruntled voters who didn't care who got their vote as long as it was a devil they didn't know.

Pride: The first of many victories I suddenly started accumulating. Coming in first on school-wide tests. Winning debates. Winning scholarships.

Sadness: But all of it tinged with the same sadness of those years after my father left the family. I couldn't shake it.

Pride: I loved the victory.

Shame: But hated the nauseating feeling afterwards that I won through bullshit. Or because the field was weak. Something always marred my victories.

Fear: I always looked around at the others in the room taking a test and could see that I was much more afraid of not excelling than they were.

Anger: I wanted to crush their lungs until they stopped breathing. I wanted to yell the answers at them in a voice so loud that it would shatter their eardrums and lacerate their brains.

Shame: No win is ever enough. This scholarship isn't enough. This first place isn't enough. Nothing's enough. And I still say and do these stupid things. Why do I do it? Like the other night I was at a Young Democrats party, sitting on the floor listening to the Beatles' White Album and letting a girl I just met paint my face with fluorescent pigments. She applied the glowing purple and pink to my forehead silently, while I blew off steam about the war. "Bob is against the Viet Nam War, whereas I'm against all war," was one of the many stupid assertions I made. The words emerged like a sudden feeling—shame, guilt, or even freedom. A minute later I felt a tap on my shoulder and turned to find Bob Turob bent over and whispering to my face, "Can I see you outside for a minute?" I followed Bob out of the apartment. Bob is usually a soft, easy-going guy. Even in his art, you wouldn't call his strokes bold, but studied and careful. But as soon as we are by ourselves in the hall, save a couple smoking a joint by the landing, he explodes in a strident whisper, "How dare you say I'm not against all wars? I go to bed every night in despair about what we're doing over there. War is just a horrible thing. Don't ever presume to speak for me again." He stormed away before I had a chance to say anything. He didn't see that I was speechless in my embarrassment. I say stupid stuff like that all the time. I don't know why. It just comes out.

Anger: Fuck Bob Turob, and fuck the art lessons and piano classes and the trips to Europe he took as a kid. And fuck you. You piss me off. Fuck your shame. It's a handicap.

Sadness: The extra weight a racehorse carries to even the odds. That's what Dad would call it. Except instead of ten pounds, it weighs ten hundred million pounds. And the track is ten inches deep in mud.

Anger: You piss me off, too. I wish I could have crushed the skulls of the kids I beat.

Guilt: I was winning, and Leon wasn't. He didn't do well in school, despite his perfect score on the SATs. He got into a lot of trouble in school, started skipping classes and then whole days. He quit the chess team after winning the tournament to decide who played first board. I don't know when he started dropping acid. Was it in high school, or college?

Fear: Losing control scares me.

Sadness: Even when he won, he couldn't win. Like when he lost the state wrestling championship in the last few seconds of the match. I didn't see it, but I heard about it enough from the old man. He was obsessed with that loss, as if he himself was the one who got pinned with a few seconds left after being up fourteen-four.

Anger: You can't believe a word that fucking asshole says. Besides, second place isn't bad. It just wasn't fucking good enough for Ed Silver. Like the time I was waiting for a call about a special test I had taken for a scholarship. The phone rang, and the asshole grabbed it and responded to the salutation with the words, "He won, didn't he?" I came in third, still good enough for a lot of money, but spoiled by his expectation of more.

Guilt: Imagine how much worse Leon must have felt ...

Anger: ... special darling that he was.

Pride: Third in this, second in that, first in something else. I racked up a pretty good record ...

Guilt: ... so did Leon ... until he quit trying.

Sadness: The scratch on the long jump, which I did see. Leon did the long jump for the Junior Varsity team. It was on his second of three tries at the City Championships. As he sprinted towards the start line, I saw a serene look on his face, as when he was in hot pursuit of a checkmate. Instead of looking around or rechecking his score sheet, he would sit motionless, his blinkless eyes fixed on the board, his lips together and turned slightly upwards as if savoring something. That was his face as he approached the line in three running leaps, each a little higher than the one before. He's at the line now, his body aligned and his legs suddenly together and thrusting forward in one powerful flight, inches above the sand pit. As his legs descend for a landing, he starts to pump them to get extra lift, as if walking on air. When he lands, all but one judge surround him. He has broken the state record for fourteen-year-olds. On a scratch. The lead judge is pointing to the starting line. The tip of his right sneaker was peaking one thirty-second of an inch onto the thick red stripe when he began his leap, which meant it didn't count. His last jump was pedestrian. He won no ribbon, and he quit the team a few weeks later.

Guilt: Thinking about it still makes me feel guilty because for some reason I am able to finish things and Leon never can.

Sadness: Once he knows he can do it, he's ready to move on. Once he has proven his mastery to himself, he doesn't need to show anyone else. He proved he could do the long jump, so he moved on.

Anger: Like the old man used to say, that's a load of horse turds.

Guilt: Leon was cut from the football team because he wouldn't learn the plays, and I lettered for two years even though I only got in for one play in one spring practice scrimmage. I should feel good about it, but when I used to look at the two large crimson letters it reminded me of how undeserving I was. The letters sat in a drawer until we moved to Chicago. Dad's girlfriend Melinda sewed them on a shaggy white sweater, which I wore one time. Same number as the plays I was in.

Shame: One play in two years, and it wasn't even a real game.

Pride: I recovered a fumble, but only because a stronger kid had blocked me out of position. But there it was, spinning in front of me like an obese dreidel. A kid from the other side of the line was a foot closer, but I dove under him—applying my father's dictum always to get my ass between the ball and the other man—and cradled the ball as five guys fell on top of me.

Shame: The coach took me out. I never got in again.

Sadness: He didn't want to see me get hurt. I was weaker than the others. I didn't like going to the weight room and could only bench press half of what the next worst kid on the team could do. I absolutely hated weight lifting.

Anger: So fucking boring. Nothing but lifting a weight up and down, up and down, up and down.

Sadness: He kept me on the team, though, because in 1944 he was a senior at Brooklyn Tech ready to lead the Engineers to a second consecutive city championship and be All-City quarterback for a second year in a row. During a routine practice, a diminutive freshman cornerback shed a blocker and slammed into him, hit him so hard he broke two bones in his leg. Coach didn't play again all year. That crappy little freshman was my father. It being football, coach held the guy who hurt him in high esteem and that rubbed off on the uncoordinated son.

Pride: The coach always had me give the last speech in front of the entire school at the pep rally the afternoon before every game. First our All-City defensive end spoke. Then our starting quarterback. Then me. I couldn't play, but I could talk. Dad said I could always bullshit.

Anger: He called it bullshit, demeaning my abilities.

Shame: I didn't belong on the team, and everyone knew it. I was in no shape to play.

Sometimes I wondered if the other players laughed at me behind my back. I was the coach's mercy mission.

Anger: Including me, there were three Jews on the team instead of just two, in a school that was two-thirds Jewish.

Sadness: Baseball was the same way. Or softball …

Shame: … since I couldn't hit a curve ball and so couldn't play baseball.

Anger: The game he refused to teach me. The one time he took me out before Little League tryouts, he said I threw like a girl.

Sadness: He showed me the proper form, his arm making a perfect right angle as he loosely flicked the wrist, pointing his toes and eyes towards the target. I could do it a few times, but then my body would naturally revert back to a kind of arm leap or I would move my right foot forward in the wrong direction, and the ball would land yards away from the intended glove.

Anger: After about ten minutes, he gave up and said he wanted to take a nap.

Pride: But I could hit the shit out of a softball, or a hardball that stayed over the plate. I always remember exactly what he said that one time he worked with me. Set yourself at the plate. Keep your feet parallel, with the front foot a little closer to the plate. Bend your knees a little and keep the back shoulder higher than the front, and then step into the ball.

Guilt: Leon would hit these tremendous shots deep into the outfield that would just go foul, but when he tried to slow his bat down or reposition his feet to compensate, he would pop up.

Pride: I hit a constant barrage of soft line drives just out of reach of the infielders for singles. First over the shortstop's head, then over the second baseman's head, then between second and first. I was always on base. By the late innings, the outfielders would play very shallow, about fifteen feet behind the infielders. I would swing an uppercut as hard as I could over the head of the left fielder and run as hard as I could for a home run.

Sadness: I had a sharp pain in my lungs by the time I got halfway to third.

Pride: I slid hard, right into the catcher's glove, prying the ball loose, then jumped up, surrounded by stunned teammates …

Shame: … who had been pissed off at me moments earlier because my errors had let in some runs.

Sadness: My arms and legs tingled with physical and emotional exhaustion.

Shame: And I was still a loser.

Guilt: What about the losers? Second place or worse, far from cheers and exultations, head in hand, or pacing claustrophobia….

Pride: At least we played the game….

Anger: Loser, loser, loser, loser, failure, lemon, flopperoo. I don't want a stupid ribbon, don't want the sloppy seconds, second best, second hand, greasy gruel at B-list parties, legless wine, polyester fabric, cloying banquet consolations, finalist who never had a chance.

Sadness: Blew the chance I had, never strong enough, never smart enough, didn't work enough, wasn't hungry, too small, too slow, too bored, too lazy, too distracted, too fucked up, I deserve to lose.

Guilt: Like the early rabbis discussing the plagues on Seder night, now we're parsing my guilt into at least three strains. My guilt that I succeed and that my brother fails. My guilt that praise matters to me. And it shouldn't. Finally, my guilt that taints all the accomplishments of the lesser loved son.

Anger: No, no, no, I'm no sniveling little piece of nothingness! I am the exile who comes back to murder the family that rejected me. I love them, but they cripple me. But I get my revenge. I kill everyone and take everything.

Guilt: Why did I get that nose for success that my father's favorite didn't have?

Sadness: He seemed to be plagued by bad luck, bad judgment, a bad sense of the odds, a bad knack for self-sabotage.

Envy: He was supposed to be the smarter one. But he's Achilles with a weak heel.

Sadness: Adonis gored by a boar, and the wild pig gouging him is our own family.

Guilt: Orpheus, torn apart by invisible harpies. He does play a great guitar.

Pride: It was the one thing at which he had to work to be good. And work at it he does! He stopped going to college to teach himself how to play. He wrote me that now that he lives off the land, he spends day after day smoking cigarettes, practicing charts, or teaching himself new tunes, mostly Mississippi Delta blues.

Sadness: The old man should be proud of him for sticking to something, practicing hour after hour, day after day, week after week. But Dad is rigid about how he defines success. Living at a subsistence level to teach yourself an instrument violently offends his sense of order. Like sports, it's extracurricular—something you do *after* you've finished meeting your responsibilities. Except to the all-knowing Ed Silver, it's an inferior occupation to pinning someone's shoulders to the mat or tackling someone to the hard ground.

Guilt: I can attend classes and read the material one time, then ace the exams with no further study. I never understood why Leon couldn't do the same. What was stopping him?

Anger: You can't ace an exam if you don't show up for it.

Fear: He would take a hit of acid every morning and another in the late afternoon. That's what I heard from a girl I met at an anti-war demonstration who, it turns out, bought some pot from him. I'm too scared of losing control to try acid. Who really knows what it does to the brain? What makes him do it?

Sadness: I remember when we shared a bedroom when we lived with the old man for those six months she was hospitalized in '64. I would sometimes hear him crying at night. We never talked about it.

Guilt: That was also my fault. I should have brought it up with him. I should have asked him what he was crying about. I should have told someone. Dad. Aunt Hope. Someone.

Fear: I was scared myself, and sometimes on the verge of tears.

Anger: I was fucking trying to survive.

Fear: But I never thought to escape through hard drugs. Didn't even have my first hit of pot until last year. I was just too scared to do it. Afraid it might do permanent harm to my body. That I might go crazy. Or lose complete control. Or have horrible flashbacks for the rest of my life. Or get lung cancer one day.

Sadness: What makes him want to drop acid every morning? He must wake up and feel something bad, some kind of burning pain in his soul. An all-encompassing sadness that makes it impossible to move.

Anger: Or is it anger that controls him? Anger that he can't strike back, because he doesn't know who to hit and why he should hit them.

Shame: Or maybe it's a desire to escape from the shame that makes him do it. The shame of knowing something's wrong with you. Knowing that others will discover it sooner or later, no matter how much you try to hide it. If there wasn't something wrong with you, why would your mother and father say and do those things?

Sadness: He places his hand into a cigar box and lifts what looks like a very thin purplish stamp off a sheet with his thumb. He licks it. His bad feelings transform to the joy of anticipation as the slightly bitter gel dissolves on his lips. He swallows slightly. He takes hold of his guitar and starts to pick at it and toggle the tuning keys. He continues to adjust the tuning long after he gets it right, for the sheer joy of hearing the slightly off notes bend into pitch.

Fear: Something soft but incessant starts to flow from his feet upwards, an osmotic rush seeping through his bloodstream into his organs, an invasion of warm....

Panic: ... leaps out of my skin, I can feel my heart, heart searing, streetlamp heart, fall faster, faster, to pieces, louder, louder, so loud it hurts my ears, can't keep up with it my skin pounding my skin, my must keep moving, lights, no lights, lights, no lights, it hurts my chest and delves into a chasm of tiny little pieces of flesh, nothingness, shivering, no, not now, not now, can't stop shaking, swimming, in my perspiration that freezes as it dries, shivering me, flashes of light so powerful they heart hurt heart, rip off my skin, burn my eyes from the inside out, every light hurting, hurting,

hurting, must walk, must walk, must fall to pieces, jump out of my skin, must jump, heart, heart, choking, choking, I have to pee but I can't stand still long enough and it hurts my teeth, my pound, pound, heart, heart, let it out, outside through the streets closing in narrow tube, pressing against my quivering ambit, sweating shadows bursting into flames, the door, the great skyless outdoors, its street lamps searing, lightning bolts, walk, walk, heart, heart, rumble cold, cold, I fall to pieces, and each piece emerges from patches of blackness, brutal heads, and walks away, bodies lug their clothes on shoulders hanging sideways next to them, rambling menace blown through streetlamp streaks, the blinking eyes of feral cats embroider other shadows, stalking light that freezes, splinters, soars, rectangular sirens blare, then fade to silence, fade to shouting mouthless goodbyes, turning gray and brittle, searching for my voice, haunted triads wince, afraid to delve a brown abyss of pasted magazines, of posters, strips of parchment, the dust is golem hiding from itself in squares, every color I can think of flashes, dreaded choking, a scowling visage rearranged by murderous rage, brows pushing inward, downward, nostrils pixilated, clenched jaw, hard stare cubed and quartered, balled-up knuckles fall apart and rearrange as rhomboid fire, as flaming coals you grasp to throw at someone hated and burn your hands in yellow bile, in acid burning through all vessels, molten khamsin blotting out the lamp inside of mind, upside-down locutions bullying past a line, shouted angry punches, pushing, shoving, baring teeth, swelling purple, side-swiping into ditches, cubes of orange blazing in the center of the fury, emboldened by persistent bursts of self-inflicted pain, flashes, ghastly chilling deadly bleak unknowns, cold, cold, can't turn off street lamps, I fall to pieces, cross the street, sporadic breathing, choking, stop and start, fall to pieces, stop, stop, heart, heart, slowing down, cooling off, cool air, slower, fall, stop, stop, slowly to pieces, sun begins to show itself as sailor's red over a lake that could be an ocean, for all the seabirds cared, for all anyone cared, it stretches into the distant pinnacle of sky, a vast shimmering blackness gradually bleaching to a peaceful, pieceless, lapping nothing.

Guilt: A sign on my forehead announces my guilt to the world for not being the favorite child, the god child, the golden boy, Apollo....

Shame: Achilles....

Pride: Orpheus....

Fear: Adonis....

Anger: Fuck all of you. I was a god, too. One of the ones who leaves home and wanders and then returns.

Sadness: To home. But that's the last place I want to be.

Anger: The last place I want to see.

Guilt: A place in the past I can never touch.

Shame: A place I can never go.

Panic: Something I cannot conceive of doing.

Sadness: Home is a house without heat, with a telephone that doesn't send a dial tone ...

Anger: ... an empty refrigerator and a sink full of crusty dishes ...

Guilt: ... that must be washed, but I have forgotten how to do it...

Anger: ...forced again to undergo the madness of a mother's self-loathing ...

Shame: ... forced to confront my own inability to control anything ...

Anger: ... forced to think about death ...

Guilt: ... forced to look at my brother and see on his face that he was trying not to think about the same thing that I was trying not to think about but thinking about it anyway, just as I was ...

Shame: ... to see his suffering in silence while the sand clock that was our mother dropped each last grain of sand on our heads ...

Anger: ...each a punch to the face that you know is coming, so it makes you flinch and still flattens you ...

Panic: ... unable to move ...

Guilt: ... unwilling to move ...

Shame: ... paralyzed, but why?

Sadness: ... still a child ...

Anger: ... angry as hell ...

Panic: ... out of control ...

Guilt: ... but ready to see it happen.

Shame: Ready to see it happen.

Fear: Ready to see it happen.

Anger: Ready to see it happen

Sadness: Ready to see it happen.

Guilt: Ready to see it happen.

NEVER A WORLD

Dear Lee,

   I'm sending this letter to your brother's address, since you told me that you don't have a fixed living place at the current moment and you are slowly hitching your way to San Francisco to visit him for a while.

   When we walked into the Prairie Post Café in Boulder last week, I was surprised to see you behind the bar making espressos and lattes. We were in town visiting my sister and her new boyfriend and wanted to hear some local country music. You told me you had taken a job at the Prairie Post for a few weeks while waiting for a festival of Grateful Dead concerts that was supposed to happen about thirty miles south of Boulder. A few weeks had now turned into eight months. I could guess why, as all the time we talked, the tall, wide-hipped woman with hunched shoulders and streaks of gray in her hair making sandwiches had her head turned all the way around and was staring at us, worry painted on her face.

   I was surprised to see you there, but not surprised to see you again. I knew our paths would cross more than once in life. Three different psychics told me so. You and I have a connection that will always make you a part of me and me a part of you. Last time I saw you was that sweet morning when we held each other tightly against a chestnut tree off Bass Road. It seems like another lifetime. But it was only a few years ago. I told you that you were not through with me, not by any stretch of the imagination.

   When you took our orders, your voice betrayed no emotion and you never looked at me. Not once. But I could tell you were still hurt and angry about my decision to marry Tyler. Of course, you would be. When we chatted for those few minutes, you looked down at your shoes and not at me. I longed to see your beautiful dark eyes. I remembered how they seethed when we were together in Macon, as if wanting to kill me and love me at the same time. But you denied me that glorious pleasure by looking away. And that cut me to the quick, and it wasn't the wonderfully sweet release I enjoyed when I cut myself as a teenager. No, no, no. After having found you again through the kindness of karma, not seeing you full faced cut me like a knife plunged into my heart. The pain was excruciating. Each luscious baritone syllable of your terse responses to my questions twisted the knife in deeper and deeper.

   And it wasn't fair of you. The world that we had—our quiet walks, our passionate discussions, our beautiful love—it was never a world meant to persist. You said so yourself. You said our love was a moment of giddy joy when flowing breeze and moving branch create a buzz of bliss, and life appears to stop in springtime's murmur, not to move again. Your exact words, which I will never forget. But it always moves again, you said. And that frightened me, because it made me realize that you would tire of me soon enough. Tire of me and move on, like the multiple hashes crossing the love line of your palm predict. I couldn't have that happen. Tyler will never get tired of me. He's too simple, and he's had things too easy. That makes him spoiled like a coddled child, and boring at times. He's damaged by the fact that he isn't damaged, just like you're perfect because of all the damage you've suffered.

You were second on the list when the open mike came. Your first song I had heard many times before, "Fishin' Blues." I laughed with the others at the overt leer in your voice as you delivered the double meanings—"Many fish bites if you got good bait, that's a little tip that I would like to relate." I clapped with the others after your note-packed solos between each chorus. But I felt as if we were alone and you were performing just for me, as you used to do in the shadows of the jack pines, joint at your lips, after we had made love in a sleeping bag on a bed of pine needles and leaves. Your playing was amazing, much better than it would have been if we had stayed together. I'm convinced of that as sure as I'm convinced that the sun will rise tomorrow.

I guess I was the only one in the place who realized that you composed your second number for me. It was an original song about loving and losing based on an obscure melody by Bach, you said. You sang it slow, wistful, almost tragic. It wasn't until half way through that I realized that the end of every line rhymed with my name. Abet. Upset. Beget. Forget. Silhouette. Neglect. Reflect. Protect. Reject. As the end of each line rolled around, instead of the rhyme my mind heard you intone my name, "Lynette," and it sent shivers through my body.

Halfway through your singing my mind drifted from the café into our nakedness together. In my selfishness, sometimes I would pull you over me as soon as our clothes were off and open without waiting, feel myself separate, fold around you, separate and fold again, the bottom of the ocean lavishly embracing the rolling weight of water, a coil of liquid fog unraveling to the soaring hawk, folding around you and unfolding, folding and unfolding, again and again, and I would start to close around you in my depths, rippling forward, and feel you tremble for control, feel you growing larger and larger within my folding and unfolding, pressing back, giving in, filling me with breathless stutter, hallucinating groan, and you always wanted to keep moving, I know, to bring me there as well, but in my selfishness I held you still, your body on mine, our tongues together, our skins burning, you still inside, quivering slightly, then shrinking slowly, sweeter to me than my own coming.

Let's remember those times, dear Lee. Let's remember that world. There never was and never will be a world as beautiful and rich and perfect as that one we shared. It was going to end one day, one way or another, and yet for me it has never ended and will never end.

Yours always,
Lynette

HASHMAL

When his cousin Pete called, Jules was reading. It took him an instant to make the passage from the world of his book to the voice on the phone, and at first Pete's words seemed even more disconnected than usual. Jules understood an invitation to go to a mikvah on Friday. The synagogue on 19th and Valencia had been sold to a real estate developer. There were no longer enough Jews living in the Mission District to support it. As part of the sales agreement, the developer allowed the mikvah to remain open while the synagogue was under reconstruction into luxury apartments.

Pete said he bathed at the mikvah every Friday afternoon with his aging-hippy lawyer friend, Gabriel. Afterwards, they would steal wood and bricks from the construction site. They were liberating the material, returning it to the people, Pete said.

Pete called the mikvah a hot tub. At first he used the words in apposition, "the mikvah, the hot tub," then dropped mikvah and referred to the ritual bath waters exclusively as a hot tub. In exchange for a few tokes of hashish, the mikvah attendant let Pete and Gabriel into the hot tub free of charge.

When Jules first moved to San Francisco with his girlfriend Elaine, he lived in the Mission. He passed the synagogue on 19th and Valencia frequently. Once he knocked on the locked door and there was no answer. He settled into the same kind of no-religious religious life he always lived. He still lit Hanukkah candles and always found a Seder the first night of Passover. About once a year he read a book with a Jewish theme, and generally avoided eating pork. He made sure Elaine hung no crosses or Christmas decorations in their apartment.

When Jules and Elaine first arrived in San Francisco, Pete and his girlfriend-of-the-moment Kat coincidentally lived across the street from them. But that lasted only a few months. Pete and Kat were on "rent strike," not paying rent for a total of 18 months until a few deputies showed up one morning. Kat quickly attached herself to the drug dealer who was their landlord. Pete was left to sleep in his broken-down car except for when he found refuge for a few days with a woman he met roaming the city or at one of the many parties he seemed to find almost nightly.

Jules was intrigued by what could still be inside the old synagogue. Old books and *tallitim*, dedicatory plaques, rolled parchments, an internal lamp, probably extinguished? Someone would have most likely removed these relics by now and buried the books with appropriate rituals. All he would see would be unconcealed joists, warped floorboards, chunks of plaster. But then there was the mikvah itself. He had never seen one before. It would also be fun to smoke a little dope with his crazy cousin.

The double doors of the blue-and-white tiled façade are locked. Jules wipes a patch of yellow sawdust from the doorknob. When he runs a finger across a dull blue tile, it picks up specks of sawdust and grime, leaving a streak of bright turquoise. At one side of the tiled façade he sees a narrow door made of pale shabby wood. To this door of a cheap motel room is taped a weathered note: *Knock for the mikvah.*

He knocks hard. He hears footsteps approach from within, then the snap of a deadbolt opening. A crack between the door and the frame appears and slowly widens, and the head of a young man peers through. He is short and thin, with a long sad face. Black down mottles his pallid feminine skin under his nose and on his cheeks. He wears a knitted yarmulke.

"I'm meeting Pete," Jules says to eyes that open querulously. Pete calls from inside somewhere. "It's cool, man. It's cuz Jules!" The wariness in the man's eyes dissolves into indifference. He opens the door. When Jules is inside, the man locks it again and trudges down the hallway, head ducked, even though the ceiling is high.

A miasma of mildew assaults Jules when he enters the dark hallway. His mouth goes dry, and a chill of nausea ripples through him. Dizzy and choking, he stumbles across a floor of mold-speckled concrete and wooden planks, grabbing at a clod of wallpaper still hanging to the wall. It crumbles in his hand, and he falls against the wall. A damp funk exudes from the plaster in waves. He staggers on. The man has not noticed his uneasiness, but plods, head down, across the long, narrow, tenebrous breach from the light outside the door to the light at the end of the hall.

Jules reaches the light, too, finally, and finds himself at a room. Pete sits Buddha-like on the worn and spotted carpet, grinning and sucking at a small hash pipe. The young man has sat down on a wooden folding chair next to a bulky misshapen object of Formica, which must have once served as a cloakroom counter. The room is gloomy, and it stinks of chlorine, but there is space here, and Jules can breathe again. He glances around the shadowy room for a place to sit other than the gritty carpet. There is another folding chair next to the man. He pulls it across to the opposite wall and collapses on it. It's warm and humid in here, but there isn't anywhere clean to place his sweater, so he leaves it on.

"What's happening, cuz?" Pete shakes his grease-sheened coarse black hair rhythmically across his eyes. "I'm tripping on this place, like broken things have vibrational insides representing physically what one never achieves, foreseeing what's happening, I'm gonna go to North Beach, he's gonna liberate me, show me how to score ten thousand dollars making buttons myself on one machine, and what am I doing with all this money is making me sweat cold stones."

"You don't have the money yet, Pete," Jules reminds him.

"It's in the bag with the button machine, and I'm sweating cold stones to the head to spend it, after going through the true love trip with Kat, like I get other women, I have the freedom to do it and I do it, but I don't dig it in a self-actualized lifestyle beyond institutions, at the party I see this other one and right away we start, and Kat checks it out, now she's pissed, says she loves me still but doesn't want to do it anymore, I don't satisfy her, what kind of mumblety-peg is that, man, just screw it, I gotta clean it all off in the hot tub, this is Noah of the hot tub."

Pete is a grubby character in his green-and-purple tie-dyed tee-shirt and his faded blue jeans, secured at his hips by a piece of string. He is short and wiry, without an ounce of fat on his body, high cheek bones and a thick, claw-like nose. It always amazes Jules how much his cousin Pete looks like Lee. Seeing Pete zoned out makes Jules think of the last time he had seen Leon, stoned to the gills and dissecting the differences between Seneca and Epictetus.

Jules glances around the room. There is nothing here, save the chairs on which he and Noah sit, the Formica relic, and the tattered gray carpet. Where the wallpaper is intact, the pink roses on an olive field seem to dance like miniature angels. Through the one window, built at ground level, light illuminates a phalanx of particles jumping up and down against a wall, an unreadable text like Daniel's moving writ.

The walls muffle the sound of splashing coming from down another hallway. "Someone's in the hot tub," Pete sniggers. "We gotta wait for Gabriel, anyway." He stuffs his pipe with green hash. His hands are scarred, his nails long and black, from his occasional odd jobs laying carpet. "Hey, what's happening, cuz?"

"A strange thing happened the other day," Jules says. "A girl picked me up hitchhiking to Oakland. As soon as I'm inside the car, she says, 'I like you. Do you want to come to my place?' 'I'm going someplace,' I say. And her leg keeps shaking, like she has to go to the bathroom. I try to make conversation, but she just stares ahead, as if she's a zombie. She just keeps saying,' I like you.'"

"Did you do her?"

"No, I didn't do her." Jules draws smoke into his lungs and passes the pipe to Noah.

"Scared of the fresh?" Pete asks in a wicked, insinuating way.

"You know it's not that, Pete." Jules tries not to sound defensive, but it comes out that way. Noah looks at him silently and takes a draw from the pipe. "I think the girl was mildly retarded. It didn't seem fair to take advantage."

"They like it, too! Was she good looking? Tell me where she lives and I'll go over right now, Petey you stud!" Pete leaps to his feet and begins to strut about the room, hands on hips, head craned forward rooster-like. His oily hair forms a flashing corona of black. He stops and eyes the wallpaper as if preening before a mirror. He flexes his brown arm muscles, twirls his body like a model on a runway. "Freedom is calling you with words of revolution, lots of pussy in my new space, but cuz Jules always has one classy woman!"

Pete offers Jules the double-slap handshake. Jules slaps the outstretched palms, suddenly feeling stoned and excited. Pete barks at Noah and points to Jules, "This man has it all, stereo, car, furniture, a Master's. He's the original Navel Hogman, our leader until he left town, I make a move and I think I have him and bam, bam, bam, he's got me, checkmate, it's over, education, books and foreign languages, like parlay-ihnen español, couchay-coo, it's happening!" Pete dances to the wall and poses.

"Do you go to college?" Jules ask Noah politely, knowing the answer is no. His listless, almost ghoulish expression tells his story: Ran away from home while still in high school to hitch around the country. Stays high most of the time. Lives in one of the converted warehouses south of Market or in a cheap residence hotel. Wastes his innate intelligence with manual jobs requiring little thought or activity, like guarding a mikvah. He's a deadbeat who takes what comes. Pete has many friends like this.

"No." Noah's first word. He takes another draw from the pipe. His face seems to collapse around the short stem.

"Is this all you do?"

"I also house-sit. The mikvah is only open Fridays and for conversions." Noah speaks from the throat, trying not to let the smoke escape."

"You sound like you're from back east."

"New York."

"The city?"

"Queens."

"Me, too. How long have you been out here?"

"I'm a Brooklyn boy," Pete interrupts.

"Six years."

It's difficult to speak with this inanimate Noah. They plunge into silence. The hash is bringing Jules up, then down, then up again. Pete and Noah discuss the politics of the synagogue closing. Although an outsider, Pete does most of the talking. The real estate developer will no longer allow anyone in the sanctuary because of the theft of supplies. Gabriel and someone named Dov have spoken to another lawyer about getting a court order to keep the mikvah open indefinitely. Another name refuses to recognize the authority of the secular court. More names emerge. The pipe keeps moving around the room, Pete to Jules to Noah to Pete.

Jules is no longer listening. He hears splashing and giggling from the mikvah. It comes as music, and Jules's stoned head explores the lapping cadences of the water. They make a jazz riff. He begins to snap his fingers.

Out of the water music emerges a reference to Noah getting home in time to have dinner with his mom and brother. Jules gazes at Noah and suddenly gleans boyishness. It is as if he's been doused with cold water. "How old are you, Noah?"

"Fifteen."

Now he sees it. Noah's reluctance to speak comes not from deadbeat indolence, but from teenage timidity. His skin doesn't reflect the irresolution of early dissipation, but the softness of youth. "What have I done?" Jules groans. "How quick I am to see what is not there, and not see what is."

The hashish pipe is in his hand, evidence of his distortions. He passes it hastily back to Pete, requiring a change in direction, but Jules refuses to place drugs directly in the hands of a fifteen-year-old boy.

"I shouldn't be smoking in front of you. I didn't realize how young you are."

"What's wrong?" Noah answers. "Jews have been smoking hashish for centuries."

"What would your mother say?"

"She smokes with me."

"It's bad for your lungs."

"And yours? Anyway, how long do we have? Aren't we all going to die in thermonuclear warfare?" Noah says this not with resentment, but in matter-of-fact acceptance.

"His mother approves, Jules, so everything is everything," Pete says.

But Jules refuses his turn at the pipe.

"Hey, cuz Jules, it's the younger generation, it's what's happening, I dropped acid at thirteen, but what a trip, like humpin', you do it but you don't really do it until you get older, like salve for the blistered psyche wandering for the experience that makes the true artist."

"I thought *we* were the younger generation. Noah, your mother must be in her forties."

"She's thirty-three."

"A few years older than me," Jules says. "Suddenly I feel old. I usually still think of myself as a boy."

"Me, too," Noah says and laughs for the first time.

More splashing and giggling from the mikvah, unstructured child's play, aquatic paddy cake.

"I have a few women now, but it's just humpin'. Kat may be coming back, what a trip to have my true love back, she can sell buttons for me in North Beach and get some bucks together, a couple hundred, you know the one who babysits her grandkids is hot and she's good to me, but her karma is getting tired and that's Wednesday. Thursday I hustle tee shirts and weed at the Mahubay, the hot tub Fridays, when do I have time for writing music? Art suffers at the hands of the unknowing, but I will continue to be an example of an outstanding personage of the times, no misconception this time restructuring the personality, or so it is said, building to the goal, and the destiny is the first goal, I need to get the addresses of people ready to buy chains. Did you bring your pieces?"

"My travel set. Do you play chess, Noah?"

"I like to play, but I'm not very good."

"Not many people are. You can be a good player and still not know the game. Grandmasters play at a level I can't begin to comprehend. They make a move which prevents their opponent from doing something twenty moves later. If I try to think more than three or four moves ahead, my mind goes dry."

"Four moves is pretty good. I just push around the pieces."

"I bet you're better than you think." Jules wants to befriend this boy, compensate for having smoked hash with him. "You know, chess is a lot like life. That's what my father always says. You make small immediate goals for yourself that will lead to the big goal. Like occupying the center of the board to capture the King later on. You're limited by your material and time, just like life."

"Chess is consistent," Noah says. "The laws never change, like the laws of the universe which are the laws of Torah." Jules is surprised at the boy's perceptive comment.

"And sometimes you win not out of brilliance, but by not being the first one to make a mistake."

"And luck is a matter of position, not fate."

The mood is suddenly joyous, and Jules feels close to this Noah. "Thought must be devoted to action," he says. "You absolutely cannot avoid making a move."

"My rabbi would call that a very Jewish statement," Noah says. "He says that, for a Jew, action is everything. All the names for God in the Torah are derived from verbs, actions that people can do. The one exception is the unspeakable word. Since we can't do the action, we are not allowed to say the word."

This remark troubles Jules. People will always believe that acts in the world give glimpses of the eternal. But there will always be the unspeakable name, the level of the two-hundredth move, which no one can attain, which is so far beyond everything else that no one can even recognize its shadow. Jules does not believe it really exists. Yet he can't break loose from the possibility of its existence.

"My rabbi says that Judaism is based on the physical," Noah continues. "The Torah does not negate knowledge obtained through the senses, as some other religions do. But we do admit that there are other kinds of knowledge beyond the senses. There is the ordering of what we sense into categories. That's reason. And beyond reason is a kind of knowledge so powerful that it is fatal to the person who discovers it. The rabbi says the Kabbalah calls it *hashmal*."

"I've never felt anything close to hashmal," Jules says. Not even when I helped the rabbi kosher our dishes before my bar mitzvah, he thinks. He remembers that they put an enormous pot of water to boil and added a large stone that had been roasting in the oven. As soon as the stone invaded its surface, the water erupted as if there were a volcano at the bottom of the pot. It was into this ultra-hot water that Jules dipped all of the dishes, flatware, pots and pans while the rabbi recited the appropriate prayer in Hebrew. He could hear strains of Dukas's *Sorcerer's Apprentice* playing in his mind and felt a special honor, as if inducted into a secret club—but not a special knowledge, not a special power.

"I bet it's like being at the center of an atomic blast," Noah interrupts Jules's flight into memory.

Pete leaps between them, one hand perched on his hip, the other waving the pipe like an aspergillum. "Hey, dudes, getting into a heavy rapside-down rap, bombs and the unknown and the beauty of life is its poetry, far out, I don't know about you guys, but hash makes me horny, stoned again!"

Pete squeezes his crotch and sneers. He irritates Jules. How can he do so many drugs, run around so much, sleep so little, and remain in robust health?

The splashing in the mikvah has stopped. The sun has sunk to window level, and its light dissects the room into brilliant glares and long shadows. Noah and Pete stare at the carpet as if counting threads.

A small boy, maybe three or four, toddles into the room and rambles around it randomly, ignoring the young men. He has curly red hair that braids down his plump, well-scrubbed face. He arrives almost by chance at the Formica counter and bangs his fists against it.

"Hey, man, what's your name?" Pete asks. The boy smiles into space and whacks at the counter. *Tzitzis* flap from his shirttail. "Man, what's your name?" Pete approaches the boy. They form a dialectic: one so clean, the other so grubby. "My name is Pete. His name is Jules. His name is Noah. What's *your* name?"

The boy pulls at his ear curls, then slurs gibberish, sounding like a pig Latin version of Yiddish.

"What?" Pete asks, and the boy gives the same incomprehensible reply. "Okay, man, how old are you? Are you three?"

The boy bleats a short sound and starts hitting the counter again.

"Four?"

Another bleat.

"Five?" Another bleat. "Twelve? Another bleat. "Man!"

The father enters from the mikvah, a corpulent man in a black double-breasted suit with padded shoulders and narrow lapels. His white shirt is buttoned at the top and tieless. The man's round, damp face seems too small for his large frame. The face is covered in thick curls, still glistening pebbles of water. Cresting this orb of coils is a beige knitted yarmulke attached by a single bobby pin. The man smiles and his open mouth resembles the darkness of a crater in the center of red lava.

These Orthodox always communicate either a great happiness or a great irritation at all things. In this case, it's happiness. Jules distrusts the joy. It comes too easily, and Jules believes it belongs in the same category as the vacuous smile of a Moonie or a Nichiren Soshu Buddhist. But the hashish controls the moment, forcing him to observe without interpreting, and he palpably feels the great pleasure this man takes in bathing in the mikvah with his son.

The man takes a rumpled dollar from his pocket and gives it to Noah. Noah puts the dollar into a cigar box and pencils a mark on the box top.

"Hey, man, how old's your kid?" Pete asks.

The man answers in a booming voice, as if he were trying to speak over a train or a waterfall. "He's two and a half. Come, son, stop your hitting." He shouts to the boy, but it is a not a yell, but rather a patient, fatherly inflection to which he has added fullness of voice.

The boy stops his banging and toddle-trots to the father. The father extracts another mashed dollar from his pants and gives it to Noah.

"The lawyer came by earlier," Noah tells him. "He wants you to call him."

"It's almost the Shabbos," the man trumpets. "There will be time for talking." He begins to rock from side to side as if praying.

"The lawyer is talking about a class action suit."

"Don't worry about it. Only good will be done. The mikvah is open today for the Shabbos." The man lifts his boy and holds him to his chest with one hand. The other hand plunges into his pocket once more, withdraws another crinkled dollar and gives it to Noah. He continues to sway from side to side.

"You got a beautiful kid, dude," Pete says. "The future, the book of life, we are working towards it, man, that beautiful thing."

The father shrugs at Pete, then shouts "Gut Shabbos" and starts down the hall, son in arm. Halfway into darkness, he returns and hands Noah another dollar. "Don't worry," he booms out. "We will talk next week. Gut Shabbos."

The man and boy navigate down the long, gloomy hall to the outside. Jules watches him stand by the door to the outside, rocking from side to side in shadows. Suddenly Noah stands up, runs down the hall, and unlocks the door.

"Go into the hot tub, Jules," Pete says with a lecherous titter. "The water isn't as hot as other hot tubs, but man, you'll be alone, unlax, take it easy, man, it's beautiful."

"I'm too stoned."

"It's a trip when you're stoned."

"I don't think I want to." Jules senses something vile about Pete dipping into the mikvah, something even viler if he did it himself. He doesn't know why he thinks this way, but the shame of it immobilizes him.

"Go into the hot tub and have a blast." Pete lets out an obscene cackle. Jules hates his smirk. Pete can slip out of his jeans and slide into the mikvah with ease. Once a few years back, they met two thirteen-year-old girls at the beach. Pete swam about fifteen yards out with one of the girls, and they treaded water side by side, their bodies pressing close, her bikini bottom floating in her hand atop the spume. Jules sat with the other girl at the edge of the water. She scraped her nails in concentric circles into the mud, like tractor blades. Water rushed into the troughs and broke their walls and she dug them out again. Foam rolled over her thighs. Jules's ankle twisted in the water swirl and touched her leg. She pressed her leg to his an instant, then pulled it away, then pressed it again and kept it there, smiling. Jules wanted to touch her again, to pull her into the deep, to do it all without saying a word. But she was under eighteen. He moved his foot away. Later the two girls went off somewhere with Pete.

One transgression drifted into the next like cloud to cloud, and Jules thought of the Greek plays he stole in college after his friend Irv Opalin, who still lived at home, brought over boxes of food and tools he pulled off the back of delivery trucks while his accomplice asked the driver for directions. Inspired by his friend, Jules walked into the college book store, placed the ten volumes of Greek plays in his inside coat pockets—two each for Aeschylus and Sophocles, five for Euripides and one for Aristophanes—and walked out the door. He had never stolen anything before, but felt emboldened by Irv's booty. When he showed Irv his haul, his friend raised his voice in shock and anger. "You risked going to jail for *books?* Are you crazy?"

"Always afraid, cuz Jules, with your apartment and your money and your books, and I have to get home early 'cause the old lady's expecting me, what's the difference, just do it!"

"Go on," Noah says. "It's a mitzvah."

"Give me a minute."

"It's nice in there!" Pete lets out a sordid squeal. "No one's watching you!"

Pete is on his feet and prancing around again, Dionysus goading and cajoling Hephaestus to take another swig from the wineskin, his arms waving Jules up. "Into the hot tub, into the hot tub, into the hot tub, into the hot tub...."

"It's okay," the boy says.

The two wave him on, stoned Cherubim opening a gate. He enters the mikvah.

But it is not a mikvah. It is another hallway, carpeted in a frayed pattern of pink flowers in a gray pasture. The floor and ceiling sink deeply in spots, and the walls blister mottled turquoise and olive. As ancient as it is, the hallway is immaculately clean.

Two rooms open off the hall, and at the far end stands a huge white door. The room nearest Jules has no door. He approaches it carefully, halting at each groan of the floor. It is a small cubicle neatly arrayed with cleaning implements: mop, broom, carpet sweeper, pail, dust pan, carpet cleaner, floor wax, cans of Ajax, boxes of chlorine compound.

He advances farther into the hallway. A disinfectant smell seeps from the other room. He opens the door and is struck first by a mirrored oak vanity table, chipped and worn, but free of dust. Sitting on a yellowed doily are some half-dozen brushes and combs. Above the vanity runs a shelf along a green wall. The shelf is lined with half-filled bottles of shampoo, liquid soap, hair conditioner, face creams, hand creams, body creams. A hand-written note taped to the vanity mirror requests that one wash all parts of the body thoroughly in the shower before entering the mikvah. The yellowed paper tape bubbles from the glass.

His eyes move past the shower stall and washbasin to the wall across from the soaps. Taped to it are peeling parchments with the mikvah prayers and directions for its use in Hebrew, English, and an English transliteration of the Hebrew. The English is a series of passive imperatives: *All rings and other jewelry must be removed. All thorns must be pulled from the skin. No open wounds are permitted. Scabs must be softened by water before immersion. The entire body including all hair must be completely submerged in water with both feet off the bottom of the mikvah for at least three seconds during immersion.*

So many rules.

He returns to the hallway and walks to the large white door. Its lever handle reminds him of the large doors to indoor pools at Jewish Community Centers and Y's. He hears water lapping on the other side.

"I should not enter," he mumbles, like someone who is trying to sing a song in unison with others but doesn't know the words. "I'm not really a Jew.

"I should not enter. I'm a Jew, but it's not proper since I won't be celebrating the Shabbos this evening.

"I should not enter. Although everything seems to be scrubbed down, I'm leery that a disinfectant smell conceals hidden filth.

"I should not enter. I do not seek sensual pleasure from a place of religious ritual, as Pete does.

"I should not enter."

He pushes down the lever and pulls open the large white door to see that the mikvah indeed is an indoor swimming pool in the form of a stout ell in white tile. The tile has been scrubbed so many times that it absorbs the bright light from a row of high windows and reflects a dull and scratchy glaze. Specks of mold grow between some of the tiles.

Steps along a rail lead down to the rectangle projection closest to the door. The railing separates the water from the walkway along three walls following the odd cantilever shape of the pool. The side without a rail abuts the door and here the water washes up onto the tiles. Jules stands there, shoes in a thin puddle of water.

He gazes into the water. Patches of light play on the surface, from which rises faint condensation. It is shallow along the edge. Even at its deepest, near the drain in the middle, it looks to be no more than a few feet to the bottom. It would take an act of will to drown at such a depth.

He steps closer. He is at the edge now. His socks feel wet. Wisps of contrail disperse into air at the surface.

An impulse to leap, fully clothed.

Will it wash away the shame I sometimes feel, for no reason? Will it suddenly wash away the anger? The undefined guilt?

The dimness of the mikvah light tells him it is nearly sunset. He has only to take another step, not even a leap.

Can we believe what we want to believe and not even question whether it's true?

Not even a step, just a lean forward would do it, a momentary loss of balance followed by an instantaneous slide into the warm and yielding stillness.

This cry for order, is it hashmal, or fear of hashmal?

Not even a lean forward, just the idea of a lean could do it.

Jules rushes from the mikvah and down the hallway and into the waiting room, where Pete and Noah are passing the pipe again, and through the hallway to the outside, suffocating from the stench of putrid cement. He flings open the door, which is now unlocked. A supernal bright late-afternoon light dazzles his eyes. A pale violet shadow of the synagogue shimmers on the sidewalk.

HER SEVENTH ATTEMPT AT REST

In the beginning, knife slash, sting at wrist, flow of blood, salty taste, bitter gas, spinning voices, father lies about the store and family and the reasons we move and everything else, mother praises sisters, one for beauty, one for brains, and brothers, too, get their share, the genius older brother, the cheerful younger ones, and none for me, taunts at my clumsiness, the mocks, the giggles, titters later when they see the body, not the oaf moving in my control to control them, to capture them, to hold them within for pulsating instants and await expected betrayal, await the new fact, the forgotten statement, returning fiancée, wife and child, the twisting inside of a blessed scalpel, the destruction of the firstborn, the brutal yammer with which I make them never forget what they did to me, what they do to me, what they will do, the imaginary spawn on which they all walk, the smell of their guilt, the smell of their lust, the buzz in my head when he spoke, since I could not be as smart as my brother, I would marry one as smart, since I was not capable of succeeding, my husband would, that other buzz, the first blow against my cheek, counting of blows, taste of blood, limping of bruised body, the spreading, the entering, the sacrament, the snipping at my womb, the beautiful pain, vicious cramps rolling over private meadows, then the sudden vacuum, the death of desire as my gathered strength propels from me, slapped and crying, a second boy, a second hope, a second curse, a second battlefield, and now my fourth attempt to start again, the bitter taste of the fiftieth pill, the test pattern hum at three a.m., the foggy, fuzzy voices, far off, blissful, the rapture when he beat me, the beautiful shame, resenting the boys when they caught us, watching the bedroom door for hours when he left, blood again, I'm swimming in my own blood, the sudden shock through my body, the many voices, the boys' echo beyond the gauze, blurs in white, floating around, waking up to a handsome smiling doctor, telling him to go to hell, begging him to let me die, another slash, this once wise and funny center, it takes my goading to get it started again, my perfection of words hurled from my victory bed: either answer begins the battle and every answer inflames it: do you like this dress? If yes, you're placating. If no, my taste embarrasses, never liked it, never loved me, never wanted me. You didn't ask me how I'm feeling. You asked how I'm feeling because you're feeling great and you know I feel like hell and you want to lord it over me. You didn't do the dishes, ungrateful child. You did them to show me how bad a mom I am. Glorious agony on their faces, snared sister, brother, husband, child, word shears snipping them away until only my thoughts remain, my logic, my reruns of their rationales, their shameful whimpers, their voices crying over the dead girl turned to splendor, her genius acknowledged, her body worshipped, surrounded by roses and gladiolas, hands wringing loudly, drowning out sobs and protestations, requiems of regret, epiphanies about wasted talent, faded beauty, the white noise.

GOD OF THE HERE AND NOW

I am the god of the here and now. Follow me.

I never think about the future. I never think about the past.

I have no time for what came before and what comes after the current moment. If I'm in the middle of doing something and it gets to be a drag, I don't wait until I have finished to start something new. Why should I? I quit what I'm doing as soon as I feel like it and start doing something else as soon as I want to do it.

If I'm at work and I want to play my guitar or take a walk by the river or smoke some dope, I blow off the job without telling the boss. If he doesn't like it, he can fire me. I can always get another job, but there is only one here and now.

I first knew I was the god of the here and now the year I dropped acid every morning and evening. In the late afternoon when the sun was falling across the plains, I would hear colors and see sounds. One of the sounds became the past pretending to be the future pretending to be the present. Another sound was the future pretending to be the past pretending to be the present. Another was the present pretending to be the future and the past simultaneously. I saw that all time walks as if its ancestors rode horses, knees slightly buckled but as light and sneaky as a cat. All time crawls past us with the haughty indifference of a salted slug. All time wears a mask that hides the fact that it is always here and now. Most people have a highly developed theology to compel the mask to treat them with benevolence—routines, plans, calendars, and clocks. I peered behind the mask and took all the power. I became a god of the here and now.

Money doesn't tie me down. When I have the bread, I spend it. When I don't have it, I don't worry. Something will come up. I'm free, my own man. Follow me, I am the god of the here and now.

I know fathers and they don't intimidate me, not mine, not yours, not his, not anyone's. A father assumes that no one can do anything correctly but him. He creates rigid rules and sets arbitrary goals, all based on his own inner fears and fantasy projections. He gets off on hovering over you and telling you everything that you're doing wrong. He responds to every move you make with a technical correction or a snide comment.

When I lived with my father, nothing I did satisfied him. He called me stupid. He admonished me for not taking care of my possessions, which showed what a jive fascist he is. Once he gives them to me, these things are mine. I should be able to do with them what I like. He always interrupted what I was saying. When I did manage to get a few words in, he criticized my ideas out of hand.

But he never intimidated me, because I always have had a secret weapon. He cared, and I don't. He worried about the future and obsessed about the past. I live in the here and now.

Last winter I saw him for the first time in three years. I refused to come to his suburban palace. I made him drive into the city to Burnham Park. We walked along the Lake Michigan shore. Harsh sunlight reflected off the untouched snow on either side of the icy path, blinding us when the route twisted into the sun. The wind blustered off the lake and made our eyes tear and our noses drip. I wasn't dressed for the weather. Just my wool sweater, the only outer layer you need in the Deep South. The wind cut through me, a knife through soft hash. I could not Zen the cold away.

Up the waterfront I could see the plastic buildings in the plastic Loop, filled with cop-out people who didn't care about their cop-out jobs but didn't know they didn't care.

He wouldn't let me get a word in. He began with the recent death of his younger brother Donald from cirrhosis of the liver. He assumed I drank too much and did drugs and warned me about the consequences. Okay, perhaps I do smoke some weed every day and drop acid whenever I can, but he doesn't know that. I resent his assumption and the judgmental way he expresses it. He has no right to call me a deadbeat. Only I can do that.

With some magical feat of transitioning, he's suddenly talking about his business. He quotes his price lists. He explains how he makes the product in excruciating detail, including the chemistry behind it. He curses the competition. He relates a few truly boring stories about his clients that he believes are amusing. If he thinks they are funny, they must be funny. He's on a real ego trip.

"The business is growing. Do you want to come work for me?" he asks.

"I don't need a job," which is true. I can always find work washing dishes or painting houses. Or I can panhandle or meet a chick with a place that needs some handyman and candy man attention.

"You'd work in the Chicago plant for maybe six-seven months—long enough to learn the business in all its aspects—purchasing, production, sales, billing, accounts payable, everything from the starting gate to the finishing line. After this apprenticeship you could move back to the South—to North Carolina, where I have a lot of business. Grow the business down there and we'll figure out a way to open a few more plants. You could take it all over some day and live anywhere you want."

I don't want to take orders from him. I want to live my own life. I want to live where I want to live. I want to live in the here and now.

I look away from him and into the full force of the wind. It makes my eyes burn. "Aren't you tired of living like a deadbeat?"

"I don't give a shit about your business."

"That's no way to talk to your father!"

I couldn't take any more of his bullshit, so I told him to fuck off and split the scene. He flipped out. "Don't walk away from me," he yelled, with the exact mix of anger and funky desperation that I wanted to elicit.

In our half hour together, he never once asked about *me*. It was all about him. His life, his opinions, his business, his ideas for my life. He doesn't care what I do or what I think. He wants to control me. But no one can control the god of the here and now.

He called me a deadbeat. And he's right. I like doing things that deadbeats are supposed to do. I like to smoke a lot of dope and experiment with other drugs. I like to drift from town to town. I like to hitchhike. I prefer balling a lot of chicks to having one steady lady. I like to change gigs frequently. I live in a teepee by the Oconee River. I hang around all day playing the same Robert Johnson piece for hours, experimenting with different fingerings and harmonics. I make my food on an open fire and bathe in the river. I like to look out the smoke hole of the teepee and stare into the distant here and now.

When I need some work, I hitch into town and look for a contractor who needs to fill out a crew. Or maybe I take steady work for a few months, make a little bread, get some new clothes, maybe take a trip to New Orleans or go to the dentist. But when I have enough for the here and now, I quit and go back to doing what I want all of the time instead of just most of the time.

Being a deadbeat means having a good time. It's safe. It's beautiful. It gives me the space to live in the here and now.

My brother is trying to be a deadbeat since he quit his job, but he cares too much about real things. He likes good food and demanding women and traveling and owning things and getting good-little-boy pats on the back too much to be a real deadbeat. He's pretending to be a deadbeat because the woman he's living with is pretending to be a deadbeat. They think that being a deadbeat is merely a matter of not working and hanging out a lot. Amateurs! She has a pension they live on, in a luxury apartment that they rent for free because they clean up and rent out the other units. Some deadbeat existence. The same woman and three squares every day in a nice place with a little spending money. That's only *pretending* to live in the here and now.

Even as a deadbeat Jules keeps to a routine and makes plans. Plans about travel. Plans about his woman's band. Plans about political action. Some deadbeat! Plans and plans, no different from the old man except in the goals, and since all goals are illusory by virtue of involving the future, not even that it very different.

That's no real deadbeat. A deadbeat lives in a here and now devoid of planning or looking back. The so-called here and now in which Jules lives is always full of the future. It's never just the here and now, never just the what-feels-good at this moment, no matter what happens next. If his next woman is a social climber, he'll buy a tuxedo. If his next woman is into organic farming, he'll be handling a hoe. Whatever it is, he'll do it well enough that nobody will think he's a deadbeat. He can't help himself. He just doesn't have the deadbeat's imagination—that ability to make no impact, to disappear entirely from whatever society he is in.

Jules cares too much about winning to be a deadbeat, which makes him a loser. Only a deadbeat can win all the time, every time. A deadbeat always wins because he never cares whether he wins or loses, or even if he plays the game, because he can change the rules at any time, meaning there really isn't a game, just a here and now with conditions different from the last here and now and the next here and now.

A deadbeat can sneak in a win, if it's really a loss. A deadbeat wins a game of chess and everyone says, "Look what he could have been. What a loss if only he wasn't a ... deadbeat." I don't play chess much anymore, except if I'm at a coffee house and someone is bragging about what a good player he is. I'll attack from the first move and pretty much beat him in the middle game. The only people who can beat me are professionals. And they don't brag. I like playing professionals. I win by losing, because I take them deep into the end game, and sometimes eke out a draw. I ran into Larry Evans in a coffee shop a few years after he won the U.S. Championship for the third time. He was playing five games simultaneously, but, after about a half-hour, I was the only one left. Three hours later, just before the flag on my clock dropped, he called me a barnacle, which aptly describes a deadbeat—something that sits around doing nothing most of the time. My father taught us the Queen's Indian, so, when Jules learned the Sicilian, he beat me a few games in a row. I couldn't have that, so I went to the library and scanned through all the pages on the Sicilian in a coffee-stained MCO. That took care of Jules. There's no point in being a deadbeat if you aren't the best in your family playing chess, the only competition in human history that isn't fixed in one way or another.

The here and now is a cool breeze that blows away warm thoughts. That's what I felt the first time I knew I was a deadbeat. It was just after I got kicked out of Truman and I was still hanging around the campus. Nash and I are walking down the halls of the administration building. We see a room with the door open and no one inside. On a folding table sits a mimeo machine. I get the idea that we liberate it from the pig community college teaching us to be pliant, contented cogs and use it to print anarchist flyers like "We're against the war and we're against the organizations that are against the war" and "Absolute freedom to do absolutely anything and everything." I also thought about stapling together books of our poetry and selling them on the street on campus or in the Loop. We take the mimeo and a half-filled box of stencils and race from the building. I get on the back of Nash's motorcycle, one hand cradling the mimeo, the other holding on for dear life, and we split the scene. Back at my crash pad, we smoke a doobie and borrow the portable typewriter of the woman I've been balling and start to type our first manifesto. But the typewriter keeps jamming, or we make typos. Before long we've wasted every stencil with nothing to show for it but a pile of crumpled paper and ink-stained hands and shirts. Nash curses the paper and kicks it around the floor, but I suddenly realize that I don't really give a shit—not about the manifesto, not about the poetry, not about my inky hands. The not caring fills me with an expansive feeling of freedom. Feelings such as love, hate, success, failure, envy, and concern depend on seeking the past or the future, but living in the here and now only conjures freedom. After Nash calms down, we take the mimeo to a pawnshop. We get thirty bucks, which is enough to keep us in food for a week, but I suggest we blow it all on a nice meal at Berghoff's. Here and now.

Most people carry a sorrowful burden of unknown events and words from a time before or after their own, a weight that slows them down to a crawl, like another person obstructing your view of nature, already constricted by walls and ceiling. But not the god of the here and now, not the deadbeat. A deadbeat carries nothing, looks at nothing. Nothing defines the core of the god of the here and now.

A deadbeat avoids thinking about the future, which never arrives, but constantly recedes into a more distant future with the desperation of a rabbit running along an Interstate pursued by a crippled dog.

A deadbeat avoids thinking about the past, which takes the form of a life-like dream as tangible and sensory as the present moment, but so unreliable that it makes you question your perception of reality. Did it really happen? Or was it a bad nightmare? Did it occur exactly as you remember it? Has desire for the past to be a certain way distorted the illusion you have of it?

Does what you wanted warp what was? Have you exaggerated the pain or joy you remember? Have you deleted anything embarrassing or horrifying?

Or has someone drummed a version of the past into you that never really happened? Do you view the past through the lens of a myth someone told you?

These questions pick at the reality of the past until it starts to bleed distortions and myths. Like lying wide awake inside a sleeping bag thinking about mischiefs of water rats and wood rats—dozens of bucks and dames, hundreds of pups—scurrying inside and outside the tent. I don't see them, but I know they are there, gnawing at nuts, seeds, and whatever morsels of my dinner I inadvertently dropped to the ground. They're running up and down my duffle bag hanging from a rope line between two trees. They slip around the tent poles. Their long slimy tails slide along every surface inside the tent. They dance across my sleeping bag. That itch could be their incisors tickling my beard and mustache. Hairy rats, foaming illness, poisonous ticks and lice burrowed among the soot and scum on their backs—a beautiful choreography of the here and now, if you ignore the possibility of disease. They're almost like pets, the perfect pets for a deadbeat, since they take care of themselves.

But even as it happens, night after night, you don't know if it's real or some infantilizing nightmare. Hours, days, years later, you have no idea whether it really happened. It's something you know, but when it comes to the past, you never know if you really know it or if the feeling of knowledge is part of the deception.

Like that night after my bro Jules flew back to Chicago from California, and I returned from dropping acid with some new friends. I find her crawling in the hall, stoned on prescription meds and wearing nothing but panties and a bra. She calls me father's name and hugs me closely. I try to remain unresponsive, but my interior voice is melting. She begins to rub me and somehow her bra comes loose. Fucked-up as I am, I can't help myself, can't suppress the natural reaction when the hot skin of a woman rubs against me. All four of our hands are rubbing everywhere on our bodies. I float through a confused state in which my perceptions dissolve into little quanta of sensation, each distinct and disjointed, floating aimlessly, unfettered by time. Now one disconnected moment touches against the disconnected moment after it, gently at first and then bristly, then forcefully. Everything happens at a distance and beyond my control—the slow movement of the bed, the sudden nakedness, the merging of skin and sweat and sighs, all faraway and impossible to touch, impossible to change. Now in the middle of a sudden warmth, a sudden rush, a sudden shudder of my entire body. Now it ends.

She touches my face and it repulses me. I leave the bed and walk for hours along the empty streets of the San Fernando Valley.

In the morning I didn't talk to her, and left the room when she tried to explain it away. I never spoke to her again. I had nothing to say. If other people were in the room, I tried not to say anything to anyone. When she called, I hung up or told whoever answered the phone that I couldn't talk. I didn't want to hear an explanation for what happened. If it really happened. There is no use explaining the past, since we are never sure if it ever really happened. I have no way of knowing. The past could be an illusion, and it certainly has no weight, nor makes a sound.

I should have told the old man. It would have freaked him out. But it's the past, so I'm not sure it happened. Besides, he would make it about himself and himself only.

Now she is dead, and I am a deadbeat.

My new job is designed for deadbeats by a government agency interested in creating work for young people who "experience difficulty finding employment because of a lack of skills or qualifications." I figure eight or ten weeks will enable me to get a room with a small bed and a nightstand for the winter, maybe a hot plate and a beat-up easy chair I cop for five bucks from Goodwill and a plain wooden bookcase for the books I rip off from the U-G-A library.

The government pays me to do carpentry. It gives me eight hours to do a job that takes only three. I know they expect me to do a bad job, but it's hard for me to make mistakes because I like working with my hands. But I manage to upset their applecart once a day. Sometimes I have to be really inventive, like putting paint thinner in the Gojo dispenser or flipping a part that isn't visible to superficial inspection. Being a deadbeat isn't as easy as it looks.

The guys at work are all deadbeats or deadbeats-in-training. Our boss expects all of us to miss work at least once a week. After all, we're deadbeats. I'm trying to live up to the expectations others have of me. The bar is so low that it's often difficult to reach. My lack of effort is heroic.

Yesterday I met a far-out girl. I wanted her to like me. I wanted to tell her that I am the god of the here and now. We were sitting on her sofa making out, our tops already off, and she pulled away and asked me what I did for a living. She found my answer clever and original. My response so impressed her that she said I was special, creative, humorous, and smarter than anyone else she had ever met. She said that she would follow me anywhere and that I could have her anytime. She showed me her wallet, full of money, and said it was all mine. My short answer to one question convinced her I was a god of the here and now.

All I did was tell the truth. I said, *I am a deadbeat.*

HERACLITUS AT THE WATER'S EDGE

Days after doctors pruned his time to months at most, we split a plate of oysters and spoke of grains he loved: kasha with noodles, barley in soup.

His hands, once precision tools, measuring, numbering, dividing, flapped like aimless claws caught in cancer's rapine anorexia.

His eyes, once sparkling mouths that swallowed things whole, pursed in languor.

Outside, the sun crawled along the brick walkway toward cooing waves.

And I thought of Heraclitus at the edge of another water: His eyes pursue a head of spume as it skirrs by in circular path and dissipates to bubbles, one of which he tracks along the streamline, gliding past rocks, between floating twigs, around a leaf, and disappearing.

WORK SITE FALLING

Did he toss the sticks that dawn? Did he read in them a time to yield? Did he conjure death reflected in his throw: retreat of ailing light from feral darkness?

Did he fling his keys—a truck that wouldn't turn—against the pile of sticks, then walk to work? Did he take a draw from clinging filtered fire, gaze beyond the wounded roof—this day's work—through stirring wind and see instinctive pattern?

Did he climb the ladder steps like *I Ching* lines, giving every rung a name and chanting every name?

Did he contemplate the piling up of bills, the need to borrow from his brother to pay the rent and get his teeth fixed again, the pattern of sweet-talking girls in bars for meals? Did the anticipated repetition of this dreary cycle make him drowsy, as he hammered sixteen-penny nails into two-by-fours?

Did noonday heat invade his eyes while parting cloud, and did it make him swoon?

And did the swoon resemble flying past unfinished windowsills, willow branches swaying under sun? Did he think of imitating ancient Greeks, conceive of taking action always as heroic deed, the throw honing the plunge?

And did he see the narrow shaft of brick along the grass and calculate the bantam likelihood of landing on this harder surface?

And did he slip, or jump?

A BROTHER'S FUNERAL

Watching aging hippies shovel dirt upon his nailless coffin reminded me of when we lay on plastic ponchos in a teepee near Oconee's weir, for years his home, and gazed through the smoke hole into the sky.

He, former science whiz, praised a spirit guarding teepees. I, arts and letters, compared Chippewa tensile construction to Old World compression techniques. We searched for patterns in countless specks of still and moving light.

I cited lines from *Meno* and he began to quote verbatim, excited, losing his *Southern*, speaking *New York* again, from Guthrie's translation, he said, his eyes connecting swarming brows to make a rolling drawbridge of thought.

A shout through trees broke his recital of Plato. "Teepee living must be awesome," says his friend come for midnight breakfast. "Well, I don't know," he slowly drawls, drawn back into his surroundings. We tramped to his corroded car. Later he made an illegal left and an officer pulled us over, and he drawled his Southern way out of the ticket.

Someone pushed a shovel in my hands. My turn now to cover his body. And I felt a sudden need for his massive craftsman arms, like when we were boys and he opened jars for me.

ALONG AN UNKNOWN HIGHWAY

Nel mezzo del cammin di nostra vita
mi retrovai per una selva oscura
che la diritta via era smarrita...
        - Dante Alighieri, Inferno

The tumbling sky shivers like my bleary body from the wind of speeding cars and trucks. Squinting drivers steer into a quivering solar ball that singes roads and signs, sears the fences, flames the crows and ducks. In my sight, glowing malls cross horizon's edge and welkin squid-ink stains the spurge and sedge, leaches roofs and building cranes, dims the city structures into specks of light.

The birth of night releases cicada humming, beetle scuffles, wind and spider throws. Moisture stumbles over dell. Wind song and cricket clatter swell and grow to ostentatious silence. A white noise knells. Time ceases giving hints of its existence.

Changeless nighttime shrouds a slick unbreaking heaven, limes the dark-cloud stars and planets. Formless, toneless, denseless, acheless time unticking strangles me in all its

.

Silence breaks with the whine of truck, the song of distant tower clock. Dark dissolves to pallid hawk-and-crow-pocked sky and a nearly urban outline. A new day leaks the *tabula rasa* of its power. Delirious from waiting up all night, I hear the road itself begin to speak, to peep my name imperiously, to brake and slow down, to tell me "Climb in," to gather me in its frock of graded concrete, to accelerate, to pitch me forward, to move through me, to take me, as if sleep itself.

That was decades ago, when I hitchhiked unafraid as my primary way to get from Seattle to San Francisco to L.A.

I was in my late twenties, mostly dawdling my way through life without a goal, looking for a signpost, waiting for a call, a part to play. Waddling on the edge of self-discovery, always on the verge of twaddling insights never made, seeking the front of the parade, waiting for a song that no one sang, a bell that never rang. I was searching for my voice, a choice to make, a road to take, a reason not to drift. Ecstatic whenever I thought I found it. Then scales would shift, dissolve before my eyes, and then another set would alkalize.

This constant readiness to be reborn is now gone, replaced by an addiction to comfort. I won't resort to roadside sleeping anymore, won't drive through night, won't wait through gray rain and insect bite. Won't stand for hours on flat feet. The truck stop slop, I won't eat it. Won't unroll a sleeping bag along concrete, won't trust to traveling strangers headed my way. I drive a Volvo, stay in suites.

I-5, Seattle or SF to La-La land, a milk run, almost a long commute. I must have scooted down a dozen times in the late seventies and early eighties after I quit my sweet job as a hot-blooded, cold-blooded junior executive suit, shucking reports and ducking meetings. After I started living off El's pension. We would thumb together or sometimes I would go by myself, to attend my Uncle Henry's family events or see my high school friends Big Irv Opalin and Robert Turob, called Bob when we first spoke in Debate Club in the last high school I attended, but insisting on being called Rob once he broke out of the closet in the middle of college. He winced and sobbed a short, polite laugh—what my father would call a tell—whenever I would slip in my squabby Rossini musical joke—"Bob Turob to Rob Turob, Bob Turob to Rob Turob, Bob Turob to Rob Turob to Rob to Rob Turob!"

Unhurried, stress-free southland trips during which I spent cayenne-blazing-hot days reading, playing chess and half-speed, half-court basketball with Henry's son Jeff, or talking with my Aunt Bridget as she scampered the San Fernando Valley running errands. Evenings flipping between sports or listening to old jazz on growling vinyl with Henry. Late nights smoking weed and prowling SoCal with Irv. I slept in their camper, parked in the semi-circular driveway that led to the front door and attached two-car garage of their ranch house in a suburban preserve dense with dead-end side streets, all of the same postcard vintage and construction on the same-sized lot, all with the same semi-curve of concrete cutting into large fenceless front yards, all with views of the Santa Susana reserve. For about six years, that camper served as my vacation hotspot. Spending a week or two at a time with Henry's family, I experienced a home in which daily life went mostly smoothly, soothing, without grimy outbursts of anger or grand emotional gestures. Henry and Bridget seemed to act in synch, never spatting or undercutting the other. Their first approach to any family problem was to think it through.

Instead of assigning blame or prattling shame, as my parents would always do, they used their children's mistakes as opportunities to learn, the kind of family I yearned for as a child. It was perfect training for my current mild suburban life with my daughter Maya and my wife May. Kind of like the life I saw Uncle Emil and Aunt Ginny lead at a distance those awful years in Miami that I never want to remember.

Emil, Ginny, Henry, Bridget, Jeff, Irv, Rob—the vastness of a quarter century warps my memory of them. They were part of the life I shed when I sped back East and shredded my past. I cut them off when I blew off El, our friends, my brother, both sides of the family, and everyone else I knew.

As I formed my plans for this Galahad trip, a warm nostalgia for the past—for what I once was—slipped through my veins. I had lost contact with so many people who had brushed my life, or gripped it. What became of them? Irv, Rob, Jeff, El's many friends, the women before El and with El, the drivers who picked me up when I hitchhiked? What are they like now? The same here-and-now as they were then-and-there? Do we persist, or is the kame-twisted river running in us no different from the one in which Heraclitus traipsed and traipsed again and said was not the same? Are we creatures of a strange past that rearranges landscapes but never reshapes essence or of a constantly shivering, disorderly present, always changing?

The reedy stalk who said he'd drive me anywhere as long as he could talk his Jesus-pop. What became of him?

The trim backstreet rock-and-roller with a great rack, forty loaves of carrot bread on the backseat of her Barracuda, headed to Eugene to see the Grateful Dead, who dared me feel her up to prove she wasn't wearing a bra, which I obliged.

The bony former all-star shortstop who wanted me to drive, so he could swill a beer and take a few more pain pills for his knee. He groaned for "One more year."

Or the shmucky kid driving a covered truck who picks up three of us and says we should pawn the shotguns in the back the first chance we can. "Cash for gas," he explains. The others smoke pot up front, and I'm riding with him in the back, spread out on the covered, low-roofed bed, napping to a contact high, when—my luck—he starts to cry a deeply-engrained pain, fiercely, insanely. He grabs a shotgun, waves it side to side, and points it at his head.

"Don't do it," I try to contain my dread. If he pulls the trigger, I might be dead, since scattering buckshot could pierce my brain.

"I'm just a fuck-up," he hoarsely sighs. "It's my bosses' truck, my sister's husband. I stole it and ran away, like the greedy, yellow-bellied punk he calls me. I've already done some time in county jail, once for getting drunk, another time for selling weed."

"No need to kill yourself."

"You don't understand. After I left school, I forgot how to read and couldn't figure it out again, which is like a crime. Then I fucked up and struck that bitch. It's my fault I put my car in the ditch, my fault they found that speed, my fault I peed in bed, my fault I lied, my fault my mother died—I know I gave her the cancer—my fault for every fucking thing I tried and failed. There's no way out, I have to die."

His confidence in this one outcome flusters me, but I must not show my fear. "Hold on, hold on," I say with some bluster, "Why do you have to die? You can always move somewhere else and give your life another try."

"But Bobber is going to clobber me and have me thrown in the can."

"Trust me, Bobber will be happy to get his truck back as long as it's not busted up," I try to reason with him. "He's absolutely not calling the cops, and you're absolutely not going to jail, trust me. You'll just lose your job. But you can always get another one," I say with all the confidence I can muster. I don't know if any of it is true, but if I were in Bobber's position, that's what I would do. "There's no need to die." My queasy stomach belies the calm I convey.

The swaying shotgun traces tiny rays in the air near his face, sometimes digging slightly into his cheek, his finger obliquely at the trigger. "I want to end my troubles the easy way—right now!" he shrieks.

"And never drink another beer?" My off-the-wall query surprises him. "Never hear another band? Never run bare feet through sand?"

Behind my glib words I am overwhelmed by the same morose fear that sailed through me as a kid every day when I got home from school, fear that I might find her impaled on a knife or passed out from an overdose, and that it would be up to me to revive her. Her attempts to end her life never threatened my own. But this kid's carnage would. Failure to convince him to drop the shotgun and park the truck, and I would end up as collateral damage. I want to stay alive.

So far, so good. He seems intrigued by my list of life's wonders. "Never see lightning or hear thunder. Never feel again the warmth of sunlit days. Never feel a wagging dog graze your leg. Never eat another steak. Never rake the leaves and jump onto the heap. Never wake from a good night's sleep. Never suck another tit. Never lay another chick. Never feel her touch your dick."

"I like all that stuff, but lots of times, it gets me in trouble. Like that girl who said I rubbed her too rough. Or when I held that cat too long under the water in the tub."

"Wait till we get to California, then give Bobber a call, let him know what you've done and where you are. I bet he'll have you drive the truck back home or tell you to leave it where it is, and he'll find a way to get it."

"I'm a no-good piece of shit, a slow-brained misfit. He's gonna want to cane me, like my Momma used to do. I deserved it for telling her lies and wishing her dead. Then the cancer...."

He sniffs and tears, points the gun to his ear. "I deserve to die!"

"Wait, wait, just think it through. It's a pretty nice ride. Bobber doesn't want to lose it. I'm not saying he won't want to tan your hide. He's pissed, but he values his truck, so he'll be cool and let you go, with any luck. So drop the gun now, we'll stop, and you'll call. Tell him what you've done and apologize."

"Apologize?" His eyes open in buggy-wild surprise, like a suddenly-cornered thug.

"Apologize. No alibies. No lies. No excuses. Just say you're sorry."

"Just say I'm sorry?" A sudden squint that makes his nostrils flare hints that he's confused, dubious.

"Believe me, it will work. You'll never see the inside of a jail. Now put the shotgun down."

He rales a rundown clown grunt, flails the weapon once more, then places it on the vinyl-lined truck bed.

"Okay, now," I exhale an intense and boundless breath at the reversal of my death sentence. "Why don't you drive again and I'll sit up front with you and rehearse what you're going to say to Bobber."

We leave I-5 at the first exit inside California and the kid calls from a phone booth in a sand pit at the far end of the parking lot of a Chevron, a dumb and toothy Clark Kent destined not to be Superman. The brother-in-law's boss tells him to leave the truck in a strip mall near the highway and get lost. Now four of us are thumbing from Yreka. I breathe car exhaust for half a day before a car stops that is going my way.

Did this hopeless dope ever get his life untracked? Is he now a well-respected businessman selling mortgage-backed securities? A filler of cavities? Monger of variable annuities? Engineer? Walmart cashier? Claim adjuster? Computer troubleshooter? A hedge fund master of the universe? Homeless because his balloon mortgage didn't burst with the bubble?

There were dozens of fellow travelers, many of whom I encountered for just a few hours, some I knew for years. A few hours was enough to pierce their veil of tears, as drivers tended to unravel their fates in monologues of buffered hopes and pied realities. A long car trip facilitates one-way conversations in which drivers, often alone for hours before, purge the accumulated steam of fenced-in complexities slipping and sliding inside them, as if they had swallowed a crowded stream of dualities and causalities. You say what you wouldn't normally say aloud, but you say it to strangers who'll never show their face to you again. Sometimes you say things that you pray were true. Sometimes you say more than you meant to say, things you swore you'd never say. Sometimes you say things you've never said before, for fear that the saying would make it true, or the fear knowing it's true, or will be true as soon as you say it. But you can bray it proudly to strangers on the road without undue anxiety. It's a free pass at the truth, or at the lie you would like the truth to be. The hitcher, often blurred and frayed from standing in the hot sun for hours or staying up all night at the side of the road, is inclined to listen more than speak, and often reaps the drivers' tales and wailings in a state of semi-sleep.

From my former life I ran without a plan and formed a brand new life back East—easy for me, because I had done it many times before. We trooped from place to place when I was a kid, more often once my father flew the coop. Four times in high school, all swooped-up-in-a-shrieking-wind, sudden and unexpected: once in the middle of ninth grade during my mother's stay in Creedmoor for twelve weeks. Once between ninth and tenth grades when we reunited with her. Six months after that in the middle of tenth grade when we bleakly departed from Queens like roadway bandits and alighted in Miami, where she made another fresh start. Back to my father again, now in Chicago, after her high hopes faded and everything blew to smithereens and she entered another mental hospital when I was in the middle of twelfth grade.

I should have made a right turn there.

Then I left my swell career as a paper pusher who managed other paper pushers to romp with El for four years. Then I left El. I went straight to Straightsville after shedding all my freight—events, people, feelings.

Each time I had to recreate my life from scratch, feel my way around like an anthropologist learning new unspoken ways, or a gambler figuring out the new dealer. At least when I left El a quarter of a century ago, it was *my* decision to throw away my old life, and I did it the right way this time, a complete excision of everything having to do with my past—my family, friends and acquaintances, all the strife and love-hate. I wanted this new life to be different from my other re-creations. I wanted my new life to be free of turmoil, free of deep-rumbling emotion. I didn't want passions to suffocate me. I didn't want to stand constant guard against embroiled cravings: anger, shame, fear, a hunted animal hiding in a cave. I had to subjugate all those old pains and turmoil that depraved my past lives. I had to run from the people and relations who summoned these feelings or who caused me to summon them. That meant everyone.

Even though I didn't have a real job save a few occasional gigs in the four years El supported me, once back East it was no big deal rigging something not-too-boring that paid a lot of cash by flashing my résumé of assorted scholarships and performing a verbal jig at interviews. It was back to pushing steeples of papers from one department to another and telling other people where to push *their* papers and how to read whatever corporate vapor landed on their desk. The first job led to the next led to the next, each one paying more and expanding my responsibility to reprimand and dismiss, an arabesque of memos and meetings, then faxes, then emails and teleconferences. Nothing exciting, which was my preference.

It was also easy to find another woman, and I made sure that this one tacked to the conventional and controlled, forward-looking and smart, lacking emotional abnormalities or artificialities, but also lacking vision to look beyond her own middle class sensibilities, a woman to whom things are what they are, and life is supposed to unfold according to a gold-standard playbook. I took the road more travelled, the one leading to a mortgaged house at the end of a cul-de-sac behind foxglove and willows, a redwood deck with built-in gas grill, a simple, sleepy life filled with slicers and dicers, toasters and composters, Osterizers and sanitizers, potato mashers and trash compactors, lawnmowers and snow blowers, hedge clippers and wood chippers, smartphones and beepers, babysitters and housekeepers, haberdashers and hairdressers, plumbers, painters, roofers, plasterers, gardeners, fumigators and electricians, stockbrokers, accountants, general practitioners and specialists, a new car every three years for my wife, with me taking hers, symphonies and seminars, plays in repertoire, piano bars in the city, boards and committees, one daughter who looks like and has the personality of her mother, as if she sprang fully armed and ready for life's ambiguities from the forehead of a modern Hera. Two fully free and unafraid women whose liberation has always led to conducting themselves as sensibly and conventionally as possible, according to the mores and folkways of the upper crust of whitebread America. That's my nuclear family. Everyone's well, thanks for asking, well-bred, well-fed and well-read, with a firm grip on their lives and achieving amazing things, but wondering why Dad is taking an automobile trip by himself for thirty days.

It was easy to start my new life, because, like all the old new lives I have ever started, I was not and am not really part of it. I am a stowaway in my nuclear family of women, like I was a stowaway in my nuclear family growing up. Always the outsider. The less favored son. The one who couldn't zing mates-in-five in his head or form an unquavering iron cross on the still rings. The one who didn't look just like Dad. When you move to a new school and everyone has known each other for years, you're a plaid-against-stripes-at-a-funeral outsider. It takes years to trace a network of associations that define your new life, years to tame the faces and spaces, norms and nuances, customs and claims, catch expressions, personalities, and sensitivities of the new place. By then you have to leave and begin the game again from scratch. The abnormality of my family kept me detached—not being able to invite friends over, not knowing how to explain why I didn't have the money to buy Gant shirts or tame my unruly curly hair with a highly-styled mop top, why it was my uncle and aunt at football games, why I always hid my shame from looks of blame I saw everywhere.

An outsider can never claim to be a real insider, but you do learn how to make yourself the consummate outsider, along for the ride, floating forward on the tide, but always faking it. Outsiders observe, even when they partic-ipate. They wait for the covert cue and hidden handshake, terrified they'll miss the secret signs and tells that glide effortlessly between true insiders. Outsiders never really live in the moment. They are too busy looking at the moment from a parallel outside.

Staying outside has its boons. Your heart won't get destroyed or ruined when everything falls apart and turns to hell, because you were never there, only observing there. Because you haven't accepted the premises of the so-ciety in which you reside, you don't truly believe its basic myths and assump-tions. You can see all too clearly its blemishes, and so can take its dismantling in stride. When it crumbles or burns, it's easy to live beyond the malaise, no matter how painful it is to keep going, because you've seen foundations tum-ble before, sometimes in a matter of days.

It's easy for an outsider to start anew. You walk away, as if from an automo-bile accident, numb, reeling, drained of affect, a bit dazed, but determined to deal with it. You walk away without a scratch, upended car impressed against a tree, transitioned from the flash of dream-world spent dissecting fenders, tires, and piston trickle near your face and hands enflamed with fear of ceas-ing movement. Frieze of jagged bird-on-branch mosaic tumbles with your skidding tug of seatbelt round around a vent in snake-skin windshield fallen, stiff, caressed by threads of blood. Who cares whose turn it is to turn away from the thud and see the maul of dead, the scrum of auto parts in duck blind ducking hurtled arrows' aching screams, of stopping wide awake to stagnant cipher, toasted sweetness reek of drunken leaves and peat becomes a thing that neither touches nor is touched, neither cared about nor caring, eternity in a speck, a speck in eternity. And then the glare of the real: You walk away, a different me in you, a me exhausted but inflexible, drained of mystery, stripped of all-impeding them and theirs.

All you have to do is shut out all the grieving you associate with the life you're leaving. It's hard the first time and even harder the second, but after a while it becomes easy to wean yourself of a former life, because, as an outsider, you never really conceived strong feelings for anything, even if you believed you fomented something as powerful as a monsoon at the moment of its perception.

I walked away not just from the ten-car collision that was my life with El, but from everything and everyone. It was a necessary decision. Emotional pain serrated my life, percolated and recirculated constantly in my mind as a bastinade of accumulated past hurts, day after day, year after year, growing up, and later with El. A world in which even the good was bad, even the happy was sad. I was tired of steaming with anger, tired of teeming with shame and guilt, tired of feeling betrayed and berated by others, tired of the feeling that I was betraying and berating. To all emotional pain, I applied the dictate of my seventh-grade English teacher, Mr. Hughes, who said: "When in doubt, cut it out." Enervated and etiolated, ready to go to sleep, in many ways my new life resembled a waking dream. I've dreamt of cogwheel-in-the-steamship jobs, dreamt of making money, dreamt of buying autos, houses, tables, stuff and stuff and stuff and stuff. I dreamt it never was enough. Dreamt of quid pro quos and falls from grace, dreamt of shambling dominoes and corporate steeplechases, all a flat and seamless endless flow, each day ambling gently to the next and the day after that and the day after that, never spiking, never dipping, all looking very much alike. Twenty-five years of living Jules Silver as a dream, of being Jules Silver in a dream, a dream that seemed as real as life, a life that seemed as familiar as a dream the thousandth time you dream it. Easy, comfortable, quiet. Never overcast. No longer a slave to my past. Nothing to threaten my equanimity, nothing passionate or zealous, nothing to make me blast anger, shame, guilt, or jealousy.

And then a brash ringtone crashes my dream in the middle of the night. Leon tripped from a dilapidated roof he was repairing, and his head landed on a concrete strip between two expanses of grass. The indurate collision instantly ripped open his head and put a crevasse in his brain. He lingered a few days in a vegetative state. I flew down alone, since May did not know Leon—did not even know I had a brother—and was busy at her law firm. I watched his moanless, motionless weight wrapped loosely in hospital greens and strapped to a dozen machines that either kept him alive or estimated what that life was producing or could ever hope to produce. The action of each machine made its own noise—a whirr, a sluice, a whistle, a groan, a gurgle, a yawn, a flop—and together they created an eerie spawn of programmed music, my brother's dying transformed to a constantly repeating pattern of mechanical sounds slowing down, getting weaker, dropping out, until all the players stop.

I was surprised at how many people came to his graveside funeral. I scrutinized a wide mix of the types I hung out with during my years with El, older and tamer now—aging hippies, fried musicians, gray-haired would-be wise guys, lame street people with burned-out eyes. Several reeked of pot, a tantalizing fragrance I have denied myself for decades. A number of hired hands who worked with Leon also came, weather-beaten house painters, bricklayers, and electricians. Everyone else calls him Lee, but I always say Leon, because it is more urban, a name that belongs in a presidential suite not a street corner, a player not a picker, less Southern, less like the shitkicker he always pretended to be. Also a handful of gamers and chess players, the only ones who didn't express surprise that Leon had an older brother up north who became a patrician at a diversified conglomerate. A few women confessed to having been recent flames, including the younger and less masculine-looking of the lesbian couple whose roof Leon had been fixing when he fell. Or was it suicide? I can't set aside my suspicions.

It was hard to keep straight this tide of names and relationships to Leon, as they glided through the one-man receiving line at the open plot. They were all jagged pieces of vitrified sand that somehow fit together into the mosaic that was the unplanned life my brother led, the same life, I surmise, that he was leading the last time I saw him decades before. I was suffering too much from the moorland heat to gather the focus to fit the pieces together and frame a unified image. It was a muggy Southern morning, not the weather for the black wool suit I wore. The heat magnified my otherness among the dozens in tee-shirts or short-sleeved casual shirts and jeans. A flaming sun tanned the rows of stone markers. I could see a tide of tiny wisps of steam rising from the grass. Behind the slow, solemnized voice of the rabbi I had hired to conduct a brief service a distant lawn mower droned stridently. When the mower came closer, we had to strain to hear, as the rabbi did not change his narcotizing low volume. He had us repeat words in English, which he followed with Hebrew prayers. The last time I had mumbled Kaddish was at my father's funeral, but I tooted every word in stride with the rabbi. I said it without sadness or snideness, but as a memorized obligation. At the beginning of the last verse, I started to feel perspiration slide down my forehead and scoot into my eyes, burning and blurring them so that my perception solidified my mood—dehumanized, stand-offish, out-of-synch, and in pursuit of my surroundings. I realized that Leon had a community, while I remained a rootless outsider to a substitute inside different from my usual, but an inside I remembered well from the past, a familiar hell that stirred memories of an inside outside of which I always fell.

I brought four boxes of my brother's possessions to the funeral in my car. After throwing the symbolic shovelful of dirt on the casket, I opened the trunk and distributed to Leon's friends this paltry lot of earthly junk— tools, books, sheet music, cheap dishes, kitchen utensils, canned fruit, audio cassettes, watchbands, his high school ring. I had to adjudicate a dispute between two women who each claimed special memories of the same maple tray Leon had made by hand. I kept a waterlogged copy of *I Ching* for myself, and his Martin for Maya, who also plays the flute, like her mother.

The night after I returned home, I found a frayed box in a colonnade of things underneath a tarp in the attic. I hadn't thought twice about it for decades. It was bound with twisted and unbraiding packing tape, which nevertheless took a sharp knife to slice through. It held photos I inherited when my mother died: the four of us portrayed in various combinations, many in the early years, only a few after my father left. I surveyed the only proof of their existence, save for references in family lists and genealogies subsisting on the Internet, and a wobbly YouTube of a song about living in a teepee a deft blues singer dedicated to Leon. The past that ceased to exist came alive again, past joys, past burning drives, past misgivings and jives, past pains and fears, past japes and jeers.

All of the photos of the four of us together share the same composition: the three of them positioned to look at each other in every frame, tensile sightlines entwined in a triangle that always stays the same, while I petition the camera with wide guileless eyes and a desperately burning smile. I remember churning through these photos in ninth grade, a few days before my mother took two hundred Librium, feeling betrayed when I discovered this overarching pattern. The photos belied what I conceived were my accurate memories of childhood, in which each parent had a favorite. I belonged to my mother and my father had my brother, or so I believed. The photos revealed a different world, one in which I was always a poorly-perceived outsider yearning to be relieved of my isolation. The outsider who outlived the insiders, like the ugly hairless, swartless hominid known as homo sapiens banished as a tot by clannish hirsute proto-humans, but who survived and, according to certain scientific speculation, came back to slaughter the lot of them. I didn't off anyone, but extrapolation about their deaths made me feel as guilty as Raskolnikov.

Underneath the stack of photos was a diary that my mother kept the last few years of her life. Always in the pile, but unseen by me before. Wept-upon pages of slights and rants tracked my mother's guileless contempt for her brothers and sisters, whom she visited on a road trip that tacked around the country the year before her final, and only successful, attempt. From Los Angeles to Dallas to New Orleans to Macon to the Jersey shore to Manhattan. She saw them all and exempted no one from her downpour of spite. She envied what she called their exemplary lives, compared to her contemptable one, their flat but satiny fight-free marriages to her failed one, the seeming ease of their children's lives compared to the hardships we endured. She analyzed it all. She freely admitted that she never stopped loving my father and never would, quilting for pages the depth of their feelings for each other. Her raw venting of hopelessness and self-hatred galvanized everything from my childhood—all at once, unfiltered. Every harrowing moment, every discontent, every pent-up fear, every flicker of guilt and slap of shame spilt into my consciousness. I ruthlessly forced myself to read through it until near the end, when I saw the statement that I can't get out of my head, a sentence that bled the sick truth of my life.

I read the chilling words again and again, until I could read no more. I ripped the diary into a hodgepodge of shapes and sizes, which I stacked against a molehill out back and lit with the long, thin lighter I use to spark the gas grill. Stacks of yellowing tooth-white sheets crackled black, then floated like monarchs and meadowlarks, swaying over glowering red, the smell of ash sweetened by dead and dying oak leaves, bleeding birch. Pages of the diary lurched apart like the baking strudel dough my mother's strutting fingers used to roll and cut and fill with apples, raisins, nuts and spices. I thought of other artful, moving-with-Kanto-slicing rites of blazing fire she made, the cutting into meat, the scraping of hardened rice and golden diced onion from the braising pan, the lazy trickle and enticing thud of chocolate bites into muddy batter, as if flaying entrails and dashing blood in an ancient sacrifice.

I fanned the air, reveling gleefully in the glow of embers, the settling of ash along the sand, the irregular weeping of hand-dripped water dousing fire. But the burning sentence spins in my mind and curdles my lips. I want to dismiss the words. But they are tattooed deeply into hidden layers of skin: "I loved Leon more, we both did. He was our Adonis."

Seeing sheets of ash break apart under billows of water spray filled me with a fleeting sense of omnipotence. I could defeat anything. I could make anything. I could meet any threat. I could cheat death.

As soon as I turned off the hose faucet and the water-borne kyrie ceased, the feeling of total power stalled and gave way to a doomsday pall of sadness. The photos said it all. The persistent outsider from the day I was born. It was my calling. It was almost preordained, a timeworn, mournful sign upon my head that made others always build a wall and hold me distant.

It was then I decided to take this trip, to slip back in time. My reasoning is still unclear. I have been a continuous being since I resigned my grimy past a quarter of a century ago. Yet I've changed so much since then. Gained a little broadness in the chest. Lost most of my hair. I sport rubicund lines around the eyes and gray tips to my beard, now short and refined, not the weird bushy mess it used to be. All of the cells that my body comprised twenty-five years ago have been replaced by new ones. Also changed—my beliefs, my tastes, my mind. I'm a completely different person, I find, from the angry and shame-purled nexus of a misfit who abandoned El in the middle of Southeast Nothingtheresville, Texas.

What happened to those I left behind?

Some people I've traced through the Internet, chased down through Facebook and LinkedIn. Some answered emails, letters or tweets. Lots agreed to meet me in their current town, surprisingly usually the same place they used to live. I couldn't find everyone—El seems never to have graduated to the Internet and I found not a trace of her, disappeared like a smirch on a wiped-clean wall. But I have a full slate of people around the country to face.

Exit the 101 at South Alvarado for the first lean into the past: fast-talking Jah Mott, Black high priest of pot who looked the part—puffed-out, short-sleeved dashiki dominated by orange and green, dark sunglasses hiding his eyes, hair comb hanging from his radically high Afro, a deep and booming, lead-the-protest-rally voice. He made his living selling choice grass from San Jose to Simi Valley. As we drove through the night, he rejoiced in what he called the unsurpassed role of weed in the world's religious creeds. "Shinto brides and grooms, they would toke it to drive off gangs of disturbed spirits, man. Mellow Hindu priests, they hiked from town to town to share proverbs about the hallowed healing herb," he rapped.

Stoned, I pealed out a high-toned happy, "Ha."

Jah was going seventy-six in a fifty-five in his back-fender-dented, high-riding Caddy, curve on curve, escarp through canyon granite, past feldspar fields of swaying yellow flowers, panoramic bowers of green and tan, windows opened, radio singing "Life's been good to me so far," the swank and planetary feeling that I've been there before and will be back again, will drive back, will drive by, will lay back, will fly by, will chill and flow, sun and fun, play and stray, embrace and be embraced by desiccated vibes propelling the valley night warmth across a twelve-lane highway.

"Folk conspired to spike it into milk and butter and they called it bhang, a silky, tangy quench for higher prayers they sang or to psyche out sacrificial wenches on the pyre," he said, which made me clang another joyous "Ha!"

"And don't forget the three wise men—Zoroastrians with a ken for hemp—they buys it, dries it, and fires it up." "Ha, ha," I laughed a one-man choir at a stony revival meeting, blurting out guffaws between each of his assertions.

"In Solomon's Temple—the priests they strolled inside dense clouds of it, just a sniffin' and a prayin' their souls off!"

"Ha, ha."

"Sufi Moslems, they puffed a bowl to conjure crowds to witness their pious testaments. German pagans smoked the holy gorse to inhale Freya's fertile force. And Rasta man, the Rasta man, he tokes to make a sacrament to Jah."

"Ha, ha!"

"I'm thinkin' Eve she cradled a baby snake in her hands, its narrow toothy maw and bony tongue gnashing and licking a bowl of sweet delicious hash." "Ha, ha!" "For them folks that calls me a drug dealer, I got a news flash. I sell the sweetest, ripest stash, a Eucharist crafted by ass-kicking horticulturalists, a talisman you put in your pipe not your pocket. My stash replaces anesthetists, allergists, cardiologists, sexologists, psychiatrists, and psychologists. Ganja is the key to god's domain. It opens heaven's bedroom door and lets us score the Virgin Mother Mary Jane."

"Ha, ha, ha!"

It was almost morning. Through a bug-smudgy window and blunt smoke, a brassy yolk of sunrise confronted us, on a freeway under a sapphire pass: brash stone, bottle brush, transparent shadows pushing against the grain. Red and purple bougainvillea through a moving window, dense, caliginous frocks of fans in prayer together, three by three, shoot after shoot climbing purple bedrock, a route of redwood picket fences, then canyon rocks, a boisterous shock of jade, the cypress and wild asparagus calmly sway, screening the valley below, ranches and drive-throughs twisting tithes of color in the green glow of rising palm, brown along the edges, greeting a surge of car echoes and the scent of drying lemons, the wild kudzu persisting, witness to balmy heat, the moon in the morning sky.

We meet decades later at a Morton's in downtown L.A. Jah—now Dr. Jonathan Mott—says he hasn't blazed a spliff since med school, because he doesn't want to lose his license to practice pediatric psychiatry. He's a specialist in boys with ADD and other behavioral malaises. He still riffs enthusiastically about his job, but now with ponderously stiff phrases.

"Neurotransmitters in the brains of preadolescent males with ADD present functional impairment. They fail at social interaction and present a locus of oppositional defiance, leading to easy distraction, minor infractions, no self-reliance, a lack of compliance, a lack of rapport, failure to maintain focus or follow instructions, disruptive conduct, quick to obstruct, quick to anger, quick to be bored."

"Sounds like my childhood."

"Perhaps you had ADD. Today we attack it with a strict regimen of counseling to modulate the emotions, a delay in grade promotion, and the prescription of ethical pharmaceuticals that we believe may act on the locus coeruleus-noradrenergic system and the mesocorticolimbic dopamine pathway."

Ethical pharmaceuticals, a fancy way to say *drugs*. Instead of pushing pot, he's shilling pills, this time to children. An anger unfelt for decades swills in my throat. He might have given me this shit when I was a kid who was always in motion. My knees were always jitterbug shaking. I couldn't stop making a commotion in class. And what would he have filled my brother's body with? I ball up my fists and set my legs and shoulders to leap across our grilled steak and Zinfandel and grab Jah. I want to break him in two, rub his bloated face in pig shit, knock his block off, rake him till his eyes fill with tears, shake his big Black ass until he realizes it makes no sense to push pills on eight-year-olds who can't sit still.

It feels good to sting inside, good to feel the homicidal jolt of rage I used to feel most of the time, as if continually zinged with low-voltage shock treatments. Something sent me into a fighting rage every day back then— some malcontent talking in a movie theatre. Jolt.

A car turning in front of me in the crosswalk. Jolt.

Some alligator-skinned dolt at the table next to ours saying protesters are traitors. Jolt.

Hearing TV reporters bray the news of the day. Jolt. Going to the suburbs—where I later spent a quarter of a century and counting. Jolt.

Thinking about religion, that fount of stupidity. Jolt.

The disturbing foppery of politicians. Jolt. Dowagers who left their mutt's flop stinking on the sidewalk. Jolt.

Thinking about El. Jolt.

Something she pestered me about. Jolt. Something she just had to get off her chest. Jolt. Something she thinks I messed up. Jolt.

Thinking about what an unhappy and routeless, rootless rut I was in with El, no fault of my own and yet all my fault. My anger was frequent and always an exalted hysteria, a jet of pure fury unsalted with guilt or regret, which always came later when the ire wilted and I thought about what had set me off.

After I split from El, I ceased to care. For the past twenty-five years I've lived in a waking sleep in which I speed blamelessly through my rebuilt life in suspended animation, engaging in half-conscious interactions. No anger, no guilt, no shame, no fear except for the fear of feeling anger, guilt, and shame. But sometimes an old song on the radio becomes an evocation of never-ending-days now decades gone. A nameless pierce of emotion invades me, not in words, but as a collection of body changes—weepy eyes, sweaty palms, tensing muscles, red face—deranged convections that briefly sweep across me, then erase themselves as I return to waking sleep.

My flash of anger at Jah is just that, a flash, momentary pandemonium in a long-persevering emotional equilibrium. No fear that anyone will ever know that I'm pissed, because I won't show it, which means it doesn't exist. Like a tree falling in the woods that no one hears.

Tree up or tree down, there is no thought outside a living mind. And inside the mind, there is little difference between thinking and living, except thinking twists in undefined and sometimes absurd directions—whisking backwards and forwards in time. You can skip steps, truncate distances, enlist memory aides, calculate and calibrate. But you miss details. After a while, everything real fades or is blurred by a refined veil of language, which never perfectly captures the real—no smell, no sight, no feeling, no scar, except as mediated through purblind words. Thinking puts everything into a box of words. Thinking while driving—a box of words within the box that is the car.

The somewhere-somewhat-somehow archive of reality mocks our sense of time. Yesterday is as distant from us as thirty years ago or thirty years hence, at least as long as you believe you'll survive another thirty. Events beyond your life—things that happen after you are gone, are never more than volumeless, heftless fantasy. The pain of the future is the easiest pain to assuage, because you can avoid it by jumping to another possible unfolding of events, bereft of affliction. Different is the past, rooted with doleful deeds as it is, which can thump you in the soul at any second.

Slow down for speed bumps.

I meet Del Gatesberg at his campaign headquarters. When he picked me up in Portola Valley thirty years ago, he was a blond, soft-faced frat-boy sporting a short shag. He chattered disconnectedly along I-280, while weaving his Ford Capri slowly between lanes so often that it was as if he were using both lanes at once. Another dealer. A popular profession in the late seventies. "I pay a brainy chem major to mix the best windowpane in Santa Cruz, which fetches an insane five times its cost when I hawk it to my psycho frat brothers, who like to goose the punch at parties so the girls will loosen up. Grab my attaché case behind you. The manila folder on top has a sheet of it if you want a hit."

"Never touch the shit," I placidly said. But I braced myself to muffle an expected shiver of death thinking about my brother taking multiple massive doses of acid. In those days, I would suddenly lose control to a morose, guilt-intensified fear when I thought of the violence people would inflict on themselves, like taking hard drugs, self-mutilation, suicide. I panicked hearing about other people's bad trips, seeing a derelict shoot up heroin in *Panic in Needle Park*, seeing a slick spurt of phony blood, a brief thought of my own demise. Sometimes it would go away quickly. Sometimes it could last for hours—hours of a metastasizing fear chasing me between tables and chairs, hours of wanting and waiting to burst from my skin. Being in a car was the worst, because I couldn't pace it off. It soon passed, though, as Del anesthetized me talking about another of his business enterprises.

"I also represent an ample junior miss who doesn't mind hiking up her skirt or letting some guy have a free hand with her, and she gives me half for setting it up. Wish I could get you a sample of that, but my partner wouldn't understand."

"I don't pay."

"Yeah, you do. You always pay one way or another, even if it's just for the pills to spike her drink. "

"That's sick. I don't have to resort to those tricks. Besides, I like my girls to come with illusions, even if they are momentary ones."

"You mean the squirrely illusion of love? Of two hearts in synch?" He gives me a churlish wink.

"I think like and respect are good enough."

"Sometimes, it's not worth the trouble. Sometimes, it's easier to lay down the cash and grab exactly what you want, without wasting time to gab over shit. Be in control. Do what you want to do, without having to ask if she wants to do it. When that's what you want, I have just the number for you"— which led to a philosophical discussion of his notion that all relationships between people reduce to transactions, quid pro quos, and horse swaps, a form of buying and selling masked by emotions and lofty aspirations such as love and devotion.

His insights, like his driving, were carelessly aggressive, but his voice so limpid and unpossessed that I doubted him when he said he sold drugs and sex. "You've been putting me on about being a drug dealer and pimp, right? It's a joke, right?"

"Scout's honor. But it's strictly temporary to bail out my betting business. I'm learning how to beat the spread, but meanwhile I'm broke—getting routed pretty bad and need the extra bread to pay the rent on my pad. I'm about to tap out my quarterly allowance from Dad. That reminds me, I better harness my horses and floor it home before my report card does so he won't see I only passed two courses."

When I meet him in his office, Del's once-portly face has thinned out and is now athletically angular, albeit marked with deep age-lines. He keeps his fine salt-and-pepper hair razor short. He puts down his study sheets and rises from his desk to greet me, automatically flattening his striped blue-and-valentine-red tie against his white shirt and buttoning the middle button of his blue blazer as he approaches for a vigorous grip of my hand. His desk is surrounded by cardboard campaign signs that read, "Open the Gatesberg to Divine Prosperity," against a background of red, white, and blue vines. Behind him on a coat rack hang two neatly pressed white shirts and another striped tie with red and blue lines.

'Last time I saw you, Del, you were pimping and shilling drugs."

"Keep that to yourself, or I'll have to have you shot." He forces a shrill laugh.

"Youthful indiscretion. I'm not going to tip the media. Besides, I'm sure they've already got the scoop."

Del tells me that, a few years after he left his third college, he heard that a group of computer nerds had created software that automated the manufacturing of silicon chips, but needed backing. Del dipped deeply into his trust fund to buy the technology and patents "on the cheap." He negotiated a long-term contract with a Brazilian manufacturer on whose board his father sat and started a company he sold five years later for the insane gain of one hundred million. Since then, he's been living off his investments in real estate. Now he's running for Congress on a self-financed campaign.

"Maybe I'll burn about twenty, thirty mill. That's why it's the House, not the Senate. I can afford what I can afford, no more, no less. I'm intoxicated by the thrill of the campaign trail, but I hate giving speeches, so I'm not going to kill myself. Politics isn't complicated, but it's as sketchy as sausage-making. If I can leverage it, great. If I can't, also great."

All the while he talks, he works his smartphone. "I have to look at yesterday's data-mining reports and approve today's round of tweets and Facebook updates. We're getting in the groove, the numbers are starting to move, but so far nothing's proved to be infectious, nothing dominating or viral, nothing spirally out of control like the PR guys promised, but it is what it is."

"And your platform?" I ask, to which he gives me a quizzical fishbowl look.

"Like I said, Twitter and Facebook."

"No, I mean, where do you stand on the issues?"

'We're still calibrating the polls we took, but whatever the voters want we'll give them—cutbacks, rollbacks, pullbacks, throwbacks—as long as we can lower taxes on job creators. Whatever's the norm, the norm, and if it's not, we'll reform it. Let's deal with the finances and circumstances we have to deal with. If it's fixed, it's fixed, and if it's not, we'll nix it or dance around the numbers, or advance a study on the cheap that shows lowering taxes on high net-worth families is the answer."

"Doesn't it bother you that you're buying the office?"

"It's not a crime, and if it's not a crime, I'm fine with it," he says with a weary aloofness, as if he thinks my queries are uninformed.

Angry again, angry to think this conniving schmo—this white-jiving fake—thinks he's qualified for office because he has a lot of dough. Angry the way I stopped being angry when I left El. Environmental degradation, mass incarceration, death of public education by government starvation, supply-side induced inequality of wealth, invasions of terrified nations, various genocides—for years, they remained nothing more than fine words that hide in newspapers and magazines, and then online. I wallowed in a stultified somnambulance, not too happy, not too sad, not too slow, not too fast. Not too good, not too bad, not too narrow, not too wide. Never thinking of the past, or of passing tomorrow, aware of days, but not of years, not too high, not too low. Little laughter, never sorrow, never tears, never angered or estranged. No moments of exhilaration. Aware of milestones, dates and celebrations, but not of change.

In the end, I don't really give two shanks of rope about Del Gatesberg, his hundreds of millions or his machinations, except for a vague hope that he loses to his rich, pampered, electorate-manipulating opponent, whoever he or she might be.

None of my past associations have any a hold on me anymore. I don't really care about any of them. But, taken as a whole, banded together, they coalesce into a force more paralyzing of the soul than Earth's gravitation, like a spiderweb capable of holding a horse or a human. Each strand—each person and each event that inhabits my memory—is a light-weight component, easy to break, but together they immobilize the victim into short, jerky bursts of setal movement, while the hypnotizing beauty of their pattern narcotizes. I see many striking irregularities and design flaws in the web, some people with but a vague connection to me, like the people I met roaming in my youth or a woman I slept with once. Others keep clawing into and out of my life from time to time, like Irv or my cousin Pete. Many connect to each other, sometimes through me, sometimes through another nexus, yaw, link, or curve, a little central star of spider silk, a bar or whirl or funnel bilked and purled so finely that it can drop out of the web, like three or thirty prime years can bootstrap out of a life. Many strands hang loose and lead nowhere, yet they also entrap their prey. The victim contemplates the irony of the interconnections, appreciates the beauty of the design, but remains neutralized in the web's grip—a bug or an ant tripped into the trap of time.

When I left El I thought I smashed the web to little pieces of silky scrim.

But maybe all I did was drive a hole through the middle and shimmy through it, thrashing and crashing, before it rewove into an asymmetric slash of dead-ends and half bends dangling in the wind, but still capable of gripping me in its sweet-and-sticky rapture. I can't help but observe the web build itself again from my memories of the people I plan on meeting on this trip, but I shouldn't try to touch it, or its clingy strands will recapture me.

Everything seems cautious and cramped, like my approach to life now. I have plotted out every day of the trip with the care of a gearwheel, so I—and May—know how long I've allotted to driving each day, where I'm staying, whom I'm going to see, where I'm eating my meals.

Uncertainty used to have its appeal. It would take hold of me and fling me into dumb adventures. No more. I can no longer live with the bedlam uncertainty of long-distance thumbing, on the ramp when darkness comes and autumn's eve turns damp and cold. I'm no longer bold enough to live with the squealing uncertainty of a fire-red Chevy's screeching halt, embedding smears of tire on asphalt, the chilling uncertainty at the sight of tanned and tattooed dopers in white tee-shirts and oil-streaked threadbare chinos swilling cans of beer, crew-cut Dale and Dennis with nothing to do and willing to take me anywhere I was headed, thinking it would be a blast to take a fast drive from Cincy to the Windy City, "Because Marley's sister's there and has some pretty good blow, and we can sail there by daylight." First they want to get another car. "The Celebee glides so smooth, and the sound system is dynamite," says Dale.

I can no longer live with the you-can't-tell-without-a-scorecard uncertainty of bounding through a beat-up part of town, soaring down pebbled streets, past wooden shanties, roofs of thatch, on sandy dirt patches, dusty paths instead of concrete sidewalks, rusted cars and rails and broken stoves gracing derelict yards. All the while, Dale and Dennis gas about "the clown whose ass we kicked last time we drove to Chi-town."

The uncertainty of stopping in a signless cul-de-sac of Loblolly pine, stucco and shingle block shacks with Confederate flags in the windows. Of shuffling out of the car with my duffel bag, scared of the drubbing I think

I'm about to take, wondering if I should start a scuffle or try to flee, or just hand these hicks my cash. The corner of one eye peers after a nearby stick or club I could use to protect myself from the bashing I'm sure to get. Not wanting to let them know how terrified I am, I swagger brashly.

Dennis Doper lifts a roller door of a ragtag garage, then backs out a Toyota Celica, mag-wheeled and painted orange like the stinger of a bee, onto the street. He cuts sharply, screech-stops in front of Dale and me, revs it up, then shuts the engine down. "One more thing, my man," he says as he points a finger to the ground and canters inside a stunted shanty.

Back a minute later, he says, "Had to kiss my ma goodbye … and grab this!," those last words bantered with the gleeful mien of a smuggler past the border, as between his fingers swings a baggie full of green.

Can't live with the renegade uncertainty of a fog-spreading night of AC/DC fading into ELP, fading into Chuck Berry, fading in my head into Cheap Trick, fading into Styx, fading into Grateful Dead, fading into Robin Trower against the whop-whop hum of eighty miles per hour in the Celebee, until they drop me at the Tribune Tower. I photograph the two of them in Popeye poses flexing anvil forearms riddled with visible veins. Dennis throws me the bag of smoke, Dale beeps a refrain of "shave and a haircut," and they drive off to score cocaine.

My curling black-and-whites of them are before their eyes now. Dale and Dennis are still best friends, no surprise. They each tip the scale at more than three hundred pounds. Their pasty faces sport ponytails. Tattoos of skulls and crossbones fill their still-muscled arms. They wear thick-heeled work boots and blue jeans, lumberjack shirttails out, concealing round bales of flab. Dennis limps "because of bad luck," he blabs. "A boozing hunter shot me in the shoes hunting ducks, like our vice president did, except we didn't make the evening news."

I meet them in front of a big-top tent that's a retreat for men somewhere in the middle of Oregon. "A lot of swearing and screaming and venting and repenting and railing and exhaling," Dennis bleats.

"A lot of stressing and confessing and repeating and brow-beating, till your throat is raw and you feel like dog meat, all of us crowded close together, overheated, nose to nose, cleats to cleats, brothers in the big tent of brotherhood, feeling the greater plan, feeling the awe of man, and a lot of wailing, yes, because I can, because I am male, because I am a man," Dale exclaims, as he beats the side of his van with his hairy, meaty paw.

They invite me to join their troop of thirty—mostly gray and severely overweight, with droopy, shirt-stripped skin showing visible tattoos—as they reenact what the leader calls the sacred rituals of the Chippewa Tent to liberate their souls in fellowship.

"I didn't understand my role as a man until my father died," Dennis expatiates, "and I had already lost control and cracked up two cars, spent eighteen years delivering eggs to convenience stores, and grew to hate the mother of two of my kids. I stagnated in my isolation from my inner track, goalless, slated for the wrecking ball. I put on all this weight, and it was hard, so very hard, to bring my inner warrior back."

Another man begins to tell *his* tale, and it's the same sob. Lots of drinking, bar fights, time in jail. He blames himself for sailing from dead-end job to dead-end job, for marrying a slob who turned into a blob, then bailing on the marriage and shacking up with her sister, staying six months in his pick-up truck, until his luck twists and he sees the light and fights back to the inner man he lost along the way.

Now a third one grunts that the hen-pecking cunts in his life wrecked his manhood. He should have stood up to them, overcome their neglect of his needs, made them understand that a man must be a warrior, a soldier, a hunter, a protector!

Dale begins to bang a kettledrum with a baseball bat. A loud and steady beat—pow, pow, pow, pow, pow, pow. Soon other drums appear, and those without drums pat on any flat surface, the ground, trees, rocks—with hands, sticks, bats, boots, rakes, joists, bare feet —and they break out in high-pitched voices—loud and senseless hoots and bleats that grow rowdy and start to shake the tent, until the leader blows a whistle to quiet the crowd.

"Men, men, men, men, men," he proudly says, "For that's what we are. Men, innocent men. When we strip away our goals and relationships, when we strip away the roles imposed on us, the parts we play for cash, the things we say, the goods we pay for, the trash we haul away, and the trash where we've enclosed our man-ness, we are innocent young sons of a king who has been deposed. Innocent as the day the world began, enslaved by our fears, drowning in hidden tears, afraid to cry, afraid to die, willing to lie, willing to pose. We are innocent hairy beasts, living in caves, worshiping stars and rain, feasting on cattle, crows, and wild grain. We are wizards enchanting the primordial rain forest with our mad raving, with our growing man-ness. Let us wash off our pain. We are initiates in the tribe of man, we are men, we are man."

All of them start to shout, "We are man, we are man, we are man...."

I have nothing in common with these bumblers. Yes, I've endured trouble with women and have had my share of tumbles, including a few knock-about rumbles that shame me to ponder. But I have never been a hunter or soldier, nor have I ever wanted to be one. At least not since I could grow stubble. I don't find joy reveling in the out-of-doors. I haven't liked to camp since Boy Scouts and used to abhor it when no ride came and I had to plop my sleeping bag in a trench at the side of the road or on a wooden bench at a rest stop. It only happened a few times. I grumbled and endured it, but now I demand a clean-and-tidy suite, preferably in a big city, where I can find someplace that pours a humble red and offers something to eat that isn't fast food, casual dining, steakhouses, or national chains. I'm not into driving trucks, flying planes, riding motorcycles, reenacting military campaigns, watching football, collecting model trains, binge-drinking, shooting lined-up-on-a-fence cans, or the other activities these men pursue to manifest their inner man. I would never let myself gain as much weight as these guys have, and certainly May wouldn't put up with it. At the first ten pounds, she would have the entire family on a steady of diet of salad, chicken breasts, and brown rice. But what differentiates me most profoundly from these riotous behemoths is that I could never mess around in wizardly enticement, could never use the device of a magic lure to try to cure what ails me, could never suppose a ritual bond with other good men would suffice to countervail my psychic woes. I do not confide in a tribe, am not the son of a glorified king, not inscribed in a brotherhood. I am an outsider.

I remember years ago when cousin Petey wanted all of the cousins to take a blood oath sanctified by cutting ourselves on the finger and mixing blood. Leon, Gary, Mike, and the others were willing to do it. Petey tied a string tightly round the base of his index finger and used the point of a Swiss army knife Gary supplied to jab lightly at the flesh and draw a drop of blood, then handed me the knife. Being blood brothers, belonging to a group tied to each other in secret, intimate ways for life, appealed to me as a child, but the idea of cutting myself for any reason terrified me. I held the instrument a long while, petrified, my stomach turning, my face burning. I started to guide the blade towards my finger, then stopped. I sighed, took a big swig of pride and said I couldn't do it. We never had the chance to find out which other cousins would perform a minor mutilation because Aunt Flo walked into the room and I quickly slid the blade into its socket and hid the knife in my pocket.

Change lanes and let that Mercedes rocket past my car.

Sometimes I would wait for hours for a ride, prancing back and forth at the side of a freeway entrance. I eyed the expanse of concrete and cars before me and started singing a song about the road, *Fire and Rain, On the Road to Find Out, The Weight*, a droning, moaning tune I crowed and cried and cripped and crooned for what seemed hours, imploding the oldie with jazzy riffs and gyrating vibrato folds, wonderfully dissonant cliffs and dips, notes expanding, subsiding and colliding, waning and waxing, until my voice went strange, like Coltrane coaxing every possible agitation from his axe, driving yelps and susurrations, voice tacking higher, lower, turning corners, climbing brimstone, diving through cold water, a sizzling saxophone hacking out taut pieces of sound, a sharpened aural chisel peeling away tone after tone, then a cello, a lush and round waterwheel, viscid, congealing, then a trumpet, stunning with squeals of strumpet tickles as long as I listened to my intentions unwind in my mind. But as soon as I stopped listening in my head and heard instead the sounds my voice was making, my ears found the notes a lazy mess of misaligned rhythms, flat and sharp at once. I stopped my warped singing, then began another game that drove me crazy. Trying to clear my bung of the song I had sung.

Soon my bored wait ended, picked up by a friendly-looking skinny guy in a tie-dyed T-shirt and blond dreadlocks asking for gas money in return for a ride.

"I'm pleased to make your acquaintance," he said. "I'm Jesse Yamana, on the road to fulfill my promise to our Lord. My goal is to spread the words of St. Thomas until the kingdom of heaven is restored. 'Woe to the flesh that depends on the soul; woe to the soul that depends on the flesh.'"

He was a fresh, unfledged college dropout pledged to driving thumbers wherever they wanted to go, as long as he could hoot to them the absolutely absurd and timeworn Christian homilies and metaphors he's read in the Gospel of St. Thomas, "Grapes are not harvested from thorns, nor figs gathered from thistles, for they do not produce fruit."

"If you're looking for recruits, I'm not the guy," I blurted out.

"I'm just looking to contemplate the Lord and emulate St. Thomas, who wandered without boots to India and converted the natives."

Jesse was willing to take me all the way to Los Angeles, but I had to live with his Jesus prose for hours, ringing crescendos of faith, rationales for miracles, sarcastic zingers at science, the friendly-fellowship innuendoes that I agreed with all he said—after all, who would doubt St. Thomas, his bloody fingers, and his wandering toes? His raving irritated me, as I was craving to doze off.

"He who seeks will find, he who knocks will be let in. For no one lights a lamp to put it under a bushel, nor puts it in a hidden place."

The car pushes through empty space, guided by white dashes scampering in front of it and quickly trailing into a dark quagmire. I occasionally nod off and half-dream of tearing Bible pages for a bonfire, while enraged vampires harass apostles into caldrons and vultures peck out their twitching eyeballs. I see mass forced conversions of pious sons to witches' worship. Teams of banshees paint the naked bodies of fainted nuns. Conspiring witches stir a pot of beaming saints.

The road rocks me back and forth, dream to word, word to dream, "A blind man ... is not sewn onto a new garment ... five trees in Paradise the night he dies ... cast fire upon the world which remains undisturbed ... light within a man of light...."

A goose-gray fog rises from mountains, streams and swells under my closed eyes, a hiss of hammam steam fills my contemplation. I'm back at the Hotel St. George pool, indwelling chlorinated dew beads dripping down dilapidated marble walls. "The person old in days will not hesitate.... A corpse is superior to the world ... for many who are first ... the worm at them ... the harvest is great...."

His voice fades to the rumble of the A train. I'm on a dim subway platform, overburdened with thick books for courses I should be getting better grades in, feeling a fool and rife with remorse, drained by school, home, everything, seeing no way out of my gray life. A bottle of aspirin in my coat pocket. Hundreds of white disks to make me drowsy, dazed, sleepy, unconscious. To whisk away my shame, my pain. My mother's way out. But I didn't take the pills, and I don't take them in my car dream. In life, I threw them on the track and took the A train to Washington Heights to see Aunt Hope and Uncle Jack. In my dream, I give them to a naked larded man on the platform who's moonbeam-gazing at Jesse's face warped to shriveled tissue, Christ-like, babbling ukases and roundelays of disconnected words hissing snake-like at me: "... Whose leaves do not fall ... raise the stone ... kingdom of heaven ... I am guarding it until it blazes...."

"Your kingdom of heaven is not real," I finally burst out in a slightly dislocated voice, warped by half-sleep and a poorly-concealed disrespect, "no matter what holy thoughts you may hatch. It's your cursed fate to die, an abject musty corpse, like all of us." I didn't want him to kick me out of the car somewhere on the long and dusty rural stretch after Bakersfield, but I couldn't catch myself.

"You don't believe in a reward after this veil of tears?" he mumbles suspiciously, surprised, as if he's never heard or conversed these words before, nor explored the thought that someone might not surmise as he did. Yet the well-wrought phrases he chooses sound so rehearsed, I supposed his guilelessness was a pose.

"I do not believe in anything," I say. "I know what science knows."

"Your science has its own boundless faith it clings to until the day it turns against itself. Once science reasoned that the burning sun and far-flung stars zinged around the Earth. Later scientists thought that an invisible wraithlike substance called phlogiston births combustion. Science once bought the thought that when earth was young life sprang spontaneously from worthless mounds of dung. Now scientists believe that you can reconstruct tiny shards of bone found in loam into enormous reptilian monsters, who, they confidently assert, once roamed the far-flung Earth before an asteroid destroyed them, and that four billion years ago strange microbial bacteria deployed themselves into long tubes of clinging cells among underwater volcanic flues and kept changing and rearranging until they became me and you. You believe life has always been a fragile shell in which selfish twisted lengths of hydrocarbons dwell. You claim that, by an unnamed chance, a grand big bang began everything and that everything expands, advances, and scatters through space, unplanned and untamed. You explain that matter is made of smaller matter, which is made of smaller matter, until the smallest dances with balls of energy. And through all these changes, you fools continue to nurse a faith that your laws of physics work the same throughout the universe."

"All based on evidence we measure with tools. As our tools improve, our knowledge does, too."

"You call it *truth*, but you're brainwashed to bray another kind of faith, a faith built on sand, a faith full of strife, because, when you die, it leaves you high and dry, alone to decay. But when you pray to a gracious god, as I do, you reach an absolute knowledge that you will take the heavenly highway to eternal life, a knowledge that stays with you until your dying day."

It was my turn to make a speech. "God's a servant of the wealthy, a bundle of myths that ruling elites elevate to convince the poor to fight in wars, to hate the poor of other lands, to adore and celebrate the president or king, to kiss the ring of power, never to question the might of authority, but to accept their fate. Without a god, who would want to risk his life or send his kids to fight? What religion does not join forces with secular authority to mistreat, deceive, and smite the common people? Christian fathers bargained deals with Constantine, and the new state religion approved the emperor's oppressions, blunders, and deceits. Ashoka's hordes beat and butchered the Kalinga, before Ashoka retreated to a Buddhist monastery. For monetary rewards, greedy Confucian monks repeated misleading paraphrases of the master's words to convince peasants to obey their perverse Ming overlords. Tryvgesson used conversion to Christianity as his excuse to plunder, rape, and raid, as he traversed the Norway coast. One of the Crusades let soldiers roll and roast Albigensians to subvert an economic rival to the Capetian Kings. Your faith always takes its toll on the poor. Your religion always helps the rich hold control."

"You've ignored the saving of the soul, the beauty of the sacrifice, the ecstasy of faith, extraction from hell, and deliverance into paradise, the heart-burst joy in knowing that you seek a blissful goal and that something larger affords meaning to your actions. You miss knowing that your soul, in whatever form it takes, fords this stormy bridge of life heroically and finds reward in the ways of the Lord."

"How soothing to believe a sentient being lavishes his precious breath weighing life and death on earth!" I spit out the words sarcastically. "What heady bliss to feel that a shapeless force treads googol miles enthusiastically through a million Milky Ways to part a sea, reveal a secret, raise the dead. What delight to praise a primal source taking breaks from enforcing natural law to settle the scores of football games. Inspiring to know its image inflames itself in every human being, setting us apart, authorizing special claims and bounties. Reassuring to realize that, after liquidating countless marine and earth-bound species, or allowing it to happen, this brave and caring, splendiferous and sibylline it-in-the-skies decides to intervene and save us."

"All it takes is faith," was his grave reply, "The gate is open wide, and all may enter, even a dissenter."

"All it takes is placing Pascal's wager. You've heard of that, haven't you? A fevered face that rampages November's fog, hacking through a shroud of visual truth, each breath cleaving kneeling clouds. In a dumb-luck cul-de-sac, the walker takes uncertain, dumbstruck steps. Will he wander closer to a cherished door? Or stumble over crumbling curb and fall? Hurtle headlong towards a moving truck?"

"You're a distrusting sinner, but the holy spirit loves you, the same as he loves me, another beaten shoddy soul trapped in a meritless, rusting, pestilent body."

When he lets me off where the 405 meets the 101, he reveals that he has two thousand hidden behind a hubcap nestled against a metal spoke, and he plans to keep spreading the word of his lord until he's broke.

Which Jesse didn't do, as he tells me at a rest stop where we meet. Jesse scoots down a ladder hanging from a helicopter cresting overhead, cell phone tooting in the pocket of his flight vest, can of diet Fresca in one hand. In a brash Texas twang he tells his tale, stopping frequently to guzzle his pop.

"After a hitch-hiker pulls a gun on me and steals my car and cash about three hours outside Houston, I drag my weary body twenty miles in the sun, my friend, pining after what God wanted for me. I finally see a shopping mall that shines like St. Augustine's City perched on the Hill. I poke along from store to store and cajole all the managers to take pity on a tired-and-broke,

Jesus-fearing soul left in the lurch by sinners. A kindly old born-again with a music store, an elder in the Baptist Church, hired me."

He takes a long swig from his can, then crushes it in one hand, tosses it onto the grassy hillside, and reaches into his vest for one more. "With the Lord as my guide, I passed years selling organs and horns, swore to the gospel of good works, and began to amass some capital. I entered holy marital bliss with a god-fearing bride, had three sons, and was pretty satisfied. When the owner died, his widow asked me to take over, and when she passed on, her will specified that the children sell the store to me. I tried to diversify—electronics, cell phones, fridges, headstones, ovens, furniture and flooring, video games and flat-screen TVs, work shirts and pants, peat and dirt, herbicides and house plants. I kept opening new stores, my friend, always in small rural towns in the South with lots of church-going folk near where major highways meet. I own a chain of 200 stores, my friend, plus a website that delivers right to your door. Jesse's Can't Be Beat Bargains."

I remember a frail, gingerbread boy who stooped his head below his svelte shoulders to be lower than his companions even when driving. Today's Jesse is hale and hearty, with fat cheeks, a prosperous gut that droops over his belt and a gyrating, bear-like butt. He's lost the dreads in favor of a dyed blond comb-over under an outsized felt cowboy hat.

"I banded with other righteous business men interspersed throughout the rural South to create a Christian Chamber of Commerce. We started spreading the good news across the land with ads on Christian radio that told folks we sold a Christian brand and practiced old-time values. We were spinning gold, my friend, like Jews. All of us started tithing to non-profit think tanks that support our stand on issues. We are fighting to overthrow the yoke of Social Security, Medicare, and other Muscovite plots to raise our taxes until we're broke, take away our guns, give away the store to the undeserving poor, and ban our religious rights."

In between slurps of his fresh can of Fresca, he chirps praise of the Christian business movement. "We pledge to provide a Christian workplace, my friend. We pledge to offer sound job opportunities to workers of the white race. We make sure we do business with other Christians of God's stock and we all work together to chase away the unions. We're the real underground economy, my friend."

He gives me an iPod preloaded with Christian rock and sermons on end times.

"No, that's okay, I'll never listen," I say sharply, determined to display my disdain.

"It would do you a world of good, my friend."

"We spent hours harping on this argument years ago when we were just out of school and both down and out. We're not expanding on what we said then. We already know where we stand."

"But the bands are really cool."

Cool? It probably sounds like Glen Campbell or The Carpenters or some other pre-fab, computer-generated, light-and-happy, country-and-western tinged major key shit. Irritating enough to put me in a fit. But the old fighting spirit doesn't incite me. Jesse and his politics bore me more than rile my anger. My old flame of fury fails to ignite.

Take this off-ramp and turn right.

The landscape's sameness submerses the fickle mind in perverse modes. Memory is the curse of the road. The present is nothing but a cavalcade of trees, signs, curves and vehicles, so the mind cascades swiftly forward or backward in time, with backwards the more probable goad, propelled by the music you hear blasting, by the unbound yearning for the past in which the sounds were first made. The road gives you plenty of time to reenact old hells, masquerading as both sides, except that, in the present version of the past, you get to prattle what you wished you had said—more clever, more lambasting, more convincing. Or control yourself, so you refrain from saying something that left others aghast. The road can help you plane down bygone days to a smooth abstraction through your many iterations of their memory. But each swell new version—fictional to some degree—taunts you, because you know it isn't true. You were not resolute. You didn't hoot words with the lexicon of a Joyce and the cleverness of a Fontanelle. You didn't act heroically. Sometimes your choice was to sit there doing absolutely nothing, like my mother's suicide attempt that we didn't try to stop. Correction, *I* didn't try to stop it, but instead sat at the kitchen table mutely drinking warm sugar water. I don't know how Leon felt because I never asked him. Even those times we would chat about growing up, we propped our feelings behind a generalized overview, such as "It was fucked up" or "Things turned to shit," never valuing any single fact or incident. We could conceptualize and intellectualize, but touching the original ordeal was taboo.

I don't know whether Leon relived any of these moments like I used to do, sitting on the side of the bed sleepless at night or waiting at the highway for a ride. Had he decided to let her die in that moment, like I did? And what did he think six months later, when she checked out of Creedmoor and we went back to live with her? Was he as delusively happy as I was to go back to Momma, ignoring the very-probable downsides? Was he as dissatisfied with New Jersey as I was? It wasn't that I didn't love my father. My misguided objective was to get back to my friends and go to the high school I was supposed to go to and live in New York again. Did he chide himself for not trying to save her? I have never been able to understand how I could be so passive, when I saw her cratered unconscious beside all the empty pill vials, and yet so smiley-eyed enthusiastic about returning to her a few months later.

Her first day out of the mental ward, she was waiting for us after school and took us back to the old house, which had a for-sale sign on it. While we ate the delicious close-faced grilled cheese sandwiches she made, she asked us if we wanted to live with her. I immediately roared "Yes," without deliberation. I don't remember Leon saying a thing, and I have always wondered whether I compelled his decision. Did I really determine our fate—two more years of an excoriating, soul-annihilating hell—or was my mother's question merely rhetorical, a way to get our buy-in, a trick to persuade us to play in a game already scored, like a corporation holding public meetings or putting together an employee sounding board to advise on minor points *after* the deal has been made.

Leon's thoughts remain hidden to me. I never asked when we were growing up, so busy was I telling him the middens of my mind. Like my whispered hysterics to Leon the time when we were still living in Brooklyn, my father toiling full-time as a lab tech and studying chemistry at Cooper Union, Momma taking in sewing. Leon liked going out on the fire escape, which was strictly forbidden. I must have been five, and he had just turned four. We were playing alone in our room. He quietly opened the window and climbed onto the grimy metal platform. In worming his way back inside, his elbow scraped a houseplant in a clay pot, which fell to the floor and shattered with a gunshot roar. In the few seconds it took Momma to unplug and set down her iron and storm into the room, Leon contrived to position himself in the middle of the throw rug and a wartime scene of toy Marines. She saw the mess on the floor and asked us who committed the crime. I said Leon did it, while Leon denied it and said he didn't know who did it, as he was looking away at the time.

When my father got home from work, he pressed us for the culprit, then decided that we would have to sit on our beds without toys and go to sleep without dinner if we didn't rap out a confession. My father warned us not to talk to each other—"Not a peep!"—or he would apply a strap to our backsides, but I spent the evening obsessively riding Leon, whispering professions of innocence and exhortations to tell the truth and stop being unfair to me. But he wouldn't acquiesce. He replied to my hectoring by sticking out his tongue and wiggling it around. Dad walked into the room to tell us to undress for bed in the middle of one of Leon's facial distortions. He made his shit-eating grin and tried to repress a gentle wisenheimer chuckle before raising his voice and asking us again who broke the pot. I remember us eating cold fried chicken but no dessert for dinner much later that night, but I don't remember Leon ever making it right. For a long time, I hurt that Leon lied and made me pay for doing nothing wrong, and would think about the dirt and shattered clay whenever Leon and I had a fight.

Turn left and follow the auxiliary road past another trap of suburban blight.

The long wait on the road sometimes drove me to madcap action. One time I stood on the shoulder of a curveless freeway and had the nerve to pop into the right-hand lane when I caught a fraction of the top of a car rising along the horizon, a shimmering abstraction, and wave for it to stop. When the drivers honked and swerved, I threw my arms out to make a crucifixion, but with two turned-up thumbs.

After a futile while, I saw a car weave into the left hand lane to avoid me. I frocked my face in a stupid smile and slid over, too, surprising the driver. Sixty feet away I could see his eyes gridlocked in rising intransigence and aching fear. He applied screeching brakes, veered back into the right-hand lane and heaved by sluggishly. It was a soft-top white Olds 88 with California plates, a smug and sneering driver, a schnooky, bug-eyed guy in uncinched tie and rolled-up shirt sleeves, checkered sports coat hanging from the back window hook. He probably wore a rug.

Darkening sky. I lugged myself back to the freeway entrance. An hour later, Dean Evidence stopped, but wouldn't pop open the car door until I swore I wasn't holding any drugs.

"Sorry to be so tough, but there's no pretense of privacy in a vehicle, so if the cops found some stuff they could cuff me for facilitation of a crime and take away my license to practice law and I'd probably do a dime, which I know the Pentagon would love to see. That's not paranoia will destroya talking. I'm walkin' the walk. I'm on their list, 'cause I pissed them off during the war. I was an expert anti-draft attorney until they ended it, and now my practice represents AWOLs and deserters, so the Feds are watching and waiting to shaft me. That's why I skate on the straight side."

When I meet him at his mountain cabin decades later, Dean tells me he now pursues a legal practice busting unions. "The longer we campaign to avoid certification," he explains, "the more time we have to win the workers' trust and impress upon them that the union's just a fusty, bloated mess that will only spend their dues and do nothing to sustain them. Show them that the company's their best friend. Meanwhile, we express the jobs south, at least that's the way it used to go. Now it's China and Mexico, India if it's tech." At his feet sit two Sealyham terriers, another on his lap. "Even if the union wins the vote, we countercheck, play for time, slam them with road-blocks, traps and bottlenecks, delays, and appeals to jam negotiations on the first contract deal. We peck away for as long as we can, trying to sap the union's resources. I've been minting money this way since Reagan wrecked the air traffic controllers."

"Don't you think it's unfair to workers?"

"The foundation of fairness rests in what we agree to value. Our system blesses private property above all else. Everyone agrees that collective bar-gaining protects incompetent pests and worthless functionaries. It restricts the rights of shareholders and erects barriers to direct communication be-tween employers and employees. Unionization resurrects class warfare be-tween the rich and poor, turning naturally peaceful allies into adversaries. Furthermore, unions cause labor costs to soar." He sounds as if he's reading from a news release.

He repeats all the deceptively pat phrases I've been treated to before by smirking technocrats—sermonized ideology and circular scat that never ad-dress the powerlessness of unorganized workers. But instead of broaching my objections to his PowerPoint messages, I take another approach. "That's a far cry from fighting the draft. Don't you sometimes feel guilty to have made the switch to helping rich companies shaft their poor workers? Back in the day, you once kept innocent young men safe."

"Honestly, if I had to do it over again I would never go that way in my ear-ly career. It's not because I no longer oppose war. I don't give a dime one way or the other anymore, but I wasted precious time not making real dough."

"It was all about contending for bucks for me, too, for maybe twenty-five years, making it and spending it, and I mucked about in a semi-dream through all of it," I admit.

"Let it be a dream," Dean says, "As long as I keep paying off my hard-body third wife's credit card and my dumb-as-a-hockey-puck second wife's alimony and feed these guys," he says, and scratches behind the ears of one of his terriers. "As long as I can pony up the down payment to lease a new Benz every two years and keep our wine cellar stocked, it's fine with me, I'm at peace."

Should I repudiate this jaded, greedy ass? But have my decisions been any different these past three decades? Just like Dean, I made sure to meet my immediate family's needs for the first-rate and the pedigreed. We were com-fortable, and I never worried about anyone else. I didn't knowingly or con-sciously help to impede a union, defile the environment, bleed poor people dry, or sell the wasteful, empty masquerade of conspicuous consumption. All I did was analyze research and write market profiles and plans. But I was, nevertheless, part of the obscene machine that ground down the dream of a social democracy that we seemed on the path to reaching in the mid-seventies. I once believed fervently in the possibilities of a social democracy overseen by a real meritocracy, where everyone had a chance to thrive, a green land that provided a minimum standard of living, and free healthcare and education to all, financed by taxes on the wealthy, something like France or Scandinavia. That was then. Has my later apathy been any different from Dean's?

Tank's halfway down. Better stop for gasoline.

A visit to the state prison outside Carson City to see Eddie, crazy drug-swilling truck driver, now in a Nevada state penitentiary for manslaughter. Years before, he picked me up outside an eatery just north of the Oregon-California border. He said he'd been driving straight for thirty hours and had another seven left before offloading his final freight at a sawmill. He offered me a palmful of pills.

"Swill whatever you like, buddy. The greens keep you up, the reds calm you down. Those yellows beans kill your appetite. You'll be cruising like a kite with the light greens. The little white ones help you fight the blues."

I pass on the pills and light a stick. He swills the mass of them with a can of Dr. Pepper, then begins to confide in me about a girl named Tracey he picked up one night who bestowed on him a blow job while he drove. He says it in a squeamish, shame-faced way, as if succumbing to taboo. "She kissed me on my special place and I, you know, right away. Nothing had ever felt that sweet before. I couldn't stop hearing my heartbeat rumble."

When he dropped her off in a park outside the Army base where she said her parents raised her, she borrowed fifty bucks and gave him her phone number. They embraced, and "she told me to call anytime I was feeling glum or neglected. But she must have swapped out some of the digits by mistake in the dark, because, when I dialed, a message barked that the line was disconnected," Eddie naively reflected. He hired a private eye to track down the right number. He started making long-distance calls to her every few days from wherever he was on the road. The first time he called, they yacked for what seemed to be hours. He said he could feel her love flow through his veins. But after the second time they talked, as soon as she heard it was him, Tracey balked and stuttered evasively and said she'd call him back after the football game. She never did. When he tried again, she hung up as soon as she heard his name.

"I couldn't explain why she was giving me the cold shoulder, because I'd be rolling down the highway late at night, and I'd see an image of her face in front of me in the space above the tractor frame. I'd feel her crazy love streaming towards me, lighting up the road from above, raising my soul to heaven. Blazing waves of love getting stronger and stronger. I knew she felt the same amazing craving for me. But when I called, she acted bothered, flustered, pissed off, always hanging up, and I couldn't figure out why, since I could feel her love coming at me like a missile through the sky."

On his next haul, he drove two hundred miles out of his way to the base in a blizzard, but the guards at the gate had never heard of her. He had the private eye find her real address, somewhere in the Inland Empire, and showed up at her door one night, hoping to impress her with flowers and a gold wedding band. To Eddie's distress, a man in a state of total undress save for a baseball cap answered, a bottle of gin in one hand. From the front door, Eddie, heart tapping a Morse code of sin, could see a shirtless Tracey on the couch with what looked like the guy's twin. Her head was buried in his naked lap. Eddie called to her. She shifted her gaze towards the door and started laughing. She blurted out in a slurred voice that he was a crazy squirt and, if he didn't leave, her friends would hurt him.

Eddie, in tears at the wheel, said he drove away sobbing. "I felt her love throbbing, rushing at me full-speed, and I swear I knew that Tracey really did care for me and was leading me somewhere. I wondered where it could be. I didn't believe those chilly lies about her not wanting me. She must be ill. Why else deny our love? But what about those guys? And then it hit me. Her ex-boyfriend was in the mob and had told her about the jobs they did. Now if she doesn't do what they say, they'll kill her. They must have made her say she didn't want to see me. They must have smacked her around. Tracey made me leave to keep me from getting whacked. It was her love for me that made her say those shitty things. She had to be convincing, or they might hack her into bits. It all made sense. Everything finally fit together. I've been running from the Mafia ever since and have to detour several times a week at my own expense, when I think I'm being shadowed on the road by the bad guys. It can get pretty intense. I change apartments every few months to keep them off my trail. I watch for letter bombs in the mail. I write letters to Tracey in code, but no reply. And I always carry this bad boy with me, always loaded."

From underneath his seat Eddie pulled out an oversized gun and flipped it vigorously in his hand, stiffened his grip, let his finger glide over the trigger, and fired a clip into the concrete road dividers.

"I'm ready for them when they bring it, buddy," he confided, "and after I kill 'em dead, I'll go and rescue Tracey."

"Steady there, Eddie, slow down. We're not in a shooting gallery," I hooted in distress.

"Hey, I ain't gonna mess with you, buddy. You're a friend, maybe one of my best. I'm just getting ready for the showdown."

I had him let me out at a convenience store in the next town.

Eddie's been in prison twenty years for knifing the Pakistani owner of a food stand, who he knows for sure was a made man. He tried to warn the FBI, but the agency was rife with corruption. "The cops who handled the case must be in on it, paid off or inside guys, but it doesn't matter now. Tracey's dead from AIDS, and I have an online wife on Second Life."

I thought I had run into another Jesus freak, but he was speaking of an online virtual world inhabited by computer geeks. "Ever since I saved enough to buy my computer, I can be found in my free time in Second Life with my online Tracey and our three fresh-faced girls, hanging out at our chalet by the creek in our Malibu compound. Sometimes we shop the boutiques for antiques. Sometimes we go jet skiing at Peek'n Peak. Climb walls at Half Moon Bay, motorbike Kahoolawe. I can pose with my posse or chill with the Chili Peppers and their clique. Or my avatar jumps onstage and plays with Alan Jackson, speaks to the roadies, fondles chicks, and listens to the fans shriek. I keep icon skis and tambourines as souvenirs. Tracey has a second life as my darling wife. Anytime I feel her love veering towards me ninety miles an hour in my cell, I don't get uptight. I just fire up the computer and take myself to my online backyard hideaway, buy an online can of beer, rake my online lawn, then watch my online Tracey prepare our online salad, while my avatar sears our online gourmet steaks."

Eddie has become a traveler in his cell, verging back and forth along the border between reality and an urgent fantasy, sometimes unaware of crossing it, dwelling along a frontier at which the border dissolves and the two sides merge.

Along an unknown highway, at an undefined hour late at night, whiling away the darkness counting trucks, car styles, lights and landmarks, stars and miles. Counting leads to reciting lists—lists that organize bits of the universe into best and worst. The game: to make them fit together and become a sign. Shortstops in the Hall of Fame, fifty favorite hits; bands at Woodstock, works by Bach and Massenet. Borders of countries, names of Vishnu, vice presidents and secretaries of state in chronological order. Countries bordering China. Moons in the solar system, galaxies in the Milky Way. Names for groups of animals—a knot of frogs, an array of hedgehogs, a sedge of cranes, a party of jays, a murder of crows, a clowder of cats, a swarm of rats, a cover of coots, a muster of storks, a kettle of hawks, a building of rooks, a swarm of flies, a charm of magpies, a labor of moles, a pack of voles, a blessing of unicorns, an unkindness of ravens, quoth the Edgar Alan, never more, never less.

That list I read somewhere of tame versions of violent phrases that mean the same: kill two birds with one stone becomes get two for the price of one—ignoring the maiming inherent to capitalism's brutish game. There's more than one way to skin a cat becomes different ways to wear a hat. Shoot yourself in the foot becomes put yourself in a winless position. Blown out of the water becomes reduced to nothing, which seems far more atrocious, connoting death, the end of consciousness, leading to another list, the ways to breathe your last: bleeding out, slow or fast, guns or fist, starvation or disease, mosquitoes or fleas, in the hospital or at home in bed, overmedicated or underfed, some painful, some pain-free, some surrounded by family, some friendless, some seeking a divinity—all equally oppressing, equally dreaded, considering that nothing follows *reduced to nothing*, and nothing follows nothing into infinity, a kind of decomposing oxymoron, since nothing has no start or end. As absurd as posing the possibility of living dead, sketchy details, an everyday sale, jumbo shrimp, boneless ribs, an accurate estimate, a definite maybe, pretty bad, happy sad, a cold fire, an honest liar, an uncharted course, a peacekeeping force. Be all that you can be, which reminds me of famous ads. I'd like to teach the world to sing Joe Isuzu. Bo knows diddley about where's the beef? Mother, please, I'd rather you pay me now or pay me later. The Uncola is a spicy meatball that absolutely positively has to turn over a new leaf. Mikey will eat anything which takes a licking and keeps on ticking off the chair against the banner and over the backboard. Tastes great less filling memories glare at photographs of the Ford in your future illustrating a song by Fred Astaire that wears your hat the way you sip your tea, the memory of all that in Marlboro Country....

Or catalogue the ways Leon and I differed. He had thick black hair. I had curly brown. His face was square, mine was round. He was short and layered with muscles. I was tall and soft. He spoke in measured tones. I jabbered boisterously. He remembered every word he read. I remembered every word I heard. He would hide on the fire escape. I balked at the danger and stayed inside.

His take on how to hitch was much different from mine. I liked to make a beeline to where I was going as fast as I could, whereas he welcomed bouncing around on side trips and breaks. Everything was like that between us, even as kids. I was always early. He was always late. I ripped through dinner before anyone else and finished every ounce. He dawdled over his food and left half on his plate. I made moves in all games right away, as if I were pouncing on my opponent, while he always took his time and contemplated the board carefully, making sure every move was explored, be it chess, checkers, or cards. He even took his time shaking the dice despite my sassing, counting to ten in a glassy-eyed trance before throwing them to the board. A total disregard of time passing.

When an itinerant photographer came to our street in Brooklyn with horses and cowboy gear, I was the Ranger and he was the Desperado. He helped dad with home repairs. I helped Mom sear meat and knead dough. He always played Haman. I always played Mordechai. I was never sick. He got everything from impetigo to pink eye. He always asked how. I always asked why. He beat everyone in chess. I beat everyone in cards. I worked in offices. He worked in sick wards and shipyards. He worked with his hands. I worked with my mind. He loved living in the South. I loved the West. He went to four schools and never earned a degree. I had advanced degrees and scholarships. He was an anarchist. I was a socialist, until I became a fatalist, or what the French might call a "Je-m'en-foutiste." He stripped his life of things to exist in a minimalist state. I lived well as the only way to prepare for the final fate.

He died young. I persist in living.

One thing we shared: we both had a long list of female bedmates.

Lists of women I have known. Women I have screwed or wanted to screw or tried to screw and failed. Women I thought I could have screwed if I wanted to. Women I never wanted to nail—that list was very short.

Women I screwed, A to Z, starting with Bea, who picked me up outside Renton, headed only seven miles. But it was early in the trip, so I took what I thought would be a quick ride in her manual VW bug. I watched her skirt hem drift up her thigh as she tugged the stick and guided her leg from gas to clutch, her knee briefly touching mine at each shift.

"I don't usually stop for thumbers," she said, "But my karma does not come from what I do in any given now, but is the sum of all I have done and how much I redirect it to my lodestar, so please don't swat a fly in my car," which led to her disconnected thoughts on meditation, while I enjoyed the contemplation of a flirty small brown spot halfway up her thigh—temptation to touch—that would appear and disappear below the skirt as she worked the clutch.

She invited me to her place for tea. "I just have to tuck in my mom and daughter. But afterwards, we can have a little space," she said, her hand lightly gracing my knee.

While I sat on a threadbare sofa drooping at its knobby feet, watching a *Happy Days* repeat with her ten-year-old, Bea fork-fed mom stew from a saucepan. I tried not to look at the sight of the old, thin, shrunken woman, one skin-hanging-from-bone arm fanning the steam away, gravy dribbling at her chin. Everywhere I looked, I saw bits of rust and patinas of dust, rimming the ceiling fan, on the windowsills, the green metal chairs, a metal hope chest, a shimmer of musty gray on the sofa pillows and armrests. Dust always reminds me of the rampant disorder of the universe, the grim settling down of all things. I wanted to skim a damp cloth over all the furniture and detail the room with a vacuum cleaner. My nose picked up the stale, peculiar odor of pine spray on a trashcan that hadn't been emptied for days. The girl drank a melting ice cream sundae from a green clamshell dish, slowly, one small spoonful at a time, her widespread eyes mooning the screen. I closed my eyes and listened to the TV scream out *Laverne and Shirley*. The frantic deadpan pranks of Lenny and Squiggy and the cranky responsa of the laugh track sank into a steadily spreading metallic white noise burling through blankness. Blankness turned to blankness turned to more blankness turned to....

I'm startled from sleep by a weight that sinks the sofa even farther towards the pinewood floor. Bea is sitting so close to me that the antiquated cushions wedge our thighs together. She hands me a coffee mug full of white wine. We clink the mugs together, but don't drink. Not a sip to our lips, for I immediately seek and fill her open mouth with my tongue.

She briefly pulls away, sighs a high-string cough, and tries to justify this casual lay: "I know I don't have to say it, but I don't pick up guys every day. I don't do it much, but it's here and now, and I've abstained so long that I don't care. I know it's not wrong as long as my atman is the happiness we share."

She isn't a beauty, but I want to feel her pressed against me, stripped naked, long-legged, small-breasted, wide-hipped, sleek maidenhair, soft and sloppy-friendly everywhere, more sensual than a beautiful woman because she seems more real, the uniqueness of her imperfections more attractive than perfection could be.

"After I put my mother to bed, I quickly tracked my daily chart and it said that I should share my heart today. Follow me," to a narrow bed in blackness, where we take that long warm swim together, naked backstroke to naked front stroke, wave after shimmering wave, limbs entangled, feeling her craving gather like rain over trees, slowly threshing, meshing, grunting, shunting, clinging, swinging, climbing, chiming, flowing, slowing. In the easy, quiet glow of our afterwards she squeezes my fingers into the burning flesh above her knees.

I hear a gentle snore, a sleeping witness to our interlude. Her daughter. I feel my face burst apart, then flame, and I'm smothered in shame. What if she woke from a bad dream and saw me nude, pumping away on top of her screaming mother?

I silently gather my clothes and dress, scrawl down Bea's number, but never call. A few weeks later, she picks me up again on a hitch around town. This time she takes me to an unlit street where we crawl against each other in the driver's seat.

Decades later, Bea drinks iced tea from a can on her break at a bake sale outside Walmart, which she coordinates for what she calls the WAC-WAC-EM-PEA, the Washington State Concerned Women for America's Chastity 'til Marriage Project. "We must protect our daughters and granddaughters. We must make sure they're taught it's smart to wait, praise the Lord," she pontificates, her deeply lined eyes and lips glowing a fleshy grayish sex appeal as she looks up from the table lined with brochures and petitions, a fishbowl for contributions. "They must reject Satan and not get caught in a shoddy, heartbroken mesh of lust. They need to know that you reap what you sow." Bea takes a slow, lazy look at the overcast sky while she sips her tea, a tiny bump poking up and down lightly underneath the creased, freckle-flecked flesh of her curving, stretched-out neck, inadvertently evoking an ad for Coke.

"You're part of my life before I found Jesus," she says, "and I pray you find him, too." I don't tell her that my god of the moment is my memory of stroking her naked body.

She leads a group of girls and women in cheeping a light-rock version of a psalm. I like this well-scrubbed sheep and her calm conviction much less than the flighty vixen she used to be. What made her change her song? What made her go from having one-night stands to believing that premarital sex was wrong? Was it a sudden revelation? Or the crowd she fell in with? The death of her mother? Or something other?

When I ask about her daughter, Bea nervously twirls a curl of her silver hair and says she's a sordid sinner who slaughtered her unborn child; she prays for both of them every day. "Hate the sin, but love the sinner," she says with the grinning self-satisfaction of all those assured of what they're saying.

"What is she doing?"

"Don't know. I lost track of her years ago, praise the Lord."

"I bet you could get her address and phone number on the Internet."

"Maybe I could and maybe I should, but I don't regret a thing. She still sees me as the slave to sin I used to be, and that's not on me. She could never get used to the saved me."

I think of my own daughter, Maya, off at graduate school in Boston, shacked up with a PhD candidate she intends to marry next year. Like everything about my current life, pristinely calculated to follow the rules. Nothing scary. I don't know jack about her sex life. My tack was always to leave it to my wife, who put her on the pill when she was sixteen to regulate her monthly flow. The first week of high school, she went to a Friday night sleepover with some new friends. She showed up at the door past midnight looking flustered, saying they were hyperventilating in paper bags and she didn't want to do it. I figured it was grass, something else we never discussed. She went out in mixed groups from time to time, trooping to the mall to see a superhero flick or a rom-com, but she never had a one-couple date in high school to my knowledge. She didn't go to the prom, but had a steady boyfriend after three weeks of college.

Bea, Bea, Bea, one of an alphabet of former loves. Sex is its own highway, with many rest stops and gift shops, battlefields and lookouts, sidetracks and roundabouts, momentary thrills that can sidetrack you for a few days, or a few years. And I got sidetracked a lot once I outgrew my teenaged doubts. I lived my youth completely in the golden age of sex without consequence, those fifteen or twenty sensual years after the spread of birth control pills and before AIDS. A lot of women were willing to sleep with me. I didn't have to extend much of an effort to persuade or keep them. If truth be told, I did worse with the ones whom I wooed ardently. My father would have been immensely proud of me. Also, his father, who bought me a prostitute on one of my trips to L.A. He drove me to her apartment in West Hollywood and waited while I took care of business. Afterwards he made me describe every detail, no condensing. As I painted the dreary picture of a quickie for money, he commenced to jab his cane back and forth through the air rhythmically. When I told him that she said I was large but made it sound like a lie, he cried out, as if he had discovered incontrovertible evidence that proved a crackpot theory, "All women are whores," a dreary, senseless statement I had also heard my father make many times before. That woman was a harlot, yes, but most women are no different from most men, creatures of habit, pretense, flesh, and fate. My grandfather and father shared a view of relationships between men and women that was offensive, old-fashioned tommyrot. I knew it back then, too, but I nevertheless still got a thrill to think they would be proud to know my how-many was a lot.

The missed opportunities: a list of women I think of more than those who slept with me. The ones I only finger-fucked or tongued and never stuck it in, or lost my nerve because I was young and inept, too awe-swept by her sophistication, or thought it was getting late, or she was too unkempt, involved with someone else, had somewhere else to go, or couldn't wait the appropriate number of dates. The ones I didn't realize were coming on to me until it was too late, a friend's mother, a next-door grass widow whose husband was stationed at Torii in Japan, the older nurse I tutored as a sophomore, the director of HR who told me that her hubby was nothing more than a roommate since she had their second daughter fourteen years before.

Or the sisters who picked me up in Reno one lazy August day, Deanne and Emma, two bony freckled-faced red-heads in cutoff jeans and scant paisley bathing-suit tops, in their early twenties or late teens, maybe younger. As Dee drove, they sang light rock songs in harmony, slanting their bouncing heads at me with bright, enchanting smiles. They were only going twenty miles, but it was late in the day, and they offered me a place to stay for the night in their farmhouse down a houseless dirt road.

Dee baked a batch of cookies and cornbread from scratch. With flips of her wrist, she poured the ingredients into the bowl without measuring, like a divinely twisted inventor, just like my mother used to do with most of her treasured recipes. While I rolled some jays, Em lined up patchouli-and-bay-leaf scented candles on the floor around the living room and poured glasses of a bad jug wine.

Our bodies made a triangle sitting on the Oriental rug with a plate of sweets in the middle, illuminated by the faintly perfumed candlelight. Dee fiddled with a mini-harp, plucking out strange but graceful peals, while Em painted their faces with fluorescent paint, then mine. Dee read my palms and declared me lucky in love; then Em read my cards, dealing me two queens and an ace.

The candles burned down to night. In the flickering shadows of al-most-spent wax, the girls kissed each other on the mouth and then took turns placing on my lips smacks as light as a kite in empty space. Em gripped one of my hands, Dee the other, and they tipped me towards them, spread my fingers, brushed them like a dusting rag against each other's blushing cheek, her lips, her nose, her closed eyes, the peak of her smallish breasts, her flamingo legs, sleek thighs.

The sound of a light truck pulling into the driveway—their parents, re-turned early from a weekend trip. They snuck me down to the basement. I stole through an open window, slipped on the ledge, ripped my shirtsleeve on a nail protruding from a pole, and fell on my face in the side hedges. My side hurt a little as I walked a few miles in complete darkness down a dirt road until I hit some concrete, and waited half the night for a ride.

I kept their names and address in a small notebook that I found under a load of papers in the attic. They still live off the same dusty road, except now it's paved and fully developed with oversized ticky-tacky haciendas and chalets, outside the same Nevada town. They have matching split-level Mc-Mansions that face each other at the cul-de-sac. I meet them at a nearby Dave & Buster's.

"We had fun with a lot of weird guys in those days...." confesses Em, glancing to the ground with a sigh of regret.

"... so for heaven's sake, we don't forget the normal ones like you," Dee completes the sentence with the same conditional expression.

Conventional describes these former wild children, living in traditional two-parent families in a Reno suburb, with matching SUVs, hair styled the same way, teased and slightly frosted, middle-aged fat stockpiled across their bones the same way, the same small triangle tat embossed above the right ankle. They're both stay-at-home moms with smartphones full of videos: overweight kids in snowbanks or fishing off piers. Overweight hubbies hoisting beers, bent over tees, sucking on cigars. Em and Dee playing guitars, both with beefy flanks and pasty, tumid eyes, puffy knees, gently jiggling flesh layered on waist and thighs. But they take their frailties good-naturedly, their physical condition as a kind of hobby.

"Everyone agrees that it's hard after three kids...." Dee starts the sentence and digs into a salad of kohlrabi, lettuce, ham, and cheese, covered in a thick tawny goop.

"... and we try and try but it's easy to cheat," Em completes it, while scooping scrawny carrot sticks in a whitish soup. "Tried the Atkins, but that meant no sweets," she says, licking her fork clean of salad dressing.

"We made it two days into the cabbage soup diet, which tasted like gasoline and gave us gastric distress," continues Dee.

They banter back and forth, listing what undermined every diet through the years, each completing the other's sentences. The one not talking shakes her head from side to side and lets go robust, high-pitched bleats and defensive sighs, as if a comic dealing one liners: "We didn't mind eating grapefruit before each meal...."

"The raw food diet—fine ..."

"... until our steaks started bleeding ..."

"... besides, feeding on uncooked veggies day after day gets to be pretty boring."

"We lost twenty pounds each on Slim-fast shakes ..."

"... but gained it right back gorging on sweets." Em fakes a retch, then starts to decimate her cheesecake.

They are as enthusiastic about regaling me with the details of their quixotic efforts to lose weight as they are about engulfing the food on their plate. "The macrobiotic diet was best for us, twenty-five pounds off our butts in three months eating beans and greens and nuts ..."

"... the only drawback was all those beans and greens and nuts."

"Too many pills with Hydroxycut ..."

"The Miami diet left us ... you know ..."

"... distressed ... the willies...."

"Weight Watchers worked great ..."

"... eighty pounds between the two of us until we stopped keeping points ..."

"... and went hog wild at the buffet joints during two weeks in Vegas."

"I'd rather eat than gamble any day."

"We're reconciled to never being sleek again ..."

"... but it's okay."

Or the fair-skinned, big-breasted blonde dream, Ceecee, another woman I never pinned, my partner on the high school debate team in Chicago. I woke up very late one Saturday after my first date with her. My father pestered me until I admitted with a broad grin that I had pressed against her breasts and thighs, both of us bare-chested in underwear, half the night on the floor right there in her living room, while her truck driver father snored in an armchair, shit-faced drunk from two six-packs, the empties on the floor. My father sneered a joy-sucking chagrin, swaggered in place, took a drag of his cigarette, and twitted me, "Did you fuck her? I bet you never tried," as if it were a crime not to have tagged her, which I had not, being sixteen and still perplexed by the social mechanics of sex.

He took graph paper and drew scaled representations to show me how and where to stimulate various states of sexual excitation. "The trick is to escalate but not to let her orgasm until after you get inside and are riding her with your dick. So she knows she's been nailed," he declared, between wails of overbearing laughter. His pornographic playbook words excited me, but repelled me, too, an inner subduction telling me a father shouldn't preach to his son to casually sleep with women, or teach him the details of a physical seduction. He made sure he and Leon were elsewhere on the early May afternoon I invited Ceecee over to have lunch and prepare our speeches. He even helped me gussy up the house spic-and-span, something that I usually did myself for the three of us.

The day came, and I heard the doorbell pulsate. We never ate, but started kissing without fanfare as soon as I closed the door. Soon we had all our clothes off, and I was touching her maidenhair, exactly as my father had said I should. With one hand still down there, I used the other awkwardly to tear open a plastic package and roll a condom over my twitching wood. I lifted my body from my side and over her body, which was moving in slight ploughshare rhythms and drenched in perspiration. I was about to penetrate when I saw an enormous image of my father standing over us, blaring in a grating, baiting tone, "That's my son! That's my son!" as he had done once or twice at Leon's wrestling matches. I gripped my dick and realized in despair that I had lost my bone. I slipped a finger back inside her glossy, waiting snatch, and kissed her mouth. But I didn't care any longer. I stopped kissing her, went to the bathroom, and latched the door to masturbate.

Another woulda-coulda-shoulda: El's best friend Gigi, the night that El walked out in anger over the clothes I chose. I sat on a dining room chair, exhausted from the verbal blows, staring into space. Gigi dropped to her knees in a praying pose in front me. She started to squeeze my knees in a mothering, consoling fashion, leaning her body over with her head high to let me snoop down her deep-scooped top and see the perimeter of her brown areolae. She gazed up at me with compassionate eyes and asked what would please me. I bolted back in my chair like a spooked colt and moved my knees to the side to remove her hands. I didn't want them on me. Threesomes with birdies El found were grand, but her best friend by myself seemed too much like a spiteful betrayal to me, especially since Gigi had already taken one man away from El a few years earlier. Weeks later, El accused me several times of sleeping with "the Jezebel." I faced the fact that El had probably planned to attack me that night to maneuver Gigi and me into the same space alone. She was testing me, or obsessed with replaying the climax of one of her favorite roles—Bette Davis replaced by the two-faced Anne Baxter.

Or the daughter of an Italian attaché who was a student in a class I taught in graduate school. Knee-to-knee we sat upon a wooden bench, reading Keats's dream of Canto Five, cool breeze lilting, high grass shuddering, trees alive with birds. Hands clenched, we slowly muttered aloud the words of Keats, who read of Paolo and Francesca who read of Guinevere and Lancelot, who read of other lovers now forgotten. We turned the page. Our fingers brushed, locked, lingered. Her cheeks flamed, her flushed breasts began to swell. My shoulders bent and quivered. The book fell. Nothing further happened.

Or the frumpish girl who picked me up outside Oakland. She spoke in drawn-out sluggish words that seemed to disconnect from sentences as if she had a stroke. She leered and purred, "You take me away and lay me." Seized by a fear that I would be taking advantage of a person with retardation, the term I had learned a few years before that was then the de rigueur phrase in the corporate conurbation. I couldn't do it. My cousin Pete teased me about it. He disdainfully said that I always did the right thing, and I felt a confused shame because I knew it wasn't true. Sometimes in the middle of a one-night fling, in the sack with a boozed woman, during or afterwards on my back with my hand rested above her breast, I accused myself of doing something wrong because I didn't love her. It was wrong when I quit my job to cruise through life with El for four years. Certainly I did the wrong thing when I said I wanted to move back to New York and live with Momma's strife. Of course, I'm conflating two kinds of right and wrong—the ethical right and wrong of sexual activity and the practical right and wrong of deciding where to live or whether to desert a career. *Wrong* as in perverted versus *wrong* as in brainless. Of course, May would assert that there is no difference between these two strains of right and wrong and explain that the ethical should be the practical, and the wrong ethical and the wrong practical come with the same result: someone gets hurt.

Better slow down. Up ahead, a truck has spilled a pile of dirt.

In a bar in North Hollywood I meet Guy LaGuy, the guy who blabbed all the way from Ojai to Marina del Rey about the women in his life, past and present, conquests all. He bagged lovers everywhere possible, in a cab, against a concrete slab, in a dorm, under a tree in a rainstorm, against a chest of drawers, under a swinging sailing mast, in a leg cast behind the reception desk in a rehab center, bent over a kitchen table, underneath a sable coat, on the front seat of a beetle, in a meat locker, in a field of wheat, in an empty subway car, in the bathroom at a bar, underneath an on-ramp, in a military camp, against a street lamp, in the Roman Colosseum, behind the stage in a college auditorium.

As Guy told it, he was always juggling two or more, one steady dish, one a side delight, his best friend's wife, his doctor's assistant when he had the flu, a waitress he knew, his neighbor's aunt, his aunt's neighbor, a divorce lawyer, a gang sawyer, the girlfriend of a jerk, someone at work, a former soap opera star, the woman who sold him his car.

For all of them he had wonderfully concrete descriptions, always in the second person—eyes that were twin islands in twin pools of clear, fresh water; breasts that bud firmly in your palm like rose boutonnieres; attentively soothing eyes of a deer greeting the dawn; the voluptuous spread of thighs across the chair when she took a seat next to you; the split of buttery buttocks when she walked naked away from you; ambrosia as if it were molasses when she talked to you; swaying like an ocean breeze on the bed; a sublime silhouette of red freckles across her shoulders; the musette sigh when you kissed her right below her neck; the savory slimy tongue that blossomed in your mouth like a mint pastille, flower-like, a blur of moldering flavor; breasts that floated beneath the touch; her steely whispered *Yes!* as she gripped your back; the clipping whoosh when you worked the zipper of her sleeveless black dress; a pussy with a cat's-paw feel, steaming like rice, a vise-like grip.

Now in her late sixties, Guy is Gail. She says she doesn't recall me, but wants to meet anyone remembering her from a single hitch years before her switch.

Her pale pink dress matches her lipstick tone, a foxtail wrap hung leisurely at her shoulders like a cowl. She's heavily rouged to suggest high cheekbones, a grandma on the prowl exuding a desperate sex appeal. When she walks, her slow and slightly owlish gait reveals she's still new to high heels. I tell her that she regaled me back then with her, or his, conquest tales, and she exhales a smothered squeal of delight.

"I'm sure I'm not the first to ask you why you transitioned." I fail at being tactful.

"Almost since I was born, I wanted to do girls' things. Wear dresses. Adorn myself with rings and pearls. Play with dolls. Peruse catalogues from Bloomingdales. My parents took me to a shrink who said I had a mild neurosis and browbeat me into thinking I was male. But I always felt choked up inside, like I wasn't really me. That's probably why I ran around and was always losing my temper with the kids. Why I abused my body with coke and booze. Failed at two marriages, and the third one was flailing in the wind. My relationship with my five kids was blistered—they didn't really trust my word, probably because I persisted in lying about the real me. It was only after I turned sixty that I realized that, despite my external adherence to appearance, I was female. And there was nothing to stop me from being myself. Two of my children reflexively rejected me, but the others respect my decision. And, strange as it seems, I'm friendly with my exes. I go shopping with them."

When I remind her that her conquest stories had excruciating detail, she emits another smothered laugh. "Although I'm woman now and I like being with men, I still like women. That part of me never changed. But male or female, sister, brother, if you relax and forget your fears, whatever it is, whoever it is, one sex is as good as another."

"It's no business of mine, I know, so don't be afraid to say so. Do you have more of a ken for women or men?"

"Most of my relationships have been with other trans, because I don't conceal my state from anyone and many cis-gendered hate it."

"I have to admit, it would be hard for me to kiss a woman if I knew she used to be a man."

"Or maybe you should say that it wouldn't be hard. I bet you've danced the horizontal Conga with a transgender woman at least once and you didn't even know it."

"Not knowing, it doesn't matter, because they were all women to me," I say in my defense.

"And they were women," Gail's fist triumphantly beats the bar with mannish resolve. "There's always slight-of-hand pretense when love is involved.

Love has evolved into a frightening game of hide and seek. You hide yourself to seek the other person or seek yourself in the other person hiding from you. In all this hiding and seeking, this colliding and peaking, this framing and concealing, this claiming and revealing, the distinctions between straight and queer and male and female disappear. People always say that God is love, but for me there is only the grace of sweet love—carnal and complete," Gail entreats thunderously, and it makes me think of El, the one and only Elaine Pallase, my four-year blunder. Deceitful El, the blowsy widow-spider singer. Wondrous El, who repeatedly fetched me other women and liked to watch me with them. El and her plundering, street-sharp, el-shaped mind and her smoke-and-booze-emboldened luscious mezzo teasing: "By the light of the Silvery Jules, he has the tools, and so he rules."

El, her isomorphic gardens resting side by side, the oval ponds, their floating olive islands riding waves, thick-fitted, taro-bloated grove within each island's orbit, wooded center centered black within the gray green of impetuous high grass swing and in the further darkened coppice sings an inflection past the one then past the other mirror image, pond and island gently mocking past perfection perfect in her iridescent imperfection. Across a pongee desert waving dusky husks, I check her shantung landscape, hear a call to float above the golden smoothly forward freckling journey over, through, along the breath-slowing Cuban sand at areola's summit, carnal crusts and bands of ground that sail by brush, by clasp, by plush ambit clinging to the flesh as air to Earth, as onrushing flow towards vale. Now disembarking into her corkscrew verdure, corms and tubers curve and twine as grappling lovers, wrapping wrestlers, dark in dark in eyeless search of creeping strands of midnight tendrils, as stark moonlight opens, twisted shadows trip and lurch in dark, in plunge in frenzied furze in repeated heightened being, gripping branches dripping, fallen rain meeting vines so thick with leaves I want to hide forever in the tangled heat.

The road purrs the beguiling deep-sleep susurration that El used to make. It makes me think of those who came before and after me. I see piles and rafters of her other lovers, one after another. And I see El's face slowly disintegrate into joy, as each man and boy smothers her body and penetrates. I try to find differences in her smile with me, to locate some nuance to tell me her yen for me had no resemblance to what happened with other men.

She told me it was different our first time together.

After talking through the night, we made love, repeatedly, in the glow of early morning sunlight through the window grate, to the syncopated beats of *Astral Weeks* and Bonnie Raitt, on the threadbare antique carpet of my rented bungalow that she would move into one week later with her knobby teak and rattan furniture I would grow to hate. The plan: she would support us on her widow's pension, so I could quit my paper-pushing job.

After that first time, naked on the floor beside me, her toes cavorting with mine, she told me she had eighty men before me and maybe ten women.

"Some were mercy lays." Between tokes and long exhalations, she spoke in a flat voice, a bit jaded, as if taking inventory of faded goods. "A truck driver on the road to get out of the rain. The rock group trains I pulled at seventeen—the Rascals, Paul Revere and the Raiders—when I was in the groupie scene. A cop or two. My husband Virgil's friend when all of us got stoned. Virgil's dad, when he dropped me home after Virgil's funeral and I didn't want to be alone. The bass player I lived with for a year. A disastrous time with a friend who didn't want to admit he was queer. With fellow actors to help create a role. Did a glory hole—one time only! A couple of times I did porn when I was broke. I liked having two guys at once, but not the third guy—the director—barking in my ear. A couple of times as revenge against an old flame. Plus an average number of nameless one-night stands, maybe two or three a year. But I never came with anyone until tonight with you, and I hate the control that gives you over me."

At the time I thought it was something she told to everyone.

I still do.

Her rollcall of lovers left me feeling empty, isolated, as if she had played me. But the feeling soon passed, as I considered how much I desired her, on a physical level, our intermeshing bodies, flesh reveling flesh, defrayed and disheveled. It wasn't that El was the best in bed. As my father was inspired to say with a lechery-infested, almost molesting sneer, whenever he saw a desirable woman nearby, "There are only three kinds: good, better, and best." El was best, but I've had several bests, including May, who excels at everything she does.

But sleeping with El was like sleeping with dozens of women, because, once undressed, I never knew what would transpire, as she could drastically change herself while remaining herself. Sometimes she was a testy, selfish ice princess slowly melting into molten lust, sometimes the slick older woman taking charge. She could play the elfish sex kitten strumming a guitar, the picky sybarite in a Jaguar, the harried, nest-building housewife with just enough time for a quickie, the elegant courtesan obsessed with style granting gifts to her favorite, the perky gymnast, the herky-jerky mannish tennis star, the barfly lush, the ditzy waif grateful for a place to sleep, the mousy, repressed secretary whose still but smoldering waters run deep, the plush, languorously-creeping Southern belle, the transgressed lover desperately fucking out her anger in a cheap motel. It wasn't that she would imitate a movie role or an actress—no phantom Marilyn Monroe or June Allison, at least not in bed—but that she would become the fiction, quell and calibrate the characteristics to fit her own tessitura of movement, gesture, voice, and diction. It was the closest I will ever come to having a harem.

Dogleg to the left when the highway parts.

Take away the rap and rumble of the road, and this is how Mozart flows from a trebly radio over the tapping sound of a bedroom curtain's early morning flapping. Scraps of light and breeze tumble through the window. The naked woman sleeping by your side is beautiful. She snores an easy sotto voce, teasing like a lapped cat purring its delight. You feel her heat when you lightly pet her scented shoulder, as it rises and falls underneath a fraying sheet resembling gray and tightly rippled clouds sighted from above, from a fleeting jet transporting the two of you away.

I wonder how my past would look to me if that first time had been the last. The torrid affair ends, and I never see her again, instead of the whipsaw between tears and joy that I accepted for four years. Four years during which she slept with other men, once a year or so, and let me know about it, which would send me into fits of soul-destroying jealousy, gave me time to heal, then did it again to toy with me, seal in me a mental pain that hurt just as badly as slowly peeling skin with a knife, as badly as the loss of a wife, torture on the rack, or being nailed to a cross. Slowly, perversely, she flayed me with her tales of what she did, whom she did it with and why, professions of love for me tossed in, which made it worse. I would make the pain I felt a thing apart from me and passively observe it, like a scientist immersed in natural phenomena—an eclipse, a planetary ring, the curve of the universe. I would sometimes want to touch my pain, gingerly, the way you rip a scab to see if it still hurts—a blazing stab that rends your organs into dirt. So you leave it alone, and in time it mends.

We would return to normal, a constant carnal *Sturm und Drang,* defined by her love of melodrama. She would jaw at me about my many flaws, my taste in clothes, my swinging-instead-of-hanging arms when dancing, that I pranced on the balls of my feet instead of walking, that I talked down to her, that I wouldn't eat her coleslaw, because I gnawed on chicken bones, because I wouldn't leave her alone, because I kept ignoring her, because my comments bored her, her misinterpretation of my off-hand remark, anything to spark a confrontation.

I usually let her harangue blow over me when first heard, like a hot but harmless breeze, which would piss her off. Sometimes I would appeal to the logic of the situation, freeze in verbal snapshots what happened and what did not, reveal the ambiguities, which would not appease her but make her squeal that I was dealing with the facts and not her feelings. She attacked again, reeling me with cruel but clever deliveries, as if it were a verbal hotrod duel, two word cars playing chicken with the road, the veins in my forehead swelling, hurting, a molten-lava anger jelling, until I finally burst into yelling, out of control, a brazing jihad boom that sounded so hard I didn't have to raise my fists, at which point she pushed me to the bed or carpet, and fucked me with the fast-burning fury of her beautiful body. She fucked my skin, my bones, my arms, my knees, my mind, my future and my past, my first and last, my insides and outsides, my yang and yin and yen, my beginning and my end, my hide and my seek, my abyss and my peak, my weakness and my might, my day and my night. Afterwards, she would fall asleep at my side, wake to first light, start another fight, leave and return hours later with an unknown woman for us to share.

Change lanes and bear to the right.

Just keep driving, alone with cares and inner riving, alone with breathing, alone with ascending and descending sun-glared asphalt bends, alone with my shadowed wending, contemplating the part of love that isn't sex winnowed from the music of the road: *Touch me, riders of the storm, once upon a time when you were ramblin' gamblin', can't you see to be that spoon, that spoonful, that sailin' takes me away to where I'm important to me, that you know you are swimming in a fish bowl year after year, running around my little runaway runaround, Susie Q sitting on the dock of the boys of summer, revved up like a deuce, another night moves working on an awkward stop in the name of better to burn than to fade into summer breeze, makes me feel like something's happening here.*

Keith Moore, industrial engineer, wouldn't go near the speed limit, and never passed a car, no matter how slow it was moving. He told me about his job approving vendors for a dozen plants that manufactured brakes, but mostly he talked about the trips he wanted to take—Grand Canyon, the banyan groves in Florida, the Cascades, the Everglades, the Poconos, the Alamo, the Pueblo villages, bison hunting on the Crow reservation, Niagara Falls, The Tall Ships, the Statue of Liberty, Awatovi, Grace Lake, the Space Needle, Bunker Hill, Boot Mills—he had a long list of reasons to pack his suitcase. It was hard for him to get away, though, the pace at work was so acute.

Now I see him at a spacious Boise big box store at his job selling work boots for the past fifteen years, ever since his company replaced him with computer software. When they laid him off, the company helped him get a loan to pursue a degree in computer technology, but he's never been able to get a job, not even an interview.

Keith is another man of my generation gone obese, wiggling, waddling, arms traced with skinfolds, a tired stupor on his bloated face and gills, lumbering slowly as if climbing uphill. Keith now bears three hundred pounds or more, and his body takes the shape of an enormous meatball. He wheezes when he talks, bitterly, of being left behind, his paycheck shamefully small, his life wrecked by global forces. Now a xenophobe, he blames his problems on immigrants, snarling his discourse with quotes from Sean Hannity and Tucker Carlson.

Never married, Keith lives with his mother. He chooses to spend his free time watching sports and Fox News, his girth buried in the cushions and folds of a threadbare sofa in the front room of a small bungalow with the same tan aluminum siding across the façade and rock garden in the front yard as every other house on the block, a pot-head on a potholed street in some crumbling suburb, shunting from game to game, alone or with a dog at his feet, in his jammies, toking away, cramming on Diet Coke and munching on tortilla chips between his jagged rants to the gigantic screen. Day and night, one hand flips from football game to football game, while the other keeps a continuous zigzag motion from a big bowl teeming with chips, which he drags through a small bowl heaped with a white sauce, then snags in his steaming mouth, one chip at a time, bag after bag after bag.

Follow the signs for the interstate.

Out to El Paso to see Roy Shane, guy with a sheathed bowie knife I picked up in the rain just outside the Arizona Penitentiary the one time I drove across the country on my own wheels, after I ditched El in Texas and hitched back to SF and rented a car.

Roy was a wiry, athletic kid with a pockmarked face—rough and scary-looking, fiery red hair, sockless in dirty flip-flops, sickled nose, and pork-chop sideburns. A trace of needle drops embossed his arms, thick with hairy muscles and sporting large tattoos of crossing anchors. He tossed his cigarette butt in the weeds and hopped in the car.

"Don't want to mislead you, man," he immediately says, "so don't have a fit. I just got out of the pen. But my bad man days are over, man. Served my time, did half a dime, so there's no point to be pissed or to start trippin' 'bout me ripping you off, man. I don't do that shit no more since I found my calling."

He opens a large notebook and turns the pages to show me. As I drive the Interstate, I give speedy glances down at his sketchpad to placate him. You couldn't conflate with high art the biker glyphs that filled his dog-eared pages—dragons in cages; skeletons; grizzly bear heads; sinewy, long-haired women recumbent in bed; vipers with fangs; preening mustangs; wolverine eyeballs rolling across fields; stylized swastika shields, serpentine instead of straight or with lines extended into shooting star horizons; paunchy but muscular long-haired men on Harleys wielding rocket launchers, ready to attack a gulp of yielding, raunchy babes, stacked and spread-eagle, all inked in classic pulp style rendered in red or black.

"I found I got the gift, man," he said without guile. "Like I excel at drawing. In the pen I had the best style. I did lots of swell stuff, man. Headed to Houston to sell it."

I didn't want to tell him he was a talentless fool, as far as I was concerned. "Did you think about going to art school?" I suggest.

"No, I'm good right now, man. Right now. In the slammer I started a correspondence course. But tests are, like, the worst. The damn things threaten me. But I'm blessed with talent. I kept working on it, man, and it kept getting better. I got stacks of notebooks, just like this one."

"Do you have any contacts who can help you find prospects?"

"Not yet, but I expect to sell my designs to tattoo artists, man, and silk screeners, man, for tee shirts or posters. Dudes in the biker scene, man. Maybe comic books and biker magazines."

"Lots of competition," I say, and as evidence tell him of the swell of mature and educated designers whose work I saw when I managed production of brochures for the insurance company before I met El. But I couldn't quell his confidence.

"I had a dream in the pen, man, and it seemed like real life. There was a party at a swimming pool, man, in the middle of the woods, and all this cool cunt was yelling and squealing, like they was at a concert. Suddenly they peeled off their tops and underneath they all wore the same little bitty T-shirt with my art on the front. It was a sign that I can sell my designs. I know it's prime, man, 'cause I see shit like this in bikers' mags all the time."

I emit a fast, noncommittal grunt.

I don't ask about his former career aspirations when I find Ron decades later at the rear of a parched-and-potholed parking lot near the Greyhound station in El Paso, sitting on a black metal folding chair in the sweltering, robber-fly-swarming sun, prune-faced, shot eyes and mouth harshly etched with hard-tack years. Flecks of unshaved gray stubble pelt his chin. He's added a roughhewn tattoo of a cross to one side of his neck. He's still thin in the chest, but sports an enormous gut. Resting outstretched near him is a grungy, slobbering mutt attached to a telephone pole by a chewed-up belt. Ron cups a smoking Camel butt and affectionately slaps the animal's mangy butt.

He says he still remembers me. "Like yesterday afternoon, man, 'cause you were the first soul I met when I got out of that black hole I ain't never going back to."

A tinny metal tune begins to shout from his shirt pocket. He peeks at his smartphone and tweaks out a message with his thumbs, then hawk-eyes the crumbling parking lot with sneaky intent and leans towards me. He lowers his voice, intoning nicotine-blotted hoarseness, "How you fixed? 'Cause if you need some jack, you could ride with us tonight. We're making a special delivery and we're short a hand. It ain't drugs, so it's all right, understand. It's wetbacks."

He coughs a long, delighted laugh that turns to smoker's hack. "There're four of us. We split fifty bucks a back, cash money, a pretty classy pay-off after splitting gas. We take about forty at a time. Ain't glamorous, but it's strong, clean work, man, once you get a taste for it."

Renewed heavy coughing makes him stand up and fold himself at the waist. The dog perks at the clamor, circles around the pole. and settles into his former mold.

"I thought you said you wanted to avoid the slammer at any price."

"Trust me, it's a riskless heist. We got friends on the inside who get a slice. Customs just waves us through. No chance of getting busted."

Roy looks at his smartphone again and bandies a trusting smile. "Anyway, we ain't been tracked down yet, not even a close shave, and we make two deliveries a week."

"Still, I think I'll pass. It's dangerous and it's illegal, and I'm fairly sure I think it's wrong."

"Wrong or right, they're coming in one way or another, man, and it's strong, steady work that puts meat in my beans and gravy on my grits. You change your mind, man, meet us right here in this spot just after midnight."

But an hour later I'm back in flight again, rolling along an unknown highway, thinking that the somnambulant years of the settled, upper-middle-class, middlebrow Jules are the ones I should try to track, instead of the wander years of youth. It's a fool's pursuit to plough so far back in time. Yet I persist in trying to connect those days to now. I insist on following an unsound method, rife with distortion. The only phenomena with which I'm dealing are two thinly cut contrasting slices of life, set apart at a distance trivial compared to ice ages, but a big deal to humans. One portion the breathing now, the other a remembered past, reduced to words and emotions that blast across decades of nonfeeling. So far, everyone I revisit reveals a course I didn't see before, a different river fed by unknown streams of time from unknown sources: a decline in hope, a focusing of desire, a diminishment of scope, the dousing of fire. A pot dealer becomes a legal pill pusher. A leftwing lawyer turns union-buster. A Jesus freak leads a capitalist life. Two roughhouse philistines get in touch with their inner strife. Many of the formerly thin grow portly. No daily splice of yesterday with tomorrow, routine repeated precisely again and again. She was that, and now she's this. He was this, and now he's that. Is he either/or? Are both then and now the real core, or neither?

And what about me? I journey like the mythic Buddhist mind ape wandering in his chariot of cloud, except my vehicle wheezes along sheets of asphalt and concrete, not above an ethereal breeze, shards of jade cutting through sky like knives through willow catkins covering grass and trees. The ape glissades on river ice propelled by breeze, while I escape in a human-made machine bellowing poison into the pristine.

When I review my own actions over my sixty-plus years, I discover nothing but discontinuities, as if I comprise a sprawl of curiosities and deformities all floating inside a black crystal ball, a different one called up in a visible band each time the globe is shaken and put on its stand. And until I left El, I had no control over which me would emerge at any moment from the quicksand riding around inside. The busybody butting into everyone's affairs. The grouch yelling venomously at cars that dared cut me off or picking a bone with people with unleashed dogs. The smooth quick-on-his-feet speaker. The foggy stoner. The wallflower feeling bleakly and obliquely oppressed standing in the midst of all the small groups that make up a noisy party. The hearty, attacking know-it-all boring others at a dinner table with a waterfall of facts. The weak wimp so afraid of the outside world that he pores over every step of the process of going to the store, considering all the possible impediments—trying to cross a wide and pothole-scarred boulevard, an hysterical parking lot argument over a shopping cart, interrupting two cashiers having a temperamental heart-to-heart—and what he might do to deal with each and every one of these hypotheticals. The pretending-to-be-evolved flirt who focuses his talk on the woman's interests and thoughts as a means to a whirlwind seduction. The highly disciplined inductive and deductive problem solver. The lazy slacker without the discipline to achieve his potential. The thick-skinned, confident expert who can spring into action and handle anything. The existential mediocrity who knows in his heart that he's essentially just a slick fraud, winging it with superficial knowledge and a few taut tricks. The favorite of mother, or so I thought. The less smart brother. Sometimes the me who emerged fit the situation, but sometimes it was a mismatch, leading to embarrassment, shame, guilt. Too angry, too wilted, too ardent, too bent, too insistent, too emotional, too devotional, too inconsistent, too curious, too acrimonious, too analytical, too metaphysical, too droll. Krishna, too, had many faces, and Shiva had many arms, yet I didn't feel like a god with multiple souls. I felt relentlessly out-of-control. Perhaps everyone feels like that to a certain degree. Perhaps our most heroic acts are getting through the day's caprice alive, still in one piece, the same person, the person we want to be.

Some people manage always to show a consistent face, and I imagine that below the glass in their internal crystal ball the one dominant persona is holding down the other frowning selves with a tight grip at all times, trying to drown them. But occasionally they slip out, like my brother's flat, regionless clip would slip from his leisurely Southern bray when he was excited about what he was saying.

Uncle Henry—he was one person who seemed never to change. Always calm, always analytical, always questioning but never critical, in an even, unperturbed modulation, never revealing a strange or deranged emotion, unequivocal and careful in his explanations, untainted by private griefs or beefs, always respectful of others' beliefs. When the extended family got together, he sat quietly, hardly noticed, while his brothers and sisters loudly argued or raucously laughed about what they had withstood and how they were seared by their hard, vagabond childhood. While they disputed whose turn it was to pay, he would noiselessly slide away from his seat, glide sneakily to the waiter, and give him his credit card.

But when it was just the two of us in their living room of French provincial furniture, listening to the jazz he was fond of—Benny Goodman, Duke Ellington, Charlie Christian, Chet Baker, Jim Hall—he would reveal political views that suggested a deep resistance to his car-and-mall-centered suburban existence. He would make fun of the dozens of upscale appliances his family would use, all purchased soon after Aunt Bridget read the product reviews: Polaroid instant cameras, time-saving microwave ovens, a coven of hand-held hair dryers, trash compactors, wireless phones that often crashed, Walkmans, name-brand VCRs, eight-tracks, Atari systems, flameless barbecues, the Simon memory game.

With a straight face, he would deliver gentle potshots that subverted this cornucopia of creature comforts, epithets that gained critical power the more I contemplated them: "I curate two sets of hairdryers given to me when my kids bought new ones with super watts," or "I thought about buying a lightly-driven gem of a demonstration model in perfect condition right off the lot, but that would mean Bridget would have to navigate the Valley in a used car," or "The problem with television is not that any of it is bad or evil or bizarre. It's all captivating, but there's just too much of it," or "Since California mandated forced water rationing, researchers now estimate it would only take the resources of eight-point-five Earths for the entire population of the world to live like we do." He was in favor of restoring high taxes on the wealthy to bring healthcare and education to the poor. His discourse easily referenced Epictetus, Aurelius, Gandhi, and King.

Every so often in our conversation, he raised a inger in the air to point out something particularly fine-honed in the music, like the halting start-and-stop piano solo in Benny Goodman's hopped-up version of "Honeysuckle Rose" live at Carnegie Hall or a Charlie Christian discordant riff. His jazz tastes froze stiffly in time where mine began, somewhere around bebop.

Once I compared him to Seneca, living in the lap of luxury while secretly aspiring to an ascetic life, and he said, "I doubt my children or wife could live without these things. Most people need material possessions as much as they do religion to give meaning to their days. Without something new to buy, they might go crazy"

From time to time during the calm-and-never-overcast decades since I left El and embalmed my past life, I sometimes regretted that I ceased knowing Henry. And now his one and only self has disappeared, submerged in the deep and slimy bog of Alzheimer's. He recognizes neither me nor his son Jeff, who brings me to the nursing home. He sits silently in an easy chair by his bed, looking fogged-over and frustrated, miming at life, occasionally flogging his hand in the air as if shooing something away, perhaps the music piping from the ceiling, easy-listening versions of the Rolling Stones. The sunshine coming through the window steals across the floor during the hour Jeff and I sit with him. Every once in a while, Henry groans and frowns, gets up and struggles to push his chair back into the sun's warm zone, and sits back down.

During the years I hitchhiked down to see Henry and his family, I saw his oldest son Jeff grow from a rude and cocky thirteen-year-old into a cool-on-a-barstool surfer dude whose low college grades precluded grad school. Soon after he graduated, Jeff offered to drive me back to the Bay Area. He said he'd pay for gas and keep us high, but we had to take the secluded, rough-hewn coastal route so that at the right times of day, maybe twice along the way he assured me, he could break out the board and try the surf. It was the first time we smoked together, the first time he was old enough. Once when Irv Opalin and I took Henry's kids to Malibu, I came back to our blankets soaking wet from a swim to find Irv and a fourteen-year-old Jeff beaming moonshiners' grins and smelling of a lid. I grew prudish and angry at Irv for toking with a kid.

"I want to test back-dooring barrel waves and there're a lot of barrels along the shore between Gaviota Beach and Tomales Point, down unpaved streets to where the crests reach fifteen feet." Jeff shouted to be heard over the highway's disjointed arpeggio roaring through rolled-down windows.

He went on, assuming I cared, or not caring I didn't, as after a couple of hits he was as impaired as I was. "In SoCal, I've ridden Zuma, Topanga, Hermosa, Point Loma, Diego, Redondo, Tamarack, Terramac, and Sunset Cliffs. I took the great San Miguel, almost lost my nerve, then skiffed and swerved through the barrel like a human caravel, then fell and thought I'd made my last farewell. I stayed a few days in Calafia in the Baja. The surf there is like a beautiful woman, peach-hair soft and curvy. But my dream, when I get enough bread, is to head to Australia, the surfer's preeminent paradise, make my bed on all the Aussie beaches, surf the whole effing continent."

By this time the pot had shredded both our mouths and minds. He started talking in grinding, tentative fragments—a disconnected exclaiming of place names and superlatives—and I mumbled that I didn't know them. We both went silent.

What a beguiling guy Jeff had grown into. He looked like his stylish Cajun mother, not his Hungarian Jewish dad—feathered auburn hair padding his ears, his toned face not too bronzed, the color of swans below a rising red dawn. He displayed a smart, athletic grace even while driving, using lissome tugs and darts of the hand to switch gears to out-race a truck or chug canned pop, like a jitterbug dancer or a high school shortstop, an unplanned, effortless movement called sprezzatura in a work of art.

A forceful sideways sway of the car as Jeff plays a turn startles me, and I realize he's talking again. "Money is the heart of everything, of course, and I want some. I'm not too dumb to realize that I'm not going to get it sitting on my bum inventing stuff like my dad. But what the hell, I bet I can sell pigweeds to farmers by playing to their needs. And I know I can act because I've had a half-dozen parts. Some guy high on blow ate my heart in 'Maniac.' I spent thirty seconds projecting torment in 'The Island of Dr. Moreau,' but my scene was cut. One of the last guys gutted in 'Alien Prey.' Three lines, then torn limb from limb in 'Curse of King Tut's Tomb.' But it's tough to find room to break through, even if you make a few contacts at the gym."

We hustled along a winding one-lane dirt road past an ancient rail bridge, down to a short deserted strand, more gray landslide pebble than pale streamlined sandbank, jutted into the water like a jigsaw piece on a blue shag rug. I sat barefoot in fleece jeans and windbreaker on a green blanket. My mind tanked thoughts and desires slow-motion into the sapphire tide. Jeff threw his board into the water, glided out almost to the horizon, caught a soaring wave, and leaned into its spire. As he rode towards shore, the water rose higher and higher above him like an unfurling flag, and curled around his form as if about to bag him, as if his sturdy body, legs spread, bent hard at knees, was a cameo pose borne in an enormous swirling liquid oval. The postcard version might have read, "Greetings from California."

He rode about six waves this way, then left the pirouetting water and staggered towards me, board in hand, shivering wet and looking haggard. I started to stand to go, but he said, "Let's just sit here a bit and watch the flow."

After some silence, I said, "This beautiful beach, these waves and their thousands of spiraling liquid spicules, this sky, it's all a trick of the eye. The waves, for example, aren't real. What we're seeing are billions upon billions of stormy water molecules, each invisible, pooling to create the form of a wave and bounding into each other to enunciate the excruciating sound."

"They're real all right—wet and cold and hard as rock when they bend your skin." His humid paraphrase of Hume—a wave at the shoreline, thin and spent. He turned away from the relentless ocean wrestle and looked to the seedy railroad trestle that bent around the sand, and hoarsely said, "And then it ends."

"And then it ends," I agreed.

"You know, I just got my college degree, just a bachelor with a bachelor's, not a PhD like my dad. But I got the embossed-and-silver-leafed certificate that's a launching pad for a professional career." Jeff now spoke in a caved-in voice that pined for something lost.

"My pal says that a degree, a short haircut, and a shave is all it takes to find a choice high-tech job, which I'm going to do after one more summer of bobbing waves. Companies south of Frisco are hiring a lot of slobs to sell big-assed computers and other electronic shit like connectors, switches, chips, wires, assemblies, monitors and power strips."

"Those are just words to me," I admit.

"No lie, me three. I don't have a clue about what this shit does. But I figure all I have to do is act like I belong, and that's easy. I can act. I can shoot the breeze. I just have to toot the corporate song and tease business jargon—that I'm teaching myself—into every part of speech. A verb, then a noun, sometimes with an adjective, and then a noun again, each word sounding techy. Check it out. It's almost an exact science. Enhance strategic synergies. Abstract compliance energies. Exploit stable cadencies. Advance preexisting contingencies. Convene adaptive market factors. I'm just pulling it out from a bag of corporate slang I saw in a mag at my chiropractor."

"You think you can pull it off by plucking a verb, an adjective, and a noun out of your hat and bet they like the sound of that?"

"With any luck. I think I have it down pat. Impede systemic rations. Orchestrate enterprise stations. Vet and benchmark flexible best-of-breed. One night, stoned on weed, I practiced that last one on my dad, and he gabbed for ten minutes about some heat activation tests he's running at his lab. Decarbonization of something or other ... fluctuation of this and that ... correlation of whatever … documentation of such and such … cybernation … commercialization…. Didn't get much of what he said, but I didn't care. It felt cool to be treated like a peer instead of his little lad. If I can fool *him*, I can teach myself to fool anyone. So what if my major was Speech? I'm going to call it Liberal Arts on my job applications."

He spoke with such determination back then that it didn't surprise me his game plan worked. Jeff lives on two acres in Crystal Cove, in a grove of palm and bougainvillea, a six-thousand-square-foot hacienda with a detached guesthouse, a tool shed as large as a two-car garage, and a pear-shaped pool embedded in an outsized patio. In the driveway sits an enormous Allegro RV that Jeff and his girlfriend commandeer for weekend trips. "It gets about three gallons to the mile," he brags, as he sips a Belgian craft beer.

After our visit with his father, we sit on canvasback lawn chairs in the shade by Jeff's pool, with his Persian girlfriend, twenty years younger, and raid an abundant spread of organic snacks—red fish and black cod sushi, honey-coated nuts, antibiotic-free cold cuts, sesame treats, blue tortilla chips, whole wheat hardtack crackers.

Jeff sports a tattoo that starts at his left wrist and continues up his arm in thick black twists onto his shoulder and part of his chest and back, an abstract effloresced track of concave curves and restless curlicues. Just looking at this extreme body mutilation gives me the blues. Maybe later on, I'll school him on why getting a tattoo is the sign of a slave. "My dad was a PhD and a top research engineer, and he maxed at maybe 250 per. Meanwhile, a lazy surfer dude like me, who still hits the waves most days, made maybe two mill last year boozing and losing golf matches to CEOs. That's fucked-up crazy," he says. His words distil the unfairness of a scientist earning less than a whistle-stop shill, but his voice reveals a delight that he has bested his pop. He retains a quaintly boyish charm and an athletic foppishness that overcome his cynicism and defuse his criticism.

"You let the client beat you, of course."

"Damn right, but what the hell! That's not the point."

"I know the point. I didn't do as well as you did, but I've scrimmaged on the field of business enough to understand that we dwell in the land of the buy and sell, and that intellectual courage is a disadvantage, unless you have the cash on hand to monetize or amortize someone else's new knowledge. It's the financier and the seller we anoint, not the inventor."

"In this country, we're nothing beyond what we own, beyond what we take," Jeff says. "It's not, I am what I do, but I am what I make—that's the conference-call-on-a-treadmill, sledge-hammer-in-a-velvet-glove guys pushing gold and diamond stones all the way up the hill each day like buttoned-down Sisyphuses—that's what they do. That's what they prize as good. They don't disguise it anymore, like they did back in my dad's day. The damn stone I shove is the sell, because what I do is sell. I am what I sell, and I sell what I am."

As jaded a tone as he takes, he still qualifies his words with a chit-chatty friendliness. "Is the survival of the fittest the rationale for the free market, or a counterfeit science created to justify it? Just because I have bought more, does that mean I am fitter than my father, with his taut wit, his systematic knowledge, and his great inventions?" His voice transmits the cheerful tension of a charismatic commander about to send his men to slaughter.

"That's why he's thinking about quitting. Aren't you, hon?" His girlfriend turns to him and rubs his knee.

"I lament not letting go every day. Yet that hasn't swayed me from going out into the real world and pretending I deserve it. Pretending that I really do believe that those who thrive deserve what they get."

"I think you underestimate yourself. You may not have a propensity for math like your dad, but you always know what to say to people to spark them. You have a genius in emotional intelligence." To myself, I wonder if the enormous body tattoo channels that mark of Cain, the mark of twenty-first century, post-industrial sin.

"That's what I always tell him," his girlfriend adds.

His smartphone vibrates and he grabs it, jumps from his chaise and relocates to the other end of the pool, where he paces, gabs, and stabs a finger at the phone. His girlfriend is telling me how they met, but I listen with half an ear, hearing instead the mournful lap of the glistening chlorinated water against white tiles. I try to conjure an image of Uncle Henry before he got sick, quietly making an acerbic, elliptical witticism at the expense of the claptrap of some pompous chap.

But instead I see my father, smirking what my mother called his shit-eating grin, an at-the-lips Chesterfield dangling below his chin.

Shimmering water baking under a dilating sun shouldn't make me think of my father, who hated swimming. My father—his life grated by cancer at fifty-six. My mother—a ghost, too, at forty-two, overdosing on nerve meds. My brother—at fifty-eight, falling or leaping from a roof, his head hitting the concrete sidewalk, shattering his brain and upper spine. All gone, their thoughts swept away, their lives cheated of years. I don't miss them, never contemplate their fears and cravings, never view their graves, never excavate their photos, never ruminate about their favorite songs or shows, never long to see them. No one mentions them to me. I don't celebrate their births, or the day each left the Earth.

Thousands birth themselves with groans and twists, tortured shades and thirsting spirits bursting forth from fiery craters of a floating mist-filled mountain, my family's souls among them, spewing from the magma. Soon we descend—tapped to live on Earth. A wraithlike travel agent reviews and stamps our cards, tags us, inspects our luggage, gives us maps, reminds the parade of spirits to stop at seven stations, then drifts away into a gap between two fiery crags. My mother, father, brother breeze through the palisades and barricades of space so swiftly, faster than the other newborn souls, shifting directions with eloquent buzz-saw fury and an unsurpassed beauty of motion that freezes the others, me included, wowed by their effortless speed. Nothing can impede their addictive need to soar. So fast that they forget to stop at good-luck tent, partially screened by hoary clouds. When the slow and careful me arrives before the good-luck dean, she says that I should reap what's meant for them to keep it in the family, a spontaneous tontine. I grasp for it and gasp—awake in discordant cold-sweat recognition: If my life had spent itself as suddenly as all of theirs, I would have missed this moment and this moment and this moment and this moment and this....

And this....

And this....

Take this cloverleaf and keep right at the Y for the summer condo of Andy Hand, another rich kid, his great-grandfather having successfully invested his bonuses from managing a copper wire factory for the Phelps-Dodge family in real estate in downtowns across the Northwest. Tall and lardy, foolhardy Andy Hand, eight years a college student, still living on his family's large estate on Bainbridge Island. Andy was one of four of us bound for LA in the late seventies, piled into the dump-salvaged Datsun of a plaid-shirted Persian graduate student named Bahadur—call me "Bad"— who insisted on taking the mountainous I-395 instead of I-5. The car vibrated round the mountains' steep and jagged ledges for mile after thrilling, Möbius-twisted mile, sweeping through a red sky dredging the valley, riding the brake downhill—all so he could see if he could work the small stake he fisted into a grand or three, hear a band for free, and buy a legal prostitute. "I'll make her cry for more," Bad said resolutely.

"You know they cry for every guy. It's part of the fee," I remind him.

"I can tell when an orgasm is real or not, even in a whore."

"You must have special powers," I roar, with my father's dismissive sarcasm.

"I have the strength of a Minotaur, and I have trained in the arts of how to pleasure a woman. I am able to remain a steel pike for more than an hour without achieving bliss myself. I can postpone for as long as I like."

At a casino of blinding fluorescent lights and a cacophony of bells and buzzers, glasses clinking, one-arm bandits plinking, piped-in Muzak drumming and thrumming, people squalling and drawling and calling across the room, others churring and purring. I play a tad of blackjack, break even, then watch as Andy, Bad, and a burly undergrad who never said a toot the entire trip, boot a few hundred each and tightly laugh it off. They souse themselves in free drinks in the hour they play. Then we take a puzzlingly circuitous way along back roads to a legal whorehouse.

It's a large parlor lit as brightly as the casino with a spritely, if messy arrangement of ancient armchairs and misfit sofas, mostly worn at the armrests. A few lovelorn cowboy hats with worn leather vests are chatting with the girls, who leave them to fall into an inviting line-up in the center of the room as soon as we enter. They parade before us in suggestive poses, in all shapes and sizes, colors and ages, in different disguises or in various stages of undress, some looking like stage versions of hardcore whores or trailer tramps, some like frat party girls, others like campy suburban housewives in faux pearls, or the girl next door. They tour the room before us. "Luscious sluts," is what Bad calls them. He picks a large-racked redhead with dark sleepy eyes, a tiny paunch at the gut, her wide bubble butt poured into toreador slacks with a gaping tear in the crotch showing panties. He follows her through a door, grinning and guffawing like a limey stevedore on leave for the first time in years.

I talk with a forty-something whore with a slight scar on her chin, dressed in buckskin and Cowboy hat, thighs riddled with a matte of thick blue veins underneath the surface of her waxy skin. When I ask her how she likes her work, she flips me a lop-sided glance, asks if I'm a cop, then tells me it's not as hard as stripping.

Andy stares with glutinous eyes at a blonde stunner named Marge, who's wearing a frayed French maid's outfit with long Heidi-braided straight hair. She has large carefree eyes circumscribed by eyeliner so thick that her pupils seem to pop out like big shiny buttons. She beams a sunny, mutton-eyed girl-next-door smile, but she answers his questions without affect. He asks her about her age, what state she comes from, any brothers or sisters, how she rates a few pop songs, she's been out of school how long, does she like Reno's oppressive hot weather, and other scatter-shot first-date topics. She looks at him heartlessly and says, "Do you want to party with me or not? A girl has got to make a living."

"I just want to talk to you. Start to get to know you. I see that you're a pretty girl from a good family. I wonder what're you're doing here."

"Earning a living, which I can't do sitting on my tailbone chewing the fat with you." Her hardboiled, unforgiving tone makes him recoil in his chair, confused and bruised, obviously unused to a woman with her you're-the-doormat-not-me demeanor.

Marge seems to be a favorite. Every few minutes, she goes down the hallway with a customer, leaving a grimly dismayed Andy squirming in a gaudy green easy chair. He stares down the hall and hears ecstatic squalls and whining behind thin walls. "Is that her screaming?" he whispers squeamishly, in despair all the time she's gone. She returns after a few minutes, reseats herself next to Andy, gives him a short mocking you-poor-baby pout and shouts at the departing john, "Stop by any time, sweets."

After she turns a few tricks, Andy says it makes him sick.

"You got to pay to play," she says. Andy brandishes a roll of bills and says, "Here's all my cash. Now don't go back there with anybody anymore."

She grabs the stash from his fingers, glowers at him. "All my cash," he repeats.

She yawns half-bored, "You just bought yourself three hours, sweetie."

Andy flashes a credit card—likely his father's—and sets it on the coffee table with a rash flourish. "How many days does a ten-thousand-dollar ceiling get me?"

Another whore peels the card from Andy's grasp and walks it to the cash register. Marge sits in Andy's lap, clasps a hand on his thigh and places one of his on a breast. He pulls the hand away and sighs, "All I want to do is have a nice talk."

She hisses a maliciously dismissive laugh, taps his face and coyly says, "Same price, same rules, delicious: no kissing, no slapping, nothing that hurts."

"I'd never hurt you, Marge. I love you," he blurts out

Yelling interrupts the lovebirds. Bad and the manager are at each other about how much Bad owes. Bad's large, sloe-eyed hooker, naked head to toe and wearing the expression of a befuddled pilchard, perches behind her red-faced supervisor, who lurches forward towards Bad, menacingly, shaking his fist as if it were a halberd and insisting he pay two hundred.

The irate Persian exclaims he ejaculated only once, at the end, and he had agreed to twenty-five for one time straight. The whore collaborates Bad's version of events.

"But love is not free. Two hundred an hour is the rate." The manager mandates his recompense. He is a short blow-fish-cheeked guy who sucks in a large-buckle-belted beer belly to expand his chest, another cowboy with long tan boots, a blue jeans jacket and a small-buckle string tie.

Bad keeps repeating like a hovering middleweight, "Twenty-five for one, twenty-five for one." The manager keeps answering, "Love is not free. Two hundred's the hourly rate." He twists to face us and says, "You boys want to pass the plate?"

Bad shoves the manager out of the way with balled fists to the chest, scoots to the entrance, and yells to us to follow him. The manager pulls a small pistol from his pocket, pursues the Persian through the door, and starts shooting, sending the prostitutes and other customers automatically to the floor, as if they've lived this scene before.

The Persian lurches behind the wheel of his car. He guns the motor and peels out, pops the clutch, engine rumbling, and heads top-speed at the manager, who tumbles to the ground and rolls away, just as Bad swerves to avoid hitting him. The car clips a headlight on a telephone pole and stops.

"Come, come, come! Hop in, hop, in!" Bad sputters, and the three of us bound past the unnerved manager cowering on the pavement and glowering at the car, waving his pistol like a fallen blind man in a gutter brandishing his stave. We cram into the car, and it pulls away, ramming into a bower before finding the road. In the harsh light streaming from the whorehouse, we see the manager's stark silhouette and the bullets exploding into darkness.

Just as the dirt becomes concrete, Andy blurts out that he loves Marge and shouts for Bad to stop, so he can hop out and skirt back to the cathouse. We try to talk him out of it. Bad lambasts him for being a fat wimp. Andy keeps repeating in a simper that he belongs with his true love.

"How do you know so soon?"

"It was like thunder from above."

"Despite the fact she's tuned a thousand men?"

"The first time we do it, she'll be a virgin again," Andy pouts.

Bad tells Andy to call him if he wants a ride back in a week and lets him out.

Andy now lives in a Pittsburgh suburb where his wife's family comes from, but I meet him in his condo at a Colorado ski resort. He's married to a friend of Marge's who was tricking in Reno while Andy was a house rep bootlicking customers at a casino. They live off his trust fund and build their lives around attending tony balls for the local gilded clique—two a week—to honor bigwigs in local charities: black-tie shindigs, art auctions, opera galas, masquerades, variety shows, casino nights, mansion tours, and aquacades. Andy tells me he's often tapped for planning committees, which involves going to a few meetings with whatever celebrities they've snapped up for the festivities, the big donors and the small business owners looking for business connections. Andy always buys a table and invites lawyers from the firm that handles his matters. Once a year like clockwork, he's in a staged photo in the society pages, sipping wine and chattering with a local jock, gripping the hand of an event honoree, or shoulder to shoulder with a stout corporate aristocrat. He shows me his scrapbook of neatly cut-and-matted newspaper clipsheets: he and his wife in formal attire as they progressively look grayer and more worn out.

The grind of morning stop-and-go past a cluster of roadside stands.

I can't keep my mind off El, like I once couldn't keep my hands off her.

El and her dray of friends. Another list: ways to play at existence. El played at boozy blues chanteuse. Her pals pined to be actors, directors, costumers, drummers, guitarists, bassists, novelists, environmental activists, painters, potters, photographers, songwriters, set designers. I felt degraded when she told me which of them she laid, men or women, even if it was long before we met. The only thing more painful than my constant burning speculation about how many of this cast of characters she had relations with was learning, little by little over time, that the answer was most. I was insanely jealous of her past, and of her future, too, since I wondered how long our time together would last.

Our house was central casting, where all of us—all of them—spent many hours hanging around, getting ploughed, dreaming out loud, giving and taking advice, planning their all-for-the-sake-of-art sacrifice, redefining goals, raking others over coals, dumping on the cop-outs and drop-outs, attacking the sell-outs and hacks, patting each other's back about breakthroughs, attacking each other over mistakes and miscues, moaning over sublime moments, groaning about setbacks and treasons. When events disappointed and plans fell through, like Swift's fleas, their reasons begot reasons which begot reasons which begot reasons of their own. I felt like an outsider to their disjointed dreams, as I had none of my own. After shining through graduate school and three promotions in two years at the insurance company, all I wanted to do was hang out, be cool, and have some fun. I stood on the sidelines, El's latest cavalier who lasted longer than the rest, who didn't have a job but always knew what to do: How to negotiate the best deals with performance venues, slash expenses, or increase revenues. How to value used equipment. What to say on an interview. How to get paid what's due. When to bend the rules. Where to find replacement parts or tools. How to fight a landlord, buy a billboard, stop a late fee, roast a turkey, write an obit, procure a permit, copyright a play, notify the EPA. One year I did the taxes for six of her friends, musicians all. I flitted without pratfall from twenty-five to thirty on my savings from the high-paying post I had quit. With food stamps, unemployment, and El's pension, we had enough to meet most of our cravings without jobs. Besides, there weren't enough positions for the Baby Boomer millions pouring out of college every year and mobbing the economy. Unemployment among people in their twenties soared, while El and I floated along a water course, sometimes lentic, sometimes lotic, pursuing rain-and-cloud games. So what the hell! Why *not* just clown around and play with a babe who let me pork her brains out twice a day and paid my way?

Stay to the left at the fork.

Driving for hours along the irrepressible sameness of an interstate can tranquilize you until your brain realizes an intermediate state between the conscious and unconscious. The Tibetan Buddhists would call it being in bardo, a transitional state between two forms of existence, a bridge from stormy *then* to static *now* on which I stand and can see every fold in the teeming, melodramatic shadow life I shared with my dream of El. If, as Buddhists articulate, empty seems the highest form of happiness, why did I beam a fierce crescendo of joy when she was full of me?

Between love and betrayal, nothing but bardo, an intermediate state of transitory pleasure between two states of pain. I imagine an ancient tree, as gnarled and knotted as my brain-constipating thoughts beside a rotting bridge of selves transforming into future selves, all wallowing in praise and blame, pleasure, pain, loss and gain, ups and downs, while El seems to slide from lotus leaf to lotus leaf down the shallow river to a waiting tiger, which she rides to a distant town.

All of life is a bardo—a delusory bridge consisting of many unplanned bridges connecting abandoned memory islands. The first is the primal bridge between birth and life. Every night, I jackknife the dream-bridge between awake and asleep. The accordion bridge that creeps across the river and the causeway bridge that is the river. The empty bridge that midwives meditation. The cobblestone bridges from station to station, from bone to bone, from joint to joint, from breath to breath. The knurled and burled bridge pointing towards sudden self-awareness of what you are and what you've done. The painful bridge stretched across death's self-anointed dawn. The bridge between this world and wild oblivion.

Get into the right hand lane and exit.

My next stop is Salt Lake City, to see Walt, who used to be part of Linebackers against Linebacker, football players attacking Nixon's Operation Linebacker Plan to destroy North Vietnam by mining harbors and bombing Hanoi. He was our next-door neighbor. He had played for a small Black college in Illinois. Not good enough to turn pro, he took a job working at a community center teaching African-American boys scholastic and life skills. He would sometimes come over to chill with a bottle of gin and a can of tonic, which we would mix and swig right from the bottle and begin to talk tilting-at-windmills leftwing politics.

When Walt got drunk, I could always anticipate the same lunatic screed, "I hate all war, the dying, the bleeding, the gore. Coaches compare football to war, and I wonder why. Sure there's a little straight-up hard hitting, but the idea isn't to push a lever and kill people or encroach with force on another country. Football is dedicated to a higher form of human endeavor, the highest, that transports us to a purer level, the purest. War assaults soldiers and civilians, but playing football exalts the players and coaches."

He takes another slug from a bottle of gin and offers it to me, but I prefer my roach, so he takes another hit.

"Nothing beats slamming the quarterback or ramming your helmet into the fullback, cold-cocking him, stopping him at the line of scrimmage or popping the end at the exact moment he catches the rock. Or watching your boys block the other side down the field, never yielding, hitting the gap, knocking loose chinstraps, spinning around defenders, finding the will to grind out that final score we need to win. No human pursuit elevates man like football, just as nothing denigrates us the way war does."

Thirty years later we sit in a Starbucks. He hands me hard copies of the magazine he edits for the National Guard, *Hooah!*, a recruiting aid sent to every high school senior six times. It looks like *People* or *Parade,* a cavalcade of star-struck celebrity articles: a photo-feature on a tattooed mountain climber and his wife, a well-endowed country-western belter splayed across a Humvee in a tight-fitting halter top, a nickel-and-dimer who claims she's not *too proud to be a patriot;* a screed against opiates; features boosting a pockmarked California drop-out who collected packs of gum, straws, and other schlock to send to the troops for protecting our freedom in Iraq; a soldier on the climb to fame as a pro gamer; an unknown grunge group with a lazy drummer and one fairly tame non-hit, "Citizen/Soldier," loosely in praise of the military, from an album Walt tells me someone else in the PR department produced.

"It's a pretty nice mag for suburban teens," Walt says.

"But doesn't it disturb you to entice kids to join the army?"

"It cleans up the streets and it's a nice career."

"You must send a lot of young African-Americans into war."

"The army is the least racist place in the country. That's one reason I'm proud to work for it."

Driving into clouds again. Walt's transformation from peacenik to war puppet brings to mind another list: Things that used to make me pissed: jerks who would make me rant for hours, raise my voice so loud my rib cage would start to hurt, throbbing blood vessels descanting a powerful rage. I frantically pounded on walls and tables, finding blame and prating fables about the injustice of it all, slammed down glasses, bawled of kicking asses, scrunched the air wildly, conjured faces clobbered with my punches, gave the dirty knaves the bird, thought of microwaving their skin or dicking their woman on top of their graves. I would feel pulses of anger, then convulsions, then a hurricane piercing deep into every folium of my blinking brain, finally falling into fierce exhaustion, a need to shrink into a ball, lost in a motionless state of non-thinking, completely drained and soaking in shame.

Like when a couple of brainless Navy boys were playing heavy metal on their boom box on the bus. El put her hand on my arm to hold me back, make me keep my poise, but I pulled away and walked up to the imposing lummox holding the radio, gave him no room to move away and yelled spume into his nose: "Hey, turn off that radio. Nobody else likes that noise."

The guy, taller than me and pretty muscular, froze up and turned red. "You can't tell me what to do, dead man."

I stood my ground and raised my voice even higher, nesting it in mean, jugular-threatening frowns. I thrust my chest forward to let him know I would not back down. "It's against bus rules, and for good reason. It's rude to everyone else."

My words were rational, but I delivered them in a hacking, strident voice, cracking with fury. I could see others standing nearby backing away, a jury finding me guilty. Those sitting folded their arms defensively against their chests, as if to ward off incoming flak. They may or may not have liked the loud music, but now they were certainly distressed, which filled me with shame but didn't make me stop. Even as I confronted these pests, I knew it was the wrong approach. I should have been barbershop-friendly, humble with a little aw-shucks bumble when broaching my concern, should have assumed they didn't know playing the radio wasn't allowed, instead of assuming they did. By exclaiming in attack mode, I set off an infusion of defend chemicals into their brains, which flamed through their cerebral mainframe. Instead of listening to my reason, they heard only aggression and responded with the same.

"I'm not afraid to whip you," the swabby said, gripping the boom box and swelling his chest the way I had. My anger was already draining, righted by a throat-gulping recognition that I would surely get beaten to a pulp in a fight. But the same gunboat force that compelled me to confront these guys prevented me from backing away. My aggressiveness had catapulted me into these desperate holes before, and I quacked a sentence which usually finessed me out of the difficulties. In a voice much more in control, blustering just a little bit higher than normal, but invested with all the confident menace

I could muster, "Hit me once and I'll have an excuse to bust you up."

He turned the radio on as loud as it could go. The crackling of the speakers salted a hole in my head. The dreadful expressions assaulting the faces of El and the passengers verified that it was all my fault. All my fault. The opposing walls of anger and shame began to close in on me, to make me gasp for breath and sweat ... feelings from childhood and my teenaged years that I couldn't forget. Like I wanted to decompose my own skin, but couldn't. Normally I shed it by pacing, but the gawks of others rooted me. All I could do was keep the gray expression of parent-hounding reprimand on my face for the brief time before the bus stopped and the swabbies bounded away. As the loud music faded into the hinterland, I felt gutted, as if I had run a marathon through quicksand carrying forty pounds.

Did you ever watch your self be someone you dislike, someone you would shun or strike, as if you lived outside yourself? How many sins and misdeeds did you commit without intention, because, preoccupied by the doing, you were not attuned to others, impeding you from feeling the damage done? How many carry wounds because you were compulsive, dismissive, defensive, aggressive? How many must you ask to forgive? How long will you beat yourself with known and unknown regrets? You will not forget those endless times you were not observing you and did not get your own wickedness. You will live outside your oubliette of skin, and rake yourself with painful shocks to guard against a further crime, as wrathful hail of a hard winter dazzles swollen river terrace, breaks apart its shelves of ice, rocks the frazil, clings defensively to floating rime, melts into waves like the self into self.

A multitude of things could drive me into such a rage back then. Cars that ran the red and threatened pedestrians ...

Those who labelled men with beards as beatniks ...

Those who loudly whined or nagged in public ...

The anorexic and the bulimic ...

Those who smoked on buses ...

Mediocre writers who critics wrote were geniuses, especially those whose novels were about writers or professors ...

Anything Disney and all fast food ...

Christian politicians mouthing pious platitudes, especially those confessing to acts of moral turpitude ...

Joan Walsh Anglund's doll-like figures with their wide-eyed solicitude ...

Multi-millionaires pretending to be humanitarians while hiding their money in Lichtenstein ...

People who cut in line ...

Try not to give the finger while passing that rude Chevy that hair-pinned into the left-hand lane to block you from passing a truck uphill and then boxed you in …

Leroy Neiman's pixilated versions of athletes …

Grimy, groveling suck-ups to wealthy elites …

Anything having to do with the suburbs—my ever-so-humble, home-sweet, not-such-a hovel for the past thirty years …

Freebooting looters and polluters and cheating financiers in dou-bled-breasted suits driving Mercedes and BMWs. Sometimes I daydreamed about filling the front of a junked VW bug with concrete, hitting the high-way and hunting Beemers …

PBS's upbeat and oft-repeated middle-brow crap with patriotic themes …

The idiotic wisdom of spending more time browsing the gift shop than strolling the museum …

People who were pro-military or anti-choice, favored banning birth con-trol and supported the Vietnam War, the Shah of Iran, the Saudi cabal, or the rich and well-fed families controlling Guatemala …

Those grinning hogs on planes, who wait until everyone in all the rows in front of them have left, before rising from their seat and clogging the aisle, while they leisurely get their bags from the overhead bin …

Seeing a tattoo would make me grumpy, and now I see them everywhere, intricate designs in red, blue, and black, on dumpy necks and faces, plump arms and legs, lumpy breasts and backs.

People who didn't believe in science always enraged me, and the news-papers are now full of religion justifiers, crooked corporate falsifiers spin-ning lies on the benefits of lower taxation and deregulation, climate-change deniers, those making false allegations about the dangers of vaccinations, rooked schoolboards that want to rewrite pages in the nation's history, vacate Darwin, or ban books.

I despised the schnooks who drove pick-up trucks anywhere but in farm country, and now there are more trucks and SUVs on the road than sedans.

I hated the stupid, gory war we got out of in my mid-twenties, and now we find ourselves in two or three, and maybe four.

I hated El when she told me she had balled other guys. It would always catch me by surprise, thinking it was too soon or anesthetized into the tan-talizing thought that it would never happen again, since it had been so long. The slattern image of him astride her, her thighs opening for him, her green eyes widening with the exhilaration of penetration, the slapdash rhythm of bed squeaks, his sweat dripping on her lashes and cheeks, her breasts swaying sideways, her skin reeking of his, her back's slightly upward arch from the bed as her shoulders frizz and her jaw goes slack—these shreds of sex would fester in me for weeks after her confession, would slash into me like a cauterized knife again and again, sear my flesh, again and again, mash my brain into a thousand wounded anima, each spinning in its own furor, again and again.

Her excuses picked at me like matadors pinning a blind bull. She was climbing the walls with boredom and had a sudden and incontrollable pull to explore. She thought of me the entire time. Assured me it made her love me more. I would start shouting at her to leave me alone, louder and louder, like a punched-out megaphone, putting so much energy into my bellowing that I soon felt as if I had run miles into a cyclone, my legs and arms groaning with exhaustion. But she wouldn't stop stoking my agitation. I would grow sleepy and scrunch my body into bed, but she'd keep jawboning through my half-slumber snores. She would put my groggy head in her lap, stroke it and say how much she adored me. It felt like a deep abrasive raking of my skin keeping me awake.

"Sleep, sleep, let me sleep...."

"How do I begin to make it up to you?"

"Let me sleep, sleep, let me sleep...."

"But I'm so broke up about my mistake."

"I'm so tired, let me sleep...."

"Not another peep if you say you still love me."

"Every bone is aching with exhaustion. Let me sleep...."

Sometimes she sounded as if she were reading lines and not living life, that she was faithless so she could play the role of repentant wife. The time she said she slept with her dead husband's fourteen-year-old nephew on a visit home. She claimed it was because she was high and the kid looked just like Virgil—the way he combed his fiery red hair, the slope of his forehead, his nose, his eyes, his wiry body—and she was seized by a sudden desire. She said it made her realize how much more inspiring her life was with me, that her days of acquiring cherries were past. She said our love would outlast this minor strife. I tried to focus on the one small part of my soul not hounded by a repetition of the scene, again and again, El supine with a boy, again and again.

The time I came home from playing softball to her confession that she had a session with her flighty ex-roomie Gigi and a guy we knew who earned his living ghost writing college papers for students from Japan. She maintained she didn't let him touch her, but they both laid Gigi, which was supposed to make me feel less betrayed. For weeks, my imagination baited me with her nakedness before another man.

Slow down. You're doing ninety-five.

Now Fog, whom I see on a smoggy Dallas day. Years ago, he picked me up outside Seattle driving to Corvallis. He was a former merchant marine turned Greenpeace activist, with the calloused hands and twisted back of a lifetime seadog. Fog had served on board the *Phyllis Cormack*, the Greenpeace boat that challenged a Soviet whaling fleet off the California coast. "At noon we saw the Russian ships," he said in a froggy boast. "We sailed our inflatables and posted ourselves between the harpoons of the *Vlastny* and a pod of whale, never close enough to collide. The waves from the *Vlastny's* engine almost flipped us. TV cameras at our southernmost side whirred and captured the *Vlastny* repeatedly flailing harpoon after harpoon over our heads, failing to hit us, which meant they also missed the pod. We were laughing our asses off, applauding their misses, lampooning them with goony, hailing movements. Cold and waterlogged as we were—and bailing out seawater like crazy—we thought we were gods!"

Now he sells commercial pod coffee systems. "The law offices love them," he crows, "because it eliminates the clods who never clean up, and everyone gets what they want, no muss, no fuss. Regular, strong, decaf, espresso-flavored, cappuccino, cardamom, cinnamon, chicory, even hot cocoa and tea. All in these sleek and convenient pods. I sell a landfill's worth every week." His vehicle is piled high with brightly colored semi-cylinders appearing to plump at the top of a clump, like in carnival tents bursting with plastic balls in red, yellow, white, and blue into which children jump head first.

Next, Danny Ambrosia, who lived across the street from us, squatting with a woman not a mate—today we would call her a friend with benefits—until they evacuated the night before the police were going to evict. They collaborated on science fiction stories for pulp magazines that sometimes paid three cents a word. He also taught English part-time at Berlitz.

One day, sitting on the stoop and passing a joint to me, he told me about his interrogation of a fat fascist who was one of his students. "He's named for the province his family owns in Nicaragua. He dresses like the stereotypic Latin American autocrat: jacket, slacks, tie, and shoes, all black but for the white in his striped shirt. A pancake-pallid, pock-marked face with a fake smile you want to wipe away with a hard swipe, fatty pink hands sliding out of initialed cuffs. Set on one finger, a weighty diamond-studded pyramid recalls the flickering band of an over-decorated silent-movie Cleopatra. I wanted to strangle him! A few weeks ago I spoke a single English phrase and he repeated, 'Some friends treated me to a steak dinner.' I make him say it again, and he repeated, 'Some friends treated me to a steak dinner,' and once again I make him begin again, again and again, until he neared perfection in enunciating the text, to which I faked chagrin. He winced a frown of dejection, and I had him repeat again, 'Some friends treated me to a steak dinner.'

"Thinking about what he must have done to his people, I wanted to rake his tongue with repetition till his head ached and blood poured forth with saliva, till his throat quaked dry, till gnats danced in his dazed eyes and upraised nostrils and beetles pranced up and down his arms, till boils sprouted on his sweat-mucked bovine thighs and midsection, till his vision oozed white with infection and he soiled himself.

"For forty-five minutes I tortured him with the one phrase, and for forty-five minutes he emitted anemic brays to echo me. When the lesson ended, he slipped one hand over mine, raised the other to my shoulder, hardened his pharaonic grip and told me how much he liked learning perfection. 'In my country, you would be a person worthy of protection,' he said. Now I teach him three days a week. His geeky bloated college boy, too, who's enrolled in the seminary. That kid has the sneaky demeanor of a child molester. I pester them both to death, striking them, smiting them, slaying them one sentence at a time, but the father keeps asking for me. The more I torture him, the more he likes it."

The deviously mind-torturing way in which Danny manifested his anger impressed me. I could be so volatile and confrontational, whereas he bored his bêtes noires oppressively and made them ask for more.

I meet Danny in a Boise sports bar. He immediately hands me his card. Gold letters on a dark blue field, which say he's a financial planner for the elderly. "I like to get my seniors into non-traded REITs—packages of real estate properties that produce a steady income. They achieve a little more yield than traded REITs. The commissions are sweet, like you wouldn't believe. It's not as safe as a REIT that's traded, because there's no market for the security, which some find alarming, ha, and in a liquidity squeeze, they could get routed and easily lose half their value in a day. But I don't say that to my clients, because it would freak them out, especially after I've spent so much time nursing them to open their purses. I doubt real estate will get weak again, so no harm, ha, as long as the client doesn't need to leave the market, it works like a charm. What the hell, it could be worse. It ain't my dime. I'll still get my cut, so I won't be grieving, no matter what."

Next I see Vinnie, a Vietnam vet I met at an anti-nuke rally outside the Lawrence Livermore Labs. He had ridden a bicycle there from Boulder, as part of a group called the Solar Rollers. From a notebook he read the crowd his poems, stark, gaudy images of digging trenches in swamps, tromping through stout jungle weeds, thumping his gun and shouting the words to "In-a-gadda-da-vida," eating ficus-seed-fed rats, hearing napalm-loaded bombs fall, watching buddies bawl like babies as they bled out. After a litany of brutality, Vinnie stretched his palms towards the audience as if giving a benediction and addressed them in a fleecy voice with noticeably careful diction, "I've seen what war can do, my friends, and there is no worse war than nuclear. Join with me and bless the world with peace."

Thousands roared, already greased and boisterous after a metaphor by the previous speaker about a quilt of peace that covers the tribe of all men. Vin asked the audience to chant, "Peace, not war, peace, not war," over which he began to describe peace as a ripe peach hanging over a deep lake on a branch out of reach unless we rise together to take it.

Now Vin is the assistant commander of an Idaho militia group, running a boot camp for his troops in the Bitterroot Range. An enormous gut protrudes from his plaid shirt. Balanced on bent and spindly legs, he moves with arthritic plods. We tramp over temporary ramparts and through an esplanade of tripods, lashed posts and army surplus tents, large mutts sleeping in front of most. Next an ascent up a hilly field where squads of men, women and teens—all white—drill in small groups or have begun to practice taking apart and putting together rifles under the stifling heat of a vitelline sun.

"This seems more like a summer camp for some of us, especially on beer and line-dance night. But it's really about getting ready to fight back after they take our rights away. We're learning how to attack a hill, scale walls wearing a heavy pack, practice defensive tracking, and simulate guerilla war with paintballs. We're also getting acquainted with surviving in a hostile topography with nothing but a gun and the pack on your back."

"But who exactly is the enemy?"

"The Blacks, the wetbacks, the A-rabs. And the federal government."

"Don't you think the government will destroy you, if you try an armed insurrection?"

"Not if there's enough of us. The Internet lets our small bands of warriors, spread out throughout the land, make connections. We'll be ready to hold out a long time when the insurrection breaks out, ready to countermand when they make that first big move, like trying to take our guns away … from these cold hands, buddy, from these cold hands."

I conjure Boschian figures tossing barbed projectiles and clouting each other with rifle butts, blood dripping onto pick-up-stick piles of jagged rebar in a roundabout landscape of flipped-over cars and jeeps, burnt-out buildings, and ripped-up skyways sprouting tree-root-twisted steel rods. Obese warriors, guns dangling from chubby arms, waddle through thick mud and heaps of smoking body parts. I scramble through the dead-and-rubble-strewn streets, the broken obelisks of brick and plastic, concrete and clay, my chest winching with dread, eyes darting everywhere at once. I amble past corners full of blown-away hospitals and schools, duck the lone snipers slinging Vipers, bands of marauders butchering, plucking off arms like burnt chicken wings, drinking blood from gaping flesh holes, clinking together severed heads in toast, roasting headless, limbless bodies over coals.

From anti-nuke vet to survivalist. From war abolitionist to war propagandist. From environmental activist to purveyor of waste. From radical squatter to two-faced financial scammer. Ideals have given way to rotten money-making. High-mindedness has yielded to commerce. Empathy has fallen to a glamorously perverse, well-healed cruelty.

But who am I to critique this decline into selfishness? Was I any different? Didn't I sell out the ideals of my youth? Take a comfortable job and buy a comfortable home in a comfortable suburb, sustain a comfortably monochrome life neglecting uncomfortable truths, like Seneca's wife protected from the hells of Nero's Rome? Aren't I driving now instead of taking buses and trains?

Do these people from my past look at me with the same disdain with which I view them and say, "What happened to him? Brother, has he changed!"

There are many ways to change, another list: To mature ... To take a detour ... To grow and leave behind what you outgrew ... To follow the lure of the new ... To free yourself from the past ... To melt yourself and be recast against the grain ... To free yourself from anger, guilt, regret, panic, pain ... To take sudden flight ... To see divine light ... To change your mind ... To stop fluttering butterfly-like and settle down ... To stop acting like a clown ... To lose your bright ideals ... To take a devil's deal ... To decide to go for money ... To please your last or latest honey ... To choose to stop caring, to choose to stop feeling ... To choose to walk away from healing ... To decide to finally live by, or deny, what is true ... To forget what you saw, what you did, what you knew ... To lose the will to fight....

A yellow pyramid bears a flashing arrow pointing right.

I won't get to see Kay, flighty heavyset housewife with no kids, who took me twenty miles through sunset in the Central Valley, chatting with truckers on a CB the whole way. She slurred and purred coquettish innuendos in CB slang with a hillbilly twang, "Meet you at Pickle Park after dark ...

"You can be the bear at my back door ...

"How big is your big rig, Billy Big Rigger? Let me look at what you're packing ...

"Any you beefcakes into swinging?" which I learned means hauling meat on a hook.

But when a voice faintly crackled, "How much you charging for a BJ," her face immediately took on a red hue, and she looked at the mic in her hand as if it were a rotting gizzard.

"Hey, take a hike, buster," she roared. "You're way out of line! I'm no snot-nosed lot lizard, no sleeper creeper you can stuff with West Coast turn-arounds and do on a skateboard. I'm a lady who won't be whored, and if you can't hear that in the sound of my voice, you can go pound a Schneider egg. If I like you and I want to meet you, you never know, I may even let you try it, but you ain't ever gonna buy it."

I find Kay on Facebook, where her photo makes her look as if she's still thirty-five and still on the prowl. "Hello, Mister," she sends a reply. "Too many world-weary people on the mend growling out there, and I'm looking for a best friend, because everything starts with friendship. I'm a country girl at heart, down to earth. One sip at a time, I like an easy pace, a very REAL person except for the part of my head in the clouds or out chasing butter-flies. I have a huge bungee-jumping heart and tend to wear it on my sleeve without disguise. I love to plunge my face in the ocean and float weightless in bunches of sweet-smelling flowers, and I have a hunch that I am solar powered."

We exchange several Facebook emails, but she never wants to fix a date to meet.

Return to the interstate.

Someone else I won't see on this trip is my cousin Petey, lost to history like El. Nothing on an Internet search, nothing on Facebook, LinkedIn, no tweets, no one in his immediate family has heard from him since the Clinton years. He never did have an address for very long. When El and I first got to San Francisco, he lived with a woman about fifteen years older than he was, but, after she threw him out for the landlord, he slept in his rusty, fenderless early sixties Ford sedan, except when he would meet a woman at a party and could sweet-talk an invitation to stay the night. Every few weeks we would have him over for dinner and let him shower and shave, and then do an odd job like caulking. Occasionally in winter he crashed on our divan, never more than one night at a time. After a year of living improvisationally, he found a small cubicle for $50 a month in a gloomy old warehouse in the potholed, slumlord streets south of Market. Dozens of people were setting up cheap households there in moldy storage rooms and spaces carved out by long panels of corrugated cardboard nailed into foraged two-by-fours. Everyone used a communal shower and two communal bathrooms. The inhabitants were mostly down-on-their luck artists, aging hippies, castaways, and roughnecks, but I did see a few children skipping through the maze of walkways running through the makeshift living spaces. Petey learned about it from another shipwreck he ran into, while waiting on line for a monthly Social Security disability check.

Someone else I won't see on this trip is my lost friend John with the deep, glossy voice, whom I met when he ripped the narration for a low-cost industrial video my department was making. During the break, we smoked some weed, scarfed a piece of cake, and peed against the fence in a downtown parking lot. He told me that he baked as soon as he got up most days and long ago forgot what it was like to live straight. We used to get high together by the Seattle quays after I got off work, our four-twenty designated at five.

He invited me to a performance of *Woyzeck* he was directing in a beaten-down little theatre-in-the-round seating forty on moth-eaten davenports and easy chairs in the unheated basement of a restaurant between Western Avenue and Puget Sound. It was a catatonic affair on a barren stage, in which all the actors spoke in thin, monotonic slurs except for an enraged Woyzeck, who blared out histrionic lines as if frantically confessing his sins, the idea for which John said he got from Schönberg's *Moses and Aaron*.

At the cast party, I got gassed and started talking to John's newest girlfriend, whom he had been praising to the skies for days, a beautiful woman with thick chestnut hair that bent over one shoulder and danced softly down her back like a half-spent waterfall. She dressed in a loose eggplant-colored blouse with tasseled shoulders and breast pockets pressed tightly into trance-inducing charcoal gray black toreador pants—built like a ceramic outhouse, as my father might have said. My chance banter about Berg's score for the opera led to talk of altos and contraltos, leading to Rossini and Boccherini, leading to the lives of sainted composers, leading to painters and paintings, Caravaggio's dramatic use of sunlight streaming through an unseen window pane in the *Calling of Saint Matthew,* the quaint decorative flourishes of a dainty Crivelli, form fighting darkness in Rembrandt, leading to the elegant lighting in old movies, leading to Sternberg, Dietrich, Bette Davis. She breaks into a discerning imitation of vain adulteress Fanny Skeffington, thrusting her shoulders back and turning her head as if posing for a bust with the same disdain, leading to her version of Charlotte Vale's awakened yearning in *Now Voyager,* then a snarling Margo Channing leading to her sad vanilla life in Centralia, Washington, as a high-school grad washing hair in a beauty parlor going mad from boredom and bad planning, before a train crushed her husband in his truck, stuck on the tracks, fried on LSD and khat, keys under the floor mat—an accident or suicide, no one knows for sure. He was home after a tour shot-gunning a helicopter in Vietnam, leading to her widow's pension, which brings in enough to let her do whatever she damn well pleases, which for her means pursuing a career as a pop queen, never mind that she's already older than most of the has-beens on the scene.

Past two at an all-night diner on Aurora Avenue, the three of us split a western omelet, real hash browns, and freshly-brewed iced coffee. John listens to our excited repartee with the satisfied smile of the recently stoned, pleased at himself for courting such a brainy and beguiling dish. We are talking about the vanishing signs of god, Isis and Adonis, the thundering replenishment of life each year, the hanging gardens and other ancient wonders, Thanatos, the death wish, the blue flower of Novalis, the search for the infinite, the Big Bang. She says my rationality is like a yin that she wants to cradle in her yang.

When John hits the head, she grips my hand, brings it to her cheek, spreads it out to let me feel her burning flesh, and slips a folded strip of paper into it. I press it into a pocket of my coat so I won't have to explain to John. It is only when they drop me off at dawn and I am combing my pockets for my keychain that I open the note and learn her name is Elaine.

A never-ending time now decades gone. Internal snippets of decayed images mash together like scenes from ancient coming attractions, flashing an instant, one at a time, then fading: Guitar, bass, sax, and drums coarsely vamp, as El parades across the stage and belts out, "Work to Do"—"Got to make it for you, got to make it for me"—in a velvety hoarse voice assuaged by shots of rum and sprays of Chloraseptic. She tramps back and forth across the stage, singing lyrics from a folded page. She draws the microphone close to her lips, then whips it away again in an obbligato of one held note, a loud and raw ecstatic yip melting to mellow sotto voce. As the sax player begins his solo, she sidles up to him and starts swaying her hips and torso in tandem to the short movements of his saxophone, her body arched from the nape to imitate the shape of the instrument, moving hand-in-glove with it as if making warm love. Then she breaks away and starts strutting along the edge of the platform ...

Dissolves to morning light streaming through the crack between drapes and palm fronds and settling in a shimmering pond around El, standing by a bookcase holding a heavy volume and thumbing through it. Her eyebrows arch, her eyes go wide, her button nose shrugs as she tugs the book by its spine and pats it squarely, until it liberates its hidden treasure, bit by bit, that makes her heave with pleasure—dried and flattened maple leaves that float to our threadbare rug ...

Dissolves to her mane of ruddy hair floating at naked shoulders along the skedaddling waves at the bottom of a sub montane waterfall, behind the crumbled shrines of Palenque, as she dog-paddles towards me. She stops swimming and starts to float, still submerged. Slowly she approaches, lightly splashing. The many small waves created by her saturnine movement through water crash as weirdly and loudly as a quetzal call. Slowly her opaline breasts emerge, spotted with droplets, then her torso, her waistline, her curving hips, the rest of her naked body, lifting slowly out of a swoon of concentric swerving waves, shifting like a sleek Xquic, the Mayan goddess of the waning moon, rising from a river and drifting towards me ...

Dissolves to her tough-girl tease for hitching curbside or hopping from bar to bar—tight low-riding blue jeans, teal vest over tight-fit tee-shirt, charcoal leather boots with reverberant three-inch heels, and a flitty, flirty frown that says, "She does what she pleases," her eyes honed to indifferent slits, her cheeks sucked in a little to highlight her cheekbones ...

Dissolves to her short spellbound gasps of glee as she turns the page of an oversized art book, delighting at the intricately stylized ramparts in emblazoned reproductions of Tura and Crivelli ...

Dissolves to her smooth large palms and satiny short fingers carefully grazing the skin of an apple, buffing gently until the fruit glows. She slowly raises it to her mouth, bites down in ultra-slow motion, chewing leisurely as her green-gray eyes look brazenly at me ...

Dissolves to her frowning face in the mirror, fussing and mussing at her hair, looking for foreboding gray like a chic Columbine, after she cut it to pageboy to accentuate her cheek line, which she thinks is eroding ...

Singing again, her debut at a B-class bar of weary, wobbly hotchpot stools and bubbling linoleum floors, substrate wood curling up in spots, slippery with pools of beer. To a blues base line and shushing cymbal brushes, her voice bringing a lush sexpot vibrato, her eyes directed at me as she said they would be, but still it gives me a chill when she trills, "We'll sit and look at the same old view, just we two, Jules and Elaine, who used to be Jack and Jill" ...

Sometimes a cruder tune she would croon while getting dressed in front of the full-length mirror in our bedroom, "What's new? Have you been screwing your Jew?" ...

Her darker moments, her bitter barks and cajoles. She hated my clothes, too straight. I needed to wear more flash, look rock-and-roll. I refused to acid-trip. I carried too much weight. I gnashed my teeth when I ate. My dancing was too stiff, especially at the hips, and I could never move my feet to keep a counter-beat. I was too cheap. I snored in my sleep. I was a slob and used my fingers too much to eat, then placed my greasy fingers on the doorknobs.

"Don't I do a good job cleaning the kitchen after I cook?" I would remind her.

"Yes, I find it prissy. I know you're not a sissy, but a man shouldn't want to clean so much. It makes me think you think I'm dirty." As usual, she's half mean and half flirty.

"I never said that."

"You don't have to say it. I took it that way," she said, with a crooked little smile.

"You remember that this discussion began because I didn't wipe my hands before touching the door handle. Now we're talking about me being a clean freak. That seems inconsistent." But right out of her standard playbook.

"Whenever we argue, you appeal to logic. You always look to pick apart what I'm saying instead of just dealing with my feelings."

Spare me your irrational spiel, I want to say. "I know your feelings. You're angry at me. And I think it's unfair."

"What's unfair is that you listen to my words but don't hear what I'm saying."

What I heard were the same surreal no-win situations that my mother always constructed to put Leon and me in the wrong, the constant fluctuation in her valuation of what we did. The sudden eructations of malignance and sarcasm. When I did A, she picked at me for not doing B. When I did B the next time, she picked at me for not doing A. Or she would tell me to do A and then lie or forget or get her orders confused and say she meant B. Or she would do A and chide me when I mentioned she was angry when I did A. Every either/or transformed to neither/nor. El was exactly the same. She blamed me when I forgot to call her when I thumbed to Phoenix for a freelance job, but bawled me out for crowding her when I asked her to call when she visited her parents. She complained that I was too proud. I talked too loud. I couldn't refrain from making historical references that bored her and my literary preferences made her feel dumb. It was my way of lording my degrees over her.

"You looked pretty slick and smart when it turned out that quartet was Mozart," she asserted after I yapped "Wanna bet" to Rob Turob's guess on who wrote a piece of radio music.

I knew I should have sloughed it off, but I couldn't help but fall into her trap. "I wouldn't have said a word, if Rob hadn't said it was Schubert."

"You corrected him so quickly, it hurt his pride. You could have waited until the DJ said something. You were showing us how much smarter you think you are." A snide verbal slap.

"I thought you liked the fact I knew stuff."

"I don't like a know-it-all."

She falsified my meanings, turning yes into no, fast into slow. Her dramatic preening—her brawling, burning, Gothic mistrals—sounded like my mother's shtick, if my mother had studied forties flicks. Especially when El was drinking and got stinking. She would furiously pound in the sarcasm and spite, take me to the brink of falling apart. I thought I had the foresight not to let my heart trip and get caught in emotional quicksand, fraught with impossible demands and constant reprimands, in no-win situations in which it's impossible to be right. Yet here I was, up to my hips and sinking.

Sometimes I fought back. In front of a party with her rock band, "The Boreads"—my name, after the children of the North Wind—and their women, she ranted that I resembled a sad ragman in my baggy pants and schlocky plaid shirt. I left the room and returned wearing nothing but my shoes and socks. I composed my sense of shame behind a grin and high-kneed strutting until a chagrined El told me to put some clothes on.

Or when the band replaced her with the drummer's sister after I set up a bunch of gigs, and she insisted we see them play, lambasting me to go with her even though I thought it humiliating. It infuriated me to watch El embracing her two-faced former band members, ingratiating herself with pleasant yakking as if nothing had happened. I suddenly shattered an empty beer glass on the table with one whack, chasing the suds and shard to the floor with a swipe of my arm. Before anyone else had a chance to react, I walked out of the bar. Several blocks away, standing against a stop sign, blear-eyed and a bit wasted, I stared at the bloodied side of my hand and wondered why she was friendly to these guys who screwed her over, and yet would ride me so hard all the time.

When I trekked into the apartment with my gear after a softball game and found El and Wynona Sage, a friend from down the hall, on the couch, facing each other, involved in light necking, both of them framed in lacy see-through nightgowns. Why, as everyone called her, was tall and well-padded, with wide hips and boyish breasts, but a flawless complexion and a pleasantly angular face. "We've been waiting for you," El said in a coy, velveteen voice. "Come sit between us."

I knew what they wanted. El had gotten Why blitzed once before and kibitzed or taunted her to reveal husband Bill hadn't touched her since his operation for testicular cancer; even before then, their dance of love had been infrequent, as he preferred to spend half the night hovering in his dark room staking crops for the photos that he spent all his weekend daylight hours taking around the city. El had told me that Why hadn't strayed yet, but El called her jumping-out-of-her-skin, always-pending-on-the-edge-of-tears needy. Bill was a good friend who worked as a sales clerk in a photography store on a seedy Tenderloin street, despite an MFA in fine arts from Yale. In his mid-thirties, but with the gritty wrinkles and gray hair of a fifty-year-old, Bill was laid-back with a note of sarcasm in normal moments, but soon became withdrawn and depressed-looking after a few drinks or hits.

By contrast, Why bleated emotional gook, always sweet and idealistic in her comments about the state of the world, never blasting or casting blame. Bill must have been a great athlete as a youth, for one day in the park we saw five young studs passing around the football, soaring perfect spirals. Bill challenged them to a three-on-four, took their weakest guy and lambasted their butts. He insisted on playing quarterback. Every receiver is able to get free for at least a split second on virtually every play, and in that small leeway of time I or the kid with us always found the ball in our hands. Bill never missed. We scored on every possession, which pissed off the other team.

Yes, I knew what El and Why wanted, or what El had convinced Why she wanted.

Why stayed for a playful night of soul-rinsing body couplings. Uniting with two women at one time made me feel like an all-powerful king of the world, a swaggering alpha male flaunting his control over everything around him. I wanted to brag to my father, Leon, Petey, Irv, and just about every other straight male I knew, regale them with the details of my two-woman roll in the hay. If I told the old man, he would bust his buttons and bark, "That's my boy"—that is, unless he decided to broadside the deed with a snide remark.

Lying between El and Why in the gray early morning, I realized—finally—that I had screwed a friend's wife. I started to feel what I would feel when I found out El had strayed and let some heel lay her— rejected, angry, above all, betrayed. I tried to follow cynical lines of justification to assuage my guilt: he wouldn't care, because he wasn't interested in sex anymore, so it was no big deal, and, in fact, he probably felt relieved of his marital duties. He had a genteel, waspy arrangement with Why that they both could stray. She was ready to step out on him and if it hadn't been me, it would have been some other schlemiel. But I kept coming back to how I would feel if I were Bill. My mind kept staging the image of a frenzied El with someone else, a masked stranger with whom she was enchained in wanton abandon. The pain I would cause Bill if he found out far exceeded the pleasure I had felt, since my pleasure was a one-time physical thing and the burning anguish he would feel was emotional and would come and go, again and again, for many tearful weeks, if not months or years, if he found out. He would drown in a swamp of regret and betrayal. I would never retain Bill as a friend after profaning his ego. I knew he must never learn of our romp.

Over a breakfast of wholewheat toast and butter, I said in a voice that betrayed my anxiety, "Of course, you won't say anything to Bill."

"Your tone displays your bourgeois hypocrisy," El flamed into an angry harpy. "We danced a beautiful, mind-expanding arabesque last night, a moment of caring and sharing, and you make it out to be something grotesque."

"I never said that," I tried to defend myself. "Did I say that, Why?" I implore her to take my side in the sudden fight. But she was hiding her views in distended silence, her Rubenesque form beautified in the early sunlight.

"But the fact that the first thing out of your mouth this morning is 'Don't tell anyone' says it all. Hypocrite!" El spat out the word as if she bit into something foul-tasting.

"You do sound judgmental, Jules," Why admitted in a curt whisper, as she pulled her chair away from the table.

"You're bending my meaning. I just don't want to hurt Bill, who is a friend."

"You have no say in that," El spat out her fuming words as if they were punches aimed at hitting me. "She can tell him if she wants to or not tell him. Their relationship is none of your fricking business. You project your bankrupt bourgeois mores on everyone else, but you don't mimic them yourself." She wouldn't stop nitpicking me with her interpretation of my meaning, even after Why had left, embarrassed at being a pawn in our argument. "Why was feeling so refreshed and in bloom, and you threw dirt all over her and made her feel gloomy about our beautiful moment."

"That was clearly not my intent."

"But it's clearly what happened," she asserted with a hateful sneer.

"I was just trying to protect Bill. Didn't you hear me? Didn't you listen?"

"By cheapening Why and me! And you, as well, which you would find out if you were willing to step out of your own dirty, perverted little mind. Some things are better left unsaid. You should have taken it for granted that Why knew how to handle Bill. They have been married for ten years. As usual, you had to queer everything with your patriarchal bullshit."

Her fit of anger lasted for days.

I was fed up with her constant berating, fed up with the cycle of anger and shame to which it led, fed up wallowing in a vast, spreading pool of guilt as viscid and rancid as the ones of my past. El would badger me as if it were a putrescent word game like my mother; blast incessant lies like my father; cast me into convoluted no-win situations in which everything I did or said made things worse like my mother; articulate perversely cruel words like my father, words that made me feel incapable of action or escape. I was caught in the dead end of my own stupid scrapes, shivering like a seal caught in a trap, knowing that the more it slithers and sobs, the greater damage it will do to its own flesh, the more the sharp teeth of the trap will mutilate its blubber, the more blood it will lose, feeling incapable of getting a job and so financial dependent on this woman who routinely fucked up my mind as viciously as she fucked my body desperately. The perverse psychodrama resurrecting itself in plot variations but always the same theme of ricocheting between anger and guilt, more than bad luck, a kind of built-in destiny to feel at fault for someone close betraying me.

I should have left her, but instead I hitched down to L.A. I spent the time glazy-eyed-and-foggy-head stoned with Irv Opalin, listening to the Dead. At about three in the morning, jogging at the water's side of the Pacific Coast Highway, both of us toasted under a full moon hidden in smog, we gaped at whirlpools of mottled dark gray and black-banded shapes—the sandbar and water at San Martin Cape. Waves rose like shadowy, misshapen crepe, then collapsed with thunderous rips into amoeba-like spasms of black bubbles. As I stared into this undulating abyss, I thought about telling Irv why I had made the sudden trip. But it would be a leap into complete humiliation. Besides, Irv had his own troubles with women, which he liked to share with all his friends. "One of my Janes said she's going camping with her friends, and I want to make sure there are no guys there."

"No trust?"

"I don't want her hanging around with a bunch of sharks."

"You think you'll bust in on someone banging her?"

"Ride with me to the park, and then I'll drive you home."

We took the same early-'60s chassis-rotted Chevy red convertible with two-tone side fins in which we rode around Chicago the summer after high school—the car we were in when the police spotted Irv doing forty-five in a school zone at midnight. As soon as he saw the squad car's red light flash, he burned rubber, hightailed it away, and dashed around a corner. We heard the siren begin to wail, but we didn't see the cop car, because Irv skittled into another nervy turn. Two blocks later he made another, and then another, and then another—left, right, right, left, right—sailing through the gridded streets of Ravenswood Manor like a hand-held maze game in which you try to swerve a metallic ball—the Chevy—along a series of curves. He finally managed to derail the cops. A few minutes later, we saw three police cars stopped on North Kedzie fantailed around a Chevy of the same vintage and colors as Irv's.

Irv was a splendid square of heavy muscle, covered in a forest of plush black hair that extended up his neck from his chest, cutting a straight line at the point the throat met his shoulders and his daily shaving ended. He had a blacksmith's reach and forearms, but his fingers were as nimble as a seamstress's. Whereas most people need a rolling device to make a perfect joint without stress, Irv could effortlessly load a single paper and roll a symmetrical fatty with one hand, while he drove like a hellcat on a hunt with the other, keeping his eyes on the road the whole time.

His mastoid juts forward, and he grins to doo-wop, the Beatles, the Grateful Dead, Pink Floyd. He doesn't say much, mostly stutters songs and gets the lyrics wrong, muttering in a beefy, stiff-lipped barbershop baritone droned through one side of his mouth, as if whispering something on the QT. "Penny Lane begins to hear and gins her sky ... She's got a thick inner eye ... Did you arrange a walk-on port in a storm for a green park with a stage? ... Wake up to find out that you are disguised as a world ..."

When we see a sign for Sequoia National Park, he juts out his chin and says, "Here we are." We've driven through the night. I have the disciplined clarity that often comes with a second wind.

Irv tramps through the campsites slowly. Fists clamped on bent knees, his vulpine eyes crawl into every tent, fearless and ready for action, swearing under cramped breath, as if stalking deer in the twilight.

He pushes his jaw forward briefly, then lets it hang slack. "They'll be here someplace, walking and talking in plain sight."

He throws back the flaps of tents and peeps inside without knocking, stares into cabin windows on tiptoes. "You can't just look inside," I keep insisting.

"I'm not stealing nothing," he says, and he persists. Failing to find a sign of Jane, he wheels towards a trail past a row of thatched hutches and strikes up a steep path, pushes past a group of tourists, and is soon deep into forest.

I follow along, grutching at him about the futility of his search. "There are so many hiking trails. How do you know which one she's on?" to which he hisses and tools on. I was used to trailing Irv on his foolish searches after a fixed idea. I had done it often the summer after high school—sailing after girls we met at dances or mixers, chasing one who threw us glances from the street, looking for a deadbeat he had sold weed to, intervening to stop a fight, or knocking on door after door to find a party to feed his endless appetite for romance. Now two hours mostly uphill, Irv chugged along, relentless in his pace, me plodding behind, flush-faced, panting and ranting that he'll never find her.

We see an opening in the sky as if the trail is going to end at the timberline. As we approach it, the opening becomes a wide plateau overlooking a sheer incline into a valley.

"Like backlight on Garbo, this sun must feel blessed to illuminate this sight," I gasp, chest hurting and joints feeling like mush, as I recover my breath from climbing two miles to reach this lookout point. I rest against a large stone, while Irv runs back and forth from one end of the crest to the other, gushing in his gravelly baritone, "Man, what a rush."

Irv casts a wide and big-boned shadow on the sedge and woodrush. Shirtless in peach-and-purple paisley shorts, he seems underdressed for a mountain breach, more like he belongs on the beach.

From our ledge, we watch the rime-lined jagged cliffs facing us, dotted with climbers scaling its side. A zig-zagging waterfall below us knots its foam into a windy creek. The glossy sun hovers above the widest peak at the other end of the falling horizon. The fiery ball grinds against the rocks slowly, sparking shadows that cross the vale, ever longer and darker, speckled with arcing northern pintail and horned lark. Complete silence, save the water attacking the rocks at the bottom of the sparkling cataract, a kind of abstract anthem repeating in ever-louder tones, noise scrawling the logic of music, as evening starts to fall.

Irv suddenly breaks into a run and skirts down another trail towards a nearby clump of trees barely visible in the failing light. He reaches between two sprawling redwoods and picks up someone by the collar of his shirt. With one hand winching the guy, Irv carries him inches above the ground about twenty yards to a massive stump. He plunks the guy's rump down like a piece of meat against the large round remnant of a trunk, fleetly whirls him around as if pushing a carousel, and says, "Why were you beating that girl?"

He's done something like this before, carrying a guy by the scruff of his neck for yards to flop him roughly against the side of a car and say, "Don't hurt my friend." It was years ago and the guy was on top of my brother, punching away. We learned later that Leon had whipped it out and was dancing around, flipping it up and down, which offended the guy who tripped him. Irv, who sighted the fight at a distance, broke into a run towards the action before I saw what was going on.

As I get to the scene, a woman drags herself from the trees, staggers towards them and yells, "Thief, thief! He tried to steal my bag!"

Irv tells the scalawag to peel off his clothes and takes his wallet from his pants. He lifts up the guy, uses the shirt to tie his hands together at the knees, and the pants to tie him upright to a nearby tree wearing nothing but a pair of light briefs and a V-neck tee.

"I hope you're not hurt," he blurts to the thief sarcastically. "Your wallet will be at the gift shop. We'll send someone 'round to fetch you."

To the sound of the would-be thief screaming for help, in the shrouded light of early evening, we slowly plow along the backstretch of the mountain, down the trail, the woman and I following Irv, whose eyes seem unaffected by night. He occasionally tells us to step left or right to avoid a sudden drop, a fallen tree, a missing guardrail, or some other threat we fail to see.

Back in the car, we blaze again, and Irv begins to expatiate about his two fiancées, both named Jane, the one he's chasing in the park, the other one waiting for him in L.A. Irv is in a bind. He knows he must choose between the two or he'll lose them both, but he's insanely jealous and can't make up his mind. He zealously computes an avalanche of attributes and what he would lose if he left each, but there seems to be little to choose between his graces. Both are fair-skinned, petite with tiny waists, pretty faces, and short blonde hair, "like the girl next door," he boasts with lecherous drool. Neither uses narcotics, and both played varsity gymnastics at convent high schools. Both work for the post office, at different branches. Both families came to L.A. from Chicago, so both retain bits of a Midwest accent. Both live with parents near Bard Lake in the hills beyond the San Fernando Valley in split-level ranches. He met both at singles dances at Catholic churches, even though he's Jewish. He has raked up guys who befriended each during temporary break-ups. Both use diaphragms, which we agree is better than damned rubbers. He has taken both to Disneyland and finger-fucked both behind the shrubs on Tom Sawyer's Island.

"Enough, enough," I sigh. Nowadays my daughter would call Irv's details TMI.

But he slobbers on. Both press him to take a full-time job instead of selling nickel bags and making short-haul runs under the table for a compression equipment jobber. Both routinely break up with him after confession and then get back together and make him sit through a boring Latin mass. Both want him to convert to Catholicism, which he'd do if he knew which one he wanted more.

Pot smoke driven by his hoarse voice streams from the side of his mouth and animates in front of me as a blushing dream cloud, gushing through a coarse black sky encoded with stars and the onrushing reflectors at the edge of the road.

Jane Edge or Jane Wedge, he asks, burning with yearning. The Jane who did the pommel horse, or the Jane who did the rings? The Jane who hums, or the Jane who sings? The one he gave a necklace, or the one he gave a friendship ring? The Jane who likes pizza, or the Jane who likes Chinese? The one who freezes blueberries, or the one who makes fresh farmer's cheese? The Jane who scratches his back, or the Jane who rubs his feet? The one who snacks on veggies, or the one who munches sweets? The Jane who gave him towels, or the Jane who gave him argyle socks? The one who watches Laugh-In reruns, or the one who likes the Rockford Files? The Jane who likes to do it standing up, or the Jane who likes it doggy style? The one with the birthmark, or the one with the mole? The Jane who likes to camp, or the Jane who likes to bowl?

After driving through the second night in a row, as light begins to fill the off-ramp, my voice starts low, but ramps up quickly to a painful shout, "Irv, Irv, Irv, Irv, Irv, Irv, Irv! These girls are not the only two Janes out there!"

Now Irv's mate is yet another Jane, a petite, pale blonde former gymnast from Chicago of Catholic background who trains mail sorters for the post office. We meet at a pizzeria in Tarzana. While his taste in Janes hasn't changed, Irv has—he's gained two hundred pounds. He's now an enormous round roast sporting a mass of fat around his waggling gut and arms—still muscular underneath—and a sandlot ass that turns his sagging pink and white polka-dot Bermuda shorts into a giant yachting flag.

When the waiter arrives with bread, Irv orders a chocolate milk. Like a silk-handed thief, he carefully sneaks the bread into Jane's shopping bag, into which he also drags a tray of butter pats and the little paper packs of sugar. As soon as the waitress sets the dark brown milk on the table, he downs half of it in a single gulp, squeezes her arm and crassly says, "It's too strong, too much chocolate. Could you add more milk. And some more bread, please."

He spreads a blob of jam on a slab of bread and orders a jumbo meat-lover's pie with extra cheese. "And please go right up to the edge of the crust with the cheese and give me extra ham," he chides the waitress. He adds a Cobb salad, with extra cheese on the side.

When the food comes, he deftly scoops the cheese in a paper napkin and swoops it into his wife's bag. He pours grated parmesan from a can over the salad until it starts to sag on his plate. "The desserts here are great, but I don't want to get too filled. I'm going to make a killing later on playing racquetball. I buy guest passes to fitness clubs all over town, play a few games down, flub some shots, pretend I'm not a threat, then lay a big bet against the best player at the club."

He lets a Beelzebub giggle out of the side of his mouth. "Look at me—don't you think you could beat me? I look like a fat old beanbag. But underneath this jiggle I'm a rock, and it is a game of skill. I love to chill in the middle of the court, almost perfectly still, and sock the ball wherever I want, and watch these clowns kill themselves chasing it up and down, back and forth, until they collapse in their tracks. I clear about a grand a week, plus another two cees standing in line for ticket scalpers, which is like twenty bucks a ticket. Pretty good jack for hanging out with chicks."

Jane whacks him in his enormous gut. "Irv, act your age!" she bandies in fake outrage, leans across the table, hand up and to the side of her face, and purrs a cheerleader's version of a stage-whisper, full-smiled and dismissively distended, "The old goat likes to pretend he's still a player, but the only thing he plays with is the remote."

Irv snorts a full-throated laugh.

He has me drive him to a party—invited by an outfielder on one of his softball teams—on a guarded plot of land by a brook in the mountains spiking above Chatsworth that smells of skunk and sulfur. It resembles a junkyard, strewn with rusted trucks and motorbikes. Maybe fifty people are there, mostly hardened riffraff—bikers, punks and pikers, arms and backs tattooed and scarred. Some guys pack hunting knives or firearms in holsters. Some rattle around nervously and aimlessly, as if jacked on coke. Some swig whiskey from bottles, some toke chronic. No Blacks or Hispanics.

A handful of women are there, some thin as rails and others portly, all wearing faded jean jackets over short shorts and fishnet stockings, painted fingernails, eyes hidden under shades. They swelter and sweat by themselves under an oak tree on yard-sale folding lawn chairs near the beer cooler, discarded soubrettes playing cards and smoking cigarettes.

Near a pig roasting on a jimmy-rigged spit, the host has dug a horseshoe pit, which immediately attracts Irv's eye. He tugs my sleeve, pokes my thigh, and grins. "Just shut up and let me do the talking."

Irv asks to play the winners. The host—a hulk with the muscular bulk Irv had when he was young, a pin through each ear and a stud in his tongue, which flashes when he tells us we have to wait our turn. Irv smokes some hash—I pass—and we stubbornly skulk around the pit, watching four games in which the same team wins, thrashing the challengers each time, earning a few bucks in bets. When they pass the horseshoes to the first losers, Irv yells out, a little peeved, "I thought it was our turn."

The players give us a disbelieving look. Horseshoe in hand, a thin kid, with a complex of tattoos covering both arms like sleeves of a mottled shirt, kicks the dirt and leans towards us, body language I perceive as saying we'd be better off leaving. Jaw jutting and hand out, Irv sways slowly towards the guy, who chooses to give Irv the horseshoe and let us play.

I've never played before and am useless. At first, Irv is, too, throwing wild corkscrews and curlicues. After a few frames of each player tossing two horseshoes at the pin, the other team builds a six-oh lead. Eleven wins the game. A group of maybe seven guys are goading us with cuts about our horseshoe skills. The din of laughter is killing me—I feel humiliated, but tense, too—these are all thugs, even if a few wear rugs and many carry immense laundry loads. I'm too old for this nonsense.

Irv seems flustered. He loses his footing at the end of his throws, one time falling on his side into the sand. He stands up guffawing about busting a rib and rubs his waistband like a foolish Buddha. A kid with farmhand arms and a big scar running down the middle of his cheek glibly says, "We should make it interesting."

Irv answers meekly, "We could make it ten bucks," and the guy chuckles, "I was thinking more like a hundred," and plucks out a wad of bills.

"Okay, good." Irv speaks in the forlornly weak and wooden voice of someone who's been cornered and has to defend by doing something he doesn't want to do or surrender his manhood. Looking nauseous, he slowly counts out five twenties and sets them cautiously in the hand of the guy holding the bets.

Irv bends his arm, takes a crisp, smooth-sliding swing and pitches a ringer, and then another. "Lucky throws," he juts out his jaw and grins like a schnook.

On his next turn, he chucks another two ringers "Maybe you're not so lucky after all," someone calls out, to which Irv replies with thinly disguised sarcasm, "Maybe I'm learning from you guys."

After the rest of us miss badly, Irv twists his wrists drastically as he lets the horseshoe fly and throws a curve to make another, and we're tied. "You guys want to double the bet?" he says with bombastic verve.

Our opponents set their eyes on the ground and mutter that they'll stick with the current stakes. On Irv's next turn, we overtake them. I begin to fret that these guys will want to bust up a couple of sixty-year-old hustlers who burned them. When Irv's eleventh ringer in a row hits the dust, he turns to our opponents and clucks broadly. "I guess you owe me a hundred bucks."

I can see that the group of them are smoldering with resentment. Irv carefully counts one bill after another into an open hand, then tucks them into his shorts. He chucks the horseshoe into the sand and begins to walk away, slowly, chest out, looking from one player to another with feral "I'm the best" eyes. "I quit. You guys keep the pit, I'm done for the day. I'm an old man and I need my rest."

As we leave the area, our backs to the players, someone yells, "Dude, you've been hustled by prunes." My spinal cord bristles with the fear that one of the rough-hewn psychopaths Irv skinned will bushwhack us with a board from behind or knife us in the back.

Irv cruises to the barbecue grill. Trailing behind, I plead, "Let's blow this joint, Irv. Right now!"

"No, I want to hang a while," Irv says. "I want to have a few hotdogs, and I need to thank my buddy. He told me they'd be throwing horseshoes."

"Irv, these guys are pissed at us, and they're not strangers to using violence."

"No one's doing nothing," he states with a firm smile, while oozing nacho sauce on an immense pile of chips on a paper plate.

"Where's your common sense? These are rough hombres."

But it doesn't discombobulate him in the slightest. "Don't throw a fit. They're not so tough."

"Irv, I have the car for a change, and I say we jet."

"No problem, just split. Don't sweat it, man. Jane will get me."

I get into the left-hand lane before the turnabout and start for I-5 to SF, thinking discretion is the better part of valor.

Riding with Rossini. Bob Turob to Rob Turob. Bob Turob to Rob Turob. A few minutes after we started our road trip to Seattle—he for business, and I to recover from another bout of El's disdain—Rob Turob, sly and cherub-faced, hydroplaned a stubby pinky underneath my rump and rubbed softly. My leg skidded away and started bobbing up and down as it did when I was a kid, like my mother's did, throbbing with the urge to move. I shouted emphatically, "Rob, you know I'm not gay."

"You're straight as the gate," he winked. "But I thought, what the hey, nothing to lose."

"It's cool whatever anyone else does, but I love to screw women, to the point that it sometimes sinks me."

He reached over and rubbed my head like an uncle. "It's your stinking fate to be a hetero slut."

"If the shoe fits," I said, with an attenuated smile.

"In a rut? Maybe you're salivating for a taste of the other side of the aisle. For something you've never tried. You could be my Mt. Everest."

"Don't be a pest, man," I replied, riled and abashed, but with a dandy revenge plan handy that I know would make *him* pissed. "Bob Turob to Rob Turob, Bob Turob to Rob Turob, Bob Turob to Rob Turob to Rob to Rob Turob!" I started to break into Rossini's melody.

"You know I despise that juvenilia, and yet you persist." Rob looked pretty much the same as he did during his in-the-closet existence in high school and college, tall, thin but not athletic with a gristless face that spoke of Cork or Limerick. He moved paradoxically, his body and head very graceful, but his wrists and knees tweaking a geeky crankcase of moving parts. As Bob, his hair carted down his neck and acne-scarred cheeks, but as Rob he had very short, part-less hair that spiked out in front a little and a strikingly burnished visage, lacking even a trace of beard or blemish.

"You look like a Bodhisattva I saw in Paris," he said, "emerging between a section of snake pit grillwork, brash as an erection, his moustache smirking perfection, but also serene." He spun his simile with the preening and mildly chiding erudition of an art critic expressing emotional distance from the subject under discussion. "No, on second thought, you're Hephaestus caught in a red figure Greek amphora—gruff, tough, handicapped but un-flappable, carrying his pain like a medal of honor."

Rob started a monologue about famous faces in art in which he found the physical characteristics of the living—Laocoön's youngest son, Donatel-lo's crusty Abraham, Verrocchio's high-strung David with his lusty eyes, Ve-ronese's surprised Venus, her luxuriously hammy arm hung across Mars's back, della Robbia's curious Orpheus, Rodin's silver-tongued, big-headed Balzac, a hungry guest at Breughel's peasant wedding, a Titian nude wrapped in diaphanous bedding, Rembrandt's ready Saskia, Walker's steady peddler.

"My first gay fling, Vinny, was a male version of Renoir's portrait of Jeanne Samary, the same serious demeanor, white skin, watery eyes, strong chin."

It made me conjure a dim memory of another Renoir—an elegant, busty, tight-grinned mother with appealing twin girls and a sleeping dog, all comfy cozy and feeling very much at home and in no way smothered within the fus-ty gilded frame hanging on the peaceful damascene wall of an immaculately clean and dustless room of an orderly gallery, its glossy, genteel floors faintly squealing out the sound of the walking real. It was after school and we were still living in New York. I often hung around the Met instead of going home to chaos.

"I once saw a woman complaining about a roadblock display the same goony insane eyes as de Kooning's Woman One," Rob said.

Rob had cut stone into moon-like landscapes as an art student and blown glass into abstract shapes later on. "But I could never build demand for my work, because I didn't have a brand. Finally, I realized how much I aped other artists. I could dissemble about what and whom my work resembled more readily than about what it was, which I understand gets you ahead in tanned and sinful Hollywood, but not in the art scene, at least not yet. I grew tired of drifting, tired of my preening revamp of past styles, tired of shifting around and sifting through piles in my mean, postage-stamp of an apartment piteously decorated in discount aisles and Pier One." The answer to his desperation was to go into business selling art to corporations.

As we drove through the discoloration of early evening's frangible light, Rob spoke with elation about his fascination with contemporary art, which he called *postmodern* and characterized as iterations not finalities, sublimely self-referential, tangible not cerebral, its birth in the liberation of banalities, spiritually broken, yet engrossed in the past. He didn't much like that artists were content to focus their creations more on the laws of process and intent than on the final outcome. "Documentation of process has subverted beau-ty and truth as the final arbiter of worth in artistic criticism," he said.

"No wonder there's a dearth of beauty in the contemporary art I see.

Most of it is a gangrene goulash," I candidly asserted.

"That may just mean you haven't expanded past your Impressionist and Cubist brainwashing."

"Make up your mind," I demanded. "Do you champion or demean contemporary art?"

"Some I hate and some is quite moving. I don't care if the artist pastes obsidian ramenta onto Peruvian flax or stacks orange peel, cornmeal and earwax onto percale sacks, if it exhales beauty, it's art, even if that beauty expresses ugliness. As long as I can feel the beauty effloresce…."

"That's a yes-and-no answer."

"You've always been more than just a pretty face," his voice betrayed a brass trace of flirtatiousness.

We were somewhere between Medford and Eugene, the sun was long underground for the evening, and I needed to decompress. I suggested that we stop in a rest area and flop our sleeping bags on top of picnic benches.

"We might get drenched or eaten by ants," Rob said. "I'll find us two comfortable beds in a clean, warm house for free at a cheap ballad bar nearby. I'll scope out some preening éclair queen with matching earmuffs, or maybe a philistine auntie, or maybe get the call from a buff and spritely debutante who'll install us in his place for the night. It'll be all right. You don't have to do a thing, I'll do all the talking—and all the balling."

"I don't know. A stagehand once let me stand in the wings to see a show of female impersonators singing Garland and Streisand with a swing band. They performed with a lot of spunk, and some of them looked grand. But a bar for cruising…?"

"Don't be bunker-shy! Believe me, no one will be confused. They know who is and is not gay. You don't have the look. But no one will care that you're not."

"You say that with a lot of certitude."

"Take my word for it, lambskin. I don't want to seem rude, but you're not what anyone is looking for."

"How do you know about a gay bar in the middle of bumpkin-biscuits Oregon?"

"Every town, everywhere, has a gay bar," he grinned.

Rob bee-lined off I-5 and drove for a few minutes to a declining downtown, where he turned into an empty parking lot down the block from a bar with a small mauve neon sign over the door starkly shining in the dark: *Off Stage*.

Off Stage was loud and reeked of pine and bad wine. Guys of all ages, colors, shapes and sizes crowded the dance floor, sashaying deliberately to a jukebox that played only anodyne slow tunes: doo-wop torch songs, some-body-done-somebody-wrong country, and American songbook croons, to which many sang along.

I sat at the bar, my chair twisted to the dance floor, and watched the show. Suggestive dancing, femme fatale glances. Flirting eyes, grazing thighs. Grinding hips, parted lips, stolen kisses, cajoling hisses. Fanny pats, teasing spats, timid hugs, coquettish tugs. The flourishes of fingertips. Covert touching, desperate clutching. This salad of mating gestures looked familiar to me, an unsuppressed cultivation of the hetero stalk of sexual prey facilitated by the constantly depressed beat of ballads. But the straight world could just as easily have been imitating the gay.

Rob was right. Everyone knew I was straight. No one asked me to dance or make a date.

In short order, Rob was talking with a tall, well-groomed man with gray-specked hair, in a wide-lapelled silk suit with vest, a silk handkerchief pluming his breast pocket. They danced and necked a bit, then they quaffed a few beers, their arms linked at the shoulder. Rob introduced me to Jim as his sister's husband and sniggered that I was "straight as the gate," which triggered a gently modulated laugh from Jim.

I drove Rob's VW bug, following a silver Mercedes to a countryside Victorian with a triple-window tower, high peaked gables, and leaded glass doors. Inside, a mix of antique and modern furniture on flowery Persian rugs on warped and slightly scoured hardwood floors. By this time it was a glassy-eyed, nearly mummified midnight. I went straight to bed in a library lined with shelves of hardcover books, in a bay window nook on what Jim said was an Eileen Gray settee that he outfitted with sheets and a sleeping bag. I took a few drags on a joint to unwind and closed my eyes, but my mind couldn't find sleep. Streetlights' illumination beat through ruffled curtains. I heard the muffled bleating and chatting of Rob and his new friend down the hall. A fleeting déjà vu invaded me—I had stayed here before, or dreamed someplace similar—lying in a makeshift bed in a pieced-out recessed corner, the sound of carefree people enjoying themselves drifting to me, artificial light from outside boring through creases in the interior darkness. My mind couldn't tease out when or where, but I knew I had been there before.

The pell-mell tones and drones of love compelled me to think of El at home, waiting for me. Was she alone?

Or?

Or?

I forced myself not to think about it. Instead, I coursed through Jim's leather gilded nineteenth-century editions of English novels—*Pamela, Tris-*

tram Shandy, The Vicar of Wakefield. Dust puffed up when I lifted them from the shelf and opened them. I drifted into a lotic millrace of floating self that became a lobby space in which I began to pace, Uncle Toby's hobbyhorse in place. Back and forth. Back and forth. South to north. The horse suddenly canters away, speeding towards the seedy, near-the-railroad-tracks apartment my grandfather shared with my mother before her final and only successful try at seceding from life. My mount has vanished as soon as I am back in 1969, now standing at the kitchen bar, famished, cutting into a cheese omelet with a fork and knife. It's just Pop-pop and me. Momma is languishing in her room.

Pop-pop wears his usual costume, an ensemble that hurts the eyes: a checked green and brown sport coat that doesn't match his blue and white herringbone pants, or his two-toned red-and-orange shirt, or his pink-field-of-purple-butterflies tie, or the straw boater he insists on wearing in the house. He speaks in a strident whine that quakes slightly, almost in synch with the unfettered shaking of his kinked right hand. "Your mother should live with you and Leon, together in Chicago or out here, where the weather is better. Families belong together. Never forget that God planned for parents and children to be linked forever."

"First of all, I'm going to be a junior, and I live in a one-room apartment." I try not to sound too evasive.

"Get a bigger place and invite your mother to live with you, honey. Your mother misses the two of you. The current situation is a disgrace."

He pisses me off. It's not hard to trace his true motivation—to offload his crazy daughter onto someone else—but I can't just dismiss his pious bluff. She *is* my mother. But a week once a year of her verbal abuses, her gas-lighting, inciting and fighting is more than enough. That same old knee-jerk shame and anger are dirking me. Who can blame me for not wanting to live with her? Yet I know the smirking phony is right. "What about money? You know her work record." I am making my excuses.

"The important thing is that a family stay unified," he pleads. "The family is the heart of everything and you are now the head of your family. If you have to, you can afford to quit school for a while, honey. Use as your guide your Uncle Emil after your blessed grandmother died."

I start to say that the only reason Emil had to quit school was because he—Pop-pop—fell apart, but I want to avoid a scene. He fights constantly with Momma, usually after he has ignited the situation by doing or saying something stupid that incites her irritation. Not closing the lid on the toilet bowl. Breaking off the door key in the keyhole. Not scrubbing a casserole dish. Not draining the tub. When she reacts with haggish intensity, he feigns ignorance, then reminds her of her propensity to get nervous and lose control.

"I'm not going to quit college, but I will think about what you said." On one level, I give the old tight-fisted twit his due: he's right. The ethical thing to do would be to invite her to live with me. But over these few days while I have visited them in L.A., her flightiness has begun to get on my nerves. There haven't been any fits or glares directed at me—just at my old sad sack of a grandfather. She has rolled out of bed most mornings instead of smoldering in her room. But the threat of an attack of gloom hangs in the air.

"Think seriously about it," he crows, "because it's best for everyone if everything goes well. I'm your grandfather. I'm blessed with a lifetime of experience. I wouldn't suggest it if I weren't looking out for your best interests. And if you don't like it, I'll give you a punch in the nose," he insists, aping a jokey false bravado as he shapes his fingers into a loose fist—thumb incorrectly inside his balled hand—and brandishes it, a Bozo gesture he has made to all of his grandchildren ever since I can recall. The fishy, wishy-washy balled band flaying the air becomes my other grandfather's black cane whipping around over his head as he tells us about his physician, who had just died at the age of forty-seven of a massive heart attack. We are sitting in his sunroom eating lox and bagels with Leon, Momma, and his wife of the time. The old man yacks over the smarmy innuendos and puns of a Redd Fox LP. "A year ago I had boils running across the top of my back and my nape," he cries out joyously. He's been in Los Angeles for thirty years, but still intones a New York wiseass sneer. "That quack sonofabitch explained that to get rid of them, they would have to peel back the skin, scrape out the infections, and cauterize the flesh near the bone. Painful and expensive, and not worth it, he said, because I'm prone to get them again, and with my emphysema and heart, I might kick in six months. That's what the ignorant prick said! Not worth it, 'cause I could be dead. Fuck him. I told that doctor I was going to piss on his tombstone. And hot damn, now I'm going to do it! He died of a heart attack a week ago, and I'm pissing all over his headstone," he hisses in victory.

He rises from his chair, cane jabbing air, and starts to totter like a jittery spinning top slowing down. I place my hand at his shoulder to stabilize him, but instead it's Rob Turob, leaning over me and softly sputtering, "Let's get trotting before he wakes up. I'm not into the brunch and munch scene after a one-night stand."

But it turned out to be far from a one-night stand, as I learn when Rob and I get together—the first I see of him since he disappeared soon after our trip thirty years ago. Rob yearned for Jim and bounced back to Oregon. They began a long, torrid, non-exclusive relationship. Jim had a band of young lovers. One of them—named Tony—made Rob "as jealous as a greedy Bathsheba at a bathhouse. A horrid little chip, always flouncing around the mansion wearing nothing but a thong, flip-flops and a sprayed-on tan." Rob wrathfully moaned that Tony was a needy little brownie queen without an ounce of real flare in his randy bones, a phony Tissot dandy. But when Jim got sick, everyone abandoned him, except Rob and Tony.

"It was such a dreadful ordeal to see Jim decline. His once appealing and distinguished-looking body now shriveled to threads and appeared to float weightlessly over the bed that confined him. Together, we sat through long nights of his retching what we fed him through a narrow tube jammed down his throat. Together we heard his coyote whines, saw infections smite his body, heard the disease eat his brain and rot his spine. Together, we watched as this divinely witty man, slowly composting into a white-sheeted ghost of pain, wrote funny roast lines to host his own memorial party. Together, we watched the lean sexpot of an intern complete his charts each visit. Together under our breaths we counted the slowing trot of his heart on the monitor after a morphine shot."

Rob's body has taken on a prosperous large-lapped corpulence, right on the vestibule of being overweight. His face has grown full, too, lines teeming around his eyes and mouth and on his neck like streams on a map of Ireland. His eyes gleam pools of empathy when he says, "I saw tenderness in Tony's eyes as he sponged Jim's abscesses or when he pressed Jim's frail hand and exhaled a blessing in an ambulance. He never shirked the hard chores, like cleaning the purulence that was Jim's body. Tony never fumed or screamed. Never a drama queen. When he reverentially described Jim's quirks and facial expressions, the ones I also always thought endearing, he zoomed right into the essential. It made me see how much alike we were, Tony and me. We consoled each other, and then love bloomed, literally over the tomb, and we've been together ever since, most of it exclusively, after the running around began to interfere. We sold Jim's Victorian and set up household in San Francisco, two chintzy old queers.

"Sometimes I walk at dawn and watch the sun tilt across the brawling hills and wonder why we never got ill, after all our tricks and sexual hijinks. It's another thing that links us—our guilt at surviving the plague, which we saw wilt so many we knew. We've built our world around blinking into the face of death, sinking ever deeper into survivor's guilt."

"How can you call yourself a survivor?" I say with the sharp-fanged scorn I learned from my father. I'm suddenly overborne and enclosed. "You're saying you banged a ton of men and you're still alive, so you're a survivor?

That's just jive!" I strive to compose myself almost immediately. I don't want to piss Rob off the first time I've seen him in thirty years.

"Okay, you're Jewish, you know what it means to be an outsider," Rob replies, at first miffed. But the longer he talks, the more a calm resignation restores his voice, as if he is telling me something he has confided to himself many times before. "Outsiders get preoccupied with their own sub-society. They come to have rapport only with those just like them. So after a while, practically everyone I knew was gay. And everywhere I saw friends struck down by horrible deaths. It was an epidemic, but it was also a gory warzone, which I survived by the luck of the draw, the same way survivors of epidemics or wars always do. Not through any special virtue, but through boring luck. Hence the shame."

Who am I to blame him for equating his experiences to war? I wasn't present, and I'm not inside his heart. No use trying to debate good and bad when it comes to calibrating the emotional parts of others, no wrong or right, no black or white. There's just what you feel, and the reasons you feel that way. There's just a gray in-between concealed by words—something neither of my parents ever understood. My mouth starts to taste like woody cotton, as it often does in a discussion with May, or Maya, for that matter. Outwitted, and feeling pretty stupid about it. But they usually freely admit when they are wrong without any emotional battering and expect the same of me. A far cry from my parents, who claimed everything that went wrong was someone's fault and at someone's expense, so someone had to be blamed, all of life a long ping-ponging of who's right and who's not. Neither my father nor El could ever admit they were in the wrong, so would fabricate and prevaricate to frame someone else. My mother did the same, but then would sometimes calculate it was *her* crime, even when it wasn't, and expected others to do the same, which never made sense, but felt normal at the time.

"You're right," I confess to Rob. "A survivor is a survivor. Your guilt is no less valid than that of a soldier, the oppressed, the starving, the smothered, Holocaust Jews, victims of rape or the worst kind of child abuse. No one can really know or say they've had it worse than others."

"Why, thank you, Jules," he smothers a jape. "Now that's a first."

Another friend I won't be seeing is Vern Jackson, who died a few years back of a heart attack, according to the online obituary I read. I knew him by face as another tenant threading through the apartment halls until the day I saw him in a three-piece suit spread-eagled against a car in front of the building, one cop frisking him, another holding a gun to his head. I briskly headed to the cop with the gun and asked him what was wrong. They suspected him of robbing a convenience store and mauling the clerk.

"I can absolutely vouch for him," I bray kindly for all to hear. "He's my neighbor."

No response. "Did someone identify the coot who did it as wearing a three-piece suit?"

"Stay out of this, or we'll haul you in, too." The cop brutally drawls and raises a fist close to my face. They cuff Vern and lead him to their police car. All this time, Vern doesn't say a word, but permits himself a serene smile. Later that day, while I'm describing the scene to El, Vern knocks on the door with a bottle of cognac to thank me for trying to intervene. We end up splitting the bottle and a few joints, as he tells us about the four times he has been hammer-locked and thrown in the slammer by police officers suspecting him of a crime.

"Why did you let them whisk you off to jail without protest?"

"When you're Black, anything you say could be interpreted as resisting arrest. If they get pissed enough, they can bust you up real bad. Best just to answer the questions and let them check my ID."

"But you're dressed so well," I persisted.

"Don't matter none if you're Black. They still mess you up. Every brother I know has been stopped by pigs at least once in his life." I thought he was exaggerating, until I started asking around—an interior decorator El knew, a friend of my cousin Petey's, a salesman at the insurance company. All had been harassed by the cops more than once in the past. While jogging on their own street. Driving into the parking lot of the hotel where they had a suite. Pulled over to have their license checked. Handcuffed, fingerprinted, and celled as a suspect. The same flabbergasting stories repeated again and again. None had ever dropped a hint of it to me before, as if they held a dark caste secret.

Vern started showing up at our doorstep every few weeks with a bottle of booze. He was always well-dressed with a nice dress shirt and an odd-patterned tie, stormy blue or purple fields covered in corkscrews and kangaroos, horseflies, or gladioli, hailstorms of cuneiforms and ensiforms, windsored and loose around his neck. His insistence on the formality of a cravat reminded me of the Black janitor with whom I worked at a TV station in Miami—a summer job Uncle Emil got me—who arrived each day in a wide-lapelled gray suit and blue striped tie and changed into his uniform before he grabbed his dustpan and broom, then changed back before he went back outside at the end of the day. When I asked him why he tried to look executive, he sighed as if I were wacky and said that clothes make the man.

An assistant professor of mathematics at San Francisco State. That's what Vern was.

Hanging around loaded one afternoon, we started perusing an old box of pop and rock forty-fives I had saved from my teen years. Lots of Motown—Four Tops, the Temptations, Marvin Gaye. Vern pulled out Dee Clark's "Raindrops" and asked me to play it.

"I couldn't get enough of that song as a kid," I said, "but now I think it's crappy. The bogus thunder in the background, the flabby violins, the sappy lyrics that sound like they're sung with a happy grin even though his heart is supposed to be broken. Completely fake."

"Not completely. Listen to the last four words just before the fadeout. In a blood-quaking instant, Dee captured the dark, God-forsaken history of my people in this land. He wails the pain of centuries, pain of smelling death and feces chained in the hull of a ship sailing west, pain of searing brand on thigh, of hours of cranking up a cotton gin, half-dead from withstanding everyday daily whippings, of gawking without protest as your trafficked children roll away from the slave mart in shotgun-guarded carts, of knowing the master sticks it to his sweetheart whenever he wants to, the pain of acting deferential to people who reprimand him for his color, the pain of losing land he plowed for years to legal tricks, the pain of fear of seeming too proud or gabbing too loud, the fear of scaring white women with his looks, the fear of beatings, lynching, firebombs, the pain of shame of his seat in his shabby, crowded, worse-than-hillbilly school, at the chilly back of the bus, the cold outside the restaurant while they grill his grub, the pain of sniper bullets, rubber hoses, ugly curses, dirt-rubbed face, the pain of whispers that assume a genetic inheritance of thievery, laziness, incompetence, the pain of being forced by the record producer to smile all the while he sings of pain, until the fadeout of an inane power ballad after two minutes of grinning through a sweet conflation of *raindrops, it must be raindrops, it feel like raindrops,* against the rising obbligato of the violins, calling forth a suddenly hoarse and harsh ear-splitting, fog-cutting cry that forces centuries of the inhumane into four short words, *it keeps on fallin'....*"

"He says all that in three seconds?"

"I hear all that in three seconds." Vern was expressing an immensely explosive anger, yet he seemed so self-composed. He never raised his voice, no matter how intense the discussion.

"Do you ever blow up and try to put your fist through the plasterboard or begin kicking the fence? It happens to me all the time," I asked.

"Can't afford to. Whether I'm going along to get along or resisting, no matter what I feel within I have to stay under control or risk making things worse because of the color of my skin. I get to keep my self-respect that way, yes, but self-protection is a much greater reward. Especially when the pigs suspect you."

"Twice I've told cops to fuck themselves and fanned the finger under their noses. They didn't flinch, either time. Completely deadpan."

"That's because every inch of you looks like The Man. And maybe one day you'll be The Man. I suppose you'll be a better man than the current Man, but you'll still be The Man."

A similar conversation with Leon. My brother believed that participating in society in any way made you part of the system of exploitation. "The rich are adroit at shaping the system to make it inescapable," Leon said. "Even those starting out with low-paying jobs, scraping by but yearning for shoddy goods that keep them on treadmills of their own exploitation, even they help to use and abuse the Third World and contribute to the war economy that subjugates other countries. People fuse themselves into the system through their pursuit of needs propagated by the entertainment and advertising industries." Leon ranted in an excited New York accent that I heard only when we were alone, otherwise supplanted by a slow and pokey thick stop-for-a-toke Southern canter. "Even today's revolutionaries evoke the happy little consumer, buying up blue jeans, Navajo tapestries, Aleutian quoits, little red books, and herbal shampoos. The more you have, the more corrupted you are, the more you feed the system, the more you do the bidding of the greedy rich, the more you exploit others. By definition. The only escape is to refuse everything and live completely off the grid, free of all material needs."

"But that's impossible," I said. "We live in a world of things. You'd be screwed if you had to make your own guitar strings, pots, razor, bicycle, tools, bookshelf, and a multitude of other things you cling to, even out here by the Oconee. If you believe that by living in a teepee you avoid the corruption of American society, you're deluding yourself."

"No, man, I don't live in a teepee to elude or cheat the system. We all live with the original sin of consumer capitalism. No, I live in a teepee because I'm a deadbeat," he cackled lewdly, picked up his guitar, and treated me to a fleet and bluesy version of "Jesu, Joy of Man's Desiring," raising his eyebrows and knitting them together impishly at each downbeat.

"Raindrops," another piece of music about desire. Another list: what was I doing when I heard "Raindrops"?

In bed sweating profusely late one muggy summer night, listening to Cousin Brucie roll through the Top 40 ...

Raindrops, so many raindrops ...

With Denny Knoll and Jerry Luft in Marty Hellman's basement, crooning it in goony voices, tightly holding pool sticks to our mouths as microphones ...

It feels like raindrops, falling from my eyes, eyes …

Jawbone aching from in-the-dark, open-mouthed, bent-over-her-arched-body kissing with Debbie Diamond on a dilapidated red roan couch at a sixth-grade party in another basement …

Since my baby left me …

Seated in a car tasting an ice cream cone, in a shopping center parking lot somewhere in Nassau County with my father's friend Joey, while we were waiting for my new glasses to be ready at Sterling Optical, feeling alone and cheated that my father hadn't come himself …

But I don't know where she's gone …

Transistor earphone to my ear and humming it as I rush into the open bathroom to find my corkscrew-faced father standing over my bawling mother, and pasting her with a hairbrush …

It keeps on falling … fades to … *the night, the waves, the sand.* … Sugarloaf's organ wells and crests on the eight-track, as El maneuvers a rented truck packed with all our possessions along a shadow-infested narrow highway through the Siskiyou Mountains. Towering rocks dressed in yellowed grass and small white wildflowers shade the lanes. Thick, almost pure white clouds overhead congest the afternoon sun. As the lead singer persuades a "green-eyed lady, wind-swept lady…" in his nervy, nasally tenor, El takes a curve. We spy a "Welcome to California" sign, as the left side of the pass fades away into a panoramic view sweeping thousands of feet into a wide valley of Western white pine and hemlock, at the same instant that the clouds dissolve into a deep blue sky mining the unsuppressed golden clarity of California sunshine: a falling away of darkness into bold light. The end of a quest. A new world ingests the old.

I wish I could recall only what I want to recall, and send what I want to forget to a dead-end wasteland, instead of tasting all of it as it comes gushing through me in all of its glorious suffering, without the buffering of my temporal distance and the words I use to link it together. But it all happened. I have the proof in photos I won't look at, photos I didn't take, in tattered proofs of birth, discharge, and death, in newsprint clips, recital notes, keepsakes—this sadness realizing former times will never come again, this sadness drenched in pain before and after happy moments, chimes of grace, sadness because of how long ago it happened, how short a time and gone, sadness crushing chest with paralyzing blow, leaves me craving circumstances cold as mind, unlinked to child, event, or love, seeking image sapped of past defined, yearning after photos, letters, music, fragrance morphed to spotless form without a sob of transience.

Every day we shed skin. Every day cells die within our brains and others are born, our minds are worn, our thoughts shorn. Every day bacterial strains inside us lurk, shirk, slink, shrink, mutate, circulate, attenuate. Every day we gain or lose weight, our skin sags a little more, more muscles feel sore, another hair turns gray. Every day our nails grow and the blood in our skein of veins and arteries flows. New cells replace old, but they're slower, less able to persevere, less able to cooperate with other cells. Skin wrinkles, legs swell, sunspots grow, liver accumulates toxins.

As things take on complex traits and convoluted whys, age chisels away the silky face of youth's easy answer, shedding persona, taming private truths, making unlike things grow alike: burrs of crystal, spikes of sand on open palm, snowflakes falling through the achromatic winter sky and striking kame. Until at last none of us is what we were, and all of us is the same.

Sometimes the present extends the past, naturally, like baby-rocking when everything you say begins to rhyme. Sometimes the present socks yesterday in the spleen. Sometimes it bends it. Sometime it upends it. Sometimes it seems to mock it. Sometimes it unlocks its meaning.

I started this trip trying to feel like a homeless Ulysses, roaming to be free, to fly free of home, or merely free of death, or at least the perception that one will die. But the longer I travel, the more I buy into Rob's idea that I'm the flawed, crippled Hephaestus, blacksmith, goldsmith, sculptor, stippler, tamer of volcanoes, the only Greek god to be exiled and then returned to heaven, to home, tippled and staggering, led back into the family fold by the equally drunk and haggard Dionysus riding a buffalo. The rejected son, who once limped away from his parents' slipshod disgust at his crimpled foot onto a sod of adventure and lust, in which he was the most powerful of the gods.

But I'm not the wheelwright Hephaestus, not the urbanite Ulysses. I never returned home, but with gratitude made my home in the nest of other birds, a brooding parasite.

Time—a blooming orchid. A flower walking on air opens to produce another flower, which adduces yet another. Do we see gradual revelation or layers smothering the essential core—the frail and vulnerable spore, pregnant with the possibility of pregnancy? We walk through time-blooms, Virgil-less except for the buoyancy of our memory that keeps us afloat and moving. Or perhaps like Repin's Volga Boatmen, we trudge through time's dry infancy with others, all pulling together the sludge-dripping mothership, even if we're trying not to, but merely struggling to escape the whip.

Tina's time is another orchid. Except for creases at her wide-awake eyes, she looks no different today from when she was taking her red-haired two-year-old boy to a commune and I picked her up in the middle of New Mexico when I was snaking back East after my breakup with El. As soon as the child fell asleep, I stopped the car, and we did the beast with two backs like wild toads against the passenger door on the side of the road. I ended up keeping house with her for two randy, sex-sick weeks, two weeks in which we couldn't keep our hands off each other, in a tent in a leased field called God's Land, inhabited by an egalitarian commune of vegetarians—a collection of tents, huts, and pieced-together cabins with no electricity. We used Coleman lamps at night and cooked on open fires. It reminded me of Boy Scouts, but I didn't find campfire meals and sleeping on the earth as appealing as I used to. Tina blamed our meager fire for the undercooked veggies. Darkness flamed with carnality, but the rest of the time passed in Hobbesian fashion, breaking our backs working the community vegetable garden or grinding corn by hand for tortillas. I faced animosity from the entire brood, when I argued for roasting a supermarket chicken. The communitarians clucked about their commitment to not kill animals for food, even after I pointed out that plants might have feelings and endure gruesome pain when we plucked their fruit or hacked off their stalks. Everyone reeked of flatulence from drinking the lip-puckering brackish creek water and itched all day from sleeping among ticks and sawyer beetles. After two weeks in which the days and diets never varied, everything about this bleak existence annoyed me in an eye-rolling way. My soul pined for open road. It was my year of destroying dead relationships. Now Tina is a public interest attorney married to another female lawyer.

Toll ahead.

Round-eyed Jaye squinted at the road through enormous oval lenses fitted in shiny orange plastic frames, under an orange-tinted bob with a horizontal braid running along one side. A graduate student in English Lit, she gave El and me a ride in Denver on our six-month hitch of the country, gabbing through a snow storm in a mountain pass about taking classes with Gary Snyder and Kenneth Koch in Greece, her show with Ginsberg and thirty other "poets for peace," the fabulous trip she took with John Cage and Yoko Ono to Japan, soul-gripping performances at happenings in Manhattan before she had to focus on completing her dissertation at Stony Brook—an analysis of fairy tales in Keats—which she hoped to turn into a book.

Jaye treated us to a recitation in a hushed, halting voice, replete with "ums" and "ers," her lips and throat groping for the words exactly as she wrote them. All were poems of hope and trust, against the war and nuclear power, lusty and lush with female incarnations—she the earth and she the sun, she the sunlight communing with her snowflake daughters, with neither pun nor wordplay, but crusty with references to folklore taken from the Egyptians,

Cherokee, and Jaqaru. Boring after one or two, but instead of the words I heard the rhythm of infectious enthusiasm, naïve optimism, love of human masses, hate of war.

I meet Jaye at the Rock Center Café, an excuse she says for her to slink around New York for the day. We watch the skaters crowd the ice rink. Her demeanor's less inflamed, more subdued, as if she's overthinking everything, and she speaks in a green-apple rural twang. She has gray-dappled hair, shoulder length with bangs. She still sports round Granny spectacles, but in clear frames. In a pastel pink pants suit, Jaye projects a few more pounds, but she's not enshrouded in fat like so many with whom I have reconnected.

Jaye has just retired from teaching at a rural private college in the middle of Pennsylvania, where she still lives and gives classes in poetry as therapy at the local Y.

"I'm preoccupied with a piece to introduce teens to contemporary poetry," she says. "It's about a wizard in the hinterlands who yearns to expand his tweet about the writing of an epic poem, which is a burning critique of a book review of a musical based on a movie inspired by a novel of a novelist's struggle to add symmetry to his critically panned novel about making a movie of a musical based on a book review, which critiques a poem about the writing of a tweet. It's a demand for authenticity and what it means to poetry, told as a sweet but grand tale of love between the author and her words on a level that tweens and teens can understand."

Jaye then and Jaye now are two more dots that do not fully connect to form a straight line. There are others, like the Klines, who spent our two hours on the road together whining nonstop about the "fucked-up" American diet and peeping about macrobiotics. Years later, she's a veep of sales for a company that franchises donut shops and he's a hotshot plastic surgeon specializing in tummy tucks....

Zee, the tall Swiss German girl with a degree in classical languages traveling around the world on twenty bucks a day. She picked me up in a used Chevrolet G20 outfitted with a mattress and curtains she bought in New York and was planning to sell in L.A. In the darkness after some uncertain stark-naked petting to the sound of cars skidding through a heavy rain, she pushed me away. She told me bitterly that her father punished her by sticking her wet fingers in an electric outlet whenever she did something not permitted. I held her through the night, but that was it. Now she's a divorced social marketing guru. She jets around the country to train people how to sell corporate assets on Twitter....

Vee, the snooty-in-a-fruity-way Professor of English El and I met at a bus stop near our apartment, who looked as if she had parachuted into the city from another century—sashes, lunette embroidery, and rosette strutted trims on her sleeves and bodice, flowing skirt, stout low-heeled block boots, pert page-boy haircut under a fake gold coronet in a wide conical silhouette, a capacious cape like Sir Francis Drake's. She was setting off for a Renaissance Faire. Vee told us that in one of her former lives she was a princess who ached after a destitute gardener and swam across a lake in a thick fog to care for the old coot in secret. Now Vee gives corporate executives seminars in brand loyalty as part of the Disney Institute....

The guy at Stanford studying the reign of Charlemagne, now a personal fitness trainer....

The distinguished Black gentleman with musk cologne who invited me to his boathouse for a drink, put *Paint Your Wagon* on his stereo, and sang in sync with Rufus Smith in a polished baritone, "Maria blows the stars around and sends the clouds a-flyin', Maria makes the mountains sound like folks were up there dying." He snagged my arm and dropped his drink as a ruse to make a pass at me. I deflected his ragtag predation with a loopy tap dance to another part of the sloop while saying I wasn't a fag, to which he replied, "I prefer to call myself *gay*, as in happy." He's now the executive director of a national Evangelical family values group....

The newspaper reporter who was visiting communities and schools using alternative fuels two weeks after the Three Mile Island leak. He spent hours exhorting me calmly in his counter pipsqueak voice about "that fool Truman's" two white papers—the one that recommended solar and the one that recommended nuclear—insisting that Truman made the wrong choice just as he did about dropping the bombs on Hiroshima and Nagasaki. He did the numbers for me with frenzied glee, showing that the federal government could indeed make photovoltaic cells economical if it used them to fill the military's need for field batteries. Now he's dressed in tweed, executive director of public affairs for an international agricultural corporation selling genetically modified seed....

Has everybody sold out? Is that the common theme of change over thirty years?—people giving up their ideals to make a buck? Changing to conform to changing ways. Changing because it pays. Changing to suck up to the boss. Changing under the influence of the mass media that glorify celebrity culture. Changing from doves to vultures. It makes me imagine a flock of elfish Hare Krishnas running around airports today chanting, "Sock your money away, sock your money, sock your money away, sock your money. Sock your money away, sock your money, sock your money away, sock your money."

Like the swans at Coulee, these pale young kings and princes with shaven heads in weird orange robes and sandals look exactly like the same ones gallivanting around the terminal three decades ago. It's not hairy-warted, pot-bellied old graybeards hopping from one foot to another and shaking the tambourines at LAX and Hartsfield. It's still the same pasty-faced, germinal-eyed young wasting my time. What happened? Could all the old-time Hares have retired to monasteries? Or did they slough off their youthful enchantment with finding freedom through the repetition of cant? Did they all become programmers and accountants?

I could ask the same question about those whose occupations have disappeared: steelworkers, assembly line workers, toll takers, mechanical drafters, switchboard operators, bicycle delivery guys, typesetters, photo lab technicians, stenographers, meter readers, bookstore employees, metal benders, lathe operators, copy boys, sandmen, travel agents. All became something different, often reluctantly. No one disappeared. No one ended up in a landfill, like countless signs of the 1970s: clogs, swag lamps, lava lamps, bean bag chairs, pet rocks, mood rings, shag carpets, moon chairs, and smiley faces—no, take smiley faces off the list. My luck. I saw one the other night tattooed on the nape of a young man with a premature pot gut under his untucked Confederate flag T-shirt, pumping gas into his bright red pick-up truck.

At the third light, take a right.

Adam, a jazz drummer good enough to work with the peak local players, picked me up in downtown Seattle while I was still portraying a junior exec at the insurance company. We hit it off, so when it leaked out that he was living in the rusted-out van he was driving, I told him he could stay with me for a few weeks. He typecast himself as the striving, slightly downcast handyman, who always did the planning, running around, conniving and cleaning up of messes for every band he was ever in. He talked only of process, doing something or getting something done, never about his personal life, his past, or having fun.

Every morning Adam compiled checklists: specs and tests on his drums and mikes, a list of club owners, their lifestyles, their likes and dislikes, the names of their tykes. A checklist for rigging the sound equipment, for organizing gigs, for planning road trips. A list of tunes that drew the most tips. He made a note of everything he had to do on little paper slips.

Adam was a tall, muscular, Norwegian-looking chap with angular facial features and yellow hair, a little slap-dash clumsy when he wasn't playing, and a bit of a sad sack. He would step on a thumbtack, slam his hand in a car door, sprawl over chairs, walk into walls, trip on an escalator, get trapped in an elevator, spill hot coffee in his lap. I introduced him to a girl I had tapped once or twice on a casual basis. I was fine, but he caught the clap.

At various times, he worked selling industrial supplies, commercial deodorizers, tie plates and risers, weights and measures, antique treasures, barb-wire, truck tires, cotton swabs, and doorknobs. Never for very long, but that was swell, he confessed one night over a bong. Just what he wanted, because he had no trouble finding new jobs. When work prospects were slim, it gave Adam more time to seek gigs throughout the northwest, a grinding respon-sibility he said typically fell to the weakest player in a quartet, "the least best," he grimly said, who he knew was always him. Adam introduced me to the local jazz scene. I'd groove with the guys between sets before I met El. I lost contact with him after we moved to San Francisco.

Now he's in a hospital, a completely bandaged left leg jacked up. Ban-dages cover both hands and arms and the bridge of his nose, plus he has a fractured back, all from driving his car into a ditch, fleeing from an airplane overhead that he thought was tracking him.

He strains to speak in a spent whisper about the dream that caused the accident. "So I'm back in country, incommunicado, and we're being attacked by lots of MIG-17's and getting our asses creamed, so I'm running in a shal-low stream teeming with vicious Rotts. I'm whacking the brutes away with boot kicks and the butt of my rifle, when one of the dogs turns into my jeep. So I get in, and now I'm trolling through mud, and the planes are in hot pur-suit, sweeping low, following my bloody tracks, growing closer. Someone's reaching out of an open porthole and shooting at me."

"I didn't know you were in the war."

"I never wanted to talk about it. I chose to abort everything in my life that occurred before the day I shipped home. But the same frozen dream of war shakes and rakes me again and again, like echoes of an earthquake. It started about fifteen years ago. I started to fear falling asleep so much that some nights I stay awake and stare at the TV, then doze off in a chair.

"So I was driving, and suddenly I have a feeling of being elsewhere. I thought I was back in the dream. An airplane swirled around me overhead in ever-tighter loops. So I zipped down a droopy country road. The plane seemed to switch directions to follow me. It swooped down towards me like a bird of prey. So I turned my car sharply, hit a hedgerow, and flipped down an escarpment into a ditch."

While he sleeps, restlessly, I learn the story of Adam's war malaise from his ex-wife Bess, who has spent her days and nights in his hospital room since the accident. Three times he was the only one of his company to return from forays, the rest burned to char or left to bleed out in the weeds. For the past few years, he swears he's been hearing hazy fragments of conversations of his buried comrades. He says they invent stories about women and sports deeds over poker games. Their frenzied clicks of cards and chips dent Adam's ears like a baby's airplane venting, driving him crazy.

I watch him silently until his head twitches and he bellows like a blind bear. He looks around and sees me. "Jules, man, it's you."

"You had a nightmare?"

"I had a scare. Sometimes my mind feels like a thousand witless monkeys. So I spend hours pacing back and forth without quitting, tracing a circle around the living room, my head spinning out of control, hurting everywhere, physically ill, and ill in my soul. I want to squeeze my life out of my skin. I'm sweating and freezing all at once, unable to stay in one place, pacing back and forth in a complete funk if I try to sit still." His description perfectly fits the panic attacks I had in my twenties.

Adam is not looking at me or at Bess, but to an undefined invisible something behind the windowpanes. As he confesses, veins on his forehead tighten grimly. He locks his limbs to his side and flexes and beats the bed, as if he were struggling to free his limbs from invisible chains. "So I pace so long that after a while my feet rub a crack in the floor and I fall through it and jackscrew into a black hurricane of blinding pain. I'm drowning, swirling down the drain of a tub.

"I've tried everything to kill this ever-lasting, teeth-gnashing fear, all in vain," he squeals. "Deep breathing, fasting, mindful meditation, swilling booze, stuffing myself with pain pills, puffing hash, talk therapy, letting a doctor drill hundreds of willowy needles into my arms and legs, you name it, I tried it! My faith that each would heal me—or help me deal with it—only led to a crash—a grand emptiness, until this thrashing anguish became a necessary part of life. A proof I'm real, an eternal presence, an involuntary rite that structures every day, like flipping on the light.

"I leap up and start pacing again, uncontrollably." Adam arches forward in the bed, then falls back and starts to march in place horizontally under his blankets. "I pirouette around the dinette set, parched but sweating, afraid to stop and sit down, threatened by every sound that's pursuing me, a caged shrew or kinkajou, offset by my greater fear to venture beyond the borders of the room, out of control, cuckooing loudly, 'I was only following orders.' Funny thing is, I bet if I were still in the war I'd know what to do. I'd know what to do, I'd know what to do, know what to do, what to do, what to, what to do…."

He keeps repeating these words. His voice veers and dips, becoming dreary, subdued, catatonic, until the words melt to blunt frets and simpers, deeply homophonic sobs, then bleary, listless grunts, then shushing sips, then no longer sounds but nervous, puppeteer-like gestures from limpid lips.

A bestiary of half-human, half-animal forms hovers over the highway and stares at me through the windshield of my speeding car. They come from all directions, all brandishing hand-held computers like pickaxes and javelins. Dog-eared dragon heads on poodle bodies sectioning the world into animated virtual playlands, toggling war zones into games and games into war zones. Bearded witches on bony chicken bodies, flattening millions of roving eyes to miniature phone screens. A lion with four cone-shaped heads cramming histamine screams into ringtones. Giant, wide-winged birds, donkey heads emerging from their tails, reshape the landscape into a bleak sameness of strip malls, parking lots, and subdivisions full of cul-de-sacs and circle drives in which every house is poured concrete and sham tile from which brew five hundred rings, different melodies but all the same jive tone, earbuds spewing fifty different pop songs, all with the same Grand Old Opry yodeling claptrap to the same static beat played by the same electronic band. The landscape morphs again, this time into the orange-coated interior of an enormous tent that stretches from sand to stars, inside of which fly by hundreds of casual dining and fast food joints with different names hawking the same burgers, wraps, and tacos, beer and pop, fajitas, wings, and sloppy Joes, grease-soaked, sweet, deep-fried batter glopping with topping, and hundreds of versions of salt-and-sugar infused meat, all micro-zapped. Hundreds of storefronts with thousands of rooms selling baseball caps, T-shirts, tank tops, yoga pants, and yoghurt desserts. Television monitors hover at eye level above the displays, blaring out reruns of "Seinfeld," "Law and Order," "M*A*S*H," and "Happy Days."

Mall after mall groan the fierce brimstone bawl and twaddle of the inked and pierced, the droning drawls and huffing waddles of the obese, ordinary human beings, but objects seem larger across the barrier of safety glass that protects me from the charge-card cyclone through which I'm trawling. Everyone seems bigger now, the average larger than before, the larger, too, the obese more obese. Many more of them, too—usually popping pieces of treats or swigging sweet tea or diet soda from outsized cups, stopping to huff and puff on city streets, riding up escalators, waiting for elevators, soughing and scuffling up stairways, lying on blankets at seashore resorts like snoozing seals, cruising salad bars, bailing cheese over plates of veggies piled precariously high, cluttering Disney Hotels and the casinos in Vegas, ambulating one leg at a time schlepping outward and forward, slowly, with no pep in the step; and on TV, being interviewed, Mr. and Mrs. Three Hundred Pounds, voluminous breasts sometimes bouncing, but more often flat against round expanding middles, jiggling thighs and sinking butts, chubby faces sometimes jolly, but often colorless and scrubbed to pink leather, as they small-step grunt or glide, their electric wheelchairs turning sharp corners, climbing lime-and-yellow-colored scarps past time-weathered eclectic storefronts, robotic greeters under warped patriotic bunting, grimy degenerates rummaging in artificial jungle waterfalls, bubbling pools of carp and dimes.

The large TV monitors are now harping the cable news version of Earth as staging ground for creeping heat: a succession of degrading images leaps forward: sailors in the sub-Antarctic scrimmage a slimy gray squid with the girth of a football field and eyes the size of dinner trays, three hundred thirty pounds of undulating arms wielding razor hooks to snag their prey. A dozen sperm whales beached on Auckland sullage whimper, as their own colossal weight crushes their lungs and kidneys. Falling snow and hale destroy a million Beijing trees. Scientists grow a fish that emanates a neon glow. A man-made disease massacres friendly bacteria. Oranges germinate in Siberia, spider monkeys hightail it to Colombia, snails blanch in the Galápagos. Twenty-one species of albatross retreat from ranching, dwindle, fail, disappear. Schools of giant Asian snakehead devour the Rock River biosphere.

Along the azimuth I drive hang mammoth spider webs clogged not with flies, but with humanity, languishing in nets, hives of tailgaters paralyzed, rhapsodizing and rationalizing the wacky shibboleths and canonized lies constructed by pettifogging corporate lackeys. Lies like the idea that successful people make their own fate and should not have to subsidize the bad decisions of the poor, the case for perpetual war, that a society cannot keep pace without a constantly expanding economy, the frequent need to lower taxes on the wealthy, the chase after more and more wealth as the sole goal of life, a husband's standing over his wife, the bewitching, divine invisible hand of the marketplace, the importance of landing credit, the superiority of the private sector, America the protector, the ghastly specter of socialism, the evil of government, American exceptionalism, intelligent design, mass murders as god's sign.

I get to the Interstate again, which is winding its way through the southern tip of Wyoming at dawn. The rolling dark hills and colluvia of night crystalize into dark brown, then gold, then olive, then deep moss-colored green as the sun rises.

Fortified compounds pockmark this fast-warming landscape. Secret fortresses on blast-shaped mountain tops or behind neat suburban gates where the ultra-rich and their Keystone Cop brain trust think they can escape their fates, survive the coming end time of wind and rain, of unbearable heat, dropping skies and leaping seascapes, melting rime and failing crops. Other compounds conceal cults and castaways scraping by and counting the days until an apocalypse that has nothing to do with the warming earth, armed to the teeth and spouting biblical phrases, dozens of groups of survivalists, re-vivalists, millennialists, mystics, prophets, government resisters, testifiers to the second coming, foot soldiers for a dumbed-down Armageddon, witness-es to rapture, cultivators of racial warfare, those who wait for redemption, those who wait for divine instruction, those who wait for alien abduction.

Wake up! Wake up! Someone rapping on my car window.

Where am I? It takes me a while to tell. It's a cop who checks my license, asks if I'm feeling well, then tells me I can go with the promise I'll head straight for a hotel.

Wide awake now. In my hand, the *I Ching* I found on the nightstand by my brother's rollout bed, which means it must have been the last book he ever read. To fix my brother's final thoughts, I imagine his swart body underneath a sheet, his shoulders ginned into pillows like my own are, as I scour the page for final words, a final sign, a final inner billowing beat. Halfway through the book, in the middle of a paragraph that gobbles on and on, I see wobbly lines of Leon's oily handprint emblazoning an edge-folded page. I can only guess at the final thread of thought the night before he crushed his head. In former times, before I felt compelled to break it off with everyone and everything, the book might be my second-hand gift by mail, and we would cobble allusions to other authors, dispel factual mistakes, fall on puns, sniff out stale or lifted phrases, cross country, back and forth, in letters and phone calls. Now debate is with myself and what I think he would have said. A small chip of wood has fallen from a tall tree of knowledge, the last this dead man felled. Flowering kernels, brooding petals, greenish fruit ripening on a grounded branch. Staring at this final folded sheet, a blanch vision propels me: this page's final phrase, this phrase's final word, it could have been his last: *transformation.*

I have no proof, but I imagine it was late at night and he was tired. He must have given up completing the endless maze of a paragraph that night, perhaps beginning several times, repeating its multi-phrases, and stopped at *transformation,* put it down, and in the morning left for the ill-fated roofing job that would rob him of his days.

I read that word, again and again, *transformation … transformation … trans-formation …* imagine my fingers thumping the page, again and again, see my eyes close, incurably tired, a sudden gasp, again and again. A wrist shudders, my heartbeat flutters, a leg jumps, the head slumps, again and again, again and again, in simulation of dying, terrified yet unable to stop my imagination coming to the word and suddenly losing all animation for all time, again and again, one harried shiver of anticipation followed by another … *transforma-tion … transformation … transformation …* and then I close the book and turn to Leon to plead, "Did you know when you saw it that *transformation* would be the last word you would ever read?"

"That's another way of asking me whether I fell or jumped," he answers. "I've sworn eternal silence on the matter, which really supposes a series of Schrödinger boxes folded one inside the next. For each we have no knowledge whether the box holds life or not. In which box is life unvexed, in which has it stopped? When would you propose volition to begin? With a mad leap? With a sudden noise? A pop? When an unexpected arm sweep-and-drop betrays your equipoise? Or the decision to climb the ladder? Or to clad yourself and come to work on a miserably hot day?"

"Any thought of it before the action constitutes a willful death," I say.

"I think about it every morning while brushing my teeth. Don't you?" His words from a conversation we once had. I've rushed from augury to memory. We're sitting underneath our transom windows on the wooden fire escape of the SF apartment El and I shared. He had made his way by thumb to San Francisco, with a more-than-slight detour in Boulder that lasted about a year to take a hum-drum job at a coffee bar where he also performed twice a week on Open Mic nights.

The one time he volunteered to make breakfast on his trip out West, we didn't eat until eleven, because he kept getting sidetracked. He couldn't speak and work at the same time, and stopped frequently in the middle of every task—chopping leeks, cracking eggs, kneading dough, forming croquettes—to take a draw of weed or a cigarette. I was used to eating a large breakfast long before eight. My inner cynicism quipped that he was waiting for the hens to lay the eggs in the backyard. I knew if I said something, it would bait him to slow down more, so I was jarred into another no-win situation. I kept sneaking into the refrigerator for sips of milk straight from the carton. That was earlier in the day. Now he sucked hard at a joint, passed it to me and stated again, "I think about it every morning. Not killing myself, but being dead."

"My preferred time is late at night, sleepless and caught in bed sheets."

"Yet it will come. The readiness is all," he said.

"I'll never be ready. I dread the thought."

"You like the things of this world, too much, Jules. For all your speculation and your reading of the peculations of the various philosophers, you still believe in reality, because you still believe in your senses." Leon stops speaking to drop ashes on the ground, stuff the pipe with weed, take a puff, and cough it out. "Even at your most miserable, when everything seems to suck for you, you still insist on feeding and fucking."

"But I'm very demanding, you know that. I can't stand crap in anything.

Not in books. Not in food. Not in music."

"Well, I don't know, man, but your schematic for determining what's good and what's not seems inherently aristocratic."

"You mean you think Neil Simon is the dramatic peer of Shakespeare? You think McDonald's is good food? Is polyester as comfortable as cashmere? Does it last as long? Do you like those ear-grating Mantovani songs our mother used to play as much as Beethoven? The tabloid press as much as *The Nation?* Is Chutes and Ladders as good a game as chess?"

"Well, I don't know, man, how can you prove that what you like or what I like is better than what you think is lame? On the most basic level, all material and experience are the same."

"Some food is healthier, like fruit versus candy, or whole wheat versus white flour. Some industrial processes pollute the environment less than others. Some energy sources don't burn fossil fuels. That's the point of solar and wind power."

"All relative, Jules, all relative. Healthier means eighty years instead of forty. Generating less pollution doesn't hide the fact that all of life on earth and everything we create reduces to a convoluted recipe for turning the sun's light into dead weight. Whatever the product or industrial process, our fate is maximum entropy."

"That's the old man's song."

"That's one thing he was right about, Jules."

"But he took away the wrong lesson. He thought the fact that everything in the universe is going to die means that the goal of our brief hours is to see who can shit the most on everyone else to assert their power. That's his definition of the fittest. An atheist who boasts that the lack of a god means he can commit any act, no matter how perverse or how much it hurts others. Quite the contrary, the lack of a god forces us to come together as brothers and sisters and use our collective wits to construct rules that fit human conduct."

"Most of which are bullshit."

"Many of which are bullshit."

"I don't want to be part of it, not part of the so-called rules, not part of the rat race, which comes down to pleasing other fools, doing what they want you to do."

Should I take Leon's rejection of the things of this world as the rational, Gandhi-like act of a shrill revolutionary, or an inflection of mental illness? If I consider him an anti-materialist, I can absolve myself of all guilt. But was it a charade? A con? How to explain his enthusiastic affection for bourgeois pleasures whenever someone else paid, or the infrequent times he had cash?

His frequent plans for musical groups, flashy new businesses, social crusades, and advanced training, all of which wilted after he did the initial spadework? To keep an idealized image of him, I must force my eyes not to see hard-to-ignore details. But when I maintain that his minimalist lifestyle manifests unresolved childhood issues, remorse never fails to course through me like a wild horse trampling a garden. Why him, and not me? I had a rocky time of it before I trashed all contact with my past, but even during my years with El—lazy, fretful, directionless—I lived well. Why couldn't my brother thrash free of the spiderweb of our crazy childhood? Why did he live one step up from the street? Why couldn't he ever complete college? Or anything? Why start so many things, never to finish? Why always so rash to act, yet so easy to admit defeat? After my father died and left us each five thousand, why did he deplete his stash so quickly, so that he was back at square one in a heartbeat?

A few times when Leon was not around, my father indiscreetly bleated to me that when Momma had her first nervous breakdown when I was two and Leon was newborn, she would beat Leon black and blue and ignore me. Does the difference between being beaten and being ignored explain it? Or that she beat him, and yet he was their clear favorite? They thought he was smarter, and he certainly was a better athlete. As my father might bray, he was a thoroughbred and I was a swayback. To be beaten and to be the favorite—what an elaborately horrifying message. We love you more, but whack!!

I was the outsider who had to find a separate track. The insider desperately believes, which in the case of our sad family meant believing in a knurling netherworld. The outsider views any society as an embroidery of good and bad, and purls accordingly. Even after he leaves, the insider stays in place and grieves his lose. Even when he stays, the outsider's world is not the same as the insiders', but a parallel same. The outsider doesn't reject, because he never believed and thus has nothing sacred to neglect. He just makes do. The insider has the inside. The outsider claims the world.

My very disadvantage growing up is what may have saved me. That thought belts me with a craven shame I haven't felt since I left El. I hit the steering wheel with my open palm, wanting instead to beat welts into my embarrassed skin, feel flaming red, an untamed urge to hide from the world, the same old guilt for being alive that used to steal over me almost daily.

Judging his actions without knowledge of his upbringing and drug abuse, I could describe my brother's life as a successful Satyagraha against the profusion of mass-produced commercial culture. He opted to live essentially off the grid, a self-made underground man hidden in plain sight. "Hold fast to the truth" is what Satyagraha means in Hindi. It was Gandhi's concept of nonviolent protest, as embodied in the boycott. Gandhi boycotted salt and linen. Leon boycotted the contest to accumulate more. He boycotted the mass consumer ideology that reduces all emotions and relationships to the acquisition and exchange of rotten, disposable, right-at-your-fingertips, got-to-have stuff. He boycotted an industrialism that rips individuality from the things we make. He boycotted the onslaught of the propaganda machines of our educational system, organized religion, and the news media that blot out meaningful dissent and remind us that we never have enough—ever. He boycotted a soul-stripping puff-and-bluff social structure in which the haves can have so much, while so many have-nots suffer.

"Leon did everything well—almost to perfection," Uncle Emil grunts and slaps his knee with paternal affection. What is my Uncle Emil doing sitting in the front seat of my car? He's dressed for ice fishing in an hibernal vest jacket with dozens of small flap pockets, chockablock with hooks, floats, sinkers and swivels, and a long-tailed pink stocking cap.

"But he was always so stinking slow about it."

"Not that welding class he took in Macon. I reckon he breezed right through that one, sure 'nuff."

"He could speed read, too." I answer in a natural voice that teases no surprise.

"I reckon he was the smartest person I ever met."

His words flush my face with an intense envy of the dead Leon in my heart. I want tartly to say, "A shit-kicking lush like you isn't qualified to judge who's smartest," but I don't know if that offensive shtick is mine or my father's, so I toyed with another start: shred him with something slick like "People always like to think that the very smartest people do little with their lives because they are sick in the head and lack common sense. It makes them feel better about themselves. They would consider themselves lesser souls to bestow the title of very smartest on someone who has actually done something important. It's a kind of a schadenfreude wish come true." But I avoid making this churlish riposte. He won't know what schadenfreude is and may guess my twisted resentment. Besides, I don't even know if this Emil exists or is a highway ghost.

Why question his presence? Let's assume my eyes are shut and I'm dreaming, not really driving a real car on a real road squeezed into a stampede of other cars. "He could steam through pages like he was looking at pictures and then repeat it almost word for word. I think he learned fast and acted slowly. As long as it was something new, he torpedoed through it like a brain machine and moved on. But when he started doing something he knew how to do, something routine or regular or bureaucratic, he decelerated down to an apathetic groove that I found to be an irritating tick."

"I reckon that would explain why he burned through welding class. If he didn't want to do something, sometimes he could move slower than molasses returning up hill in winter."

"Too bad he couldn't earn his living in a job in which all you do all the time is learn something new."

"Ain't no such job. After a stint, it's always repetition."

Which pretty much describes my current condition. I display the same limited erudition to troubleshoot the same few tasks at work each day, based on the same few suppositions of management I've mastered, always on an even keel, before repeating the same scoot home on the same freeways to eat—with zeal—the same limited selection of meals—always prepared deliciously with fresh ingredients—or go to the same few French restaurants May and I like for veal and soufflés on Saturdays, repeat the same few actions in pursuit of a handful of genteel hobbies, see the same few plot variants use the same few techniques and the same brute double entendre in movies and plays, listen to a limited selection of music, all "good," encounter repeatedly the same heroic themes exemplified by the same set of archetypical characters in books I read, enjoy enormously the repetition of the same semi-acrobatic sexual choreography with the same woman every few days. There's something soothing and even fulfilling about this haze of repetition. I'm conditioned to drama-less overlays of regularity that prevent the cognition of anything abnormal which could fill me with shame or contrition. And while there may not be the ramjet thrill of discovery, there is still the anticipation and joy of the understood. Even if you know exactly what you're going to get. It's still good.

"I like to repeat my days, too," says my Uncle Jack, who has replaced Uncle Emil in the passenger's seat. He wears a sailor's cap, although he's never been to sea. He has a model of a sailboat in his lap. "Now that I'm retired, I always get up at the same time, eat the same breakfast, and take the same train to Columbus Circle. I walk up Broadway to West 86th Street, always stopping at the same McDonald's to get my iced coffee with one of my twenty-five-percent-off coupons and nab some free packages of sweetener. Then grab a seat in the men's room on the second floor of the H&M. I often chat a few minutes with one of the guys selling newspapers or a Lincoln Center usher on break, or give directions to a gushing out-of-town gaper or a video-taper, then hop the train home to beat the rush hour."

"Maybe repeating the same walk every day might get a little boring, especially since you have the whole city."

"It's always different in the nitty-gritty. Different people wearing different clothes and using different words and ways. Different people striking different poses. Holding different objects. Different things in the store windows. Cranes and scaffolding at different buildings for different reasons. Different birds and different weather on different days in different seasons."

"Does your amazing ability to see something new in the same-old-same-old explain why you didn't mind counting change all those years in your job? It would have driven me crazy."

"Drove me crazy, too, but it was the best I could get that didn't require me to hurt other people. I never wanted to order anyone around, or fire them, or deny them a raise, or assert authority and make them work on Sundays, bully protégés, end up a liar, or decide between résumés who not to hire."

Uncle Jack the imaginary passenger repeats what he said to me when we were on a coffee quest, when the family was waiting for Aunt Ginny to expire from cancer. It started in her breast and spread through the rest of her once-voluptuous-but-now-brittle body. The reason Leon and I had flown to Georgia—on my dime—a week after he had shown up at our doorstep in SF. The last time I saw any of them. My other uncles—Henry, Emil, Hal, Morris—had been boring six or seven cousins with tired tales about the career decisions they had made when they were the same age as us. We were anywhere between eighteen and twenty-nine, and none had the benefit of a career or calling, and they were trying to get at least one of us to commit to something. Correction: I had started a career, then quit.

Both Emil and Morris fawned over what was for them a wise fit—settling in a small town, in which an aspiring professional would spend just a bit of time becoming a big fish in a small pond. Henry advised that we would never rue doing what we loved to do, wherever we wanted to do it. Nothing to it.

Jack silently bonded with the tweedy green wallpaper during the conversation, but now it was just the two of us in a vending canteen, feeding coins into the coffee machine. "I never had the desire to compete and flatter for the next promotion," he said. "Winning or losing didn't matter, but I was never mean enough to do something that I knew would purposely hurt my brother worker. When you win, someone else loses. Winning is always about hurting others."

"All of life is winning or losing." I tried to smother the thought, but I blurted it out, feeling a sudden libertine shame, knowing that I was a loser who became a winner who became a loser again and didn't see much difference to choose between the two. And now—decades later—I'm a winner again. For me, winning is routine. I've spent so long cruising in the winner's circle that I have forgotten what it feels like to lose.

"Maybe life is winning and losing when you're in charge of the game, but not for most people. For most people, it's a matter of how badly you are going to lose," Jack said.

"I like to win," I said. Documents my department detailed helped my company to prevail in the battle for tens of millions in sales, which meant other companies were losing, which tormented hundreds of their workers, who wouldn't get a raise, or would get fired or not get hired, or become saddled with debt. Or have their house repossessed. Or see the company fail. Twice, ideas I had were instrumental in sending other companies into the sunset. One company was already in rapid descent, and we merely issued a messy coup de grace. The other time, though, we out-finessed an old-line company for a quartet of large contracts over the course of two years. I took a no-tears, lion-over-still-warm-zebra-meat satisfaction in the conquest. Whenever I confessed a moment of lament in another's defeat, May pleaded that I was a technician, a professional with a code of honor that demanded I always seek to do my best.

"Which is exactly what Krishna entreats of Arjuna," Leon says, reeking of weed, having taken the place of Uncle Jack in the passenger's seat. "Act rightly, according to your code of conduct, and think not of the outcome of the action, but of the purity of the acting, win or lose."

"But all things being equal, it's better to win," I say to this ghostly relic of my dead brother.

"All things being equal, winning and losing are equal," he responds, playing with semantics. "All things being equal is the second law of thermodynamics."

Sockless peat-stained sneakers, seedy denims, grease-streaked rainbow tee shirt, busted glasses, pockmarked, long-haired point of a fragile coil of thought.

And me? I'm still wallowing carelessly in the post-war American original sin: the will to drive. Original sin balances on an enormous chassis, as I follow a hairpin curve headed nowhere. The original sin of brakes screeching, original sin of noxious gases embalming the fallow landscape, original sin of vrooming down the warm road through sun glare and thunderstorm, zooming past the scene it's in the process of entombing. Isolated original sinners roaming America in half-borrowed steel and cast plastic rolling domes. Original sin of the hitcher, who doubles the payload, participates in the sin while assuaging it by his farrowed virtue of not driving, an outmoded contriver roaming the eroding highway, winging it, rebelling by not owning. The original sin of the car clings to the hitcher like the stinging smell of gasoline to the surface of the road.

Yet I persist in this trip back in time, insist in cobbling my checklist of little freeze frames of the past by which I hobble the present, persist in trysting with wistful feelings at the places where I stop. Gasoline blasts through my veins, and I feel my mitochondria gobble carbon dioxide as if it were a last meal. Drive fast. Drive into the past.

A quaking limb shackled by shifting blanket, the constant cramp where back meets legs, my prickling forearm numbness each time I start to drift. Outside, cats stalk grackles along the windowsill, tires lisp through damp, welkin wrings a rain from clouds. Now I count, now I conjugate. Now, to clear my ramshackle mind, I investigate a drip that grows beyond precision to mackling sleep and real, a cell phone cackling Mozart, the yearning of overpowered lips for sweeping kisses, sunflowers in deep senescence ensconced in the stupor of their desiccation, their soporific crackling escorted by cerulean flyers, a weeping, almost Gregorian susurration that could be slowing down, or seeping into an all-enfolding silence, or the end of that sweet cycle of oblivion....

Clank! My head leaps forward, lucid, nervous, the covers on the floor, the room cold.

Better get gas and maybe check the tires before I hit the road again.

That slow nomadic trip we took via thumb, El and I, six months bumming around America. We started out with five hundred dollars and that sick vertigo that gripped me when she said she could always turn a trick if we got desperate for dough. The fear soon passed, as she treated me differently from in the past. She didn't provoke fights. No casting herself as a drama queen. No nasty ridicule or ironic bitterness when she spoke to me. No tasteless, mean flirting with other men, then sadistically rubbing it in. Nothing melodramatic, nothing grubby, nothing that hurt. When we walked in the street or talked to anyone, she laced her fingers into mine or slipped an arm around my waist. When an underfed-looking actor whom she knew asked her to dance at a club in Merced, she said "No," and affectionately stroked the top of my head.

Nearly the first thing she drawled to everyone who picked us up was that I had a photographic memory and recalled everything I ever read, saw, or heard. She said it proudly, as if something I was born with could make me heroic. I would bluffly say, "Not everything, but a lot." It would make me think of my dead brother, who never forgot anything he read and could virtually wink at a page, close the book, and recite it robotically. Lots of drivers shot questions at me, trying to stump me about their field in college or their favorite hobbyhorse, but nothing tricky. It was all the small and simple stuff lumped into survey courses. It felt good to be lionized instead of cauterized for being a know-it-all.

Early in the trip, while we were still in the East Bay, we celebrated my birthday. I was thirty. El was on the brink of thirty-four. She gaily sang another of her slinky, kinky double-entendre tunes at an open mic, "Take the J train, to get to my sugar hill." Pressed close against me naked in two zipped-together sleeping bags on someone's floor, she quipped she would spike her drink with an overdose of cyanide the first time she saw a trace of age on her face, a wrinkle or a tip of gray on the side. I said I couldn't believe someone so given to debauchery would erase herself.

We did it everyplace on that trip. Smothering our noises in a stall of the men's room in an old-line folkie club in Berkeley, after El melted the audience belting out "Silver Dagger"—"Don't sing love songs, you'll wake my mother"—and I passed around a half-folded thrift-shop felt fedora hat.

Ripped on cheap red wine among the grapevines running up a moldered garden wall in the dead of a sweltering hot night in Coalinga to the sound of a caterwauling cat.

Under full-moon shine on the cold beach north of Monterey, the night before the annual motorcycle races, hiding under the cover of a pride of Harleys.

Sliding across a polished hardwood floor on a throw rug in the den of the house of Jim and Nancy, whom we met at an IHOP in Brawley.

On top of an abandoned wicker sofa in a field of wolfsbane and goldenrod near a bus stop underneath a Texas sky wide with constellations: fly, archer, crane, fishes, scorpion.

In the back of a soup kitchen after I finished washing dishes, to the mundane plodding of an endless freight train, for so long and with such pot-inspired jubilation she said we were bleeding ichor, the ethereal blood of ancient gods.

In a barn outside Todd Mission, Texas, waiting out a sudden thunderous downpour, perched against a tractor.

In the cloakroom of a church in Taylor, another small Texas town.

On the floor at four in the morning with a woman named Arlene, who found us in Taylor and drove us to Abilene, where she planned to crash with her pregnant sister Sandy and Sandy's old man Chuck, who wasn't the dad. We arrived when Sandy was already in labor and all of them stoned on hash, the midwife paralyzed into a chant-humming lotus pose. Sandy panted and thrashed on the floor, clad only in a ratty old plaid sweater exposing most of her form, a dumbfounded Chuck frozen in place, standing over her, eyes wide with terror and truculently fretting, "Oh shit, oh fuck, it's coming, oh shit, oh fuck, it's coming...."

No one wants to call a doctor. "Do something, Jules," El implores.

"I can call an ambulance," I say. "Where's the phone?"

"Five miles away outside a convenience store," someone bleats.

"Oh fuck, it's coming, oh fuck, she's going to die," Chuck keeps repeating in guillotine moans.

"No one's dying," I say with swagger. "El, find a large pot and start boiling water. Arlene, bring me any type of cloth that's clean. Anything—towels, underwear, dishrags." My directions lifted from my memory of a windbag obstetrics nurse who had come to a party directly from her shift, quivering with hyped-up details of having just assisted a delivery.

There is something about grave situations that clarifies the mind, slows it down, and simplifies thoughts so they flow smoothly. Like when that kid was waving a loaded shotgun threatening gore. I was terrified, but I figured out soothing words to pacify him. Or when confronted by frowning, night-stick-wielding cops at an anti-war demonstration, my kinetic clowning molli-fied them. They couldn't stop laughing at my sloppy, jokey, fake magic tricks. Even as a boy, some analytical drive in me would kick in. Like when Leon slipped and fell down an Olympic-pool-sized open ditch, and I had him out by the time the firemen arrived. I kept Momma alive three times with my careful thinking. But then there was that other time. I just sat in the stinking kitchen drinking hot sugar water. Sat there waiting for her to die, knowing I ought to do something but unable to move, shrinking from thought, dumb, drained of desire, emotions drummed down to a numb, brainless groove. Years before I bottomed out, years before I decided to shut out my past strife and start anew, again and again I succumbed to this knife at my aorta, this moment of zero's zero, this maximum entropy of shame and strife at not being able or willing to act, maximum entropy of blame at my shortcom-ings, at just sitting there and letting her die, maximum entropy of my fear of death, and of life.

All Arlene can find unsoiled are some lacy pillow cases and tie-dyed tee shirts—blobs of fluorescent colors like soft and psychedelic John Cham-berlain constructions—which I rip apart and sterilize in a pan of boiled water. I order Sandy to close her eyes and brace herself for intermittent pain, keep her knees up and spread, turn her head to the side, purse her lips, and breathe deeply, then drive her hands into the floor for traction and to push out at each contraction. I get El to pace her breathing and wipe down her face with the dark fluorescent rags. Meanwhile I wait and watch the space between her thighs. The others observe me with pot-laced stupefaction.

"Vocalize your pain," I command Sandy. I fret to myself about how tight-ly my hands need to pull to complete the imminent extraction—not too much to injure the baby's head, but I realize the longer it takes, the worse for all concerned. It's a fine balance that I haven't had time to rehearse. There's so much involved—a universe of universes. My face begins to burn and my throat to scratch. I need a glass of water, but I dread dispersing my focus. I want to snatch the baby out as soon as I spy its head. Sandy looks at me with a wry cosmical yearning. I've noted that thatched look before, that emotive combination of assertion and vulnerability. It coated my own face in the photos of the four of us, looking away from my family's inbred swampland, away from their stymied abjections, gazing beyond the camera with my passionate demand to make a connection somehow, someway.

"Slowly, like you're swimming leisurely," I say to Sandy in the most soothing inflection I can muster. "Stroke after stroke."

Sandy's sudden seizure and anguished croak, her knees desperately pushing into air. A trace of the fontanel pokes into view. I hover in, squint my eyes, and pull it out slowly with sterilized pillow cases. It's a girl, soaking sheening blood and placental material, which I carefully wipe off. I hold the new life between the mother's legs in one hand and use a sterilized bread knife to tear the umbilical cord with the other, then offer the crying girl to Chuck, who wears a pickled, churlish mien and immediately gives her to Arlene.

Afterwards, while mother, child, midwife, and stepdad sleep, we lounge on the couch basking in the glory of the newborn, and share a spliff. A choir of bells chimes four somewhere in the distance. Arlene and El debate the existence of a divinity. Happiness skiffs through me, the man of the hour, possessed of a sublime masculinity that everyone admires. Something I haven't felt in a long time, not since I pulled my department at the insurance company from a technical quagmire soon after they hired me, six long years ago, before I knew El.

Arlene takes a deep hit, pivots over El, presses her lips to mine and fills my mouth with pungent smoke and her slimy limpet-like tongue that seems to swell and grow as it rockets around my palate. Her face smells of afterbirth, of paschal blood and chaparral. As soon as she pulls away, El kisses her and begins to rub my thigh. Soon the three of us are naked on the floor colliding in intricate mirthful embraces. Soon I'm inside El, inside Arlene, inside El again, inside Arlene again, until they converge into one graceful, earthy succubus into which I plummet, submerge and emerge and submerge and emerge and submerge and emerge and submerge....

My eyes open to cold darkness. Pins and needles bore through my backwards-folded arm and hand. A woman's head rests on my shoulder. I hear her snoring lightly in my ear, and further off, hear barely audible squeals. I close my eyes again. A sharp ache begins creeping up my arm, but I don't want to move. I want to keep feeling the gently breathing weight of her body against me rise and fall, keep hallucinating dislocated vibrations from someplace on the other side of my sleeping. But I have to shake out the arm numbness.

I lean forward and see a naked El propped on Chuck, gliding the way she's moved on top of me a thousand times, her shoulders swaying, her eyes glazed with the same distant, half-baked, incandescent ecstasy, her fingers raking his cheek and playing with his chin, her breasts flopping to her side in the same lazy but incessant way.

I seize El by her torso and push her off, jump astride Chuck, crunch his arms to the floor with my knees and start to pump punch after punch at his nose.

"Stop it, Jules! Stop!"—the distant fuzzy tremolos of the women.

My face is breaking into frozen chips of flesh, my brows threshing inward, outward, downward, into echoes of echoes of the women's miles-away yips to stop. Blenching nostrils, clenched jaw, squared-off stance, all rip apart and rearrange as rhomboid fire, as flaming coals you grasp to hurl at a frantic, gigantic reptile and burn your fingertips, a spreading rage, a yellow bile, an acid stripping any vessel. I inflict a steady barrage of burling blows to Chuck's head until I see red at his lips.

Another leap in time. I remember feeling Chuckie's part, my arms pinned to the floor and immobile, hearing my heart beat somewhere deep within my brain, helpless as my brother strangled me after I gloated over a game of Monopoly. A bittersweet guilt invades me, followed by resentment, fear, loneliness, in a darting panzer movement. My hand is full of black blood. My tongue feels like cement, tastes of peat and mud. My punches turn soft, and I get off Chuck, who curls into a fetal position with his hands ramparting his face. El extends her arms to embrace me, but I fleetly pull apart from her.

"Jules, please, let me explain," she entreats me.

I get dressed as fast as I can ...

"Wait, don't flip out, it was nothing ..."

... stuffing my socks in my pants pockets and slipping into untied shoes ...

"Don't split, it was nothing, I didn't mean to hurt you, just a sudden itch ..."

... not bothering to tuck in my shirt ...

"Okay, I admit what I did was bitchy ..."

... all the while exerting my inner minotaur to stay in control and ignore her hurtful and hurting exhortations ...

"Yes, it was a dirty thing to do right in front of you. Can't we talk about it?"

Talk about it? I don't even want to think about it. I grab my backpack and walk past her and out the door. Five minutes later, I'm in a Buick blasting down the Interstate in the rain, half listening as a stinking-drunk, rinky-dink franchise salesman jealously lambastes an absent colleague over linking up with kinky jailbait. I'm still half dwelling in the moment of my visual recognition of her final betrayal, a swell of shape and color crystalized into the image of the two of them together, her ballet of duplicity. Her game of shame in which her transgressions tilt me into guilt, as if I did it, not her. Just like the lot of them—father, mother, brother—braying words that salt my wounds. No matter what I do, no matter what they do, I always feel pain because it's always my fault.

It's the last I ever see of El.

That's when I tore away from my past and began anew, a newborn with a thirty-year-old's experience and virtue. I slammed close a door that blew open the window into my second life of quiet—not of Thoreau's quiet desperation, but a quiet robed in strifeless rationality. Was this the consolation Job felt about his second family and his second set of riches? As if he had strangled his past emotional twitches and could dwell forever in the comfort of his second life? Did he ever miss his first wife, his first set of sons and daughters, his first flocks of goats and ewes, the fruit of his first fields? Did he ever mourn losing them? Or did he shield himself from his blame and shame for the loss? Did he ever toss off forlorn comparisons to the wife, kids, and new-fangled possessions of his second life? Did one beat the other? Or was it all the same to him? I avow that the pain was so maiming and the anger so mangling that Job eschewed repeating those early memories, never allowing a fleeting thought of them while reveling in the sweetness of his now.

On my way to see Gigi, the fifteen-year-old runaway who rented a room in the house El shared with a struggling bass player before she met me. Gigi soon supplanted El in their bed and El moved out of the place. For some reason, Gigi remained El's pet. She gave the younger woman advice about everything—clothes, hair, manicures, drugs, amour. El served as a mentor who abetted Gigi's peccadillos, an older soubrette exposing a newcomer to sure-fire lures. Gigi blew the bass player's coop after a year, and weeks later ended the marriage of two actors El knew.

Gigi had a face and carriage that could staunch a thousand relationships: flawless skin, high cheekbones, and outsized lips posed permanently in a flirtatious pout, her long unkempt raven hair, sometimes tipped with outrageous color, swept back and up. At six feet in height, she stunned most men and women at first sight. Long legs that rose to a haystack ass, wide thighs, and a voluptuous hourglass figure she touted in platform flip-flops, form-fitting V-neck sweaters, and knockabout slacks. Thinking about it after three decades, I regret not taking a chance and slipping it to this body without flaws the one time I had both opportunity and cause, the night El left us alone after rip-sawing my ego. Memory can desire the impossible.

Gigi was quite deft at detonating break-ups and then leaving the dope humiliated and bereft of hope and money weeks or months later. Her style was first to play the deep-eyed innocent. But after a few weeks or months of a searing romance with her new man, she turned into an easily-bored coquette, flirting with other men and talking condescending dirt about him to his friends. Overnight, she would transform from willing marionette to whorish martinet. Gigi explored Seattle's artsy lithosphere for years, living with one guy or another, never working, always high or looking to score.

Gigi's flawless cheekbones now look worn and thatched, thick make-up shellacking her skin to a used-leather shine embossed with cracks. Her hair is now a short blond frost and is cut above her slack and freckled neck. Her voice, once laid-back and feline, now scratches alcohol. She supervises the greeters in a Tahoe casino, where I meet her at the grand bar. She smells a little sauced and has a whiskey neat in hand.

We hug a long time, full body to full body. She's packed on a little weight everywhere, a luscious padding swaddling her ageless curves.

We post ourselves on barstools, and she swerves her seat towards me. Her hand chances to tap my arm and she grabs my wrist, brings it to her face an instant, then advances it to her lap where she wraps my hand in hers. She asks how I'm doing, with the unreserved cheery grace of a glad-handing hostess. But before I can answer, she turns teary and says, "I have to tell you something. Something sad. Something crappy. Deep breath now—here goes! No dancing around it. El is a ghost—gone three years now. Breast cancer."

Breast cancer. Like my Aunt Ginny in Georgia. A dark confusion spreads inside me, a thick trance-like desire not to think about a dead Elaine. All my deeply embedded baneful feelings for her—jealousy, anger, shame, love— fire to the surface of my brain for a brief perception of soul-shriving pain, before I swallow them to keep from planing out of control. I had connived not to see her on this trip, yet I couldn't stop scrolling through memories of our dime-store-novel prime together.

"I saw her often before she died. When she wasn't in a morphine fog, she spent a lot of time complaining bitterly—you know how she always went on and on, mostly just venting—about her parents, her sisters, the doctors, her friends, her dog. She had a long list of people to flog. But she never meant any of it, she never did."

Why do I feel a sense of guilt, as if it's engraved in me? I haven't shared a quilt with El for decades. Didn't even think of her for years, until I decided to hit the road for this trip. Her death doesn't forgive the long-faded pain she gave me, her degrading masquerade she made me make my own.

"Cancer is not a cabaret. She wasn't beautiful any more, but gray, shriveled and sexless, almost surreal. It was eating away at her from the inside out, peeling away her body, layer after layer. She went bald from the chemo. Her skin turned mealy. She said she never thought she would get to play Camille."

Other fatalities from the past, other people close to me, other people I try never to ponder, breath-deprived personalities whose dense modalities seemed to wander at times, but flowed inexorably in one direction, towards death. The thought of each breeds a radioactive liquid breaching the containment vessel of my mind and reaching the taunting facts of their realities. Father, mother, brother? What did they ever want, any of them? Kindness, love, acceptance, control, respite? All of them wanting all of it. Or maybe none of them wanting any of it. Maybe it was me wanting these banalities, or wanting them to want them. They had an appetite for something else, something haunted to which I have applied and denied a wide series of flawed and flaunted theories, but never got right. Something I never knew, never understood, never could know or understand, always being on the outside.

"One day near the end," Gigi continued, "she let me talk about the old days and said she had no regrets, but then corrected herself and said she never expected you to leave her and that she would never forget or forgive herself for hurting you. Next to her hospital bed she had set a photo of herself at thirty-three in front of the apartment you shared in Frisco. She stood silhouetted in a red sunset, her long chestnut hair down to her waist. Her flirty demeanor in the grainy photo made her seem to reign like a queen accepting the loud acclamation of an adoring crowd. Next to it lay the pasty El, drained of animation, all bones underneath a flimsy spread, dull, hollowed out eyes that seemed to desert the world, mouth wasted with pain...."

Gigi begins to cry. I put an arm around her shoulders to console her. She twists to face me and I can taste her sloppy tongue trolling at my lips. Her warm breasts roll towards me in floppy submission, her eyes opened wide, her heart racing so hard I can hear it in my chest, her green-polished fingertips tracing circles between my thighs. Still an angel of permission. Still a test. Why not a late-in-life, what-happens-here-stays-here conquest?

But no way. Not now, not ever. Not as long as I'm with May. Not as opportunistic pleasure, nor long-sought treasure. Not as a tawdry try to balance past books, nor a desperate attempt to recapture youthful looks. Not as an affirmation of living, not in a moment of giving. Like years before, when she pestered me after she had witnessed an unrepressed shouting match I had with El, I pull away.

Pretend indifference, like a Buddhist monk who shoves spoiled mullet guts down his gullet and pretends it tastes like life. Life that cuts real enough to touch, smell, bend, boil, eat, feel pain, have weight, and is always ripe. But it's an endless illusion that struts ruthlessly to conceal its lack of substrate. All of it, nothing but tripe! A delusion you don't want to teach. A conclusion you don't want to reach. But you will, sooner or later.

Give it up, ladies and gentlemen, for death, that fierce truth that explains any shibboleth and peels away all illusion.

Death. The absolute truth that's also a contract. Receive eighty succulent years and the agio you pay is eternity. A worse return than at the Bellagio! And it's eighty, if you're lucky. How about these moonstruck numbers? Do they take your breath away, these Pythagorean computations importuning a Kabbalah of nothingness: mother at forty-two, younger brother at fifty-eight, father at fifty-six. And now at sixty, the woman who ruined you and made you live beyond ruination.

Better than nothing, but still, too soon.

And everyone else who didn't die? Everyone became someone else, something else, in the interval between two moments thirty years apart. Or was I the only one who changed, and in so doing, purged a deranged view of others, saw the veil of yen ripped from their hearts and their real selves emerge?

Did I abandon all these people by changing? Did they abandon me?

Or are all of our lives a drift between different states of the same crystalline matter, careening between lean and fat, flowing amorphous and serene, bubbling to gaseous shapelessness, a boat floating away into an abyss, escaping into before and after and that great gaping now that lies in-between. Another list to note: natural drifts that make and unmake the universe— clouds in sky, leaves in rake, preening mist in woodland, ice on lake, gusts of rumbling sandblast, gallivanting spider-cast gossamer, dipping and slipping isomers, the resonance after dulcimer notes, tectonic plates on upper mantle, the clip-clop of hip-hop vibrating borders, dye in teardrops, throw of die, disorderly ideas, planetary traveler, Milky Way's chaotic dust, times to come before they happen, lust for beauty, bleary memory at the border of teary dementia, a rusting mind immersed in catting around or booze, eyeless, battered weight losing itself in drift for thirty years. A lump of primate matter. Meaningless hoots from a mind ape who wanders in his cloud, like the ratty monkey in the Chinese epic pondering recent aberrations.

The dead fill me with rage. By saying and doing nothing, the dead say and do everything possible to re-engage my guilt for persisting. Guilt for not being crazy, guilt for resisting mental illness, guilt for having learned not to hurt myself. Guilt for having lived a life full of many adventures, wins and hurrahs. Guilt for finding thirty years of peace by forgetting the dead ever existed.

The dead disappoint. They jilt my nights and tilt my days. Do the math. Their numbers overwhelm, like silt and nurdles clogging waterways. Their actions, entirely passive, the act of not acting, the thought of not thinking. The act of being in the way of a gun or a germ, on a crumbling berm, under wave or fractured stave, in a fight, a fall, or flight, or a smothering pall, a poisonous snake, the squeal of brakes, bite of rat, gobbet of fat. Or a concrete path.

Or a grim thought. Try as I may I can never imagine not feeling what they are not feeling.

The sound of pain, I can hear it everywhere. In the incessant squeaking of a wheelchair, the tentative creaking of the door of a bare cupboard, the discordant blasts and blares of warfare, the bleak stare of loneliness, the weak and furtive peer of the defeated. But the sound of death? Fleeting ocean echo, canyon bluster? White noise bleating in the basement of a hospital suite?

None of these.

The sound of death is the sound of the heart that does not beat.

Nothing frightens me except seeing the passage of time, that monstrously amorphous aura of now replacing now replacing now. Memory is a kangaroo court that imprisons us, while future time flees us at the same moment it fills us with fearful anticipation that time will continue without us.

Nothing will make me ready for the day of nevermore, windless soundless take-me, creeping jackal, stations of annihilation, nature's way. Nightly shiver horror hackles heart sore endlessly: the end the end and after that no after-that. Words brattle many years. Words. Words in nervous tenses bow to me, battling in a final but-when, in a stark final finale finally not free, knelling endless no in between no after no after after's afterwards. Oblivion nods, not as long and roughshod freefall, but as closing bark. *Ready or not, come to me, music-of-the-dark.*

Never ready? Not even if someone told me the exact time and day.

If you knew, what would you do?

Would you drink your favorite brew, eat your favorite dinner, if you knew today was your last day of life? Would you say goodbyes, play your favorite tune, screw a woman or two, stay stewed on gin and wine? Would you pine away the ticking time in panic? Would you chase your last volcanic heartbeats, rue the time you've wasted, calculate your final sums—days you've lived, hours, seconds, number of women, number of times, all together and in your prime, countries you've seen, where happy times have been, people you knew, or those you remember—the rest a blur?

Would you review your wins and losses, phone and email last adieux, toss out or go through family albums, recalling your kids when they were young, recall their play, their toy-doll chalet, their science fair displays, the rungs they climbed, the songs they sung? Would you gather them 'round with their children, pets on ground, make your goodbyes, apologize, forgive their lies, give your final okay, say the things you always wanted to say?

Would you pray to your god for its mercy? Or contemplate the terror of nothingness, curse the obliteration of your consciousness? Would you purse your lips and sigh in resignation, look forward to it, tired of aches and pains, tired muscles, tired brain, tired of watching other people die?

Or maybe you would sit in a chair on the porch, feel the breeze and sun, watch the clouds gather, watch the rain, smell the clammy land after thunder passes, watch a smattering of birds bandy about, skirt wet grasses, start to chirp, dozens of them bounding, in a symphony that grows so loud that it could drown out the sound of death itself.

No more stops planned. Just keep driving until I get home.

That time El and I ate hash brownies and roamed the New Age Exposition in the old Moscone Center. We entered into a rainbow honeycomb of booths and tables filled with superstition and unabashed deceit—the after-birth of the commercialization of god—and wended by the many swindlers pretending expertise and looking for suckers worth fleecing. To these wordy charlatans we talked in phony French accents, pretending not to understand half of what they meant, making them give a second recitation of their absurdities, so we could share a secret mental laugh, except about what El believed, like transcendental meditation.

We descended into a cavalcade of belief. Something for everyone, from the easily persuaded to the jaded to the pining to be remade in subservience: Meher Baba, the reluctant father of grief; the dreamy and fashionably feathered Swami Mukaananda and his unbending beam of divine radiance; Elizabeth Clare, redeemer of the self-made soul living freely with ascended masters; David Moses and his renegade Children of God; Hilda the spiritual weather forecaster; the dreamy and fashionably feathered Swami Prabhupada and his holistic New Rishikesh to mend the soul; Jehovah's Witnesses asking us to wade in the water and become one of the lucky 144,000 to be saved; the Reverend Sun Myung Moon, then just another in a crowd of shady pretenders; loud serenading from the Assemblies of God Pentecostal Church; dowdy matrons of the Divine Light Mission spreading friendship;

some very rowdy Jews for Jesus baying *What a friend we have in Jesus*; priests of the Rosicrucian Order who swayed stiffly to Mozart; staid test proctors from the Church of Scientology; doctors in Bibleology from Mother God's Abiblical Society; the feisty California director of the American Atheists Association on a tirade against Christ; Iskcon Center mentors recommending the principles of bhakti-yoga; a parade of retread monks panting Hare Krishna Hare Krishna, Krishna Hare Krishna Hare; beautiful girls in pearls enticing loners to knoll tiny bells and chant *Nam-myoho-renge-kyo, nam-myoho-renge-kyo*; handmaidens of the Radha Krishna Temple; the Mahikari-No Waza's divine invisible energy extending a purebred era of fairness; Santeria's shrunken rubber heads; ECKANKAR the trendy science of total awareness; Grandmother Divine, the spiritual advisor blending Tarot, astrology, and E.S.P.; Actualizations' expensive personal goal maximizer classes to help you get what you're missing; the Silva Method of teaching mind control, a band of White Power punks in bowling shirts showing pecs and hissing racist invectives, ready to fight anyone who upbraided them; the last reminiscences of Gus Hall, looking a faded wreck; a Baptist preacher on a crusade to mend lost souls; pyramid power intended to control your destiny; the kisses of Princess Kundalini consoling primal energy and trolling after bliss.

Many mongered products, all meant to improve your life, to get you in touch with the constructive you, the younger you, the restrung you, the groovy you, the improving you, the essential you, the reverential you, the experiential you, the better you, the fret-free, debt-free you, the balanced you, the wild you, the child in you, the spiritual you, the astounding you, the grounded you, the unbound you, the new-found you, the you you used to be, the you you could be. We saw the Samadhi isolation tank for deep meditation while sounding salt water, plastic ankhs, compartmentalized tote bags to organize your life, biorhythm feedback machines to anesthetize strife, Zen thank-you cards, Pacer Mat platform tables for working out, kits for the fat-free sour kraut diet that stank of green-mold bread, holistic medical practices, astrolabe placemats and Mandala tack boards, Shiatsu acupressure, Shaklee vitamins and Amway cleaning supplies, vaporizers, ionizers, polarizers, graphology analysis, herbal cream for psoriasis, books on ludology, agathology, explanetology, spiritual homology, psychosis, cirrhosis, kyphosis, and autohypnosis, Islandia Free University of all things devotional, bodywork classes for untrammeled energy, academic degrees in the language of ocean mammals, Dynique Aloe Vera rage-healing lotions, processed treats and potions for the atomic age, promotions for the Neuropsychic Institute for treating caged emotions, the John F. Kennedy University graduate program in concrete consciousness, the footsie roller to massage the bottoms of tired feet.

On stage between country rock groups working hillbilly harmonies behind blasé, barefoot chick singers and the fierce fingers of silent smirking banjo players, a stooping gray-haired man with a drooping face as red as Georgia clay, cracked brown around the eyes and lips, Kutenai tribal headdress on his head and a feathered breastplate, stared skyward and recited the open letter from Chief Seattle to Franklin Pierce, as if praying. "Perfumed flowers are our sisters, the deer, the horse, the great eagle, these are our brothers, the rocky crests, the dew in the meadows, the pony's body heat—all belong to the same family."

His words ambled in the air slowly, every syllable carefully enunciated, with neither anger nor presumption, in a deep but brambly voice that likely appreciated the depredations of excessive gin consumption. "All things are connected. Whatever befalls the earth befalls the sons of the earth...."

It knocked the breath out of me, or maybe it was the taste of hash. My body filled with a sudden oneness with the chief—ersatz or authentic. In a flash, I transcended myself and inhabited the same body as he, and as El, too, as everyone around us, and everyone living, and everyone who ever lived in our messy Rorschach mash. I, cynical unbeliever, felt at one with all these calabash folks—these benighted perpetrators and followers of balderdash, trends, and hoax, these freaks and charlatans. I kenned oneness with the peeling paint, with the steel and brick, with the hedges and the building ledges, with the concrete ascending into sky, with the sun coaxing fronds and ponds and the bending rivers feeding wide fields, with all things broken and all things healed. I felt a bond with the vagabond horizon and with everything beyond, with everything coinciding with beyond and everything beyond, beyond all things visible and all things hidden, the kind of oneness I never apprehended outside of sex—or maybe one time when my mother and father saw me drag an upended-and-on-his-side obese kid across the finish line and win a three-legged race at Dad's company's picnic and a oneness with everyone and all things drained me of my pride for an instant. A oneness in which you retain an amplified self and yet blend with all the other selves around you, not apart and fearful, not an outsider, not tenuous or disingenuous, not slyly looking out for yours, not clutching your bag and hiding your swag, not forever taking bigger pieces, thicker slices, not staying-at-home-all-day alone, not moaning an after-mourning Kyrie, not alone in a crowd or a play, not concealed from the world in moving glass and steel along an unknown highway.

A oneness I have never felt again.

Nor do I want to. I can't do it.

To melt myself into an all-embracing oneness with all, to give up my transitory resistance, transcend the physical, and cease to care about the aches of existence, find peace from all I've ever felt, I could never achieve this state of grace. I would never want it, since it involves the eradication of every trace of consciousness, a release from my awareness of myself and of others—these vibrant interfaces with the illusions that comprise the physical world. I am too committed to rising and repeating every day, eating, making love, walking the marketplace, talking with other people, making noise, sharing joys, showing off bling, wandering far and wide, pondering the glowing stars, trawling through the enthralling imprisonments and effusions of natural and human-built space. I love every breath of it too much to give it up for oneness with all things.

I don't want enlightenment. I don't want heaven. I want life without death.

Yet I understand that this real world of mine is nothing but a weeping phantasm, since at every turn it is lost in the deep and constant chasm of time, abruptly supplanted by the new world of the new instant.

The past accumulates as a kame of isolated mental snapshots that quickly freeze and get slotted into words, a broken chain of fusions and allusions, some pleasing, some heartsore and unforgiving, dots on an imaginary map of a city I used to live in. I remembered exploring places and neighborhoods, but forgot how I found them and how they fit together. The spaces between them blot and blur, so, instead of a unified whole, I see a litter of remote island shores floating on top of the water of a crossed territory, or, in the case of memory, of tossed time, a profusion of distortions, a confusion of moments that came before. Only the present is real, and yet the soaring reality which I chase changes constantly, from nanosecond to nanosecond, with no encore. The embrace of reality is the embrace of illusion, a pinafore of many colors that burdens the body until death, when it disintegrates as if attacked by moths. Release from the weight of the fabric eradicates our being, since all we were was in the cloth.

The landscape of ago is an archipelago of these elliptical images floating in a sea of forgotten heres-and-nows. Let me embrace them, no matter how painful I envision them to be, even as I live in the current one. Let me unfold anfractuous memory, monstrous twisting swarm of failure, rage, hostility, shame, decline, futility, betrayal and vows, place-names, epochs, and melodies endowed with sad fragility, beyond my touch, beyond redemption. Let me plow each memory into points of feeling—selected pearls of rain and not the rain itself: lover's kiss, child's embrace, father's legs-on-shoulders tote —remembered briefly, set aside before metastasis to anecdote. Let me take each filament of memory, hold it close, grapple and clasp, let it grow inside my grasp to the fullness of its story, let it grow beyond its grief, let it grow beyond its brief imperfection, transform to lover's arching brow, crumbles of an ancient coliseum, toddler's lisping answer, something beautiful beyond belief. I'll take the entire lot of illusions I'm allowed—the past, the present, the future, the real world and my projection of it, all five modalities of knowing and not knowing, I'll take them, because the totality of it feels so good. Even the pain is worth it, at least once I've plowed through it and stored it compactly somewhere deep in my lumbering brain.

The now? The now! The now....

The now when I say goodbye to my cousin Pete before returning East. He is naked as a beast under a sheet with his six-foot-tall live-in girlfriend Petra in a small bed—a wooden plank with some padding—that you can only reach with a ladder. It is built close to the ceiling, above the shelves and drawers where they store their things in a subleased locker smelling of yeasty concrete in the shell of an old unheated warehouse converted into crash pads and artist studios south of Market Street. Somewhere in the building a rock band beats out fragments of a Tower of Power cut. Squaw-jawed Petra, called Peter before her operation, bellyaches in a husky, smoke-raked masculine voice. "I'm a heartbeat away from a painful death, sweetie pie. You absolutely have to pick up a pack of Kents with the vodka," she entreats, and begins to nibble on a rice cake.

A radio down the hall wails "Satisfaction" and it reminds me of another time with Petey, in his halfway house after his stint in jail, sitting on a bed swilling lousy wine and watching the action as Pete and his fellow parolees trade pills.

Petey's space is essentially a padlocked walk-in bulkhead with a long work surface in rough unfinished wood, covered with Petey's stuff, including a button-making machine he bought, declaring with guff that he could make a million dollars in a year selling slogans like "Freedom is calling you with words of revolution" and "Make love, not war" at Ghirardelli Square. This venture lasted a week, but even a few years later, the machine and raw materials are sprawled on the long counter among piles of balled-up white underwear, packets of tie-dye, and buckets full of boggy water, vestiges of another business idea that went nowhere. Also spread out are piles of dog-eared papers scrawled with words, beginnings of novels, plays, poems, prayers, and performance pieces. Leaned against the wall to the extreme left of this mess stands a makeshift ladder hammered together from irregular knot-filled boards leading up to Pete and Petra's bed.

Pete jumps from the bed, bounces a time or two on the concrete floor, shakes his hair in the air like a wet bird, and quickly throws on blue jeans. "I was about to get ready to catch some life, cuz, need to get out and figure out what I've heard in the weeds today before it's yesterday's absurd turd, work over some new words to unglue and seed my internal energy avenue renewing what our needs need, 'cause our needs need as much as we do."

"Pete," Petra's husky falsetto gives a comfortable, cat-snug-in-a-high-place purr, "don't forget to get a bottle of scotch, too, and maybe one of those little bottles of the herb-infused vodka."

"Jules, cuz, discovering booze has given new meaning to my what-am-I-doing-here. That's why Petra's the love of my life blood and the life of my love blood."

"What do you mean, discovering booze?"

"I mean discovering how easy it is, no hustle, no hassle, no taboos, you just go to the corner store and buy it, man. What a concept, go to the corner store and buy it. No scam, like eating candy with a baby, no meeting the man who may not come and here he is with excuses and shitty shit, but you can't lose it, and you try to sell it for the smoke to get high cleaning and rolling and bagging and hitting the corner of my eye, maybe get ripped off, rock rocker taking a beating up the side from some guy with tattoos where the grass makes you so high you blow it on some blow that's cocksucker cut, and maybe the cops are cruising the sky and bust your ass. Much easier with booze. You go to the store around the corner, and you buy it, whenever you choose."

"Come on, Petey, booze has always been legal, at least in our lifetime, and available in every supermarket. I refuse to believe you didn't know."

"Yeah, man, I knew, but I didn't know. There's knowing something that you park in your head, and there's knowing in a way that makes you do or think something that may impart real knowledge or self-knowledge or self-storage of what you know, not in the dark of the brain where you know you know, but in the other part attached to your lost shoes and missing keys that spark you like art or open-mouth kissing from time to time to the new birth of an old quark. So I knew in that way, but not in the other way that Petra started."

The now when my brother calls to tell me our father has died of liver cancer.

"We're orphans now," Leon jokes.

Any fishtail answer drowns in a wordless lake for what seems like a very long time. I listen to each of us inhale and exhale, until he breaks the shivering silence. "I took care of him the last three months, after he knew the chemo failed."

He arranged his meds, made his meals and fed him, cleaned and preened him, dressed and undressed him, changed his messes, screened his visitors, smoothed and squared his sheets, soothed his twitches with hot compresses, scratched his itches, patched him up after he hurt himself flailing his limbs against the walls during a nightmare, set up his games of solitaire. Talked to him and walked him for his exercise. Emptied the old man's bedpan and prepared his drip. Gripped the phone while he terrorized his employees. Listened flippantly as he recounted old adulteries.

Leon gave the details with a deep Southern twang, cool and noncommittal. "I watched his vital signs begin to fail, like I used to watch the dying patients when I was a bored hospital orderly. It was grueling for him to talk or move, and when he awoke for brief instances during the last few days accorded him after the cancer attacked his brain, he insanely wailed and railed some drool about a wrestling match I lost in high school."

After years in which he never spoke to our father, Leon has done what I never could, or never would. He has observed a deathwatch over him, a counting of days and hours until a parched-and-choking, tucked-in, done-with-treatment, in-a-drug-induced-trance body, chest weakly advancing and retreating, in a bed enclosed in bent and bleating ducts and vents, greeting cards and flowers, stops its movement.

"At least you had a chance to come to an understanding with the old man, Leon."

"About what, man? About what a piece of shit he was? He paid me two hundred a week and room and board for three months, and that was it." I could hear a well-fed sneer. "I let him talk about whatever he wanted, which was mostly the horses and skirts he used to stalk. I appeared to care about what he said. Why argue with the dead? Now I have all his shirts and pants that fit, and all his shoes, and enough to get by for maybe a year."

The now the last day I see my father before he dies, in Baltimore during his first round of letting the docs pump poison through his veins, while there is still hope of stopping the growth, before it spreads to his brain. We eat plump raw oysters at a dump on Chesapeake Bay, like we used to do, in what looked like an airplane hangar along the Rockaway shoreline, decades ago in another now. While his second wife and El groom in the bathroom, he slumps his head to the plate and whispers, "I'm scared," in a lifeless voice that comes from the tomb.

You and me both, I think.

"But I'm fighting to win." His straining vow to beat the cancer makes him cough. An unnaturally brilliant sun stream jumps the bay directly onto the remains of his face, revealing a bony yellow lump of skeleton.

You and me both.

And I think of Heraclitus at the edge of another water: His eyes pursue a head of spume as it bores by in circular path and dissipates to bubbles, one of which he tracks along the streamline, gliding past the rocks near the shore, veering between floating twigs, around a leaf, and disappearing.

Now a barely breathing body connected by tubes and fat wires to a vast array of flash-cube blinking, brashly bleeping machines on the verge of humming the same flat-tone dirge. My Aunt Ginny, once so urgent and voluptuous, now another thrashing sack of shrinking sandy bones submerged in covers. My Uncle Emil, stinking of his days-long, coffee-jacked vigil, sits next to her, holding her emaciated hand, head sinking into his chest. The entire family has converged on Macon, all my mother's living brothers and sisters and their spouses and children stashed in a waiting area near Ginny's room, purging their fears and catching up on family news, ignoring my grandfather, who sits in a corner, eyes closed, looking a little smashed. One by one, Emil has called the families into the room to say goodbye. Now it's Leon's and my turn. We stand before the bed silently. My hands grip one of the safety bars. The room is dark, all the objects grainy as if textured in serge, illuminated by a small reading lamp on a table by the bed. I have no urge to say anything, but I know I should: goodbye, or thanks for being good to us. "Thanks for taking my brother in," I manage to intone.

"You know, she loves you like her own," Emil says. I don't protest, but I doubt the words. I know the difference between your own flesh and blood and an outsider, even for someone with a heart as stout as Ginny's. I know there's a line you can never cross that divides a nephew from a real child. I know the difference between inside and out.

"I know it, Emil, I know it," I hide my unbeguiled reaction to his sentimental epithet behind a grim smile and look at Leon, his shoulders raised to his ears, his angular face looking at the floor, eyes glistening and cheeks glazed.

The now when I sit on the couch in my Uncle Henry's house in the San Fernando Valley after my mother's funeral, debating the rabbi about the theology of his eulogy, a kugel of spiritual nostrums and slouchy, self-ingratiating analogies. He insists that the Torah creates freedom, and that, the more one follows the Torah, the more freedom one has. "But, Rabbi," I taunt in an infuriated boom that I want everyone else in the room to hear, "the Torah consists of more than six hundred do's and don'ts. Freedom is about doing what you *want* to do."

The rabbi persists in his position, so now I argue to humiliate him. "You have conflated the *feeling* of freedom with what freedom is, because you, your congregation and everyone else in America rate freedom as the greatest good. The Torah restricts action and interdicts freedom. Sure, a person who follows the Torah's many edicts may sense a special glow—an Apollo-like ecstatic transfixion animating what we call freedom, similar to driving down the highway, windows open, and feeling the cold wind blow, or peeling off your clothes and jumping into the sea. But to call it freedom is a lumpy fiction."

I'm talking so loudly, and with such double-fisted anger in my voice, that the entire house grows silent. Everyone is looking at me, which makes me happy, makes me want to admonish even more hatefully, as I take apart the rabbi's cherished simile.

The now when my father raises his hand to me and I catch it, bend it back and pin it to the wall, at the same time raising my other arm to attack, which he grabs in midair. We stand face to face like two entwined and deadlocked Grecian wrestlers, muscle against muscle, feet stuck in bedrock, lineaments straining, my hand staying his fisted hand and his hand holding back mine. We tussle in the kitchen of the small apartment which Leon and I occupy, next door to the place he leases with his girlfriend Melinda. It's Yom Kippur, but no one is celebrating. He has vehemently tried to bully me with lying, so he can win an argument. When I tell him to fuck himself, the wrestling match begins—or rather, the wobbly embrace of balanced push and pull. I'm no Jacob among angels, but at this moment my stocky father ceases to occupy a higher sacramental space to me. I am as strong as he is. We push against each other, frozen, as if put into the background of a monumental altarpiece. I increase the pressure, really put my will into it. He starts to sway and lose his footing. He releases my arm, so I drop his, and he races away.

The now when a black, obese leviathan of cloud begins to break into pieces like a thick wave making shore, heavy waterfall of rain as packed as dirt against a grave, fanning out quickly across Coral Gables' palms and willows, murmuring like a sickly banshee folding clothes. It flows down the street about a mile away, headed towards us. Together, we sprint, listening behind us to the storm's ever-growing racket as it plunges cars and houses into mesmerizing slacks of water, glinting at the surface of the street, splintering, bouncing up and down like jumping jacks, turning flower beds to mud, settling into potholes, pooling into mini lakes and flashing floods without reliction … until the pounding grows so loud we know that it is about to overtake us. Together we stop, let our arms go slack, and feel the friction of the tepid water drench us like a benediction.

The now when we try to dribble the basketball, but it won't bounce on the waterlogged playground. Instead it flounces and floats on zigzagging provisory streams. At each shot, the wind blows the ball around like a leaf.

It feels good to be wet and cold and running around on concrete, just two boys goofing around, feeling careless. The storm sighs a high, reedy requiem through its harmonium of blending, almost floating trees. For a wet moment, I am free of the bad dream in which the television blares and our mother lives on Librium and ice cream.

Now men on first and second with no outs, top of the fourteenth. Orlando Cepeda clouts a hard liner that Roy McMillan spears near second. In the smallest of nows imaginable, McMillan invokes the tag-up rule, stepping on the bag, and in one searing motion rifles the ball to Ed Kranepool at first, sealing a triple play. My father points at a swayback gibbous moon tacked on a black sky above the right fielder and says, "It's late, and this game isn't ending any time soon. We'd better start back."

The now when Leon's crying in bed wakes me from dreamlessness. I lie under my spread and listen, but say nothing. I empty my head of everything but the sound of his tears. It is soon after we begin living with my father for half a year, after the winter day we come home from a Boy Scout trip and discover my mother lying folded over, comatose from an overdose of meds she has amassed. The time I did nothing. Did nothing, said nothing. Decided not to try. The time I waited for her to die.

The now of our first breakfast in our three-bedroom, brick-veneer A-frame with a curved gray travertine walkway and a yard to rake on a traffic-less street in the easternmost part of Queens, my mother's lifetime aim, the first and last home my parents buy together. It is an arctic, morning-starred day in early fall, but we have the back door open. "Let's enjoy the clean air and clear sky," my mother exclaims with seraphic gaiety. The coffeepot sputters. In a kitchen still cluttered with boxes, she makes pancakes and lean bacon, dramatically singing along to a phonographic record of Sigmund Romberg songs between munches of zwieback. The sweet philistine aroma of frying butter and pork bombards the downstairs. The taste of it fills my mouth as I chew the crisp, almost black pancake edges. While Leon, my father, and I eat stacks of thick, piping hot pancakes and long strips of crisp bacon, my mother serenely flips more on an old griddle she says her mother used. Her hair is pulled back and held by a green plastic band. She has no lipstick on. She wears one of my father's polo shirts tucked into a pair of pedal pushers, and pink slippers with fuzzy white balls at the toes. Everything grows more intensely realistic than usual, as if in a dream experienced as profoundly real. Under this spell, the blasts of breeze kick with more bite than usual. The morning light glides through the tall kitchen windows, brighter and hotter. The milk I sip is colder, the orange juice bolder. The bloated smells of butter and bacon grease more pungent. The syrup-swelled pieces of pancake warmer, sweeter, and lighter, as they slide down my throat. My mother's spatula movements fleeter than usual, graceful, rhythmic, forceful, rote. My father's words more heroic than his usual course. He's talking about something called "the float," combining two of his favorite subjects, the laws of thermodynamics and horses.

Now I tread off the lake shelf into the deep, unable to swim, the water surface now inches above my head. Despite my terror at hearing my heart quake underwater, I sweep my knees up like I'm high-stepping and let myself sink down, until my feet touch bottom. I embed my curled-down toes into the silt, push as hard as I can and leap up, head and shoulders breaking the shimmering surface, remaining above long enough to bellow "Help!" before sinking back below. I repeat this tricky maneuver again and again, pogo-sticking up and down for what seems like a long time, before my waist is suddenly engulfed by a faceless savior's arms, which pick me out of the water and carry me to shore.

Now under the Livonia Street El in the early morning, my arm tight around Leon's shoulder, both of us wearing burly winter coats, gloves and winter caps flared with furry flaps, toothy carousel smiles blowing steam into icy air.

Now I'm flat on my back in a bathtub full of warm, soapy water, a wet facecloth covering my face. I feel something touching the other side of the cloth in a series of light pats—pat, pat, pat. Pat, pat, pat. Like the rub of a cat's paw. It feels warm and liquid. I move away and swish the facecloth off to see Leon peeing on me and hissing impishly. I push his naked body into the water, stand up and start pissing on his face, without giving him the protection of a cloth barrier. He stands up and aims a urine stream in my direction. "The Burns and Allen Show" is playing in the background. George has just said, "You're fired, Harry," and the orchestra is pounding out the opening bars of "Love's Nest," the Carnation evaporated milk theme. We stand in the Dial-silky water, two wet and zestfully naked toddlers beaming radiant joy and pissing on each other, until Momma comes in, lets out a flabbergasted scream, then a laugh, pulls Leon out and says it's the last time we'll ever take a bath together.

The now at the beach, just the three of us. Momma holds my left hand tightly and Dada holds my right one, as they guide me into the cold tide. A plush wave creeps towards us, growing as it slides, reaching my father's waist and towering over me. Just before the rush of water is about to greet me full-faced, my parents lift me over it, so I can gracefully ride the crest. I totter when my feet hit the swirling mushy sand below the foam. We giggle together, and my mother says I'm bold. Another steep wave comes, and they lift me up again, this time with the help of a small kicking leap I make. We roam a little deeper. There is no fear in me, only happiness to be standing in ocean wet, holding my parents' hands. A wide-sweeping wave breeds in the distance. It picks up speed as it heads towards the shoreline. A tingling-bright sun entwining the sky behind it makes the water glow and sparkle. My parents lead me towards this rapidly growing liquid jet gushing rosettes of light. I feel the lush salty spray on my face. Without fright, I bend my legs to spring up at the last moment before the water crowns, but my father's strapping-strong arm holds me down. A wall of cold water crushes me like one hollow-sounding, stinging slap at my whole body, head to toe. I'm immersed and floating free. My flapping mouth swallows part of the flow and I start to blow out water and cry.

The now in which I stare dog-faced, eyes agape, from our playpen towards the casement window sill, where Leon is using his small, ball-shaped fist to unlock the window latch. He rocks and knocks his body into the glass until it yields to the push and opens like a door onto the fire escape. Now he is crawling on the metal grate, and scapegrace-smiling back inside. Something seems amusing about the scene. I must have seen it before, because instead of my brother's danger frightening me, I find it beguiling. He's doing something wrong, I know that, and the idea of danger comes to mind. But what does that feverous word mean? It's something Momma and Dada remind us is wrong. But some wrong things are wrong and bad. Others are wrong and unrefined. What Leon is doing is wrong and—the word they use—dangerous. But what is danger, they refuse to say. I won't do it because I'm a good boy. I won't abuse my freedom. I want ice cream for dessert. Leon seems to be having fun, but I don't see the rhyme or reason of climbing out of the crib, up the radiator, and cruising along the window ledge. I like it fine, tumbling in the playpen with my big red ball. A passing El train rumbles its sleep-inducing saraband. Leon starts knocking both open hands against the glass.

The first now, the first moment knowing I exist. I'm on top of a makeshift bed consisting of a stack of linens on a dark-stained wooden bench built into an alcove in my grandmother's apartment. I must be around two. Persistent loud laughing frightens me. I fling off my shroud of covers, slide off my makeshift bed, and walk in my pajamas towards light. My father and his six older sisters crowd around a dining room table, staring at something, oohing and cooing. Below an overhead lamp lies the object of their attention: my baby brother swaddled in blankets, babbling joyous nothings. They begin proudly to pass the baby to each other, each one holding him close to her face and singing twaddle for a few minutes, or giving him his bottle, or ringing a little red bell in front of his eyes. My father finally spies me standing by his side, takes hold of my hand, and leads me back to my makeshift bed. I ask him when Mommy is coming home. He pats my head and quietly, almost gently, pleads with me to sleep. I close my eyes and consciousness recedes.

More nows emerge, thousands of them surging through my head, bringing confusion, anger, fear, sadness, guilt. I start to purge my mind of each and every past and future now. Only this now is now.

I clear my mind of then. Only this now is now.

I clear my mind of next. Only this now is now.

I clear my mind of soon. Only this now is now. Only this now is now. Only this now is now.

I want to embrace this now for as long as it lasts, to bind its evanescence. Taste, smell and touch its essence, croon to it and spoon with it, make slow, soft, lazy love to its presence. But it doesn't last long enough to do anything else but graze the ambit that surrounds it before it dissolves into the next now.

Now travelling solitude. Now drift in moon's amplitude. Now lifting over a mossy cauldron in a lasting beyond. Now cast in the abiding rift between lewd and prudish diffusion. Now unraveled delusion at a failed crossing. Now lightning's loss of biting foresight. Now a frightening obstruction. Now earth stripping away. Now the long view tripping over glossy chaos. Now ripped in birth throes. Now abundant radiance shedding the skin of a kindred spirit. Now a vast and nurturing cryptic honeycomb spreading the finite. Now an appetite centered in the direction of a newfound home. Now contentment in a new light. Now power over a loam-bound flight.

Now at the lookout over Pine Creek Gorge. I instinctively kill a fly sniping around my face. Thoughtless, breathless swipe, and squeeze. When in the coarse brutality of sounds I didn't trace, couldn't sense or tease, the consequence of a buzzing fatality occurring long before forging fuzzy thought of any consequence. One breath sooner, one breath later, it might have been a diary of a different death.

Now at the top of the hill. The view is worn down, aching, ready to surrender on cue and reawaken to another view of things untouched. I want to confront the forces that clutch and crush me, face to face, old friends brushing into each other with nothing more to say. The sublime is fearsome, violent, combustible air, then grounded in ground, burning baize then waterlogged clays, the turner turned against itself, but always.

Now somewhere along the Hudson on the side of a dark highway that ranges along the river. Flat tire, and too tired to change it.

I aim a cry at scatting river flow.

The waters of the night reply with a thousand fractured lights, stars and lamps matted down by rain and dredged through rivers flowing west through cities in the plain.

The stars reply as well, sleepless dust brooding sparks along the damaged slopes. Dancing terebinths reply in taupe-gray silence. Other answers paint the dusty, self-effacing darkness. From the tainted river towns, barges, rust-stained eaves, and murmuring pools of oil reply. Each bridge leaves its version of reply, skewered lines of wood and coiling metal groaning faintly. At every distant light, humans drone replies throughout the night.

Now on a bench in Central Park, underneath cherry trees in full red bloom, watching people zoom by. A bed of tulips, still and stolid, random combinations of velvet red and purple poking out of stalkless chambray leaves. Gawk at that a week or two, see the petals curl and shed, the plant heads fade and fray, the slow decay of stalk. Each stage invokes a cavalcade of questions on what things are and what they're made of, of what they may become in time. Unquenched questions one could pose for hours about the next trench of flowers by the next park bench, or the one after that, or the one after that, about the meaning of every budding branch of every greening tree that lines the streets, about the weather-blenched building figurines, the iron grillwork, the stone and brick facades, the wrenching curb where sidewalk meets roadway, the curiosities and singularities of women and men, of anything on this high-rise island towering over ocean, or anywhere else on this Earth of possibilities.

A muggy ocean breeze teases with its wheezes. It glides between the buildings, reminding me the seas are near. It fills the streets with sticky nuzzles and the puzzle of the clouds: will it drizzle, will it drench? Will it shroud the roads with fog undulating emerald over square and circle beds of pink and yellow heads, blinks of purple hidden in clover?

Twists of conversation ride the wind—"Well, I mean, like, so, anyway, you know, you see, no way, it's, like, I go"—as meaningless to my ear as the chirp of birds. Invaded by a damp tranquility, water hides in air, a shadow blanket reminiscent of an untroubled April years ago. Not déjà vu, but déjà *senti*. A burst of sun soon breaks it up, as if it were a bubble.

My hand and forearm sense the emanations rising from a beautiful woman who stops to look through binoculars at the birds, the cilia on her skin floating gently like invisible wheat, orchard's perspiration, spicy soaps and vineyards, bitter of her coffee, the savory smell of her sexuality skittering luxuriously—a scented warmth clinging to her outfit. I get a momentary erotic freeze, as her body quickly brushes by mine and forces me to penetrate her ambit on a path between the people on the benches and the thrushes on the trees.

Now bursting with life's constant rehabilitation: myriad species of vegetation, mold, manifold bacteria, birds, worms, horseflies. bees, bats, rats, squirrels, cats, dogs, frogs, lizards, fish, humans walking, talking, meeting, sitting, knitting, eating, sleeping, reaping, peeping, keeping beat, repeating, deleting, hoping, coping, longing, wronging, belonging, sowing, rowing, growing, going away, staying, praying, graying....

Now scent of jasmine blossoms, four in the afternoon. I sit beneath a tree in a state of not wondering. Not wondering what to do. Not wondering what comes next. Not wondering if the journey upstream has ended or if I have stumbled upon another dream.

Now cold air wakes me from this latest nap. That much I know, but where am I trapped exactly? It's getting late, and I feel lost. I can't find myself on the map in my mind. There are no place-names, no center lines, no billboards, no road signs.

But what would the name of the place matter? Whatever it was called, it would be the same. I would still feel the sun cool off as it descended, still shield my eyes from its acute glare. Still sense the tack of pollen at my nose, still hear deranged swarms of black and yellow bees snacking on the red and purple flowers in the furrows. Still endure the weight of my backpack. Still see the sky change from a feathery blue to red to black. Still alone and yet, with all the others, together.

Now my arms, like trembling gossamer, ride along Spring's thermal updraft, lift high and, spider-like, release, float upwards, downwards, sometimes height of hands, sometimes over birds that fly to unfamiliar lands.

ALONG AN UNKNOWN HIGHWAY

Acknowledgements

An earlier version of "Hashmal" appeared in The Jewish Literary Quarterly, July 2015. Several sentences originally appeared as poems or parts of poems in the following literary journals: A capella Zoo, China Grove, Curbside Review, Ellipsis, Janus Head, Mississippi Review, Peralta, Poetry in Performance, Recourse au Poème, and Slant. I would like to thank Gene Hayworth and everyone else at Owl Canyon Press for shepherding me through the publication of my first novel. To Sonja Boyd, Michael Herschensohn, Juliet Neidish, and Will Torphy, I owe a debt of gratitude for reading and commenting extensively on various versions of the manuscript. I reserve my final thanks to my life partner Kathy and my son and daughter-in-law, Ezra and Sarah, for their emotional support during the hard, dark years of writing and editing.